Wonder, adventure, and mystery abound in these exci[...]

In a strange country in a distant fut[...] negotiate a contract between two [...] by Elise Stephens

Sometimes the gods are cruel, and sometimes they are kind; sometimes they need a person to show them the difference— "The First Warden" by Kai Wolden

A kindly old murderer on a doomed ship finds himself pitted against an evil god as he battles to save mankind—"The Damned Voyage" by John Haas

Idealists generally start revolutions—and either die in them, or are condemned by the men they fought for—"The Idealist" by L. Ron Hubbard

Li is struggling to defeat God, but is he following his own will, or is he just another one of God's puppets?—"Thanatos Drive" by Andrew Dykstal

At the edge of a faraway solar system, an android with noble intent finds that they must rob the dead to aid the living—"A Harvest of Astronauts" by Kyle Kirrin

It's tough to be a disabled girl struggling to live on the moon, especially when your best friend is in danger, but having a great attitude helps—"Super-Duper Moongirl and the Amazing Moon Dawdler" by Wulf Moon

Beneath Lake Mead lurks an ancient warrior—"Lost Robot" by Dean Wesley Smith

When aliens take over the world, one father decides to take vengeance on the people who bullied his daughter—"Are You the Life of the Party?" by Mica Scotti Kole

Would you kill a child?—"Release from Service" by Rustin Lovewell

Those who can see the beauty of math sometimes find it overbearing—"Dark Equations of the Heart" by David Cleden

Buying your first submarine is always exciting, but it can also be a struggle—"Yellow Submarine" by Rebecca Moesta

When Claire's father cuts down the old tree at the edge of the garden, it was because the old enchanter had an itch for something he couldn't quite describe—"An Itch" by Christopher Baker

There's a lot to be learned from the crotchety old wizard who lives in the trailer house at the end of the road, but perhaps the most important things aren't what he is trying to teach—"Dirt Road Magic" by Carrie Callahan

Walter has always loved his wife, but is his love for her more enduring than time itself?—"A Certain Slant of Light" by Preston Dennett

Read on to discover amazing tales from some of the most talented new authors from around the globe, along with gorgeous art and timely advice from our panel of blue-ribbon judges.

L. RON HUBBARD

Presents

Writers of the Future

Anthologies

"Not only is the writing excellent . . . it is also extremely varied. There's a lot of hot new talent in it." —*Locus* magazine

"Where can an aspiring sci-fi artist go to get discovered? . . . Fortunately, there's one opportunity—the Illustrators of the Future Contest—that offers up-and-coming artists an honest-to-goodness shot at science fiction stardom."

—*Sci-Fi* magazine

"Always a glimpse of tomorrow's stars."

—*Publishers Weekly* starred review

"The book you are holding in your hands is our first sight of the next generation of science fiction and fantasy writers."

—Orson Scott Card
Writers of the Future Contest judge

"This is an opportunity of a lifetime." —Larry Elmore
Illustrators of the Future Contest judge

"The road to creating art and getting it published is long, hard, and trying. It's amazing to have a group, such as Illustrators of the Future, there to help in this process—creating an outlet where the work can be seen and artists can be heard from all over the globe."

—Rob Prior
Illustrators of the Future Contest judge

"The Writers of the Future experience played a pivotal role during a most impressionable time in my writing career. And afterward, the WotF folks were always around when I had questions or needed help. It was all far more than a mere writing contest."

—Nnedi Okorafor
Writers of the Future Contest published
finalist 2002 and Contest judge

"I really can't say enough good things about Writers of the Future. . . . It's fair to say that without Writers of the Future, I wouldn't be where I am today."

—Patrick Rothfuss
Writers of the Future Contest winner 2002

"If you want a glimpse of the future—the future of science fiction—look at these first publications of tomorrow's masters."

—Kevin J. Anderson
Writers of the Future Contest judge

"The Writers of the Future Contest is a valuable outlet for writers early in their careers. Finalists and winners get a unique spotlight that says 'this is the way to good writing.'"

—Jody Lynn Nye
Writers of the Future Contest judge

"The Contests are amazing competitions. I wish I had something like this when I was getting started—very positive and cool."

—Bob Eggleton
Illustrators of the Future Contest judge

"Speculative fiction fans will welcome this showcase of new talent. ...Winners of the simultaneous Illustrators of the Future Contest are featured with work as varied and as exciting as the authors."

—*Library Journal* starred review

L. Ron Hubbard PRESENTS

Writers of the Future

VOLUME 35

L. Ron Hubbard PRESENTS

Writers of the Future

VOLUME 35

The year's twelve best tales from the
Writers of the Future international writers' program

Illustrated by winners in the Illustrators of the Future
international illustrators' program

Three short stories from authors
L. Ron Hubbard / Dean Wesley Smith / Rebecca Moesta

With essays on writing and illustration by
L. Ron Hubbard / Mike Resnick / Rob Prior

Edited by David Farland
Illustrations Art Directed by Echo Chernik

GALAXY PRESS, INC.

For information, contact Galaxy Press, Inc. at 7051 Hollywood Boulevard, Hollywood, California, 90028.

Interior Design by Jerry Kelly

ISBN 978-1-61986-604-1

Printed in the United States of America.

CONTENTS

Introduction

BY DAVID FARLAND

David Farland is a New York Times *bestselling author with more than fifty novels and anthologies to his credit. He has won numerous awards, including the L. Ron Hubbard Gold Award in 1987, and has served as Coordinating Judge of the Writers of the Future for more than a dozen years.*

*He has helped mentor hundreds of new writers, including such #1 bestselling authors as Brandon Sanderson (*The Way of Kings*), Stephenie Meyer (*Twilight*), Brandon Mull (*Fablehaven*), James Dashner (*The Maze Runner*), and others. While writing Star Wars novels in 1998, he was asked to help choose a book to push big for Scholastic, and selected* Harry Potter, *then helped develop a bestseller strategy.*

In addition to his novels and short stories, Dave has also assisted with video game design and worked as a greenlighting analyst for movies in Hollywood. Dave continues to help mentor writers through the Writers of the Future program, where he acts as Coordinating Judge, editor of the anthology, and teaches workshops to our winning authors. He also teaches online classes and live workshops.

Introduction

Welcome to *L. Ron Hubbard Presents Writers of the Future, Volume 35.*

In this collection you will find twelve outstanding stories from new authors that we've discovered from around the world, and it was my pleasure, as Coordinating Judge of the Writers' Contest, to dig through the piles of manuscripts and discover these new writers. Each of the stories is also illustrated by an artist that we have discovered through our sister competition, the Illustrators of the Future Contest.

Every three months, thousands of writers and artists send their entries to the Contest (usually submitting their work online), and then I get to read the stories, sift through them, consider them carefully, and then pass the top eight stories on to our panel of blue-ribbon judges, who vote for their favorite stories.

In the field of short fiction, there really aren't other contests quite like the Writers and Illustrators of the Future. Sure, there are other contests, but none of them offer quite so much as these do. Yes, the cash awards, payment for publication, the training of new writers and illustrators, and the opportunity to get published are all great. In fact, the Writers of the Future Contest has become the premiere vehicle to help new authors launch careers into the professional marketplace.

Not only has the anthology become an international bestseller, topping many of the sales charts for anthologies of short stories, but it has also begun winning awards based on its high quality, as I mention in the "Year in the Contest" article at the back of this book.

But this year I want to focus on just how *long* this has been going on. This is the 35th year for the Writers' Contest and the 30th year for the Illustrators' Contest. That means that if you are reading this, the chances are excellent that these contests have been going on since before you were born. (The median age for all people is only 29.6 years, so statistically, odds are that you're under that age.) That's unprecedented for this kind of talent search. As a young writer in college, I began searching for writing contests to enter, and every year I might find one or two, but all of the ones that I entered passed away long ago. Only this one endures.

As a collection of stories, this one is unique. As an editor, the stories are submitted as "blind entries." That means that I don't know who wrote the story, whether the author was male or female, old or young. I don't know the author's race, religion, or nationality. I don't know anything about the entrants. All that I get to see is an assigned number on a story—nothing more.

Of course, we accept submissions from anyone, anywhere in the world. Because there is no cost to enter either contest, no matter how humble the means of an author or illustrator, or how far away they are, anyone can enter. So we tend to get a lot of winners from around the globe. In fact, we had five winners from the UK this year (the most in any volume ever) along with one from Canada.

Since the judging is blind, I get to focus on the various qualities of the story—the power of its concept, the exploration of themes, the author's facility with story, the stylistic strengths of the piece, and the use of voice and tone.

I can't judge the stories based on any hard standard, I have to look at each story in the competition and then compare them to one another. Ultimately, I go through several rounds of judging and make my picks, and that can be hard. I might be trying to compare a comedy to a thriller, or a story with a strong futuristic voice to one that has a great historical flavor. In other words, I am comparing apples and oranges to bananas and kumquats.

Some of the stories will be among our eight finalists, another few stories will be semi-finalists, perhaps thirty or so will be Silver Honorable Mentions, and others will be Honorable Mentions.

The Honorable Mention awards are becoming more and more coveted, and part of me wants to give more of them out. Very often we will get fine stories that really don't have anything particularly wrong with them. I sometimes wish that I could do more to encourage some of those writers who have their work "rejected." In short, I see a lot of fine work by some dedicated writers who don't place.

At this point, I like to give young authors a hint about what I am looking for, and there is something that I have never mentioned: I search for stories where the author has a strong grasp not only of how the world works, but how it *could* work better.

Let me explain that statement. Some people, when they write a story, will show characters with problems, and often those problems remain unresolved in the story. I might have a story, for example, that deals with a divorce, or with a broken legal system. But if an ending doesn't resolve well, it worries me. One of the most common endings in stories by new authors is that the protagonist in the story faces a huge problem and gives up—usually by killing him or herself. I won't publish those stories. I'm not looking for authors who recognize *problems*; I want authors who are bright enough to see *solutions*. I want authors who are not only capable of talking eloquently about problems, but who can ultimately, if they desire, have a positive effect upon the world.

So, in this volume, you will find a dozen stories of wonder, intrigue, and even horror. They span several genres and subgenres, but they all share one thing in common: they're all winners of the Contest, and all of the authors show tremendous promise.

If that isn't enough, each of the stories has been illustrated by one of the most talented new artists in the world, winners of the Illustrators of the Future Contest.

On top of that, we have fine advice on writing and art from some of our celebrity judges—Rob Prior, Echo Chernik, and Mike Resnick—and we've got some delightful stories from other judges, Dean Wesley Smith and Rebecca Moesta—along with a powerful piece by the Contests' founder L. Ron Hubbard.

I hope that this year's presentation will make you laugh, make you cry, astound and delight you, and ultimately fill you with wonder.

I know it has done that for me.

Cover Art

BY BOB EGGLETON

Bob Eggleton is a winner of seven Hugo Awards and eleven Chesley Awards. His art can be seen on the covers of numerous magazines, professional publications, and books in the world of science fiction, fantasy, and horror across the world including several volumes of his own work. He has also worked as a conceptual illustrator for movies and thrill rides.

Of late, Eggleton has focused on private commissions and self-commissioned work. (The latter was the genesis for this year's cover art.) He is an elected Fellow of the International Association of Astronomical Artists and is a Fellow of the New England Science Fiction Association.

Bob recently completed nineteen paintings for The Foundation trilogy. And he is currently working on a new book, The Art of Frank Kelly Freas.

Bob has been an Illustrators of the Future Contest judge since 1988. He has participated as an instructor for the annual workshops and as an art director for previous anthologies. As a judge of thirty years, we thought it fitting that his work grace the cover of the anthology celebrating the thirtieth anniversary of L. Ron Hubbard's Illustrators of the Future Contest.

BOB EGGLETON
One of Our Robots Is Missing

ALIYA CHEN
Untrained Luck

ALEXANDER GUSTAFSON
The First Warden

ALLEN MORRIS
The Damned Voyage

BRIAN C. HAILES
The Idealist

11

QIANJIAO MA
Thanatos Drive

SAM KEMP
A Harvest of Astronauts   13

ALICE WANG
Super-Duper Moongirl and the Amazing Moon Dawdler

JOSH PEMBERTON
Are You the Life of the Party?

15

EMERSON RABBITT
Release from Service

VYTAUTAS VASILIAUSKAS
Dark Equations of the Heart

DAVID FURNAL
Yellow Submarine

JENNIFER OBER
An Itch

19

YINGYING JIANG
Dirt Road Magic

CHRISTINE RHEE
A Certain Slant of Light

The Illustrators of the Future Contest Directing the Art

BY ECHO CHERNIK

Echo Chernik is a successful advertising and publishing illustrator with twenty years of professional experience and several prestigious publishing awards.

Her clients include mainstream companies such as: Miller, Camel, Coors, Celestial Seasonings, Publix Super Markets, Inc., Kmart, Sears, Nascar, the Sheikh of Dubai, the city of New Orleans, Bellagio resort, the state of Indiana, USPS, Dave Matthews Band, Arlo Guthrie, McDonald's, Procter & Gamble, Trek Bicycle Corporation, Disney, BBC, Mattel, Hasbro, and more. She specializes in several styles including decorative, vector, and art nouveau.

She is the Coordinating Judge of the Illustrators of the Future Contest. Echo strives to share the important but all-too-often neglected subject of the business aspect of illustration with the winners, as well as preparing them for the reality of a successful career in illustration.

The Illustrators of the Future Contest
Directing the Art

The most valuable award from winning the Illustrators of the Future Contest is *not* the most obvious. The twelve winners each year don't only win a monetary prize, and a fabulous ceremony in their honor, as well as having their name permanently added to a prestigious collection of past winners who have gone on to successful careers. Along with their victory, their work is published in the bestselling *Writers of the Future* anthology. The best of the best emerging writers and illustrators are published in one fantastically supported annual book and this year is the thirty-fifth volume.

This article, though, is about something these artists win that may be one of the most essential gifts they could be given: *they win the gift of experience from artists who have come before them.*

The winners of the Illustrators of the Future Contest spend an entire week in Los Angeles learning from industry giants, hearing stories of success (and failures), and discovering what it really means to make a living as an artist. They participate in workshops and lectures. They get to sit down one-on-one with the likes of Larry Elmore and Ciruelo, who will eagerly share their experiences and advice. They are inundated with more knowledge in a shorter period of time than they have ever had before.

When I took over as Coordinating Judge of the Illustrators' Contest a few years ago, it became one of my primary goals to infuse the winners with industry knowledge and experience that was difficult to get elsewhere, to really make the experience invaluable for them. Much of the week-long seminar is focused on the business of being a working artist. Whether they are looking toward a path of being a freelance artist or working on a team or in a studio, they will have to learn how to work with art direction. Working with an art director is a skill that is learned over time. During the week-long seminar, the winners work on a project with an art director from concept through timely delivery.

Their experience with art direction, however, starts even before they arrive in Los Angeles. Upon receiving the exciting phone call that they are a winner, finalists are individually assigned a story that complements their artistic style. The story they receive is one of that year's winning stories from the Writers of the Future Contest. From that story, they will illustrate a new piece that will be published and credited to them. This piece serves many purposes. They will experience, possibly for the first time, the process of creating a published work of art with professional art direction. It will also be a publishing credit for their résumé and not many artists can claim to be a part of a bestselling book. This published work will be judged and will contend for the Golden Brush Award (a Grand Prize check for $5,000 and a beautiful trophy) announced at a grand Hollywood gala. Maybe most importantly, the published piece will be a landmark portfolio piece—helping each winner earn their next job.

As the art director, I work with each winner to help make their piece the best it can be. Being a good art director takes balance and practice. The goal is to work *with* the artist to guide them to conceive and create an amazing piece of art. An art director should *not* tell them what to paint.

The winners are given thirty days to complete their illustration from start to finish. They first submit their concepts as thumbnails or loose drawings. The artist describes to me what their final vision is for each sketch. It is usually pretty easy to pick out the most exciting one, as the artist is inherently more excited about one or two of them. I then talk to them about details, focus, and composition. What elements should they make sure to retain when transitioning from sketch to their finish? What colors and shapes (both positive and negative) will really draw in the viewer? What elements of symbolism and position are there, and do they give the viewer the correct impression of the story? Is there a way to deepen the story and push the piece further? What sort of foreshadowing can be added into the illustration? Is the viewer's eye traveling around the piece in an engaging and entertaining manner? Can the artist justify the choices they make in their vision?

That one work will be judged for their vision and execution, but their career will be judged by their professionalism and ability to work with art direction.

Eventually, as their careers progress, that once stellar piece will be replaced in their portfolio with new works and the prize money will be spent. But the big thing that will remain and be built upon is the experience and knowledge they gain from this special week. It becomes a part of their foundation—strengthening them to become that much more magnificent in their future. This is the gift that I, and the other judges, strive to give the winners, made possible by L. Ron Hubbard and the Illustrators of the Future Contest.

Untrained Luck

written by

Elise Stephens

illustrated by

ALIYA CHEN

ABOUT THE AUTHOR

Elise Stephens was raised on a steady diet of fairytales and Disney musicals. Early involvement in the theater left Elise with a taste for dramatic, high-stakes adventure while frequent international travel gave her an awe and respect for foreign cultures. When she fell in love with the intricate plots and strange worlds of science fiction and fantasy novels, her fate was sealed for the writing life. She graduated with a creative writing degree from the University of Washington where she was awarded the Eugene Van Buren Prize for Fiction. She attended Orson Scott Card's Literary Boot Camp in 2014.

Through her fiction, Elise strives to discover beauty within brokenness and unlock healing after devastating loss. She intends for her stories to offer light and strength for facing the darkness and disappointments of this world. Becoming a mother five years ago added a ferocious affection to her storytelling, and themes of self-sacrifice, legacy, and family ties currently permeate her work.

Elise lives in Seattle with her amazing husband and two rambunctious kiddos in a house with large windows for letting in the sunlight that she constantly craves, both literally and metaphorically.

ABOUT THE ILLUSTRATOR

Aliya Chen was born in 1998 in Buffalo, New York, but calls California her home. From an early age, Aliya fell in love with both reading and drawing, and she found a hobby in reimagining science fiction and fantasy stories through her artwork. She discovered digital painting and animation in middle school and became fascinated by the idea of bringing characters and worlds to life on screen.

This fascination led her to pursue computer graphics at the University of Pennsylvania, where she is currently in her third year. Although she loves to explore the intersection of technology and art, her ultimate passion lies in capturing moods and telling stories through her illustrations.

Untrained Luck

Mag forced herself to think about anything except the crescents glued inside her boot heel while the immigration officer addressed her in Hinshee, the official dialect.

"What brings you to Palab?" His black eyes studied her face from beneath his green wool cap. She smelled desert dust on his jacket. Overhead, an icy stream of conditioned air warned of crackling heat outside. Even here, she tasted the bitter tang of Palab's soil. Mag had thought her previous visit to this country had been her last. Life and survival had other ideas.

"Business," she said.

"Your line of work?"

"I'm a mediator. I've come to resolve a dispute."

"Really?" His eyebrows twitched. "And who are your clients?"

"I can't ... say." She grasped fleetingly for the Hinshee word for *disclose*. That would have sounded politer. Then again, disclosing the identities of her clients, with their reputations for violence and disregard for the law, would endanger Mag's own safety more than a mild discourtesy.

The officer nodded. "Did you take classes for this? A university degree?"

Mag shrugged and turned her palms skyward, as per local custom. "Some skills I taught myself, for others I took lessons."

She'd built the bulk of her mediation skills from a childhood spent pulling her parents off each other. The day she'd come home to find her mother's neck broken, body limp on the kitchen table, her father showering in the bathroom, she'd pulled her eleven-year-old sister Nika onto the Firebrand and gunned the bike out of town.

The officer tapped an unlit cig against Mag's pack. "Anything to declare?"

She opened her jacket and laid out her handgun, permit for the gun, echo tin, snoop, and wallet. The moonblade tucked into the small of her back remained hidden and undeclared, as did the crescent coins in her boot. She'd learned from her first time inside Palab's borders that extra weapons and secret finances were always wise. As she began to unclip her therma-pin from her lapel, the officer flicked two fingers to dismiss the effort. He nodded at the items on the counter and she put them away while he lit his cig.

"Do you think your clients will find an agreement?" he asked casually.

She shrugged again. "If the Eye shows mercy."

"If the Eye shows mercy," he echoed, grinning, and reached for his stamp, then paused midway and shook his head.

Mag's relief froze in her chest.

"My apologies," the officer said. "You must go here first." He motioned her to a curtained room labeled Secondary Questioning.

As Mag entered, the room wafted scents of dust and disinfectant. A woman wearing a starched blue scarf sat behind a table. She pointed to Mag's arms. "Roll up your sleeves."

So the Palabi government was searching for simpaths now. Mag had seen the same witch-hunt play out in Palab's neighbor, Kesh, which had required simpaths to publicly register last year. All that had done was spur a wave of mob killings: death by bloodletting and eye-gouging. Mag held no high hopes of enlightenment for the days ahead.

She doffed her riding jacket, baring her forearms. The female inspector met Mag's eyes with disinterest, then set to swabbing her arms to check for concealed simpath heat-scars.

Mag's mind pinged back to her first run-in with a simpath. She'd been young in her career and hadn't yet earned enough to purchase a therma-pin's protection. The simpath had emotionally pushed Mag into negotiating an imbalanced divorce settlement in which the already traumatized children were placed in the neglectful parent's custody. Her throat tightened at the memory and her mind's eye still burned with the sight of the simpath's whorled heat-scars peeking out beneath his shirtsleeve as he'd sauntered from the room. Mag had known then what he'd done to her, but it had been too late. She'd sold her mother's necklace the next day in order to buy a therma-pin. Never again. Palab's government appeared to have taken a similar stance.

When the inspector felt satisfied with her scrutiny, she waved Mag to the room's egress with a flat "Welcome to Palab." Mag shrugged back into her jacket.

She'd wished for a gifting as a child, but now felt grateful to bear nothing. As her boots hit the pavement outside the customs station, a wave of heat engulfed her. She retrieved the Firebrand, swung onto the seat, and drove for the border town of Ajrah. The sky above her was not yet stained with purple-and-black stripes. Then again, by the time the storm stripes appeared ... "May the Eye show mercy," she muttered under her breath.

Minutes later, Mag snapped her kickstand onto the oily asphalt of a fuel station. The air was a filmy haze of petrol, honey-roasting pistachios from somewhere nearby, and burned rubber. As she topped off, she ran down her mental list: she'd already changed the bike's oil, filter, coolants, and checked her tread depth. One and a half days' ride to Ellawi City, do the job, get paid, then buy space in a bunker to hole up for the storm.

After refueling, Mag headed for the dingy lavatory and moved the crescents from her boot to a concealed money belt. Her reflection in the bathroom's cracked mirror halted her. A dull orange light burned at the tip of her therma-pin. She tapped the sensor twice to reset it, but the pin flashed three more blinks and then went dead. She hissed. The ultrasensitive temp sensor and proprietary pattern-recognition software made therma-pins expensive and costly to repair. Of course, today was when the device would finally stop working.

While a simmer could heat or cool a non-bio liquid, and an empath fed emotions into the subject's mind—always with a discernible "push"—a simpath bore a blend of both gifts and regulated sweat, blood and other bio-fluid temps, causing an imperceptible emotional sway that was limited only by the simpath's line of sight. Simpaths bled excess energy from their hands at wavelengths with unique hot and cold signatures, the effect of which eventually scarred their forearms. Therma-pins detected these simpath heat signatures. Mag's work could not be done without one. At least not ethically.

Her clients would doubtless bring their own pins for security at the upcoming negotiation, but now Mag would have to add repairs to the list of necessities piling up behind the expense of a two-week bunker stay. And asking to borrow a therma-pin for her own mediation might erode her clients' respect. Mag was cursing to herself as she exited the lavatory when she saw the kid.

As a child, Mag and Nika had spent hours at fuel stations like this one, begging for spare change. This seven- or eight-year-old kid wasn't a street urchin; those always traveled in twos or threes. He was alone. His clothes were grimy and tight shirtsleeves hugged his narrow arms instead of the region's customary loose tunics. Hair straggled, lips chapped, eyes round with wariness.

In a border town like Ajrah, child trafficking stats gave mere hours before a vulch snatched him. Sure enough, lounging against one of the fuel towers was a man in a long tunic with sunglasses trained on the kid.

Mag chewed her tongue, then shouted her best Hinshee curse at the boy.

"Where have you been?"

The eyes of the other customers swung to her like magnets. The boy gaped.

Mag stabbed her finger downward. "Come here. And don't even think of leaving my sight again."

The kid stumbled forward, his arms held warily at his sides. He had the sense to be cautious. Good.

"Go wash your face. Your father's missing work as it is!"

Mag pulled the kid into the lavatory and slammed the door. He sprang against the far wall, arms barring his face. From the shape of his eyes and his delicate nose, she guessed he was Keshian.

Mag knelt. "Listen," she spoke slowly, trying out her Keshrindi. "I won't hurt you."

His eyes sharpened with understanding, but his arms stayed raised.

She said, "There are people outside who want to …" Mag searched her vocabulary, "who want to do bad things to you."

He frowned and turned out his empty pockets.

Had she just said someone wanted to rob him? She shrugged.

"It's your lucky day," she told him. "I'll take you somewhere safe. But you must act like we know each other, like we're friends."

"Friends," the boy said, using Mag's native tongue, Darik.

She slanted him a sharp look. Had he recognized her accent? She shrugged. It didn't matter. She'd made her decision and she'd ride it out. She'd find the kid a youth hostel on the way out of town. He'd chosen to trust her. For his sake, she was grateful.

"What's your name, kid?"

"Lio."

She shook his hand. It was slick with sweat. "I'm Mag."

She re-pinned her hair, smoothed and tucked her headscarf, then marched back into the sunlight with Lio's hand inside her own. The man in sunglasses had already backed away, as if sensing defeat. He made no move to follow as Mag buckled on her helmet and motored away.

Lio locked his arms around her waist and the Firebrand growled with hunger for the open road. Mag bit her lip. The youth hostels in this border town would be just as sketchy as the fuel station.

She twisted the throttle and let the town's neon lights and stone spires blur into a dappled stream behind them. "You'll stay with me tonight," she told Lio.

The Firebrand roared, and the kid dropped his head between her shoulder blades to brace himself for speed. Mag felt a crisp charge in the air: the promise of imminent, destructive change.

The Firebrand overheated three times that morning, which was unusual, but she'd never liked the Palabi climate.

At about noon, Mag gunned her throttle at a railroad crossing to clear the tracks just ahead of a train wearing rattling acid shields. Once across, Mag's shaking arms forced her to pull over. Despite the close shave with the train, the jitters surprised Mag. A few long drags on a cig restored her calm, but Lio clung to her even with the Firebrand idling, his thumbs biting into her stomach. It was then that she realized he wore no helmet. She'd actually thought she was protecting him while she rode recklessly. Her cheeks flamed as she banked down the off-ramp to the next town.

The mint tea she purchased from a street vendor was lukewarm, despite its "iced" claims, but even with its chalky residue from a cheap acid filter it was better than her canteen slosh.

She walked Lio and the Firebrand past stalls of quick-harvest grains and outrageously priced cuts of meat. They passed two vendors in a shouting match. Mag's ears told her that if the first paused long enough to listen to the second's complaint, the matter could be quickly solved. She halted at a shop purveying breeches, chaps, gloves, and helmets.

Lio pointed out a gray helmet emblazoned with a dagger on an aspen leaf. "Like you," he whispered reverently.

Mag snorted. It was cute that he wanted to match her, but LeafBlade brand didn't come in child size. She parked the Firebrand and chose instead a scratched green helmet that had been discounted, then handed Lio her tea while she haggled. She was so absorbed with blocking the vendor's clumsy empathic pressure toward a higher price, she didn't notice Lio's sulk until the purchase was tucked into her pack beside a bonus tube of silver decal paint. She'd still probably overpaid.

She took her tea back and drained it. It had cooled nicely inside the air-conditioned shop.

Lio's mournful stare followed the LeafBlade helmet halfway down the street. The vendors were already rolling up carpets and boxing wares, though the afternoon was still young. Lightning forked in the distance. She sniffed and smelled ozone on the wind. Days or hours now.

A man in a black jacket with gold thread cuffs monitored the traffic from a street corner. That would be a peacekeeper, employed by Nalib Rinwahl, one of her clients in the upcoming negotiation. Power and strength were Rinwahl's trademarks.

Mag buckled the helmet onto Lio and fought the urge to twist hard on her throttle. If the rains broke in the next hour, recklessness wouldn't get them to Ellawi in time. Nothing would save them if the storm hit them on the open road.

The highway grew more pocked and oilier with each mile, worming like a ravaging parasite into the humid gut of Palab. The smell of animal carcasses rose with the heat, and the still-living beasts prowled the roadside, lean bodies sharp against a blue sky that was starting to turn a disturbing shade of purple. Mag pulled over once to tear off a sprig of wild sage and tuck it inside her visor where its scent repelled the stench of death.

She'd charged twice her usual fee to account for the travel and low-visibility clientele of this job but, more than that, she'd charged extra for having to travel near the storm's onset. Then again, she might have charged four times her standard, had her references not been fouled by two failed negotiations in a row.

She'd lost her latter-half payment for both of those gigs, and had barely managed the bills to repair her hip, a casualty of one job's violent implosion.

She knew her problem's source, but like a loose bolt without a wrench, she couldn't reach in and fix it. Mag had lost her grip six months earlier when she'd received news that Nika had died of infection after a cut-rate abortion. Just like that. Words on a screen. Little sister gone.

She should have taken a break, but she'd needed the money. So she'd entered those last two jobs with deadened reflexes and paid for it dearly.

When the job from Rinwahl and Nasheed had hit Mag's inbox, she'd groaned at the Palabi address, but reminded herself she was still far from being able to afford a storm bunker. She'd accepted.

After another three-hour ride, she and Lio stopped briefly for jerky strips, bread, and water, then pushed on. When the sun had sunk almost to the horizon and Mag felt sand between her teeth, she checked her mileage and pulled off at the next campground. When she twisted to look at the kid, she saw bloodshot eyes, skin like a dried apricot, and trail of crusted blood at the corner of his mouth. Not one complaint.

At the campsite's check-in box, she inserted her coins and a red cube tumbled out of the lockbox's base with her campsite number. A small cabin would have been nice, or even one of the sturdy canvas tents, but after-hours entry removed such options.

"We'll be roughing it," she told Lio. She switched to Keshrindi when she saw his blank stare. "We'll sleep outside tonight. No one will trouble us here. The eyes and ears of a crowd—"

"They guard us," he broke in, finishing her sentence in Darik. "For now," he continued, still in Darik, "we speak your words. I understand enough." Pride quirked his mouth.

"Fine by me."

They washed at the campground restrooms and Mag moved her holster to a conspicuous position on her good hip. She walked with the Firebrand and Lio past amber-orange flames and the sweet mesquite smoke of late lingering fires, nodding to fellow travelers. Mag had noticed more pink rivulet-scars on faces and hands than when she'd traveled to Palab a year before; one in three now bore some mark of storm rain.

At the campsite, she pushed the cube into its metal socket and a solar orb cast a thin glow onto the gravel lot, sweeping the base of a red cliff at the far end, the edge of a woven tent on the right, and a battered aluminum trailer with hand-painted Hinshee proverbs on the left.

Lio chucked gravel at the cliffside and watched the dust puff. Light twinkled on his throwing hand, a bracelet. Not diamonds. No one put diamonds on a kid this young. Unless it wasn't his.

After wiping down the Firebrand, Mag spread out her kerchief with flatbread, dates, dried apples, jerky, and water.

Lio eagerly folded his legs under him. As he chewed, Mag let the humming generator from their neighbor's trailer drown her words.

"I have some questions, Lio. But first, I'll be up front."

He frowned, then asked with a full mouth. "In front of me?"

"Up front. Honest," Mag said.

He nodded.

"I want to help you, but helping costs money and I don't have extra. Do you have anything you could sell? Like this?" She pointed to his bracelet.

Lio swallowed his food, then clamped his hand over the bracelet. "This is my luck," he said determinedly. "My stars of—of when I was born." His voice shook. "My mother gave it."

"Okay. It's lucky. I get it."

"Luck is everything," he said.

"How did you come to Palab?"

"I ran."

"On foot?"

"Yes, on my feet. I am fast."

"Was someone chasing you?"

His eyes didn't leave her face, but a part of Lio slid into shadow. He said, "They come for my mother, in our home. She was sick. Could not go, but she told me run. She told me promise not stop until I see gold dome."

The old site of Ajrah's Gilded Palace. So this woman had made her son flee.

"Was your mother in trouble?"

He looked away. With flushed cheeks, he said, "She is good person."

Mag was silent.

"She *was* good person," Lio said. "They drained her."

"Spirit's blood," Mag cursed softly. "I'm sorry, Lio. I'll stop prying now."

He looked up at the darkening sky. The clouds were beginning to pile in the distance, but the wind was low. Not tonight.

"Here," Mag offered, digging in her pack. She slid her echo tin out of its wooden box and placed it in the center of the emptied kerchief. "Courtyard in Milyan," she whispered into the box.

The shiny sides flipped down and a small globe, bright as a blue day, burned in the open.

Lio's head whipped side to side as the walls around them sprang to soft, colored life. The box projected a bubbling stone fountain and the slap of water on flat stones. The cliffside, trailer, and tent flaps were eclipsed by bright awnings and spotless storefronts selling richly dyed clothing, fruit in bright neat rows, and a bakery window piled high with sugar-dusted puffs. The sky above them glowed luminous.

Lio opened his arms wide and laughed.

Mag smiled. She'd captured the scene herself when her purse had been fat enough to keep two young women in Milyan for a full dry season. Though hard times had often pressed her to sell the echo tin, she'd always found means to keep it. It stored up to fifty scenes. This courtyard was one of her favorites.

While Lio amused himself by poking at items in the three-dimensional projection and watching his hand pass through, she laid out her statements from Nasheed and Rinwahl to study.

From what she'd gleaned during preparatory interviews, the two duja tycoons had made a deal a few years ago, with Rinwahl controlling sales of the addictive duja north of the Hebra River while Nasheed sold to the south, but something had soured.

ALIYA CHEN

Citizens had been killed in crossfire, and her clients now faced a government ultimatum they couldn't afford to ignore. Mag smirked as she read Nasheed's handwritten comment: "I was happy to hire you after hearing your former client Jave Nillim say you pinned his collar with a blade-tip pen when he repeatedly broke your ground rules. You have a knack for making people listen." The story was true, and though it hadn't been her most levelheaded choice, calculated risks were often necessary.

Duja sales were illegal in Palab, but due to low levels of violence and generous contributions to the government, Rinwahl and Nasheed had kept free of official intervention until this recent rash of killings.

She looked up. Lio was poking his head out of the echo tin's projection the way a cornered rabbit might peer out at a fox. Whether he was a refugee, or fugitive, or something else, he wasn't about to tell her. She only knew he'd lost his mother. Gentle pity filled Mag's chest. She heard Nika's voice mocking her, "Bandage up that bleeding heart." Though she felt sorry for Lio, if the kid had been Mag's client, her instincts said to fact-check every single thing he said. She returned to her notes.

When Lio seemed sleepy, Mag leaned over the tin and said, "Night mode." The Milyan scene faded, replaced by a faint golden glow. "Two guests. Set perimeter alarm."

The tin chirped softly.

Mag rigged sky-cover from her travel tarp and gave her riding jacket to Lio. She wriggled into the smelly woolen jumper she'd stolen from her father on her last day home and promised herself that when she reached Hotel Alikesh, she'd use the in-house laundry to transform herself into the mediator her clients expected.

The night was quite warm for early spring, another sign of the storm front.

Mag rinsed her mouth, brushed her teeth, then checked on Lio. He'd already curled up beneath the tarp and was zipping himself into her jacket with his knees tucked. He looked like a leather egg.

Lio fell asleep quickly and spent the next half hour filling the makeshift tent with noisy, unapologetic flatulence as if to say, "Don't get attached to me. I promise constant irritation."

An hour later, Mag rolled away, desperate for clear air. The desert night was thick with the scent of night-blooming cereus and the taste of coming rain.

She hurled a pebble, listened to it dust-skip, then lit a cig and brought out the tube of silver decal paint. She loosened the tiny paint brush taped to its side and held Lio's child-size helmet at arm's length. After a moment's study, she began.

The instant Mag woke, she felt the void. She reached for her pack. Canteen and food gone, wallet empty, and both the riding jacket and boy had vanished.

She crouched, blinking, then mechanically closed the echo tin and packed it away. No one had snatched him. The tin's alert hadn't marked his exit. Lio had wanted to go. She looked at the small helmet she'd painted with an imitation of the LeafBlade logo. She'd meant to surprise Lio with it in the morning. She cursed herself for being a sap.

Mag washed at the restrooms, finger-combed her hair, replaced her scarf and allowed herself to mourn her riding jacket for one caustic minute. Then she smoked a cig and, when she was sure she'd calmed, returned to the campsite.

At least she'd tucked the ignition key into her bra. He hadn't had the nerve to grope there. And the crescents were still hidden in her money belt.

Mag took her time packing up, then as she picked burrs off her boots, a motion caught her eye. A face watched her from behind the Firebrand. She bolted to her feet, neck hot.

Lio's face was crumpled. He pointed to her campstove and she saw coffee boiling in a pot. The pickings of her wallet sat beside Lio's shoes. He mutely offered a bunch of wild yellow primroses.

She waited for a blubbering excuse, but instead Lio met her eyes and said, "Before the sun, I walk away for one hour carrying your things. They much heavy in my hands, so I come back." He squared his shoulders. "Decide I am not thief."

He held out the riding jacket to her. She drew the leather to her nose, then pushed her arms into the sleeves and crossed to the coffee. She poured a cup and took three slow swallows, letting him stew in his guilt.

"My world runs on second chances, but not third ones." She cleared her throat. "If you weren't so cute, I'd have already shot off your thief's hand. Also, primroses are my favorite, you little shit."

He grinned. Sheet lighting flashed behind him in the morning haze.

She raised a finger. "One more chance."

Lio nodded, then unclasped his bracelet and held it out.

Mag pushed it back. "You need all your luck out here." Then, after a moment's hesitation, she showed him what she'd painted on the helmet.

"Beautiful!" Lio shouted, cramming the helmet onto his head. He caught her in a wild hug, then seemed to remember himself. "Thank you," he said, bowing ceremoniously.

"You're welcome."

As she made a final sweep of the site, Mag's fingers brushed her matchbook, tucked inside her jumper pocket. What kind of eight-year-old thief knew how to start fires without tools? Exactly how worried should she be?

As she was securing her pack on the Firebrand, Lio touched her arm.

"Maglin Grayhawk," he began, sobriety plain in his green eyes, "I want to ask. If you . . . if you help me to learn who I do and am better."

Mag flinched at his use of her full name. Then she remembered he'd ransacked her wallet. So the kid could read Darik as well as speak it.

She said, "By 'learn' do you mean 'school'? You want a teacher?"

His face brightened with relief. "Yes! A teacher." He swallowed, then said with deliberation, "For me."

Mag noted his strange intensity, then squatted to bring their eyes on level.

"If this job goes well, I'll have enough for room and board in an Ellawi bunker to wait out the storm. I'd wanted a spot with a private kitchen. But if I don't really need that kitchen, I could find space for two."

I must be losing my mind, she thought. *I'm making a generous offer to a kid who just tried to steal me blind.*

But the words continued pouring. "Maybe, once the storm has passed, I could find you a school with late enrollment." Mag activated the Firebrand's choke. "How does that sound?"

"Find a school," he repeated.

"Did you understand anything else I just said?"

He wagged his head unconvincingly. "Most?"

Mag folded the kickstand. "Get on."

The multi-spired outline of Hotel Alikesh was the grandest sight for miles, including Ellawi's three-hundred-year-old cathedral. Gleaming ramparts and polished roof tiles glowed the color of sunset and resembled a flaming crown.

Mag and Lio agreed that they'd pretend, if asked, that he was her personal attendant. At the city gate, Mag balked at the gatekeeper's exorbitant entrance fee. As she reached for her wallet, palms sweating slightly, Lio leaned around to stare at the gatekeeper. The man smiled at him and offered a discount on behalf of her hungry-looking kid. Mag was happy to take whatever kindness she could get.

The hall clock read five minutes after one in the afternoon as Mag turned her room key in its lock. Lio sprang across plush carpet toward the array of complimentary fruit and nuts. Mag stashed valuables in the room's safe, sent a bag of clothes to the laundry, then locked herself in the bathroom for a thorough washing. Half an hour later, the laundry returned, pressed and steamed. The Alikesh almost certainly employed a simmer.

Mag dressed, then noted the emptied food bowls. Lio lay curled on the bed, eyes closed. Perhaps his flatulence of the previous night had been his stomach's distrust of a full meal after prolonged starvation. She tapped his shoulder and suggested that he bathe, then called Petrin Nasheed's room and acquired permission to borrow his therma-pin for the negotiation. She took a slow stroll through the hotel's courtyard, noting the sky's deepening shade of purple while she relished a cig, then returned to the room.

Lio was asleep atop the bedspread. His wet hair smelled of orange-blossom soap, but he'd put on the same filthy long-sleeved shirt again. She reached to touch his forehead, then stopped herself. She seated herself at the room's desk, back to the sleeping boy, and fixed her eyes on her notes.

Big. Important. I see in your face. What you do today?" Lio asked. Mag sat at breakfast with him in the courtyard. He'd been slipping dried dates into his pocket.

She said, "I'm going to help some angry people find a way to agree."

He leaned in. "Angry people are dangerous, yes? You bring gun for shield?"

She smiled. "No guns. Just mouths for talking and ears for listening. And brains for thinking. Hopefully."

"No one have guns?"

She shrugged. "Well, someone usually smuggles something in. But I keep tempers in check so that no one uses them."

Her hip throbbed in bitter protest.

"Then you take this." Lio held up his lucky bracelet.

The conference room's twin chandeliers reflected on Mag's polished boots. Her buckles, buttons, even her gold nose-ring, were freshly shined. Lio's bracelet weighed heavy in her pocket. She'd purchased an expensive black scarf from the hotel boutique in order to wear Palab's traditional color of power.

Mag had left Lio in the hotel room with plenty of vids and snacks, and stern orders to stay put. She entered the conference room an intentional five minutes late.

All were in attendance. The ice-blue marble floor was streaked with white branches and black flecks, resembling a dark snowfall. A double row of brown earth-stone pillars lined the hall like an orderly forest. Two tables faced each other, seating three delegates apiece.

Before introductions, Mag silently scrubbed for bugs with her snoop, calibrated the borrowed therma-pin, then strode to stand at the room's far end.

She mentally summoned her clients' profiles as she surveyed them.

Nalib Rinwahl had held a national monopoly on duja sales for fifteen years. Five years ago ceded sales south of the Hebra River to Petrin Nasheed. Lost wife to stomach cancer within the last year, but still wore a silver wedding cuff. Known for his severe temperament, Nalib Rinwahl was also a traditionalist obsessed with reputation and honor.

He sat to her right, flanked by his two adult sons, Ush and Isma. He wore a well-trimmed beard, black suit, and digital signature band on his right pinkie. Ush, Rinwahl's eldest, dressed like his father, but the younger Isma wore an azure collar beneath his jacket. Isma stared at Mag for a long moment, then absently rubbed his little finger as she turned aside.

Petrin Nasheed had been raised by his uncle after losing both parents in a maglev wreck. Opened a business consulting firm at age nineteen. His acute intuition for social scenarios had routinely roused suspicions that led to repeated tests for empathic abilities, always with negative results. His unofficial slogan: "I'm just good with people." Seven years ago, left the consulting world to enter the duja trade. Business had thrived steadily until a recent outbreak of violent run-ins with Rinwahl had burned bridges and dragged the government into the fray.

Petrin Nasheed sat between his advisers Murelle Dijab and Liata Greensword. Nasheed flashed Mag a grin while his fingers spun a ballpoint pen in a complex weave. Both advisers' headscarves were flame orange. Dijab wore half-moon reading lenses and wrote on a tablet while Greensword watched the room with sharp, bright blue eyes.

Mag drew a breath. "As all of us know, we're here to resolve the rift between your two enterprises. As mediator, I'll work to facilitate terms that are well balanced and acceptable to all. I offer the following: One, confidentiality on all matters discussed here. Two, voluntary participation—I will not force you to concede any point. Three, neutrality—I promise an unbiased stance. I will channel and facilitate discussion. I will not advise.

"The rules: Listen. Don't interrupt. When you do speak, strive for courtesy."

She cleared her throat and paused. Nasheed seemed attentive, though his eyes were slightly reddened from lack of sleep or possibly substance indulgence. Rinwahl wore stoic skepticism. Mag's gut said Rinwahl would be her stubborn client.

She continued. "During my separate meetings with each of you, I established your objectives. Mr. Nasheed, you seek a stop to the recent wave of violence. Mr. Rinwahl, you seek renewed adherence to your original contract terms, specifically that sales of Mr. Nasheed's duja remain strictly south of the Hebra."

Both sides nodded curtly.

Good. No time wasted there.

Mag said, "Four days ago the Palabi government instated a 5,000-crescent fine for each day that this dispute remains unresolved. This adds incentive to proceed with efficiency." She paused.

Of course, the fact that no one had yet been jailed for the murders meant that the government was still being generously paid off, to some extent.

Rinwahl was clenching his jaw in agitation.

Nasheed raised his hand. "I'd like to make an opening statement."

Mag nodded.

"We're here about the killings," Nasheed said. "The trend began two months ago when Rinwahl provided his so-called peacekeepers with assault-mode scatterblitzes. This ridiculous stance of martial authority puts my vendors at a constant disadvantage." Nasheed looked sidelong at his advisers, then added, "I'm well aware we could meet the challenge with bigger, better guns, but I've read too much history to think an arms race will solve matters."

Rinwahl grimaced, motioning for attention.

"Is there anything you wish to correct in Mr. Nasheed's statement?" Mag asked him.

"No. But I'll supply details that he blithely glossed over." Rinwahl leaned forward, elbows brushing the tabletop. "I issued those scatterblitzes after multiple safety complaints. My employees are like family, and I take their safety seriously."

The younger Rinwahl son rolled his eyes. Familial discord.

Rinwahl said, "Five years ago, I ceded the southern half of the country to Nasheed's sales. But he hasn't been satisfied with that. He's flagrantly stolen my customers. Then, when he resented my means of protecting my people and territory, he tainted a batch of duja during its bottling, which made my customers have violent nausea."

Counselor Dijab read from her tablet. "The precise contract terms should be noted here. The agreement appeared fair, but a close inspection of Palab's population density reveals the division of customers was steeply tilted in Mr. Rinwahl's favor."

Rinwahl seemed ready to rebuff the claim, but Mag said, "Yes, the population disparity between the North and South surfaced in both our pre-meetings. The gist of the contract was that Mr. Nasheed would buy raw duja product from Mr. Rinwahl's greenhouses at a minimal markup that was only to rise with the country's standard inflation rates. Mr. Nasheed's sales would be restricted to the South, which was less populated than the North."

"Significantly less," Nasheed muttered. "And the clientele is poorer and less civilized, if I may be blunt." He locked eyes with Rinwahl. "But I surprised you. Instead of withering, my business thrived. But to address the accusation of tainting your duja, I suggest improving your quality control, since another bad batch could impair your credibility."

Reading between those lines was simple: Nasheed had a man inside Rinwahl's manufacturing plant. When Rinwahl used his new guns, Nasheed had signaled his man to tweak a batch of duja that then sickened Rinwahl's clients. If Rinwahl's product could be made to seem unreliable, his customers would flock to Nasheed.

Counselor Dijab handed Nasheed a simple, unadorned echo tin. He murmured into it. A projection of a scuffed brown-glass bottle spun into view.

"Most of us know Rinwahl's duja," Nasheed said. "It comes in one flavor and one strength—highly intoxicating. All well and good, if that's what you like. But this is my duja."

In the projection, a velvet curtain enclosed the room and a polished table appeared at the room's center bearing gold-etched glass vials.

"The projections can't carry smell, but I have vanilla, mint, and sandalwood scents, among others," Nasheed said, "with intensities to match any passion. I proposed this product to Rinwahl seven years ago. He turned me down. Then, after I'd grown a business that was successful enough to worry him, we signed that stilted contract. He wanted to cut me off from his best cities and customers. He thought I'd dry up. But I didn't."

Mag said, "Is it fair to say, Mr. Rinwahl, that you underestimated the potential of Mr. Nasheed's business model?"

Rinwahl hesitated, then nodded. "It's dishonorable to begrudge a man his success, but I believe I can criticize Nasheed's disregard for terms. I've spent my life growing things, you see." He took out his own echo tin. It was twice the size of Mag's own, filigreed with spiraling swallows. He murmured into it and the conference room was domed by glass and steel girders. Lush, raised beds lined the ground in rows, bearing lime-green stalks and tan blossoms.

"Furthermore," said Rinwahl, "my customers include the most influential families of Palab. I may not have a flashy product, but I have a time-tested tradition. I cannot abide the brazen attitudes of your vendors, Nasheed, slipping across the Hebra, enticing customer migration, having no scruples about whether your goods are resold up north."

"I'm not shooting people at every chance I get. Let's be clear on that," Nasheed snarled.

Rinwahl reddened. "If you call self-defense a—"

"Self-defense?" Nasheed laughed coldly. "And this, after you raised the cost of my raw duja to triple the rate of inflation, leaving me with no recourse but to swallow it?"

"Okay," Mag raised both arms, "we're at the heart of it."

"No." Nasheed stood. "The heart is that my good friend Brussin Seff was murdered yesterday because, despite this upcoming meeting, you still didn't call off your dogs."

Mag absorbed this new information and watched Nasheed's face flush as he shoved a chip into his echo tin. She crossed to him and placed her hand firmly atop the box. "Wait a moment," she said.

Nasheed's eyes were flaming, but he eyed her unyielding stance and relented.

Counselor Greensword whispered something in Nasheed's ear. He shrugged and replaced the chip in the echo tin with a different one.

Mag turned to Rinwahl. "A man's broken word is quite an insult. Mr. Nasheed's contract violations have destroyed your respect for him, correct?"

"Absolutely." Rinwahl spoke coolly, eyes on Nasheed's face.

"And Mr. Nasheed, you seek an end to bloodshed. A peaceful way forward."

Nasheed cleared his throat, struggling to speak.

So the murdered man had truly been a friend. Even in Palab, where hyperbole was everywhere, he hadn't exaggerated this.

Nasheed said at last, "Yes. Of course."

"Can we agree that peace and mutual respect are worthy goals?"

Mag let the awkward silence hang until both men gave verbal agreement.

Then Nasheed said, "Now let me explain, Rinwahl, I'm trying to do good business. It's no secret that my duja is more popular. But your 'family' are harassing and shooting my vendors at the mildest provocation. And they're not just killing my guys. Children were hit by crossfire more than once. My wish is that duja sales *throughout* Palab would flourish, but that's too lofty a goal for today. I'd settle for keeping my people safe on the street and a fair cost for raw duja." His eyes glittered for a moment, then Nasheed added, "I'd thought to share a view of the alley where Brussin's body was found. Instead," he glanced at Counselor Dijab, "in better taste, I give you the medical examiner's report." He whispered into his echo tin and the report spun as a single page in three dimensions. "Read it for yourself, but I'll highlight the thirty-seven bullet wounds, all delivered from the back. His tongue was cut out."

The room hung still until Rinwahl said, "Though this man's death was a mistake, I must say that threats to those under my protection will always be treated seriously."

Mag knew Nasheed's next move before he took it.

"No apology," Nasheed muttered.

Mag held her breath.

A nasty grin contorted Nasheed's face. "Shall we talk about what's really threatening your family?"

Both the Rinwahl sons flinched. Isma straightened.

"You've been trying to cover your son Isma's gambling debts for years now," Nasheed said as Greensword nodded beside him. Dijab handed Nasheed a tablet. He read it quickly, then said, "Today we see he's not even wearing your family dig-sig anymore, which means you've cut off his independent spending."

Mag flicked a glance at the finger that Isma now held studiously still. How recent was this development?

Nasheed continued, volume mounting, "You supplied false reasons for raising my raw duja cost because you needed funds to placate the casinos. You've even started selling your wife's jewels. I don't know what kind of deal you made to get those scatterblitzes, but it's obvious you aren't thinking with a level head."

Rinwahl had flushed from red to purple, which was notable given his bronze complexion. "How dare you bring in my personal matters?" he growled. "You're not trying to make peace! You're trying to tear me down!"

Mag said loudly, "We're going to take a recess."

But a clatter of chairs drowned her voice as Rinwahl, Nasheed and their supporters took to their feet.

A rapid assessment of both sides' confident postures told Mag that concealed weapons were in the room. The weapons' presence wasn't usual, but if anything went off, even assuming no one was injured, the negotiation failed and Mag lost her payment. Of course, if she was dying of a bullet wound in her gut before the storm hit, affording shelter would be pointless.

Mag gritted her teeth as she strode to stand, arms wide, between the two tables, hoping for a nonfatal shot if she was going to be hit.

The elder Rinwahl son had one arm extended, bent at the wrist, probably readying some hidden dart gun. Nasheed brandished a pistol in plain view. Mag thought briefly of her concealed moonblade, but a knife was little help here.

"Eyes on me!" Mag shouted. "I said eyes on *me*!"

Nasheed responded first, but not as she'd expected. He tensed and bent, as if to run. She looked at Rinwahl, whose eyes were wide with a similar terror. Ush caught his father by the arm, face full of concern. A sudden mood change in both leaders.

Mag's skin chilled.

Not now. Please not now.

The therma-pin beeped three sharp notes. She turned its glowing light toward her face. "The device has registered a simpathic heat-signature," she announced. "The pulse was erratic. No further activity detected."

"You hired a simpath, Nasheed?" Ush Rinwahl spat with disgust.

Counselor Greensword glared at him. "Do you really think he'd have hired a simpath to attack himself, too?"

"It could be a clever ploy," Isma Rinwahl suggested.

"This meeting is canceled," Rinwahl growled. "Simpathic sway compromises everything."

Mag rapidly scanned the room, silencing her panic with pragmatism, noting where a simpath might hide. Making rapid decisions, she said, "Here's what we'll do: Put those weapons away—out of the room. Take an hour lunch break. You can channel your anger into creative problem-solving. Regroup among yourselves and I'll arrange private meetings. I'll also re-secure the premises. Send your own security teams, too, if you like."

"I agree with Rinwahl," Nasheed said. "Simpathic disturbance should nullify this now."

Mag crossed her arms. "Is that really what you want? To schedule another negotiation date, rehire a mediator, all with those daily fines?" She turned her palms up. "It's your money, not mine."

She refolded her arms to hide the shaking. She wouldn't consider a reality in which this negotiation was canceled. Not yet.

"All right. One more chance," Nasheed said. "The simpath pulse was erratic. Perhaps it was circumstantial. Perhaps room security will solve it. I'm not comfortable, but I hate delays even more. I'll risk a little for the chance to be done with this."

After a pause, Rinwahl grunted agreement.

Mag set up private conference times as the delegates prepared to leave. As they exited, storm dust swirled into the conference room. Mag stood in the empty room while her heart pounded manically.

Boiling coffee on a stove without matches, an overheated engine with an excited young rider, her own uncharacteristic fear after the close-call railroad crossing.

The instances hit in a stinging stream.

Tea that went from lukewarm to chilled, the strange discount at the Ellawi gate, and—of course!—the religiously worn sleeves that concealed the forearms. She really should have known.

Mag pressed her palms to her cheeks.

Secure the room first. Obscure all line-of-sight options.

There were no windows. The walls had no doors or alcoves. This left the ceiling air vents as the only place a simpath could feasibly maintain visual contact and stay hidden.

Mag enlisted two boys from grounds keeping to fasten dark sheets over all air vents, then headed straight for her hotel room, heart in her throat.

Do you have any idea what you almost did in there?"

Lio sat cross-legged on the bed, eyes innocent and wide. He hadn't even bothered to replace the air vent screws; they lay loose on the bedside table.

"Lio," she grabbed his shoulders. "I know it was you. I know you're a simpath."

He twisted away. "You needed me," he said. "I saved you. Weapons were too dangerous. My lucky bracelet not enough."

He'd interfered while she stood in harm's way, revealed himself as a simpath in order to protect her, and at great personal risk. Warmth bloomed in Mag's chest, but she resisted it, holding tightly to her rage.

The kid must be ignorant of the horrors that greedy bastards inflicted on child simpaths. Or was he? Had Lio's mother been killed for birthing a child with simpathic abilities? Keshian law now forbade the union of a simmer and an empath.

Her words trembled. "If you meddle again, it'll be worse for me than if I were shot."

Lio twisted his mouth in disbelief and Mag seized his collar. He whimpered.

"Stay out of this," she hissed. "That's an order, not a request."

He seemed to shrink as he nodded, face pale, shoulders drooping. Mag found a maid and paid her generously from her dwindling purse to watch and stay with Lio. Of course, if Lio wanted to use his gift to dismiss the maid, he could. But Mag judged by the stark fear in his face that he'd respect her wishes.

She crammed a handful of nuts into her mouth on the way out the door. From there, she had five minutes before her first client conference.

I'll speak frankly," Nasheed said as Mag joined him and his advisers at their courtyard table. Machinery groaned above them as the Alikesh unrolled its roofcap to prepare for the storm. Dust thickened the air and purple streaks were darkening overhead.

Mag coughed to clear her lungs and accepted Nasheed's offered bread and dipping spices.

Nasheed said, "Rinwahl is a bully with no creativity who can't even control his own sons."

She smiled crisply. "Mudslinging only hampers resolution. Contrary to logic as this may seem, now's your time to make Mr. Rinwahl a unilateral offer."

Nasheed snorted. "And why would I want to do that?"

"It's your best chance of getting an offer from him."

He stared at her for a moment, then straightened. Counselor Dijab readied her writing pad.

"Your vendors and product sales are his main point of contention," Mag said. "You might focus there."

As she stood to leave, Nasheed said. "That's all you have to say?"

"I strive to guide and facilitate, Mr. Nasheed. You have some very intelligent aides to advise you."

As she turned to go, Counselor Greensword flashed her an approving smile.

M̲ag had purposefully given Rinwahl the later time slot. Despite Nasheed's turbulent emotions during the negotiation, she judged Rinwahl as the man who needed more time to cool off. He was on the rooftop veranda, smoking a cigar over the remains of his lunch while his sons sat in tense silence. The roofcap above bore an artful projection of a clear blue sky over far mountains.

When Mag suggested Rinwahl make Nasheed an offer, he balked in similar fashion.

"He's not getting any more land."

"Territory isn't his objective," she reminded. "He takes issue with your new weapons and the increased violence."

"Removing my people's protection would only invite more problems."

Both Isma and Ush seemed ready with comments, but Rinwahl only glanced at Ush and shook his head. He ignored Isma completely.

"If I may have a word," Mag said suddenly.

It was an impulse, but she felt confident as she led Rinwahl to the balcony railing. He dangled his cigar over the open air and watched the hazy trail. The wind had dropped to dead calm. The storm was poised and ready.

She shivered, pushed the thought away, and lit her own cig in the silence. She said, "This is the truth: you'll poison your future more quickly by choosing favorites between your sons than you'll ever lose to granting Nasheed a few concessions."

Rinwahl pulled his cigar from his mouth, wordless. She left him still frowning.

Unbiased empathy was the mediator's best and most delicate tool. Mag took a minute to refresh herself in one of the Alikesh's powder rooms, prayed for the eighth time that Lio would stay put, then strode into the conference room with a show of confident optimism.

Nasheed seemed relaxed. He was smiling his trademark grin again. Rinwahl sat with a son on each side, all three men had their heads held high. He nodded to Mag and she knew he'd spoken to Ush and Isma.

This was the moment in the endgame when Mag compelled herself to truly love her clients, to feel Rinwahl's anger at Nasheed's affront, to grieve with Nasheed for lives needlessly lost. She became a genuine advocate for both men, esteeming them as people with histories and souls. Mag summoned her own grief for Nika's death as she met Nasheed's eye. "You lost a good friend to an early death, and yet you're here for peace. This takes courage."

He nodded and looked down quickly.

Next, Mag summoned the gnawing betrayal of the day Nika announced she didn't need Mag in her life anymore. She met

Rinwahl's gaze and said, "You've endured a broken contract and the shame of family disloyalty, yet you've chosen to hear out your opponent. This reveals honor."

Rinwahl frowned and rubbed his knuckles, but Mag knew she'd hit her mark.

The therma-pin remained blessedly silent as she continued. "A successful negotiation is a dance of give and take. You'll likely compromise more than you planned. Now is the time to make a request and, perhaps, an offer."

The chandeliers flickered.

"Consider that a warning to work quickly," she added dryly.

Nasheed began immediately. "My northern sales are a point of contention. Some instances of resale will remain beyond my full control; however, I'm offering today to relocate my three main duja distribution centers an additional ten miles south of the Hebra, which will decrease the proximity issue. In addition, I'll impose a fine of five hundred crescents for vendors I catch selling product across the river. I ask that you replace the scatterblitzes with something less destructive which will still give your people the protection they deserve." After a pause, Nasheed added, "I can't stop the migration of customers coming south, but I can offer you my consultation services for improving your product's marketability."

That last bit was a cheeky move, but Rinwahl didn't seem to mind.

Rinwahl said, "I can't confiscate the scatterblitzes. It would make my people feel vulnerable. I can, however, mandate training and make a selective protocol for who is permitted to carry such arms with severe consequences for breaking the protocol. I will set strict terms of engagement for weapons. In addition, I request a cessation of all marketing campaigns aimed at customers in the North." He leveled a glare at Nasheed. "You know the ones I mean."

Nasheed grinned.

Rinwahl added, "I'm pleased to hear you've already considered stricter guidelines for your vendors' sales. I wouldn't want more accidents to befall those who venture beyond our defined trade zones."

Without skipping a beat, Nasheed returned, "And I'd hate for another bad batch of duja to destroy your customers' trust in you. I doubt you could afford that right now."

There. Both men had made their thinly veiled threats as means of insurance. Not the brightest outlook, but they had an understanding.

"All right," Mag said. "I've written the offers and demands on the board. We'll finesse the wording until we reach something acceptable to everyone."

As she lifted her pen, distant thunder rumbled. The negotiation's worst might have passed, but not the storm's. Her mind returned to its rattling question.

What am I going to do with you, Lio?

Less than an hour later, the agreement was being sent to print. Mag watched Nasheed cross to Rinwahl's table to shake hands with him and his sons.

It wasn't warmth that passed between the two factions; it was a fragile bridge. But it was enough.

Rinwahl had offered to personally make restitution to Brussin Seff's family and this small gesture had sped the negotiation's completion.

Once the document was officially signed on both paper and dig-sig pads, Mag set the therma-pin on the tabletop and addressed the room.

"Congratulations. You have managed to stop tearing down and to start building up. This is how great nations are built. You should feel very proud."

A murmur of assent swept the tables. Then the moment broke and Rinwahl approached Mag. "You've addressed not just the problems at hand but given me a new mirror to examine myself as both leader and father." He smiled, and Mag sensed the rarity of it. "Wisdom has bloomed today. May the Eye show mercy and success on your future work."

She bowed.

Nasheed caught her in a firm handshake as she turned. "You're at the top of my list now, though let's hope I don't have to hire you again anytime soon!" He laughed loudly.

After one more round of gracious farewells, she ducked out and headed for the elevator, forcing herself not to run.

Mag needed no warning against forming an emotional attachment to a simpath; the foreboding pulsed like poison in her blood. The kid might well have used his sway on her during the entire trip to Ellawi, but in this hallway he couldn't see and therefore couldn't sway her, yet Mag's determination to shelter him remained.

To her surprise, she found Lio sitting on the hotel room floor playing a game of tallit with the maid. She rushed to hug him wordlessly, then paid the maid and locked the door.

"Pack your things," she whispered. "The storm's almost here."

Lio's stare indicated his need for explanation.

His words echoed in her mind. *Help me to learn who I do ...*

She said, "Thank you for trying to protect me. I realize now that when you asked to 'learn' you meant simpath training. I don't know where to start, but I'll try to help you. For now, I have to get us someplace safe."

He nodded.

Thunder clapped overhead, and the clouds burst. Too late for safe.

Mag hastily double-checked the new numbers in her account, then pulled up the address of the bunker she'd researched the day before. Though she might have squatted for a time in the Alikesh foyer, she knew the hotel would have found a way to charge her beyond her means, and Lio wasn't safe in a crowd. They needed a bunker's isolation.

As they left the lobby, Mag grabbed a gilded mirror off a wall and hoisted it above her head, muttering to Lio, "The things I do for you already."

The bunker was two blocks away. The acid rain wasn't

pounding yet, but slanting lines in the purple haze were racing toward them.

Lio pushed the Firebrand and Mag shielded them with the mirror. Lio froze the first time she screamed. The acid was eating her hands.

She cursed at him. "Don't stop till you reach that blue door!"

She wasn't sure she had more than bones left on her fingers, and her shoulder blades flamed where her jacket had melted away, but they made it.

The place smelled of bleach and scrubbed steel. She wrapped her bleeding hands in bandages given to her by the bunker's proprietor, parked the Firebrand along the back wall of their private room, wiped the bike down, checked the fluids, then arranged echo tin, snoop, gun, some ration food packs, and Lio's bracelet on a wall-ledge. She eyed the window. She'd paid extra for the slit of green glass, but now she wished she hadn't.

Lio strained on tiptoe, trying to improve his view of the outside. He must have never seen the stormwall, but surely he'd heard the stories? Mag had spoken to a few storm survivors. Sometimes the rain melted flesh, sometimes it melted the mind. The Alikesh had its retractable roofcap, but most Ellawi citizens couldn't afford such things.

Well, there was no hiding it from Lio. They'd be stuck watching this for two weeks.

Bruise-purple clouds were throbbing above them. Mag put a bandaged hand on Lio's shoulder and was surprised by the dullness of her pain. She'd savor the effects of shock and adrenaline while they lasted.

First came the hissing acid pellets, sizziing semisolids at the storm's head. Then the small fires as a few pellets found wood. A minute later, glass cracked somewhere beyond. With the glass broken, the storm whipped into homes. Then the screams.

After an awful minute, Lio touched Mag's arm.

She said, "Want me to set up something on the echo tin?"

He nodded.

They retreated together into the Milyan courtyard. Lio curled around his helmet and shut his eyes while Mag thought of the storm she'd escaped only to hole up with a different kind of peril.

Lio needed training. The kid created his own kind of luck, but untrained luck like his was a hazard to anyone near him and a magnet for power players. She couldn't just turn him loose when the storm was over, could she?

Mag forced herself into the present. At least this room kept Lio safe for now. Folk hatred for simpaths and the black-market value of young ones were bleak realities. Two weeks without a cig. Best not to think about that, either.

She slipped out of the projection and stood again at the window. The bunker's proprietor had warned her that the grid shut off for the first few hours of storm, and that after the stormwall passed, the first electric light outside became a sign of hope.

Wails and roars thudded dully against the bunker walls.

Even in this short string of days, Lio could betray her. He could twist her mind against itself and bolt, leaving her with nothing. Simpaths were famous for that. All her charity, all the risks she'd taken for him, could still end in curses and suffering. Yet the kid had tried to save her life when he'd thought it endangered.

Mag leaned her forehead on the glass. She always took more chances than was wise. It was her nature. Some risks were worth it.

Sometime later, Lio leaned against her side. He was cradling his helmet on his chest.

"Look," Mag whispered, pointing.

High above, strung between two crumbling apartment towers, a single line of white lights glowed bravely, like stars.

The First Warden

written by

Kai Wolden

illustrated by

ALEXANDER GUSTAFSON

ABOUT THE AUTHOR

Kai Wolden is a writer, editor, and fantasy fanatic from Northern Wisconsin. Home-schooled as a child, Kai started reading at an early age and writing not long afterward. Kai aspired to be an author at age ten and completed their first novel at age twenty-two.

Kai has a Bachelor of Arts degree in English and writing from the University of Wisconsin-Superior, where they graduated cum laude in 2015. Kai has three short fiction publications in the literary journals Red Fez *and* The Nemadji Review, *and is a two-time winner of the UWS Women's and Gender Studies Essay Competition. Kai is also an alumnus of Sigma Tau Delta, the International English Honor Society.*

Among Kai's (many) inspirations are the works of Anne Rice, N. K. Jemisin, Garth Nix, and the great Ursula K. Le Guin. Kai's other interests include cosplay, Dungeons & Dragons, and traveling everywhere possible. Kai lives in the Twin Cities, Minnesota, with their partner and spoiled cat, Clawdia.

ABOUT THE ILLUSTRATOR

Alexander Gustafson is an illustrator, concept artist, and maquette sculptor. Growing up in the icy mountains of Vermont, he enjoyed drawing, telling stories, and playing Dungeons & Dragons to ward off the cold. He also spent hours in those formative years admiring the works of modern masters like Todd Lockwood, Chris Van Allsburg, James Gurney, and Brom. All of this eventually compelled him to seek out a career in fantasy illustration, where he has the freedom to create worlds and tell stories with pictures. He graduated from Savannah College of Art and Design in 2008 with a master's degree in illustration, and continues to pursue his passion for fantasy, sci-fi, and steampunk art.

The First Warden

When I was very young, a sickness struck—the sort that spreads like fire, consuming everyone it touches. I remember terrible heat, terrible cold, a drifting sensation, and something I can only describe as bliss. It would not have been a bad death. It would have been an ordinary one, and I have never felt the disdain some feel for the ordinary.

I thought I was dreaming when I opened my eyes to see a blurry figure wreathed in light. He bent over me, long hair brushing my face, and asked me if I knew him. I nodded. I did know him, though only from afar. He was Shae, our magus, the vessel of the gods. He replied softly that he knew me too. Then he told me he was going to take me away.

"To the Afterworld?" I asked—or something to that effect. And he laughed the most delighted, silken laugh. I recall being unsure if he would be able to lift me; he was so slight. But he did so with ease, letting my soiled blankets slide to the floor and bearing me out into the cold daylight in only my nightshirt. My eyes watered in the sunlight, so my family's tent blurred as I took my last look at it over his shoulder. And then, all at once, it burst into flames.

I cried out, only half sure the flames were real—they wavered and danced so phantasmically. Names spilled from my lips—those of the people we'd left inside—though now I cannot recall them. Shae murmured something meaningless and calming, holding me firmly as I struggled. And as we departed, I saw that all the tents around us were burning. The air shimmered, flakes of ash gathered in Shae's long hair, and for the first time in ages, I felt warm.

ALEXANDER GUSTAFSON

We did not go to the Afterworld. When I came to myself, I was buried in soft furs and the air was sweet with wood smoke. The canvas that arched overhead glowed softly in the afternoon sunlight. My body felt languid, boneless, and my mind was pleasantly muddled. I would have described the feeling as drunkenness had I been old enough to enjoy the pleasures of wine.

Voices reached me faintly from outside, rising and falling in a lulling manner. It took me some time to identify one of them as Shae's and to realize that he was angry.

"I have done my duty. The north side of the camp is cinders."

"Your duty was to eliminate the plague. Not to bring it into our midst." This voice, I did not know.

"I knew when I saw him that the child would live."

"And what is to be done with him now? No family will take a child of plague."

"He will stay with me." The words were cool and placid, but for the taut silence that followed, he might have shouted them.

When the man—I was sure it was a man—spoke again, his voice was thick and pent. "You think that is wise?"

"It is not your concern whom I share my home with, Councilor. Now I ask that you leave me be."

There was another fraught pause, and then the man—who I now suspected was Councilor Glenn—uttered stiff departing words, which Shae politely returned. I lifted my head as the dim tent was briefly flooded with light and then darkened again as the door flap fell back into place. Shae's slender figure approached me, and as he passed the fire pit in the center of the room, the flames within sprang brightly to life, illuminating rich carpets and polished wood furnishings the likes of which I'd never seen.

It frightened me to see the fire flare so suddenly. I buried my face in the luxuriant furs. But my fear flickered out as I felt him settle beside me, replaced by curiosity. He smiled as I peeped at him, and the effect was truly startling. He had a face like no other: smooth, sculpted, and ageless. Tawny skin and ink-black hair that fell in a rippling curtain to his waist. And when the light caught his eyes, they were jeweled amber.

"I suppose you heard all that," he said. His voice made me think of clear water. "But I don't want you to worry. You are my ward now, and no one can take you away from me."

"Ward," I repeated the strange word, pleased by the way it rolled out of my mouth.

"It means you are under my protection." Smiles came to him so easily; it was as though his face were made for them.

But, overwhelmed by the strangeness of my new surroundings, I could not share his joy. Turning my face back into the furs, I whispered that I wanted to go home. He answered calmly that I was home, and I started to quietly cry. He stayed beside me until I hiccupped myself into silence. Then he asked me if I wanted something to eat. I sat up and nodded, suddenly ravenous. I never asked to leave again.

The following days passed, dreamlike. The sweet, heavy wood smoke made me sleepy and the tea Shae brewed for me, thick with honey, made me feel light and dizzy in a not-unpleasant way. It would take me time to grow accustomed to this muddled state of being that I would soon learn was simply the way Shae lived. It would take me time also to adapt to the luxury, the softness, and the warmth. I had lived a harsh life before coming here, though the details of it were fading fast. Sometimes, I was woken by terrible nightmares in which faceless people called my name and reached for me with skeletal hands, black with ash. But he was always there, a quiet presence in the dark, and his soft, even breaths would lull me back to sleep.

He bathed me in warm water and patiently trimmed the mats out of my hair. He clothed me in his spare garments at first, which were long and silken and trailed behind me on the floor when I walked. He laughed to see me stumble about and promised to have proper-fitting clothes made for me. One day, a woman came to measure my arms, legs, and torso, though she didn't look me in the eye or touch me directly. She murmured something strange and stomped in a hurried circle before entering and leaving the tent.

"Superstition," Shae said when I looked at him questioningly. I did not know this word, so he went on, "She believes that you have cheated death, so death will forever seek to claim you. She believes that this curse may cleave to her if she comes too close. She asks for the gods' protection."

"And will the gods protect her?" I asked.

He shot me a conspiratorial look. "The gods do not entertain such foolishness."

"Then I am not cursed?" I pressed with a cautious hope.

"No," he replied, placing a warm hand atop my cropped curls. "You will live a long life and you will never suffer sickness again. But it will take others some time to see that. You must be patient with them."

I nodded, forever anxious to please him. When the clothes arrived, they were perfectly fitted and made of the richest fabrics I had ever felt. There were soft underthings, thick tunics for winter and lighter ones for summer, trousers and leggings, and fur-trimmed cloaks. There were boots as well, of supple deerskin, and leather belts with pouches for keeping whatever trinkets a child might wish to keep. Shae watched with quiet delight as I marveled over it all—I could tell by the way his eyes danced. They were like crystallized honey, enchanting.

"You will never want for anything again," he told me, snatching the finest of the fur-lined cloaks and swirling it around my shoulders.

"Where does it all come from?" I asked, clutching the thick fabric around me. I meant not only the clothes, but all the wonders the large and beautiful tent contained. And I truly asked not where, but why—why were these things here and nowhere else?

"It is gifted to me in return for the service I offer the clan," he answered.

"But I thought you served the gods," I said. With my returning health, my questions had grown bolder.

He smiled that secret smile that made me feel privy to something I didn't understand. "I am a magus. I serve all but myself."

Often, his answers confused more than they clarified. Of magi, I knew only what every child knows. Magi were granted power by the gods. This power they used to protect and guide the clans. Each clan had only one magus, and he or she was regarded with honor. Shae's name had forever been spoken with reverence in my hearing. Though it was true he possessed the power to call or quell storms, to spark fire from nothing, to summon and ward off sickness, to control animals, and to foretell the future, he was not to be feared. Magi were benevolent and wise beyond measure. This was all children needed to know.

But I was no longer an ordinary child. I was ward to a magus, and I wanted to know more. "Is it true they share your body?" I asked him. "The gods?"

He appeared surprised, but not displeased by my forwardness. It was a look I would come to know well—the sort one might give a small animal if it suddenly spoke. As time went on, I would come to suspect that he knew very little of children and had expected something far tamer than the whirlwind I turned out to be.

"In a sense," he replied with that unshakable steadiness. "But it would be truer to say that they are me. The gods and I are one."

"Then when I speak with you, I am speaking with the gods?" I uttered, awestruck for an instant.

"No," he chuckled. "The gods do not speak. They do not need to."

"Oh." I was relieved; it had perturbed me to think I might be plaguing an ancient divinity day in and day out with childish chatter.

"They listen though," he amended, watching my face. "Not to your words, but to your heart. And they know when the two do not align."

I received this not with the shock he clearly expected, but rather with skepticism, for it seemed to me a very adult thing to say. "Are you only saying that so I won't lie to you?"

His face, I thought, took on a special sort of prettiness when he was caught off guard. All at once, he broke down laughing and grabbed me and tumbled me to the floor, where all my lovely new clothes lay strewn about, and rolled me around in them until I was breathless with giggles.

"You'd better not lie to me, Noch," he scolded, collapsing beside me at last. His hair had come loose from its binding to cascade over his shoulders. "I'll always tell you the truth."

I peered at him from beneath the cloak that had enveloped me. "I won't lie," I promised, and I meant it. Inside, I felt a spreading warmth like the sort one feels after a sip of whiskey. At the time, I did not recognize it as love, but as comfort, kinship, and the feel of home, which I suppose are not all that different.

No matter how sharp my tongue became, he was gentle with me. I tested him sometimes, as children are wont to do, but he met every challenge with unwavering kindness. He regarded me, it seemed, with the same cautious wonder any new parent might feel for their delicate and mysterious offspring. But I grew strong again quickly under his doting care, and soon my stunned complacency was overtaken by restlessness. I questioned him incessantly, maddened by his secret smiles and careful replies. I began to slip off when his back was turned to wander the nearby lakeshore and woods. I always returned before I might give him cause to worry, though. Privately, I dreaded disappointing him.

The rest of the clan avoided me as a rule. When people passed me, they averted their eyes and hurried their step. Occasionally, I spotted children peeping at me from the safety of their doorways. I pretended not to notice, but my skin prickled with shame. Shae said it would pass; people would forget. People forgot everything in the end, he told me. Even things that had once been insurmountably important. I knew he was right, because when I tried to remember my life before Shae, I was met with a gray blur and a dull ache that I couldn't place.

For months on end, we were left entirely alone—except for the people who brought food, drink, and whatever other comforts Shae could think to ask for. But this was not to last forever. One morning, I woke to hear again the stern, disagreeable tone of Councilor Glenn outside our door.

"Don't you think this has gone on long enough? You've made your point, had your small rebellion. Now, for pity's sake, put an end to it."

"I don't know what you mean," Shae replied unassumingly, his voice like cool grass to the councilor's gravel. "Caring for a child isn't something one can simply 'end.'"

"Give him to someone else—they will take him if you insist."

"It does a child no good to be shunted from caregiver to caregiver."

"It does a child no good to be raised in a home shadowed by death and enchantment by a caregiver with one foot in this world and the other in the next!"

A short silence followed that for some reason made my heart race. When Shae spoke again, his voice dropped to near inaudibility. "I assure you this place is no more shadowed by death than your Elders' Lodge where death warrants are signed, stamped, and sealed."

The conversation ended abruptly, and I had to quickly feign sleep as Shae burst inside. I waited until he had stopped his pacing and settled down near me to cautiously raise my head.

"Why does he want you to send me away?"

He shot me a wearied look. "Why aren't you ever asleep when you ought to be?"

I kept quiet, knowing he would answer me sooner or later.

Finally, he sighed and said, "He still thinks of me as a child. I suppose he thinks I'm unfit to care for my own. It comes as no surprise—the Council and I have never seen eye to eye."

Watching his face, it dawned on me that Shae was quite young. Up until now, I had simply categorized him as an adult. It had never occurred to me that his quietude and eternal patience might make him seem older than he was.

"Like you, I was left parentless very young," he said after a moment. "I had the Council, the occasional caretaker, and all the luxuries a child could want. But no one to call my own. I suppose that's why I brought you here. It's selfish, really. I'm sure someone else could give you a better life."

My eyes must have widened in alarm because he smiled and added, "Don't worry. I don't intend to let you go. I think even a magus deserves one selfish act in his lifetime."

I allowed this to comfort me for only a moment. "But won't it cause trouble? Defying the Council like this?"

He shrugged. "Perhaps. But they'll let it go eventually, as long as it doesn't interfere with my duties."

I reflected on this and quickly realized that I had never seen Shae do much of anything. "What duties?"

He laughed self-consciously and said, "The ones I've been neglecting."

I gave my best stern look, but he poked his tongue out at me and my efforts were dissolved. "You'd better start setting a better example. Or I'll grow up to be lazy like you."

He sighed. "If you say so. But if you knew how dull Council meetings can be, you'd have more sympathy for me."

"It's no good feeling sorry for yourself," I declared, perhaps echoing a mother or father I'd forgotten.

He gave me that pretty, startled look. "I thought children were supposed to be fun."

He started to attend Council meetings after that. Sometimes, he would be gone all day. I didn't mind the solitude at first. I relished the small freedoms it offered. But after a while, I began to miss him—especially at night when the fire cast shadows and my dreams crept up on me. It was always a relief to wake and find him soundly asleep beside me. The Council meetings made him unhappy, I knew, though he never told me much about them. If I ever asked, he would sigh and say he didn't want to think about it; let's play a game, let's roast chestnuts, let's go outside and count the stars. I stopped asking, but I didn't stop wondering.

It turned out he was right about people forgetting; slowly but surely my exile ended. Soon, people looked at me and saw only a child—if a mysterious and well-dressed one. Others my age no longer watched me from afar but began to trail after me in groups. Now and then, they called out questions: "Is it true you live with Shae?" "Is he your brother?" "What's he like?" I started to make up stories of fantastic magic I had seen: beasts of flame and shadow, feasts produced from thin air, and whatever else my wild imagination could conjure. Before long, I had friends, though part of me would always remember when all the clan had turned their backs except for him.

So, the years began to pass in comfort and strangeness, and I grew up as any child of a small, secluded clan might—despite sharing a home with the gods. Shae went about his duties as magus, which he kept largely private from me. In fact, I believe he told me nothing of his dealings with the Council, except to complain of their dullness, until I was around the age of sixteen.

"There is war in the South," he informed me over dinner, after returning from the Elders' Lodge one night. "Beyond the realm of the clans. Its refugees are moving northward."

I stopped chewing and stared at him, startled by his sudden forthrightness and baffled by such foreign concepts as war, refugees, and a land beyond ours.

"They are not a warlike folk," he went on, "but they are hungry and desperate. There has been some thievery and violence. Far away from here. But they will keep coming north."

"Will the clans not offer them shelter?" I asked, having swallowed my mouthful at last.

"Some will," he answered. "Some will not. A few newcomers is one thing—many is another. They carry with them new beliefs, new ways of living. Any clan that accepts them is bound to find itself changed."

"Is that a bad thing?" I pressed, watching his face. He gave me a small, weary smile. He was always tired after dealing with the Council.

"It depends," he replied enigmatically, and I got the feeling his short burst of honesty was drawing to a close.

"Why are you telling me this?" I demanded before he could retreat completely.

"Because if change comes—good or bad—I don't want it to catch you by surprise," he said with an air of finality. "Now, let's talk about something else. Who was the girl you had here the other day?"

I averted my eyes, chagrined. "She only wanted to see the place. She was more curious about you than me, really."

He lifted his brows at me skeptically. "Well, if you're going to give out private tours, at least give me fair warning next time. Perhaps I could put on a magic show."

I snorted and returned to my dinner, hoping he would drop the matter. He did and retired early, leaving me to see to the dishes. When the fire burned low, I crawled into bed and watched the light play on the screen that divided his bed from mine. It was a pretty and delicate thing of paper—a common furnishing in households that valued a small measure of privacy. I had despised it at first. For the first month we slept apart, I had stubbornly crept into his bed nearly every night. He never sent me away, but at some point, I stopped of my own accord. With age had come distance. But the sound of his breathing still lulled me to sleep.

Over the next few days, I pondered his talk of change. It was a strange thing to hear, coming from someone who never seemed to change at all. He must have thought it important since he'd bothered to share it with me. But he didn't bring it up again, and with time it sank to the back of my mind. People forget everything in the end. But the tumult beyond our borders did not cease just because I ceased to think of it. And I would be made to remember it soon enough.

I was walking with a friend, Jemma, on the outskirts of camp one day in early spring. She spotted it first—a huddled form on the ground perhaps a stone's throw from the camp entrance.

A dead deer, we thought at first. But as we came closer, we saw that it was a man, lying face-down with arms outstretched before him as if he had been crawling. I could tell from a glance that he was not a clansman; his tattered garb was foreign to me and his matted hair a sandy color I had never seen. I hurried toward him at once, ignoring Jemma's cry: "Noch, wait! There's something wrong with him!"

I knelt beside him and turned him over to see a dirty, pallid face that glistened with a sheen of sweat. He did not open his eyes, but his skin was hot and damp to the touch, and a pulse fluttered against my fingers when I pressed them to his neck.

"He's alive!" I called to Jemma. "Go fetch Shae from the Elders' Lodge. I'll stay here with him."

She gave me a wide-eyed, frightened look, but turned and dashed away. I remained beside the man, murmuring to him that help was on the way. A truly awful stench rose from him; I had to open my mouth to breathe, and even then, it seemed I could taste it on my tongue. When I caught sight of Shae approaching in the distance, I made to rise and half-raised a hand to hail him. I was caught off-balance when a force struck me hard in the chest, knocking me flat on my back.

My head struck the ground and I bit my tongue hard. Stunned, eyes watering, I sat up to see that I was now several feet from the man on the ground who did not appear to have moved. I gazed at him for a bewildered instant. And then, before my eyes, his body caught fire. With a wordless shout, I scrambled to my feet and lurched toward him. I would have plunged my hands straight into the fire had they not met some unseen barrier that would not yield. Within seconds, the man was reduced to ash, and I fell to my knees shaking beside the smoldering heap.

"Get up," Shae's voice said close to my ear, and when I did not obey, his hand closed on my arm and dragged me to my feet with alarming strength. We were walking then, swiftly, through the camp, he with a firm grip on my wrist as though I were a wayward child.

"He was alive," I kept repeating uselessly as he shunted me along.

"Did anyone else see you touch him?" he demanded in a low, fierce tone. "Other than the girl? Can she be trusted to keep quiet?"

"What are you saying? What does it matter—?"

"Do you wish to be again the child of plague? Shadowed by death and shunned by the living?"

"I survived the plague. You said I would never suffer sickness again."

"We do not know this sickness! It is not of this land!" We reached our tent. He pushed me inside and sealed the door flap behind us.

"You will stay here," he said, "until I can confirm that the stranger's sickness has not touched you. Let us hope word of this does not reach the Council, lest they order your banishment. Councilor Glenn has forever sought to be rid of you; he needs only an excuse."

He sat me down by the fire, brought me the wash bin, and bade me wash my hands. When I did not do so thoroughly enough for his taste, he knelt before me and scrubbed each one until it stung. I was silent, vaguely ashamed that I had thought only of helping the sick man and not of the danger he might pose to my clan. Still, I could not block out the image of his burning body and feeling of horror and wrongness it brought me.

As if he'd read my mind, Shae looked at me with jewel-like eyes and said, "Don't hate me for this. I did it to protect you."

I could think of no reply. He moved away from me and sat watching the fire with his arms folded around himself. After a while, I noticed that he was trembling slightly.

"The day you brought me here," I proffered quietly, "I remember tents burning. I thought I must have imagined it."

Without looking at me, he answered, "You didn't. The north side of the camp, where you lived, was overtaken with plague. It was spreading quickly. The Council had to act."

"So you burned them," I concluded. "Alive."

"Some were alive. Many were dead. All had suffered. Fire was a mercy."

"And the people in my tent?" I asked, feeling cold. It was something I had thought I would never voice aloud.

"They were still," he said softly. "I do not know whether they were alive. But they did not feel the flames."

I put my head down on my knees and did not answer. After a period of silence, he added, "You were my small act of defiance. Somehow, I thought if I saved you, it would make everything all right. The Council still thinks I only kept you to spite them. But really, I kept you because I needed you. Their disapproval was only an added benefit." He smiled somewhat sadly, and I felt a softness in my chest in spite of everything. In the end, there was nothing he could say or do to make me love him less.

In sudden fear that he would think he had lost me, I crawled to him and put my arms around him. He stiffened at first, but then relaxed and let his head drop to my shoulder. He was smaller than me now, and it felt strange to offer comfort to the one who had comforted me all these years.

The foreigner's sickness did not affect me, but he plagued me in other ways. I dreamed again of fire, skeletal hands, and blackened figures crawling toward me. Such visions had not haunted me since childhood. Shae was distant from me; though he knew I had forgiven him, something had changed between us and I suspected he suffered over it. He was away more often, and some nights went straight to bed upon returning, ignoring the supper I'd laid out for him. I tried not to be hurt by this, telling myself it had more to do with the Council than with me.

Jemma and I did not speak of the stranger we had seen, and no one seemed to notice the black scorch mark on the ground where he had lain. But, of course, the man was not the only newcomer to have wandered so far north. Reports came from neighboring clans of small groups of nomads passing through their lands. Some even settled down to stay. My clansmen were intrigued but not worried by the strangers. After all, they were only a few.

Inevitably, we ourselves would play host to foreigners. They came one day—a group of seven, each thinner, dirtier, and poorer than the last. My clan welcomed them, offering food and drink as was our custom with travelers. They spoke a strange tongue, though one who seemed a leader knew a little of ours. She, a tall tow-haired woman, offered us thanks for our kindness and promised us peace. It was summer and fair weather, so fires were lit outdoors at the camp center as they would be for any celebration. The clan gathered in full force to look upon the newcomers, who huddled together, eating ravenously. Two of them were children, two elders, and all were so alike in appearance they might have been kin.

Our Council members sat and conversed with their leader—to the limited extent they could. Shae sat with them as well, silent and watchful, shining hair and rich garb standing out in bright contrast to his drab company. It was no wonder he drew their eyes—the grubby little children who gazed at him in wonder. They meant no harm, I'm sure. One of them whispered in that strange tongue to the old woman beside him, who in turn whispered to their leader.

She smiled slightly and spoke haltingly to Shae, "They wish to know if you are a prince."

He smiled in return and said, "We have no princes in this land. I am called a magus."

They did not know this word.

"Sorcerer, magician," one of the councilors tried. "Servant of the gods."

They shook their heads in confusion. Shae stretched out a hand—more for show than need—and from the fire emerged a bright bird of flame that took wing and swooped over our heads before shooting off into the sky. My people murmured in pleasure as they watched it go; so rarely did they get to witness the power of our magus.

But when my eyes returned from the sky to the faces of our guests, I saw something I could not have imagined. It was horror—there was no other way to describe that raw, twisted fear. One of the children was crying silently, and the old woman beside him clutched him with a shaking, claw-like hand. Their already pale faces were ashen and their large, haunted eyes round with fright. They looked ghastly to me all of a sudden; I couldn't fathom how I had thought them only moments ago not so very unlike us.

"Devilry," their leader whispered huskily. "Evil."

And as our Council members protested all at once, Shae got up and left. I followed him immediately, only half listening to our Councilors' weak insistence that magi were not to be feared. He went straight to our tent, and I burst in after him, needlessly declaring, "They're wrong."

He was setting a kettle of water to boil and smiled at me in mild surprise. "Maybe," he said with a shrug. "But that doesn't matter."

For once, I didn't argue, but I thought it mattered very much.

Despite their terror, the newcomers stayed. They were housed in a tent on the edge of camp, not truly part of us but not truly separate. No one knew how long they would linger. But Girah, their leader, could be spotted now and then coming and going from the Elders' Lodge. "To promote peace," some said. "If we are to share our lands with these southerners, they must understand our customs and we theirs." Others said it was abominable to let an outsider sit beneath the Council's roof—let alone one who denounced our magus and our gods.

In any case, for this reason or for one I could not guess, things went truly sour between the Council and Shae. Due to his characteristic silence on Council matters, I was not made aware of the falling out until many months had passed. It was winter when Councilor Glenn made another unwelcome appearance at our door.

"Shae is not here," I informed him, making no effort to disguise the chill in my voice.

"I know," he replied. He looked, if possible, grayer and grimmer than I had ever seen him. "It is you I am here to see."

I crossed my arms against the cold, refusing to invite him in. "What can I do for you, Councilor?"

He looked about us and grimaced. "Perhaps you would accompany me to the Elders' Lodge so that we might speak more comfortably?"

My first instinct was suspicion, but this was quickly overtaken by my age-old curiosity. "Very well," I said. "Let me get my cloak."

I had never been inside the Elders' Lodge. It was a privilege few were offered. I could not help but feel a little awed as I stepped through the dark doorway after Councilor Glenn. It was dim inside and hazy. A fire burned low at the center of the oblong room, permeating the air with smoke. I had to cough as I breathed it in; it was strong and herb-scented. Around the fire, figures were seated on rush mats laid on the bare earth floor. There was no luxury here. I recognized each Council member, though their faces were strange in the smoky half-light. As we drew near to them, Councilor Glenn bade me sit.

I knelt on the empty mat before me, and he took his place opposite the fire. The full Council was present, and I realized that the place I had taken must be Shae's.

"I thank you for agreeing to come here, Noch," the councilor said, his voice oddly muffled by the stuffy silence of the lodge. "You have become, as we'd hoped, a reasonable young man."

I had to stifle a laugh at this, thinking that I never would have reached manhood if the Council had had their way. "Certainly. Now, what's this all about?"

"As you may have noticed," he replied grimly, "Shae has ceased to attend all Council meetings."

I blinked, trying to hide my surprise. I had noticed nothing, but they needn't know that.

"This is not the first time he has opposed us—as you well know," Councilor Glenn went on. "But I fear the consequences if this goes on much longer. Magus and Council must act as one. Without proper leadership, the clan is at risk."

"I'm sure he'll come back eventually," I said with no small measure of defensiveness.

"I admire your faith," he said dryly. "Unfortunately, we can never be quite sure of anything when it comes to Shae. He has always been willful, temperamental—but lately he seems to have passed beyond all reason."

"If he has forsaken you, I'm sure he had reason enough," I replied sharply.

"Child," the elderly woman to my right broke in. "We say this not to vilify Shae. It worries us to see him isolate himself like this. Shae's well-being is essential to the clan's well-being. We merely wish to reach out to him."

"If you could speak with him," Councilor Glenn added, "reason with him, encourage him to return ..."

"You wish me to speak on your behalf?" I scoffed, amazed at their gall. "To act as your liaison?"

"We ask you to act on the behalf of the clan," the councilor said sternly. "To set your personal feelings aside and do what is best for all."

I felt sick then, wondering if these were the precise words he had spoken to Shae before my family had burned. The smoke seemed thicker all at once, and I was stricken by a feeling of entrapment. Overcome with a need to be under the sky, I rose to my feet and left. I could not say what I wanted to say: that my loyalties lay not with the clan but with Shae. To speak such words would verge on treason, and this would not help Shae in the least. Already the Council mistrusted him enough to come to me behind his back. I dared not give them a reason to mistrust me as well.

It took me what felt like hours to find him. He was by the lake, gazing out over the ice-crusted waters. I couldn't guess how long he'd been there, but his hair and clothes were wind-tossed and he was not dressed for winter.

"What are you doing out here?" I demanded, removing my cloak and wrapping it around his shoulders. "It's freezing."

He glanced up at me with a vague smile. "Haven't I ever told you? I don't feel the cold."

A dozen questions rose in my mind, but I pushed them aside. "Let's go home," I said.

Without my cloak, I was shivering by the time we reached our tent. Shae brought the fire to life as we stepped inside and nudged me toward the circle of warmth. But I turned to face him, arms folded.

"The Council has discovered a use for me at last. They wish me to act as their agent. I am to attempt to reason with you—for the good of the clan, they say."

He showed not the slightest bit of surprise. "Yes, I thought it would come to this. I'm only surprised they waited this long."

"You could have warned me," I exclaimed. "I never would have gone to that musty, old lodge in the first place."

"It's no good to defy the Council," he answered with a shrug.

"You're one to talk! They say you've abandoned them entirely."

"I have."

"Why?"

He sighed and brushed past me to approach the fire. "How about some tea?"

"Don't do that," I snapped. "You promised to always tell me the truth."

He paused and gave me a bleak look. "I was stupid then. I didn't know."

"Didn't know what?"

"That you would grow up to be a person. That everything I said and did would affect you, and you would remember it all."

I didn't know what to say to this. I splayed my hands hopelessly. "Of course I remember. You were my whole world. Everything I am is because of you."

"That's what I'm afraid of," he sighed. "Noch, sooner or later the Council will ask you to report on my actions and words. I want you to tell them the truth. Be as difficult as you must be but never disloyal. I want them to keep you in their confidence."

"No," I replied sharply. "I will not spy on you for the Council, nor on the Council for you. I will not act as your go-between or as their lackey. Speak to the Council yourself, Shae, for pity's sake."

He lifted his brows at me. "If the Council wants a lackey, they will have one. You're already attempting to reason with me, just as they commanded."

"Because you're being unreasonable," I shot back. "Just go to them—show them you're all right. They think you've gone mad. They talk about you like you're dangerous."

He let out a soft laugh. "Are they wrong?"

"Of course they're wrong—"

"Noch, I burned your family before your eyes. It didn't even occur to me that you would remember. I gave you nice things, kept you warm with that same cursed fire, and held you when you woke up crying without even bothering to wonder why you had so many nightmares. How can you tell me I'm not dangerous?"

"Is that what this is about?" I spluttered. "Shae, that was years ago."

"Twelve years. Almost to the day. I have you to remind me— every winter when I see you've grown a little bit taller."

"Because you saved me," I reminded him, voice trembling. I didn't know why, but there was panic rising in my throat. "You walked into a plague-ridden tent to get me. When no one else would come within fifty feet of me, you held me in your arms. That's right, I remember that too."

He gave me a wan smile. "You were never any threat to me. I am immune to plague, and cold, and fire, for that matter. In fact, I think there's hardly anything that can kill me at all. It wasn't out of kindness or self-sacrifice I saved you. I saved you because I hoped you could save me. And, in a way, you did."

I didn't want to talk anymore suddenly. I wanted to drink tea or play a game or do anything that didn't feel like saying goodbye.

"I'm sorry," he said after a heavy pause. "I never meant to deliver you into the hands of the Council. But the curse of being mine is that you are also theirs. I should have foreseen that."

"I won't serve them," I said thickly.

"You will," he replied. "Because if it isn't you, it will be someone else, and I need it to be you because you are the only person I trust."

This confused me. A cold draft from the door brushed me and I shuddered.

"Come here," he said as coaxingly as he might have in those early days when I was as wary as a half-starved animal. With that same caution, I moved toward him into the fire's warmth. He shed my cloak, which was too long for him, and placed it back around my shoulders. It was surprisingly warm.

"Noch," he said quietly now that we stood face to face. "When I die—"

"What?" I interrupted him. "You're barely thirty!"

He raised an impatient hand to silence me. "I didn't say it was going to be tomorrow. But I want to say this now just in case."

"Who says I'm going to outlive you?" I demanded. "I'm much more likely to fall in the lake or choke on a walnut—"

"Noch, listen to me," he said sharply, and I fell silent. "When I die, another will be chosen to take my place. It will be a child—the age you were when I took you in, or younger. The child will know nothing of the power they have been granted and they will be frightened. I need you to be the one who finds them. I need you to care for them, shield them from the Council, and make sure they don't grow up in a big tent full of lovely things with only the gods for company. I need you to make sure they grow up human. I can't tell you how easy it is, with power like this and no one who loves you, to become something else."

"You're human," I told him firmly.

He smiled, eyes glowing liquid amber in the firelight. "Because of you. And that's why I need you to do this for me."

I melted; I couldn't help it. "I would do anything for you."

"Thank you, Noch." He dropped his gaze and suddenly looked tired. "And I will return to the Council. I'll give you freedom for as long as I can. But when they call you, you must answer."

With that, he moved as if to leave, but I caught him quickly by the shoulders.

"Don't go tonight. You offered me tea. I fear I'll catch cold if I don't have some."

He awarded me a shaky laugh. "Of course. It's the least I can do."

We drank our tea by the fire as we would on any other night and talked no more of dark things. But when he retired to bed, I sat awake for hours with a cold stone of dread in my stomach. Unconsciously, I glanced again and again at his motionless form as if to make sure he was still there. And when I finally nodded off, I dreamed that something monstrous lurked outside our door, sometimes in the form of Councilor Glenn, sometimes in that of a pale foreigner, and sometimes in no form at all. Whatever it was, it sought only one thing—to take away Shae and leave me alone in the dark.

Nothing ever felt quite the same after that. Shae returned to the Council and the clan went about their business as usual. But I could not shake the sense of foreboding that seemed to hang over it all. When the snow melted, more Southerners came. They came in droves rather than family groups now—vast caravans that spanned the horizon. Occasionally, they stopped to speak with us, eat our food, and drink our wine, but mostly they passed us by. They were searching for someplace to call their own; Girah, who acted as translator for us, explained. We hardly understood this, having never laid claim to the land beneath our feet.

The small family of foreigners stayed with us, and we made no attempt to discourage them. They served a purpose for us whether they knew it or not. They showed the other newcomers that we were not afraid of them, and that they need not fear us. Yet they did fear us; the seven of them stayed huddled in their tent and watched us from a distance with their round, colorless eyes. They were dependent upon our kindness, and in that sense, they were our prisoners. I felt strangely sickened to see their thin forms skulking about the camp. They were like dark omens.

A settlement grew to the north of us—it almost seemed to spring up overnight. It was closer than any clan would have settled to another, but these newcomers knew nothing of our etiquette. Our hunting grounds would overlap, and the more they expanded, the more they would drain our resources. It was this that shattered the fragile peace between Shae and the Council at last. Shae proposed that we move. It was not uncommon for clans to uproot and wander; many never set down roots at all. But the Council, set in their ways, would not hear of it. They suggested instead we discourage our neighbors from lingering in their chosen place. A drought ought to do it, but if they would not budge, then perhaps a storm or a wildfire. Shae refused, saying that he would give them no more reason to name him "Devil."

I learned this not from Shae, but from the Council themselves. Because, as he had predicted, they soon turned to me on account of his rebellion. I became what I had sworn I would not be: mediator between magus and Council, spy in my own home. The willingness of my subject made it no less strange. I made no secret of my distaste for the role but showed no disloyalty to the Council. I did what Shae needed of me, and I would not change it even now. In fact, it was my honor to take at least some of the lifelong burden from his shoulders.

There is no telling which of our many visitors first brought the blight. It made itself known slowly: a cough here and there, a child running a fever. Thus, it crept quietly from tent to tent, afflicting family after family, and by the time we took notice, there was nothing to be done. Plague had us by the throat again. This was a new sort of sickness. It attacked the lungs, causing one to cough and gasp until they spat out blood. I knew this by Shae's word only; he would not allow me to leave the tent.

From our doorway, I could see the greasy gray smoke trail that issued from the funeral pyre day and night. Our part of the camp had not been stricken, but it would be. Helpless and useless, all

I could do was wait. Shae was away most of the time, helping where he could or conferring with the Council—the crisis had incited a cease-fire between them. Trapped at home, I was not privy to these meetings, and he told me nothing of them. He hardly spoke at all, nor ate, nor slept. But then, neither did I.

I found myself sitting by the fire, half-awake, half-dreaming, for hours on end. Sometimes, I fantasized that I saw things in the flames or imagined for an instant that there was someone near me when I was in fact alone. A few times, I came to myself suddenly with an overwhelming sense of déjà vu, as if I had slipped briefly into another world and promptly forgotten it upon my return. Always, it seemed there was something on the edge of my consciousness, some nagging and persistent force just beyond my realm of perception. Still, I wonder about this; I have never felt anything quite like it since. Perhaps it was simply that worry and sleeplessness had stretched my mind to the breaking point. Or perhaps it was that the veil of death lay so heavily over the camp, the line between this world and the next had wavered and my thoughts had begun to seep through or vice versa: something from the beyond had reached me.

Whatever the case, I must have fallen asleep well and truly one day, for I dreamed the most vivid and memorable dream. I was lying with my head in a woman's lap, and she was familiar to me though I could not name her—a mother, a sister, or an aunt perhaps. She had my curls, black, thick, and untamable, my copper-brown skin, and my almond-shaped dark eyes. She was murmuring, "Don't be afraid, little one. We will all go to the Afterworld together." And I felt entirely safe.

The feeling lingered for a moment as I came awake, and I felt certain then that I was not alone but surrounded by the warmth of those who loved me. But as reality came creeping back, a cold sense of dread took hold of me and I sat bolt upright, convinced that something was wrong. The moment I stepped outside, I saw it: a wavering haze of heat in the distance that was sickeningly familiar. Gray smoke billowed against the blue sky, reaching upward and outward like ghostly fingers. A strange silence lay over the scene; where one would expect to hear shouts and cries, there was nothing, not a whisper. But I needed not see flames or hear screams to know the camp was burning.

Without thinking, I took off for the Elders' Lodge. I saw no one on the short journey; all was still and quiet. Now that I thought of it, I had not seen Shae for what felt like days—I had lost track of time. It seemed as if I were the only person left alive in the world. But when I burst inside the lodge, there was Councilor Glenn, and I had never been gladder to see him. Only two other Council members were present, and the three were hunched over the fire with their heads bowed. The air was thick with the smell of sandalwood and sage and I could hardly see for the smoke.

"Fire," I gasped, voice husky from lack of use. "There's fire in the camp!"

They did not respond, and I wondered for a wild instant if they were asleep or in some sort of trance. But then, Councilor Glenn stirred and raised his head slightly.

"It is contained," he said in a dry, dull voice. "It will not reach us here."

"What?" My head whirled, and the strange sense came over me that I was still trapped within a dream.

"We are safe now," the councilor went on quietly, as though speaking to himself. "The clan will carry on."

"Shae," I responded, no longer listening. "Where is he?"

Councilor Glenn shook his gray head and seemed very small and insubstantial suddenly—the dried-up husk of an old man. "I only wanted what was best. Why couldn't he ever see that?"

I turned and left, knowing now that visiting the Elders' Lodge had been a waste of precious time. I went straight to the lakeshore, where I had found him last time, and spotted his slim silhouette standing waist-deep in the water. The surface of the lake was as still as glass, and his fine, silk robes billowed out around him. His hair in the sunlight shone like ravens' feathers. Without hesitation, I plunged into the water, scarcely feeling the cold, and waded toward him.

When my ripples reached him, he turned and smiled over his shoulder. "I thought you'd come if I waited here a bit."

"How could you do it again?" I demanded, voice coming out raw and hoarse. "I thought you regretted what happened back then. I thought ..." I broke off, words catching in my throat.

"Of course I don't regret it," he replied calmly, turning away to look out over the lake. "How could I possibly regret something that gave me you?"

And then, for the first time, I was angry with him. I was angrier than I had ever been, and it swelled in my chest, red hot and heartbreaking.

"You're killing them!" I shouted at his turned back. "You're killing them again, and you don't even care! They're your people—you're supposed to protect them!"

A twitch went through his shoulders, but he did not look back at me. "I protect the clan. When the clan is threatened, I purge the threat. You've always known this. Why is it different now?"

"Because—" I floundered for words, but for some reason all I could think of was the woman in my dream who had held my head in her lap. "It's terrible. It's monstrous. Better we all die together than this."

He looked at me at last and his eyes were wet. "I cannot allow the clan to perish. The magi must preserve the clans, for without the clans, the gods would be lost. They would wander, bodiless, mindless, and forgotten until the end of the earth. They are our masters and we are their keepers, and if that makes us monsters or devils, so be it. We are what we are. I didn't ask for this."

"Well, I didn't ask for this either," I cried. "I didn't ask to be plucked from my family or raised by a magus or subjugated to the Council. I'm not cut out for any of this. I don't have the heart for it."

He bowed his head, and a long stream of hair fell forward to hide his face from view. "I know you don't. But you will. You will do as you must, as I have done what I must. I forced this life upon you, and you can hate me for that. It's a burden I'm willing to bear."

My chest tightened and for an instant I felt that my heart would stop. "Don't be stupid," I choked. "I love you. I've always loved you—you never gave me a choice in the matter."

He lifted his chin at this and gave me a weak smile. "Thank you. That means more than you know."

I steeled myself against the warmth his smile always brought me and said, "Put out the fire, Shae. Please, for me, save the ones you still can."

His smile vanished. "I can't do that, Noch. It's too late. The fire must run its course."

"You have to try," I insisted. "Please, even if you can only save one."

He turned slowly to face the lake again, and I knew by his posture that it was hopeless. "I hope you can forgive me," he said so quietly I hardly heard.

I left him there, standing in the lake. I forced myself not to look back as I slogged to shore, and I don't know if he watched me go. I think probably not; he was looking ahead.

I ran, dripping and breathless, through the silent camp toward the blooming smoke cloud. At first, it seemed I would never reach it; it appeared farther, then closer, then farther again as though I were running in circles. But at last, the fire reared up suddenly to either side of me as if I had passed through an unseen barrier. My steps faltered as a wave of heat assaulted me and the air was stripped from my lungs. Coughing, eyes stinging, I stumbled forward while flames flicked out at me hungrily from the burning tents.

Desperately, I began to call out for anyone who might still be alive. I burned my hands pushing open door flaps to find only roaring flames on the other side. Some of the tents flaked to pieces at my touch, and others were smoldering skeletons already. I could see no human forms. Despair crept up on me all at once, and I stopped in my tracks, bringing my stinging hands to my face. I thought madly of crawling inside one of the blazing tents and dying the way I was meant to. It would be fitting, wouldn't it? It would break Shae's heart, and maybe he deserved that. But I had not the courage to face death alone. And even here, in the midst of such destruction, I could not wish harm on Shae.

Something happened then—I caught it in the corner of my eye. A tent blazed brighter than the others and, with a rush of hot air that nearly knocked me off-balance, it collapsed. I turned to stare at the heap of blackened remains that still sputtered weakly with flame. An explosion of some sort; perhaps a barrel of whiskey had caught alight. But even as I told myself this, my feet moved, carrying me toward the site.

As I came closer, I saw amid the burning debris a small, huddled form. Flames flickered in a perfect circle around it but ventured no closer than that. And beneath the charred, smoking rags that hung from its thin limbs, the figure appeared unharmed. It raised its head as I approached, and I looked upon the soft, genderless face of a child with matted black hair and enormous tawny eyes. They gazed at me with a calm, calculated expression unbefitting a ragged child squatting in the wreckage of its home. And I got the sudden sense that it was not only a child who looked at me and that whatever ancient essence appraised me from behind those golden eyes knew me very well.

Scarcely thinking, I extended a hand and said, "Come here."

Something shifted in the child's gaze; a question had been answered. They stood and stepped forward quickly, dirty bare foot plunging straight into the ring of flame. But before I could cry out in alarm, they were through and apparently unhurt. A grubby hand reached out and caught mine, closing firmly around my fingers.

"Who are you?" they inquired bluntly, gazing up at me with eyes like an owl's.

"I'm Noch," I replied, but they only continued to stare. A word rose unbidden to the front of my mind—a title the Council had offered me once that I had refused in disgust. "I'm your warden."

The child tipped their head curiously. "Warden?"

"It means you are under my protection," I explained.

They appeared satisfied at this; the trace of a smile even flitted across their face. "Noch," they said with that same forward tone, "why are you crying?"

Startled, I brought my free hand to my face and found that it was indeed wet with tears. "It must be the smoke," I said, doing my best to wipe them away. "Come on, now. Let's go."

"To the Afterworld?" the child asked, eyes threatening to swallow me whole.

"No," I answered with a small, broken laugh. "Let's go home."

The Damned Voyage

written by

John Haas

illustrated by

ALLEN MORRIS

ABOUT THE AUTHOR

John Haas is a Canadian author living in Ottawa with his two wonderful sons. Since the early days of elementary school, John has been an avid storyteller, though mostly only told those stories to closest friends, family, and the occasional pet. Once the above-mentioned wonderful sons entered his life, the need to write kicked into high gear, fuelled by a desire to be something his boys could be proud of. In the past eight years or so he has had fifteen short stories published in various excellent publications, and seen his first novel, The Reluctant Barbarian, *a humorous fantasy tale released by Renaissance Press. Since the sales were made to small presses that don't pay professional rates, he was still eligible to enter the contest at the time. The sequel,* The Wayward Spider, *will be released in 2019. John's goal remains to become a full-time writer (rich and famous would be nice too, but one step at a time).*

ABOUT THE ILLUSTRATOR

Allen Morris was born in 1991 in the Mississippi Delta, growing up surrounded by endless horizons.

Long hours with books and role-playing games after school with friends solidified his love for exploring foreign worlds. Art, since a young age, would offer a different avenue to fulfill that explorative need through creation. He continues to travel and practice his craft daily.

The Damned Voyage

The Southampton docks were bedlam, people shouting and gawking, cursing and rushing. Beyond all this a stream of first-class passengers boarded. The ship would soon be underway, to where I neither knew nor cared. I needed to be aboard.

Gusts of warm, brisk wind forced their way around us, and I shifted more weight to the ever-present cane. To my right, Singh, companion and best friend for more than a quarter century, stepped closer to offer support. I took an equal step away, which was met by a resigned shrug. Singh never *had* understood stubborn English pride.

"It is here, Doctor Shaw," he said.

It was. I'd felt the damned thing calling to me, insisting, as soon as we'd arrived. "Yes. It's aboard the ship."

The two thieves must have boarded earlier with the lower classes.

A brief sigh escaped me. This mad adventure was better suited to someone half my age. At sixty-one I should have been in front of a fire, penning memoirs no one could ever read. Memoirs of death, madness, and an ancient evil mankind was better off not being aware of.

Singh stepped into the crowd, one hand under his robe on the concealed dagger. Always ready. People took one glance at the massive Indian's emotionless face and created a path while I followed in his wake.

The first-class passengers boarded in a steady stream across what was more wooden bridge than ship's ramp. At the base of this bridge I plucked at Singh's robe, stopping him from forcing his way to the deck above. He turned.

In 1878 I had helped rescue Singh from a final holdout sect of the Thuggee cult, a cult we had thought long broken, destroyed. Now, three decades later, no trace of that orphan boy remained, having become a man of solid muscle and determination.

And now I had to leave him.

"I'll be taking this voyage alone, old friend."

A flicker of anger passed over Singh's face, arms crossed over thick chest. At six and a half feet, the man towered over me by almost a foot.

"You need to go to London," I said, holding up one hand. "In case I fail."

Singh's expression didn't change and I nodded my understanding. Aboard that ship were two men who had stolen an item he had vowed to keep safe, as he had vowed to keep me safe. Now I was asking him to abandon both.

Perhaps he understood English pride better than I thought.

"Go to the Prince's son," I continued. "His father knew the dangers of this book and so does he. Warn him it's loose in the world again."

Prince Albert Victor was dead now, as were most of the group that had come together in Whitechapel twenty-four years ago. They'd done their duty, retrieved the book and earned their rest, all except myself and Singh, of course, who were charged with keeping it out of the wrong hands, and Kosminski who would rave in an asylum until he died.

"He may be illegitimate," I said, "but he will have the resources to help."

"He will listen better to you."

"Perhaps, but I couldn't endure the carriage ride, much less handle the horses. I only made it here through your skills."

I'd walked with a limp for more years than not and forgotten what it was like to *not* carry a cane. Getting about was not a problem, controlling a carriage would be. On top of this, the breakneck trip here had taken its toll, though I struggled not to show it.

"The book calls to you, Doctor," Singh said. "Will you resist when it's in your hands again?"

"My leg is lame, not my mind," I snapped.

Missing last night's sleep had made me irritable and short-tempered, and Singh's blunt words were too close to the truth. The damned book *did* call to me, *had* called ever since I'd opened it and read those few words twenty-four years ago. We'd followed that calling over the space of miles, from Cambridge to here.

Would I be able to resist?

I closed my eyes and calmed my mind.

"You've taught me well, Singh. How to meditate and block the voices."

Singh heaved a deep sigh, the only sign he would give of his frustrated resignation. He knew this was too important, that precautions needed to be taken.

"How will you get aboard?" Singh gestured toward the deck above.

Fair question. We'd had little money in the house, certainly not enough for a first-class ticket. I'd taken all we had, grabbing my doctor's bag as an afterthought. There was one possibility as I saw it.

"Ships like these allow first-class passengers to have friends and family, even their doctors, go aboard to see them off."

All these well-heeled passengers milled about, chattering their inane conversations, making sure not to give the appearance of being in line to board the ship. They were far too important to queue up.

Singh strolled the length of this line that was not a line, acting like one of many dock workers. The rich ignored him. Twenty passengers along Singh stopped, made a sharp about-face and headed back. Where he'd turned stood an elderly woman, some aging dowager, stooped and wrinkled, perhaps ten years my senior. She fanned herself against the unseasonal heat while waiting to move forward, alone.

"Best of luck, Doctor," Singh said as he passed.

I headed for the woman.

ALLEN MORRIS

"Good morning, madam. Archibald Shaw at your service."

She started and glared around at this intrusion. I waited for my appearance as a plump older gentleman to register as unthreatening. My receding gray hair and squared lenses completed the image of a latter-day Ben Franklin. Her glance dropped to my doctor's bag then back to my face, a smile cracking her features.

"Oh, Doctor. A pleasure."

"The pleasure is mine," I assured her. "This heat is quite unbearable, is it not?"

That was sufficient to get her going on a lengthy diatribe of problems, starting at her sore feet and working up, leaving out none of the aches and pains of age. I offered her an arm for support and we ascended the ramp side by side. It had been years since I'd practiced medicine, but I still recognized this lonely woman for the hypochondriac that she was. She would have a bagful of medications when what she needed most was someone to listen. I made sympathetic clucking noises and tut-tutted in all the right places, trying to identify the perfume she wore. L'heure Bleu?

In the course of the one-sided conversation, moving slowly up the ramp, I was able to discover the ship was headed for New York after a couple of brief stops.

Reaching the deck above we found no less than the captain waiting to greet us. My companion introduced herself as Mrs. Penelope Hooper, then the man held a hand toward me, a dubious expression on his face which was quite understandable. My style of dress hardly measured up to first-class standards.

"Captain Edward Smith, sir."

"Doctor Archibald Shaw."

The other man's expression changed, the smile more genuine. Everyone trusted a doctor. He appeared ready to continue the conversation but a crowd had accumulated behind us in our slow journey here. These guests requiring the captain's attention worked in my favour as too much scrutiny from this man wouldn't do. We moved on.

On the docks below there was no sign of Singh, on his way back to London already. I was well and truly alone, a thought which both saddened and frightened me.

My new companion continued chattering on about her medical woes while I half-listened, scanning the passengers around us until I saw one that would suit my purpose.

"I beg your pardon," I said as Mrs. Hooper took a breath. "I'm afraid I see a patient of mine I must speak with. May I look in on you later?"

"Of course, Doctor," she said with a smile.

The man ahead had about an inch height over my own five foot eight, but I beat him by ten pounds in weight. Other than that we were similar in build, and he seemed to be alone.

He would do.

Only the amount of passengers making their way through the halls slowed him, but it was enough to keep pace. I was able to catch up as he reached the door to his cabin.

"Excuse me," I called.

He gave a jump and turned towards me, an annoyed expression on his face which quickly passed.

"My apologies, I didn't mean to startle you. Ship's doctor."

"No harm done, Doctor. Can I help you?"

"A couple of routine questions if I may?"

"Oh, of course. Please come in," he said opening the cabin door.

Everyone trusted a doctor. Of course it was easier if that doctor looked like someone's grandfather.

Glancing left and right I followed the man inside, allowing the door to close behind me.

The cabin was decorated in mahogany panelling and furnished better than my house. A bed with nightstand, a heavy wardrobe, a sitting chair, and a table with two chairs for taking tea. This would be one of the smaller first-class cabins, still a most comfortable way to cross the Atlantic.

I placed my bag on the table.

"What can I do for you, Doctor? Not to be rude but I do still need to change."

"Yes, of course," I said, glancing over at the massive chest at the end of the bed. "You are travelling alone?"

"I am. On my way to New York for business."

I gave my most disarming expression, recollecting the basics of doctoring, building the trust of the patient. "First time across the ocean?"

"Yes." The man shrugged. "Travelling in style."

He glanced at the clock sitting on a chair-side table. As his focus changed I drew the sword concealed inside my cane, thrusting it forward in one fluid motion. The blade pierced the man's heart, a killing thrust.

He looked at the sword protruding from his chest, expression changing from surprise to rage.

"Fall, damn you," I said, withdrawing the sword and stepping back.

Blood gushed from the wound, but not shooting out as it should have. Not the immediate killing stroke after all, but fatal nonetheless.

The dying man rushed at me, hands outstretched. We landed on the floor, him on top with hands closing on my throat, his blood squelching between us. My sword skittered across the cabin, stopping against the bed's leg. Strength left his grip, but not quickly enough. My lungs burned with the need for air while my heart pounded an irregular, terrified throb in my ears. With each beat the world went more gray, moving toward black.

Singh, I'm sorry old friend. I failed.

It would be up to him now to find the book and keep it out of the wrong hands. God knows we'd tried to do that over the years, moving from place to place, keeping away from those searching.

The black deepened, then receded back to gray. The man's grip on my throat relaxed, and I gasped. The world came back into focus and I pulled one rasping breath into a burning throat. For several minutes we lay on the floor, the dead man's weight pinning me until I mustered sufficient strength to move. Rocking him back and forth I eventually rolled him to one side. With the weight off I was able to draw more air into my lungs.

"Damn."

How had I missed the artery, the entire heart? But raising my hands, so unaccustomed to precision work now, I knew how.

I lay on my back a long time, exhausted and hurting, needing a rest but having so much to do. Using what strength there was left, I crawled to the sitting chair and pulled myself upward with the help of that heavy furniture. Halfway to standing, I slumped into the chair. My head leaned back and eyes closed even as I tried to get moving again.

Perhaps a few minutes rest then.

Bastard.

My eyes opened and I focussed on the dead man's face. "That I am, my friend."

You're no friend of mine.

"Why don't you cross over?" I muttered, the room fading.

Then everything slipped into the blackness of unconsciousness.

The door to the small room lay before me and on the other side was the next woman I would question. It was a vast conspiracy, a spider web of cheap, brazen women, weathered and beaten down by fate, ready to grasp anything to give meaning to their lives.

The last woman had given the address for Mary-Jane Kelly.

Nearby, hidden in an alley, Singh and the others waited, making sure I would not be disturbed.

When the door opened and I saw the young lady on the other side I almost lost my nerve. This was no old whore in her declining years. This woman was lovely.

"And who sent you then?" she asked in an Irish lilt.

"Annie."

The lass started, blonde hair bouncing around her face. "Annie's dead."

"Yes, she is," I responded, stepping forward.

Mary-Jane Kelly did not die easily. It took hours for her to convince me that she was not part of the cult.

By then her death was a mercy.

My eyes snapped open.

I was cold and clammy with the sweat of nightmares, my body still thrashing against the soft upholstery of the reading chair.

Nightmares.

I hadn't medicated before napping and those damned dreams, those memories, had taken me by force.

Aches and pains echoed through my body, unaccustomed as the muscles were to such strenuous work and of sleeping in a chair.

My glance drifted to the clock beside me.

"8:30?"

I bolted to my feet, all aches forgotten. It had been a few minutes before noon when we'd entered the cabin.

"No! I've slept more than eight hours."

In that time the ship had not only launched but had come and gone from its first port in France.

You sleep well, for a murderer.

"You don't understand," I said, looking at the dead man's body. "The thieves could have disembarked in France. I would never catch them now."

I stood still, listening for the presence of the book.

"It's still here," I said.

Of course it was still aboard, the nightmare alone should have told me that much. Without the book's presence I would have had a peaceful sleep.

Twenty-four years ago, when I'd brought the book home from Whitechapel, I succumbed to curiosity. I opened it, read from it. The first word threw me into convulsions. I read on, unable to stop. Another word. A full sentence. The words leaping from my mouth in lunatic screams.

Ph'nglui mglw'nafh Cthulhu R'lyeh wgah'nagl fhtagn.

Singh had batted the book from my grasping fingers and I collapsed, spending the next weeks raving about ancient evils that no human mind should try to comprehend.

Those words still echoed inside my mind.

I tried to strangle you while you slept. The voice was hateful. *I couldn't touch you.*

"Of course you couldn't. You're dead. All you can do is observe."

The angry spirit gave a long mournful groan.

Using the furniture for balance, I made my way across the cabin to retrieve both sword and cane, then headed for the dead man. I wiped the sword against his chest.

My favourite jacket.

"You've no use for it now."

The front of the man's jacket, like the shirt underneath, was a mess of sticky blood. An inside pocket held a billfold which in turn held his ticket for this voyage. Both had been narrowly missed by the sword thrust. I pocketed the billfold after wiping it against the man's jacket, and opened the ticket.

Bastard, the voice said.

"So you've said and I didn't deny it," I read the name on the ticket. "Stephen?"

I will kill you.

"No, you won't. You can't even touch me."

You're a monster.

"Perhaps."

Stephen was silent a moment before replying in a low whisper. *Why me?*

"Convenience. I needed a cabin, ticket and clothes. You were close enough in height and weight."

You killed me for my luggage?

I felt no desire to explain to this spirit, but if it would give him the closure he needed to move on ... "No. I killed you to stay aboard this ship, and I would kill a hundred more like you to get this book back."

Stephen sobbed and I wondered at a ghost's ability to cry but left it.

There were some unavoidable tasks before I could leave the cabin to start my search. The sleep had done wonders and I found myself full of energy, though also full of aches and pains.

Heading for the trunk, I flipped the lid up, throwing contents onto the bed.

Not enough to have murdered me? Now you vandalize my belongings?

I didn't reply, continuing until the trunk was empty. Now it was light enough to be dragged across the cabin, my left leg giving complaint but I'd lived with that pain enough years to ignore it. Once it rested next to Stephen's body, I tipped the trunk onto its back and opened the lid, then getting onto the floor next to the dead man, I used my good leg as a brace and rolled him inside. Rigors had set in, giving trouble with the bending of limbs, but there was no need to be gentle about it. In the end Stephen fit inside his own trunk.

A choke of outrage had initially come from the disembodied voice, but Stephen had since fallen silent, as if at a loss for words. That wouldn't last.

Getting the proper leverage to flip the trunk back turned out to be more difficult. The trunk needed to be rocked back and forth several times before rolling back onto its bottom.

Stephen laughed meanly. *You are too old for this.*

"I'm fine," I snapped.

A sensitive topic. I look forward to your heart attack.

I stayed silent. Stephen couldn't affect the physical world but words had a power of their own.

My clothes looked as if I'd been in the operating room, catching Stephen's dying blood between us. I washed up in the water closet, then changed into some evening clothes from the jumble on the bed. The fabric was of excellent quality, much better than what I'd been wearing.

Is there nothing of mine you will not violate?

"Why should this matter to a dead man?"

Well, it does.

A knock sounded on the door and I jerked in surprise.

Come in, Stephen yelled. *Quick. Help!*

"No one can hear you," I said in a low voice, then louder. "Coming."

Gathering my ruined clothes, I threw them into the chest, covering Stephen's upturned face, then closed and latched the lid. On the way to the door, I inspected the cabin. All seemed in order.

Outside was a young man in ship's uniform, smiling as the door opened.

"Good evening, sir," the man said. "I will be your steward for the trip. My name is Thompkins."

This man murdered me, Stephen screamed. *Get the captain.*

I greeted the steward, forcing a smile onto my face though Stephen's shrillness hammered my brain.

"I knocked earlier," Thompkins said, "but there was no answer."

"Ah, yes. I took a nap. It has been a long journey."

Damn it! This man is a lunatic.

"You need to see my ticket?" I asked.

"Oh, no sir. We'll ask for those after leaving Ireland tomorrow."

"Of course," I nodded, trying to appear the experienced traveller. The last time I'd been on a ship was as a doctor in the army, travelling to India and back.

The thought of India reminded me of Singh. Damn, but I missed the man. So many years I'd relied on him.

"I wanted to introduce myself," the steward continued, "and to see if you needed anything."

"I suppose I've missed dinner?"

"Yes sir, I'm afraid so, though the *a la carte* restaurant will still be serving. Or, I could bring food to you."

"Perhaps just some tea. I want to stroll around first though. Say in an hour?"

"Yes sir. I'll leave it on your table if you aren't back yet."

"Thank you."

The steward left, retreating down the corridor.

He couldn't hear me.

"No, I told you as much. Only I can hear you." I stepped into the corridor. "You will find you are confined to this room as well."

A lie but, with luck, one Stephen wouldn't test. I needed time to think and couldn't have the dead man following me around the ship, moaning about his fate.

Damn you.

"I've been damned a long time."

And now you've damned me too.

"You're not damned, you're dead."

Stephen fell silent and I reached for the door's handle.

Please don't leave, he said.

I stopped. Stephen's personality had an annoying inconsistency. Depressive. Hateful. Now pleading? Was it an inability to cope with being dead?

There is a voice ... It whispered to me all day, telling me unspeakable things.

"A voice? That is the book you're hearing."

I knew the power of that whispering. I'd heard it, resisted it, for years, but with a tie to the physical world which this spirit did not have.

Yessss, Stephen sighed.

I felt unsure if he was responding to me or not.

"Stephen, where is it?"

Silence.

I waited, hoping for a response, until it grew obvious none was coming. Unfortunate.

"You are correct, I am not your friend," I said to the empty cabin. "Let me give you some advice as if I am, though. Move on to the afterlife."

With that I left, closing the door on the morose spirit.

First class occupied an incredible amount of the ship and, moving at my speed, it took some time to travel around it. Even after my tour I'd seen no more than half of the deck, though I did discover the name of the ship which meant little to me.

While moving about I'd become more certain of the book's location being somewhere below my current deck, on one of the lower-class levels, but could not get an idea of how far away or whether it was closer to the front or back of the ship. I would need to get closer, but that was a different problem.

Passage to the lower decks was marked by waist-high locked

gates, each of them attended by stewards, ensuring no one made the social faux pas of mixing with the wrong class.

I continued my investigation, hoping for another way below to present itself.

Around me a vague atmosphere of gloom and despair had descended on the ship like a fine mist. At this point, few would be aware of it, but that wouldn't last. Below, it would be worse. In all likelihood the book would be in the lowest levels. It called to the uneducated and backward, the psychotic and disturbed, the easily swayed.

And which was I?

It had called to the Thuggees in 1878. The cult was a throwback to a more brutal time of Indian history, a final holdout against the purges. The cultists hadn't been able to read the book, but from the illustrations inside, they concluded the book would bring about the Kali Yuga, a time when their brutal goddess would rule the world. What they presumed to be the many arms of Kali were the tentacles of a much more ancient, more terrible god.

At that time I was a doctor in the army, knowing little of cults and nothing of ancient, sleeping gods. My regiment assaulted the cult's cave hideout, intent on wiping them out. The Thuggees threw themselves at us in a fanatical wave before being broken. These sacrifices played their part though, giving time for several of their number to escape out the back, leaving behind the too old and young.

One of the initiates left behind was a boy of ten taken from the streets of Bombay, already on his way to learning the art of assassination. I took on the job of rehabilitating him.

As I educated Singh, he educated me, telling me about the cult and what had happened within that cave, telling me of the profane book, an object of pure evil that only the highest in the cult were ever allowed to touch.

It was true. Inside those caves there had been a tangible malevolence that was more than simply the evil of men. The book was a danger, but the remaining cultists had fled with it and the army declared the Thuggees broken for all time.

The book was forgotten until our return to London.

Shaking off the memories of those more carefree times I headed for the *a la carte* restaurant the steward had recommended. The smell of cooked beef and melted butter set my stomach rumbling.

When was the last time I'd eaten?

I ordered the first item on the menu, something which would come quickly, then watched the people around me. The passengers acted as one would expect, chatting with friends and family, enjoying the novelty of being aboard such an incredible machine. Occasionally there were furtive glances on one of their faces, eyes darting as if expecting some unseen danger. They would then return to what they were doing, unaware of their brief unease.

These would be the more sensitive people. Artists and romantics.

The food arrived, a hot beef sandwich, and my focus changed for the next fifteen minutes. It had been some time since I had enjoyed a meal so fully ... enjoyed anything for that matter.

Sipping an after-dinner port, my thoughts returned to the book and thieves. Speed and mobility was their advantage but aboard a ship, even one this vast, that advantage became less relevant.

Only if I was smart about it though.

They couldn't know I was aboard, but any search of the lower decks now would draw attention. All they would need to do, if they became suspicious, was keep ahead of me and disembark tomorrow in Queenstown. Without Singh I couldn't give chase.

I wandered the deck, thinking, planning.

Tomorrow, after the last port of call, I would find a way past the steward and into the lower decks. There would be some way, and if not, I would create one. For now I would wait, and I was skilled at that, having done little else for the past twenty-four years, guarding the book while waiting for death to come.

Standing at the rail, watching miles of water pass without truly seeing it, I found myself starting to doze and was surprised to see the time close to midnight. The decks around me had cleared off in April's chilly night air.

How long had I been standing here?

Sighing, I headed toward my cabin. "Better to sleep in bed."

With luck Stephen would be gone.

Five steps toward the cabin, a wave of overwhelming fear and horror slammed into me like a train. It gripped my heart and squeezed. Staggering against the rail I stopped myself from falling to the deck.

I knew this sensation.

"No! Oh, God damn it, no."

One of the thieves was reading from the book.

Then it was gone, as quickly as it had come. The reader had been interrupted after only a word or two.

I waited for more but none came.

Behind me the door closed with a soft click. Inside the cabin, the chest had been returned to its place at the foot of the bed, and a silver serving tray with teapot and cup had been delivered. I'd forgotten about that. Not much hope of it still being hot.

Ooooohhhhhhh, the mournful groan came, filling the cabin.

Damn. I should have known better than to hope Stephen would have moved on. Mary-Jane Kelly had haunted me a full year before going wherever the dead go.

What have you done to me? Stephen said, his voice pure misery.

We both knew the answer to that question, but I wasn't sure he was even talking to me. No, something had changed in Stephen in the past few hours.

The moaning increased, coming from every corner. A disembodied wailing.

The darkness. The evil. IT PULLS ME.

Of course! The thieves had read from the book, awoken its power. Stephen, being all spirit, took the brunt of that influence, greater than the most sensitive artist would experience. Earlier it had been whispering to him, but now it was screaming.

Oh, God! It's driving me mad. I am damned!

Something hit me across the back, staggering me forward. The pillows from the bed were on the floor behind me.

107

It's pulling me apart!

The teapot lifted from the table and hurtled across the cabin, crashing against the entry door. Next, the clock soared past, missing me by a foot and colliding with one wood-panelled wall. I dropped to the floor, my leg screaming at the sudden rough treatment as the cabin came alive with every object not secured. The two chairs from the table. The silver serving tray. Cream and sugar containers. The soap flew from the water closet, shattering against the table and showering me with soap splinters. I too felt myself being pulled upward and crawled under the bolted down table, grabbing it as an anchor.

The damned book had awakened an ability in Stephen, turning him from ghost to poltergeist.

Chairs, clock, teapot, soap splinters, and more, all flew in a swirling maelstrom around the cabin, accumulating objects. Across the room the trunk flipped onto one side and stayed there.

Stephen's screaming increased to the point where I needed to choose between holding onto the table or covering my tortured ears. If anyone could have heard those wails they would have been breaking down the cabin door.

The long scream became a word.

Cthuuuuuuuuuulhuuuuuuuuuuuuu.

"Oh God!"

I opted for covering my ears and was immediately pulled out from under the table.

"No!"

The scream ended, cut off mid-syllable, and I returned to the ground with a bounce, fighting to catch my breath.

"St … Stephen?"

No response.

Another full minute on the floor, recovering, watching the objects around me.

"Stephen?" I repeated.

Still nothing.

With the help of the table's edge I was able to get upright again.

The room was still.

Stephen was gone.

Absently, I moved around, cleaning the damage while thinking about what had happened.

Cthulhu.

That word chilled my soul to the core, more thoroughly than a winter's night would freeze my body. I knew the name, remembered it from the words I had read.

I shuddered.

Stephen had connected with the force of madness and power that was the book, and his soul had been destroyed because of it.

"No," I whispered, making my way to the sitting chair.

I collapsed into it, my thoughts resting on grim subjects. Killing innocents was a horrible but necessary task at times, and as I'd told Stephen, I would kill a hundred like him if need be.

Being responsible for the destruction of an immortal soul was too cruel a weight to bear.

I closed my eyes, slipping into a meditative state and calming my mind, focussing past the constant whispering.

In time, sleep did come again.

*D*reams *of sleeping gods lying in their sunken kingdoms.*

Deeper and deeper I descended into the stygian blackness, past pale loathsome things swimming. Things which had never been seen on the surface.

A pyramid of dense obsidian, ancient when the Valley of the Kings was young, came into view, each brick etched with a language as dead as the god it held.

No. Not dead. Sleeping.

That is not dead which can eternal lie.

Through an opening massive enough for a ship to sail, along ink-black corridors where I could see nonetheless, until I came to face the pyramid's sole inhabitant.

Eyes opened, glaring at me, shrivelling my soul like a raisin.

"COME!"

APRIL 11

Standing at the rail of the ship, I watched those disembarking, wondering how many had planned such a short voyage and how many had horrendous nightmares they'd taken as premonitions. The artists among them would have for certain.

Nightmares. If theirs had been half of mine, they were wise to leave. The morphine in my bag would have provided a dreamless rest, but I'd allowed myself to sleep without it. I knew better. Singh had been able to push the book's influence from his mind through meditation, but the best I could manage that way was to subdue the voices.

I stifled a yawn.

Tenders shuttled people back and forth, the docks at Queenstown being unable to accommodate the ship. This gave only one avenue of departure.

None of those milling about, preparing to depart, were the thieves I chased, not that I expected them to leave without some sort of push. There was more to this than the cultists reclaiming their evil tome. They had an agenda, some reason to cross the ocean. Were they headed for one of those cursed New England towns heard only in whispers? Innsmouth? Dunwich?

"It is beautiful, isn't it?"

I turned toward the source of the voice to see Captain Smith also looking at the tenders. He stood with the excellent posture and bearing of the career sailor, one hand on the rail, the other by his side. The man had an air of authority and power which came as much from personality as from station.

"It is indeed," I agreed, though unsure whether the man spoke of the ship or the sea itself.

The captain breathed deep of the salty air, serenity clear on his face. "So much comes together to make a successful voyage. Ship and crew, the course laid, even those tenders below. If all works to plan, then most of it is not noticed by the passengers."

It all seemed to be running like a German train.

"I apologize, Doctor," Captain Smith said. "Get a sailor talking about the sea, and he drifts away."

If the pun was intentional, the man gave no sign. I was more focussed on the fact that he remembered I was a doctor.

"How is Mrs. Hooper?" the captain asked.

"Mrs. Hooper?"

"The lady you boarded with. I had assumed you were attending her."

"No." I shook my head, forcing a smile. "Just two slow-moving people coming up the ramp together."

"Ah, I see." The captain nodded, watching the proceedings below. "Please excuse me, Doctor, I have tasks to attend to before we sail."

"Of course, Captain, you must be quite busy."

I felt happy to see him go. Though he was an amiable sort, having the attention of the most powerful man aboard ship made me uncomfortable.

A few steps and the captain turned back. "Doctor, would you join my table for dinner tonight?"

Damn it. More attention, and not the sort that could be rejected.

"Thank you, Captain, I would be honoured."

After departure from Queenstown, I headed back toward my cabin, frustrated.

The gates between decks remained closed with stewards always at hand. I had tried the direct approach, simply asking for entry and when the steward explained this was impossible, I demanded. The man offered to call the captain and I'd relented.

Thoughts of killing the steward and forcing my way through itched at my brain, but too many people milled about. Even if I wasn't apprehended immediately and *could* retrieve the book, then what? It wouldn't be destroyed. I'd tried enough times over the years to know the damned thing didn't burn or tear, and submerging it in water didn't even smudge the ink.

No, once it was in my possession again, I would need to wait until New York. That meant retrieving the book as quietly as possible. A murdered crewmember couldn't be left on the deck, or even thrown overboard, without complications. Second class would also have a gate and steward blocking my way into steerage.

Killing had to be a last resort for now.

I needed to return to the cabin and think on this.

As I neared it, a wave of pure malevolence dragged me from my thoughts.

All around, passengers went about their regular business. Nothing strange. I slowed to a stop and another man some thirty paces away did the same, making a show of searching through his pockets. In all outward manner he appeared a typical first-class passenger though overly tall and thin to the point of malnourishment. The clothes hung from his frame, yet one finger tugged at his collar as if the shirt were too tight.

I continued forward, as did my chaperone, a consistent distance between us. There could be no doubt he was following me, and was the source of the terrible sensation as well.

At my cabin door I stopped, turning to face the man who again came to an abrupt halt, his eyes darting. A full half minute we stood this way until he shook his head several times, like a man fighting to clear his mind, and stepped toward me.

That loathsome sensation increased, wrapping around me like some great, constricting fist. Evil and corruption accompanied this man in an aura reminiscent of the one surrounding the book, coming off the man in erratic waves, like the heat from a fire.

I was looking at one of the thieves.

How had *he* found *me* though?

Gripping the head of my cane, I was ready. The man stopped in front of me, staring down with piggy eyes. One sinewy hand reached over and rubbed at his opposite arm, but he made no move against me.

This was no casual evil surrounding the thief. He was not

a man who cheated the poor or beat his wife. No, he had a blackness to the centre of his soul and it was one I recognized.

He had read from the book, just as I had, and he'd found me by following that shared link. The same link that allowed me to recognize him.

Now what? He'd still made no threatening move.

"We gots the book," he said in the twang of the uneducated.

A faraway quality rested in those eyes, worse than an opium sot, a look I recognized from years earlier after coming out of my own ravings.

"We gots the book," he repeated.

Was he boasting? Taunting?

No, he waited for a reply.

"Yes, I know," I improvised. "Where is it?"

"Safe. Safe ... yeah, safe."

"Yes, of course," I said as if that all made perfect sense. "Where is your partner?"

A glimmer of normalcy flickered in the man's eyes and he spoke as if I were the lunatic. "Wit' the book. Keepin' it safe."

Of course he was. The other thief had not read from the book and could be trusted with its keeping.

"Was lookin' fer you. Goin' to yer cabin."

"Right. My cabin."

Why would he ...? A flash of insight hit me and I almost gasped with sudden understanding. This man wasn't coming to *my* cabin at all. Another conspirator was aboard the ship. Because of our shared link and his confusion, this man thought I was the other.

Thoughts swirled in my mind. This thief had knowledge that I didn't. If I could get him inside the cabin ... "We can't talk out here."

The taller man gave his head one quick shake, eyes darting again as if surrounded by people trying to eavesdrop.

No one who passed spared the briefest glance at my companion. It seemed that clothes, no matter how ill-fitting, did make the man. Was that how he'd been able to get into first class? Surely he needed more to get past the steward. Perhaps this unknown conspirator had greater influence than I did, enough to allow a steerage passenger into first class.

I reached for my door handle.

"Where you goin'?"

"My cabin."

Confusion creased the expression of the thief's face. "On A deck."

"I beg your pardon?"

"Yer cabin. It's on A deck."

Suspicion replaced confusion and his hand darted into the jacket he wore. The motion reminded me of Singh and I knew there was a concealed knife.

Damn.

"Oh yes. My cabin was changed at the last moment," I tried. "Very inconvenient."

The mind worked behind the thief's madness. My advantage was disappearing and I threw the cabin door open, backing inside. The thief followed, sniffing at the aroma of death within my cabin.

"You ain't him. You ain't."

I shook my head, backing farther into the cabin. "No. I am not."

The man drew his weapon, a blade curved much like a snake. A ceremonial kris, and a better weapon for close-quarter fighting, but I didn't dare draw my sword anyway. This man could lead me to the book.

Dazed or not the man moved fast, rushing forward, bringing the blade up then down again. I dodged to one side, but not by much.

The advantage of distance gone, I retreated, skirting the table. The tall man swung his blade again and I deflected it with my cane, though the blow was staggering. I scrambled to get the table between us.

He launched forward and I took another step away, my back pressing against the wall. The blade swept down with savage ferocity and sunk deep into the wood tabletop. He worked the kris, trying to free it.

Seizing the advantage, I swung my heavy cane around, the arc finishing in a meaty thud against the side of his head. It didn't have near the force hoped for, but it was everything I could muster, and it was enough. The thief's eyes rolled up and he dropped like a poleaxed cow, tumbling to the floor. The kris, now free, clattered next to him.

I watched this unconscious man, expecting him to jump up and continue the attack.

Now what? I had no rope to bind him. In my doctor's bag was a hammer but no nails.

The man groaned.

Soon, this opportunity would be gone, but inspiration struck as I looked at the bed.

Would it work?

I threw the blanket off the top and pulled the sheet underneath from the bed. Laying it flat on the floor next to the unconscious man, I flipped him onto the sheet and started rolling, making the package as tight as possible. His arms needed to be pinned. When the job was done, he lay face-down, and I gave him one final roll.

Open eyes stared back at me.

He thrashed against his bindings, which were not near as tight as I'd hoped. I bolted to the table, grabbing his kris and returned to place the cold metal against the skin at his throat. He calmed, the disconcerting grin of a man dedicated to his cause, creeping across his face.

Lucidity floated in those eyes for the moment. It wouldn't last.

The man's smile widened, revealing missing teeth. "You're him. The hider."

"Yes, I kept that damned book hidden."

"The blasphemer. The heretic."

The thought of that *god* I blasphemed gave me a cold shiver of repulsion.

"The *Ripper*," he whispered.

115

"Enough! Where is it?" I demanded.

The thief giggled, his sanity wavering again now that he was fully conscious. I added pressure to the knife in warning.

"Safe from you," the man said.

"Who is the man you were looking for?"

More gap-toothed grinning, nothing less than expected. Questioning this man could take hours, but I knew I could get the information I wanted. I thought of the second largest scalpel inside my doctor's bag.

What to put inside his mouth to muffle the screams?

"Cthuuuuuuuuuulhuuuuuuuuuuuuu," the man whispered in an eerie echo of Stephen's wail from last night.

I pressed the knife still harder against his throat in warning, a bead of blood appearing under the metal. It was sharp as any scalpel and I fought the urge to just be done with this.

The thief giggled, then shoved his head forward, pressing the blade more forcibly into the skin of his neck. He jerked his head quickly left, sawing through his throat and the artery there before I could react.

A jet of blood spurted from the wound, covering me, the sheet and a good portion of the opposite wall, adding to the gore with each heartbeat.

"Damn it!"

Using the table's edge I pulled myself up and collapsed onto one of the chairs.

"What a waste."

I could have drawn so much more information from him.

His dead eyes and lunatic grin mocked me. I felt seized with the urge to kick him, but that seemed like too much effort.

"Stupid old man!" I said, slapping the table with both hands.

So what information *had* I found out?

The thieves were not alone in this. Someone in first class was their contact. Someone who had boarded in Queenstown? Maybe. This man would not be uneducated or psychotic. What else? Without this second thief it would complicate the two sides coming together. Both would wonder what had happened to him, assuming he was with the other. Would that give me time?

I got to my feet and approached the thief, grabbing the sodden mess of sheet that tied him and cut it free with his own blade. Inside the jacket pocket was a scrap of paper soaked through with blood. I unfolded it, frowning at the now mostly obscured words.

Mr. W—
Cabin—
A Dec

Mr. W? Was this his first name or last? And how many men had boarded with names fitting either? No, there wasn't enough information, and this Mr. W didn't have the book anyway. Not yet.

This left me where I started, needing to get to the remaining thief in steerage.

After jamming this second body into my wardrobe and cleaning myself and the cabin, I took a bottle of rubbing alcohol from my bag and poured half on the thief's remains, the other half on Stephen. That would mask the growing smell for now.

I returned to the closest gate leading to second class and stood at a nearby rail, watching. This steward was most attentive to his duties. One couple who had taken a wrong turn, perhaps on purpose, arrived at the opposite side of the locked gate. The steward spoke with them pleasantly, explaining where they needed to go.

If they'd arrived dressed in first-class clothing would the gate have been opened for them? Had the thief made his way through this way?

Hours of watching, wandering from one entrance to another, I came to the conclusion that there was no simple way to get past those gates. There would be *some* way to get past that gate, but did I have the luxury of time to discover it? It was as expected, but I still returned to my cabin in a foul humour to change into dinner clothes.

The dining room was a sea of tables on two levels, made all the wider by mirrors lining two opposing walls. The captain's table was foremost. Serving staff weaved their way around tables, chairs and passengers, bringing food, filling glasses and being as unobtrusive as possible.

Seated on Captain Smith's left, I made idle chitchat throughout the many courses. The captain's affable manner lulled me into relaxation and I found myself enjoying our conversation when he wasn't engaging the other guests.

"Mr. Wainright," he said to a man who had done no more than push food around his plate since sitting down, "are you unwell?"

Wainright? Mr. W?

"Hmm? Oh, yes, Captain. I'm fine, thank you," he responded, glancing up. "My first cruise. I suspect being on a ship takes getting used to."

The captain smiled, understanding, comforting.

"I didn't sleep well last night," Wainright continued. "Strange dreams and all that."

Smith's smile faltered and he stared at the man, nodding mechanically. I noticed around the table other guests had halted conversation mid-word at the mention of the dreams.

"Yes," the captain said finally. "Just need to get your sea legs, I'm sure. It will be better tomorrow."

Wainright seemed to accept this, though didn't eat more than he already had. This would not be the Mr. W associated with the thieves. That man wouldn't have suffered under the weight of nightmares.

The captain steered the conversation away from the topic and the meal ran its course without further mention of dreams. After dessert the captain excused himself, needing to attend to duties of the ship.

Before leaving myself, I made a quick tour of the room, overhearing conversations with three different Williams and a Wilson. Too many names starting with W to be of any use.

The circuitous route back to my cabin took me past each of the gates once again. As expected, they were still well attended by the stewards. No plan presented itself for getting through, other than the desperate one of killing the ship's crew.

Annoyed I returned to my cabin, turning possibilities over in my head and discarding them as quickly. There would be some way below that wouldn't lead to my incarceration. I just needed to find it.

APRIL 12

The sound of knocking woke me, an insistent quality to it saying it had been going on for some time.

"One moment," I said, voice too low for anyone to hear.

The deep slumber of morphine had left me with dry throat, as well as a certain fuzzy-headedness. Both would clear soon enough.

"One moment," I tried again, louder.

The knocking ceased.

With a muted groan I pushed my feet from under the covers, reaching out for my cane. Crossing the cabin provided enough time for my head to clear, and on opening the door found a ship's crewman I didn't recognize. The man shifted from foot to foot.

"Good morning, sir," he said in a quick, clipped tone. "The captain asks for your presence at his cabin."

"Now?"

"Yes, sir. I've been asked to escort you personally."

Why would the man be sending for me?

"I'll need time to dress," I said.

The man opened his mouth to reply, then took in my nightclothes and gave a nod. He stood, hands behind his back as the door closed on him.

"Damn it," I whispered.

This was the sort of attention I was trying to avoid. How did Smith know which cabin I was in, anyway? No, forget that. The man was resourceful, and if the ship's register had a different name assigned to the room, he would assume I had taken it from a friend.

Quickly I dressed in day clothes, sparing a glance at the clock. A few minutes before nine. A longer sleep than expected, more than I'd been able to get in years.

I opened the door. "Ready."

The crewman started up the passageway and I tried my best to match his brisk pace but soon fell back.

"I apologize, Doctor," he said, embarrassment sliding over his face as he slowed. "I'm anxious to get you to the captain."

"Has something happened?"

"The captain is ... distraught."

We continued on in silence another ten paces before he spoke again.

"There is something about this voyage ..." He shook his head, perhaps unsure how to complete the thought. This time his silence held until he led me into the crew's section of the vast ship.

A knock on one door was answered by it opening a crack, one eye filling the gap.

"It's Johnson, sir," my guide said. "I've brought the doctor, as requested."

The door opened and Captain Smith appeared, gaze shooting left and right. The quiet dignity and affable demeanour were gone. What word had the crewman used? Distraught?

"Doctor, come in. Come in," Smith said, stepping aside to allow entry, then pulled himself to full height and settled his gaze on Johnson. "Thank you, Ensign. That will be all."

The command in his voice was unmistakable. Johnson snapped off a salute which the captain returned before closing the door. Smith deflated into a chair, waving an arm toward a matching seat across from him. I sat.

"What has happened since last night?" I asked.

"Doctor, I fear I am going mad. You heard Wainright at dinner. Dreams. Nightmares."

"You've had nightmares?"

Of course he had.

"No!" Smith laughed, a sound I didn't like. It was too close to the lunatic giggle of the dead man in my wardrobe. "Calling them nightmares is like calling this ship a raft."

"And you want my opinion on these nightmares?"

"Yes," the captain said without making eye contact.

I weighed the options. If the captain were incapacitated, would the ship return to England? No, more likely we would continue on with a new man in command. The attention on me would be gone at least, but was that the wrong way of thinking? This man could be a source of information.

"Often dreams are the hidden topics of our subconscious, our desires," I said.

Smith jumped up with a cry and paced.

"However," I continued, "more often they are influenced by outside stimulus which we are unaware of."

Closer to the actual truth than Captain Smith would ever be aware. His romantic view of the ocean and sailing life made him more susceptible to this evil influence.

"A rich dinner, for example," I added, "can provide a night of vivid dreaming."

Smith came to a stop in front of the cabin's one small window, watching the ocean outside pass by. Two full minutes passed while he, hopefully, absorbed the concept. He nodded once. Another minute passed before he would nod again and turn toward me.

"You are telling me there is more of gravy than of grave about these dreams," he said.

Dickens has always been a favourite author of mine. The fact that Smith had been able to make a joke, as much as the joke itself, gave me hope for the man. The captain took a deep breath and exhaled the hold of last night's dreams.

"What does your ship's doctor say on the subject?" I asked.

I knew the answer already. The captain would not have brought this up with a member of his crew for fear of losing their confidence. It was why a passenger had been escorted to this cabin. The other man focussed on me with such intensity that I was sure I'd asked the wrong question.

Smith said, "Of our two doctors, one is asleep and will not wake."

"Won't wake?"

"He sleeps, fitfully, thrashing and mumbling, but nothing rouses him."

And nothing will, not during this voyage at least. "And your second doctor?"

"We have no idea." The captain returned to his seat. "He disappeared in the night."

Disappeared. Three of the most important men onboard affected by the book's influence.

"Captain, given present circumstances, I recommend a return to England."

Anger flashed in the man's eyes, his mouth becoming a slit. For a moment I feared being struck, then the storm passed and Smith shook his head. "I can't do that. The shipping strikes at home have caused too much difficulty. I have my duty to the company and crew."

"How can you continue without a ship's doctor?"

"Yes, quite right." The captain drummed his fingers against the arm of his chair. "Doctor Shaw, I know it's an imposition and you are here to enjoy the voyage, but would you consider filling in until we reach New York?"

Refusal perched on my tongue, but then an image of the gates flitted through my mind. I closed my mouth with a sharp *clack*. "Of course, Captain. We all do what we must."

A sigh of relief. "My thanks."

"I would need a note from you," I continued, "to pass to any section of the ship where I am needed ... unless you have a uniform in my size."

At that Smith laughed again, but a genuine thing this time that broke the last of the nightmare's grip on him. He went to his desk and wrote a hasty note which he handed to me. "This will do."

I opened it and read:

To whom it may concern,
  Dr. Shaw will be acting as ship's doctor until further notice.
Please convey every courtesy to him and allow access to any area
of the ship he deems necessary.
                    Sincerely,
                    Captain Edward Smith

I tucked it into the inside pocket of my jacket. "Now, my first duty is to prescribe something for you to sleep."

"Nonsense. I'm fine."

"And the ship needs you to stay that way."

The captain mulled this over before throwing his hands up in surrender, mumbling, "Never argue with the ship's doctor."

"Quite right. When are you due on the bridge?"

A look at the clock and he jumped to his feet. "I should be there now."

"And when will you return?"

"Before dinner, but I need to be at my table."

"Fine. I can give you something after dinner to sleep through the night."

I headed for the nearest gate in high spirits.

The captain's letter turned the impossible task of getting through into a simple one. Each of the stewards read it then rushed to open their barrier.

Now I stood at the base of the stairs in third class, eyes closed and listening for the book.

"Damn it."

My mood plummeted in the span between heartbeats.

The book was indeed nearby, that much was obvious. It should have been simple to pinpoint now that we were on the same level. It wasn't. Unlike first class where the location had a constant downward sensation to it, now it felt to be everywhere.

Its power was growing.

"God damn it to hell."

All around me were people who had spent their every penny for this voyage, full of hope for a better life, but one of them was not what he appeared to be.

Would he be recognizable when I saw him? Would the book call to me when I got closer?

I had to hope so.

Announcing myself as ship's doctor I started talking to the nearest people. These third-class passengers expressed surprise that any attention was being paid to them by the ship's crew. They knew their place on the ladder of society.

Word of a doctor in third class would precede me, and that should offset the surprise of a first-class passenger being down here. I didn't want to alarm the thief.

Many complained of general ill-feelings, lack of energy and, of course, the expected nightmares. One passenger who had boarded in Ireland muttered that the voyage was cursed and there was no arguing against that.

The rest of the morning and all that afternoon was spent in a slow circuit through third class, eliminating many as suspects but nowhere near enough. Too many had a natural distrust of the upper-class, which matched how the thief could be expected to react. There was no sudden recognition with any passenger, and no pull from the book.

Calling to the damned thing might knock me into another coma or destroy my mind completely.

Was I desperate enough to try it?

No. Not yet.

In the end, I made my way back to first class, tired and frustrated, ready for a meal and knowing that finding the book was no closer than it had been when I first boarded the ship.

The dining room was three-quarters full at most. Every table held one empty seat at least, and those present were more subdued than the previous night. Captain Smith spoke with his table guests but it was forced, the man exhausted.

After dinner I accompanied him to his cabin as promised and shared some of my stock of morphine. There had been precious little in the ship's stores and it had already been added to my own. Keeping the captain in dreamless sleep would mean exhausting these supplies faster than expected, but I needed him in his right mind, both to keep this ship on schedule and to retain my ability to get through those gates.

APRIL 13

The next morning, I found myself summoned to the captain's cabin once again.

Captain Smith stood erect, commanding, and in control. The perfect image of an experienced sea captain. He sipped a cup of tea. "Good morning, Doctor."

"You slept well?"

"Can't let a few dreams stop me. I have a job to do."

"Glad to hear it."

Smith sat and gestured toward the other chair and the tea. I poured myself a cup.

"Last night, three first-class passengers needed confining to their cabins," he said.

The crewman, Johnson, had filled me in. "People who were trying to harm themselves or others, as I understand it."

It would only get worse.

The captain sighed. "Our sleeping doctor is gone as well."

This was new information. "Gone?"

"He woke and scrawled a message on his wall, in blood no less, presumably his own."

"What did it say?"

"Insanity. Voices speaking to him. Sleeping things waiting to rise. Nightmares." The captain shuddered without noticing. "He concluded by saying he would fling himself off the ship."

"Did he?"

"I would say so," Smith shrugged. "Apparently he went from his cabin to wherever he ended up without a soul seeing him."

We sat in silence a moment before he spoke again. "The crew is calling this 'The Ravings.' Doctor, what is happening on my ship?"

Nightmares notwithstanding, I doubted this man was ready to hear that the doctor's wall scrawlings were true. I could be confined to my cabin, if I tried.

"The Ravings is as fitting a name as any," I began. "I've seen a similar illness before. It attacks the mind, affecting it with a temporary alienation."

"Temporary?"

"Yes, until the patient is removed from the cause. In this case, the ship—or something on it."

The captain mulled this over before replying. "Very well. We'll need to keep these people confined to cabin until we reach New York then, and keep an eye out for any other strange behaviour."

"Unless you are willing to turn back."

Smith shook his head. "Even if I could, it would be a moot point. We have reached the point of no-return. We are closer to our destination now."

The captain put his cup down and got to his feet. "Doctor, please look in on these affected first-class passengers before doing anything else."

"Of course."

Leaving the captain's cabin, I headed straight for steerage.

The first-class passengers were a waste of time. There was little I could do other than sedate them, and I wasn't about to waste morphine on overly sensitive, easily influenced people. My time was better spent with continuing my search.

Smith's words rang in my ears as I walked: *We're closer to our destination now.*

While I was no closer to finding the book.

"Where the hell is it?" I said, stepping into second class. "Where?"

The book's presence hammered into me, pulling a groan from my throat. It was everywhere on this level, as it had been yesterday in third class.

"No! No, no, no."

I rushed for the gate leading to steerage. This sensation in second class *could* mean the thief was on the move, or . . .

I flashed my letter at the steward. "Let me through."

"Are you well, Doctor?" he asked. "You seem . . ."

"Yes, yes, yes. Just open the damn gate."

The man complied and I started to the next level.

"No. God damn it, no."

The thief *wasn't* on the move, but the influence of the book *was*. It had spread like a pestilence, covering the lower two levels. Soon it would occupy the entire ship.

Time was running out.

Like diving deeper into water, the pressure of evil was greater down here, and the effect on the passengers was evident. Many were lethargic, eyes haunted by visions only they saw. One man leaned over his gathered family speaking in hissing whispers, warning them. Another stood in a corner, back to the wall and eyes darting, ensuring nothing could sneak up on him.

All stared at me with trepidation.

How had none of the ship's crew noticed this?

"I'm here to help," I managed.

Those that would speak to me told me about their nightmares. I knew what those visions would hold and moved on, searching for the one who would be less affected.

Some asked if *I* was well, as if *I* were acting in a demented manner.

Insanity.

I spent fruitless hours searching for the thief in this way, but there were too many people, and missing one in that crowd was easy.

"Where is it?"

Would finding the book be enough? There were still two more days at sea.

Two more days under this influence.

A ghost ship would arrive in New York.

I laughed, without knowing the reason why.

Could I throw the book overboard?

"It wouldn't stay there though, would it? No, it needs to be hidden. Guarded. This ship full of people is fair exchange."

There! That man was suspicious.

"You!" I rushed at him, drawing the knife the first thief had carried. "Where is it?"

I had the man pressed against the wall, knife in one hand.

"Where is that damned book?"

"What? I ..."

"Daddy?"

I turned to see the terrified face of a five-year-old boy. He hid behind the doorway, staring up at us.

"Go back inside, Jamie," the man said.

No. That wasn't right. The thief wouldn't be travelling with a child, wouldn't care about his safety.

I backed away from the man, seeing the terror in his eyes matching his child's.

"No, you aren't him. You aren't."

I turned and headed down the hall, making it ten steps before men were on me. They wrestled me to the floor, taking my knife away.

"No! I must find it. Can't you feel the evil?"

"Someone get the steward."

I lie there, under the weight of all these people, warning of the danger surrounding them. Couldn't they feel it for themselves?

"Doctor!" The gate steward, three other men in ship's uniform standing behind him.

"The Ravings," one muttered.

A second one added. "Another doctor affected."

They pulled me to my feet, my arms held fast.

"Help me find the book! Help me find the thief!"

"Yes, of course, Doctor."

They said they would help, yet they herded me toward the stairs.

"No. You don't understand."

"Easy with him," one of the crew said. "He's a friend of the captain's."

The next I knew I was being eased onto my bed.

Then I started screaming.

Dreams *of blood, death, and destruction. The entire world and everyone I'd ever cared for destroyed and defiled.*

Archibald Shaw revelled in it.

Piled before me were all the bodies of those Whitechapel women, and many more that had only been possibilities. All of the men who had gone into that part of London with him there too, torn apart, eyes vacant and mad.

And Singh. The boy I had rescued. He lay, disembowelled on an altar.

In my hand, the long ceremonial blade of the thief, dripping with redness, my mind dripping with madness.

NO!

This was everything I'd fought against, everything I'd dedicated my life to preventing. This was not me. I rejected it.

I am not the Ripper.

Not anymore.

APRIL ??

In my desperation to find the book, I had called to it, and it had answered. I saw this now that I was awake again, now that the madness had passed.

How long had I been unconscious?

I retrieved my cane from the floor and hurried to the cabin's one window.

Still at sea, and the sun only starting to set. I'd regained my senses before it was too late.

The clock on the table said 6:00. Beside it sat a meal, lunch by the look of it. Cold to the touch.

The door to the cabin was locked, which was no surprise. People with the Ravings were being confined to cabin.

I shook my head, trying to clear the lingering fog, and paced the confined space. My body screamed in complaint and reminded me about the morphine.

Did I still have my bag?

Yes. On the trunk where I'd left it. Luckily the stewards had ignored that when they'd dropped me here. I crossed the cabin and opened the bag, pulling out a syringe.

For five minutes I gazed at it, wanting it, before sliding the drug into my jacket pocket with a regretful sigh.

No, I need my wits.

What I needed more was to get out of here.

How though? I lacked the strength to break the door down, and the window was no exit.

Until someone came I was trapped in here.

While waiting, I changed my shirt and pants, the current ones being soaked in the sweat of madness. In the end I sat in the reading chair, facing it toward the door and eating the cold lunch, though I had little appetite. My cane laid across my leg in a casual manner.

A little over an hour later, the handle twitched as someone unlocked it from the other side. A deep breath and a mental reminder to be calm and unthreatening.

The steward, Thompkins, entered, a platter of food to replace my hours old lunch balanced on one hand. When he saw me out of bed, he stopped, then turned to leave.

"I'm fine now, Thompkins," I said. "The fever, or whatever it was, has left me."

Thompkins nodded, coming no closer. "I'm happy to hear that, Doctor."

After another moment's indecision, he stepped forward to place the meal on my table, not picking up what remained of the previous one. He wanted to keep his hands free around me. Sensible.

"Can I get you anything, Doctor?"

"Just some news if you would."

"News?"

"Yes." I tried to keep any impatience from showing. "What

has been happening on the ship in the hours I've been locked away?"

"Hours? Doctor, I'm sorry, but ... you've been in here since yesterday morning."

I'd lost an entire day? "No. God damn it."

Thompkins took a step back and I forced a calming expression to my face.

"Sorry. I was thinking of all the people I could have helped in that time."

The steward relaxed, somewhat.

"Have there been many more afflicted?" I asked.

"Yes, sir. I'm not sure on the number, but quite a few. Both passengers and crew."

"The captain?"

"Oh no, sir! Captain Smith is rock steady."

"Good," I said. "That's good."

The captain had slept through the night without relapsing into his nightmares. Perhaps he'd found something in the ship's pharmacy to help.

I leaned on my cane and got to my feet, suffering at least half of the effort I let Thompkins see. The man took another step back toward the door but looked embarrassed for doing so.

"Obviously you can't let me out," I said, "but would you take a message to Captain Smith for me?"

"Of course, Doctor. Is it urgent? I have other meals to deliver."

"After will be fine."

I crossed to my nightstand and scribbled on one of the papers there, then folded it into four. Turning back I headed for Thompkins, the paper held out in two fingers of my free hand. As he reached for the note I dropped it.

"So sorry," I muttered. "Must still be weak."

"Quite all right, Doctor."

Thompkins bent to retrieve the paper.

"*So* sorry," I repeated.

I took a step back, pulling the sword from my cane. Thompkins must have heard the soft whisk of metal on metal, but gave no sign of understanding its meaning. As he rose, innocent, unsuspecting smile on his face, I lunged forward and skewered him through the heart.

This time, I did not miss the killing stroke. Thompkins pitched forward and collapsed at my feet. Dead.

I waited.

No angry ghost. No wailing.

Thompkins had followed a different path into the afterlife than Stephen.

"Rest in peace," I muttered, not sure what that even meant.

No sense in hiding this body. Unlike the other two, Thompkins would be missed in time. I had to hope that, with the amount of people experiencing madness, the crew would be too busy to bother with one missing steward anytime soon.

The hallway outside was empty except for a cart of meals, which I wheeled into my overcrowded cabin.

"Now what?"

I locked the door behind me, picked a direction and started walking. In motion I could think.

The captain's letter allowing me run of the ship was gone. Even if I did still have it, the crew would know by now what had happened to me. An alarm would be raised if I approached any of the gates. I couldn't be sure the book was still in steerage anyway. Stopping to sense, it told me it was everywhere.

The decks were now mostly empty, and those that were around gave signs they would also rather be left alone. I took up residence in one of the more secluded deck chairs, staring at the ocean.

"Now what?" I repeated.

After sunset, I worried less about being recognized and moved to the rail, chill night air pushing at me as I continued contemplating my next move. The last option of killing my way to the book was still available, and might be my *only* option now. If only I knew for certain where it was.

Lacking any better ideas, I decided to return to the gate, see if anything had changed. Two steps into that direction, my mind was assaulted and my body hammered to the wooden deck.

"Evil. Evil. The evil. The horror. The sleeping death. Cthul …"

I stopped myself. My words had grown from chant to near frantic scream.

"No. No."

I wouldn't allow that. Not again.

Between rail and cane I was able to get back to my feet.

Waves of hate and evil assaulted me, but I was ready.

"They're reading the book again. Reading the words. Reading …"

Stop it!

Yes, they were reading it again, but this time they weren't stopping at a word or two. Oh God, they kept reading and my head felt like it would burst.

"No! Oh, sleeping gods of ancient death …"

The morphine! I fumbled the syringe from my pocket, stripping my arm bare and injecting the needle. Fear and desperation said to depress the syringe the entire way, but I stopped at just enough to dull the assault.

The attack eased, my brain feeling less like it was being squeezed in a giant fist.

And I knew.

They were on this deck now.

Following the sensation back to them was simple. Two men, standing at the extreme bow of the ship.

The first was one of the people from steerage who refused to speak with me. He had been suspicious, but no more so than any of the others in steerage had been. The other, holding the book open in both hands, wore the splendid clothing of someone who had come from formal dinner, completely incongruous next to the thief. He was familiar too. Weston? No, Wilson.

Both had their backs to me, Wilson reading from the book.

Ph'nglui mglw'nafh Cthulhu R'lyeh wgah'nagl fhtagn.

"No!" I yelled, not thinking.

Wilson paused in his chants, turning first to me then the thief. "Get him."

The thief pulled a blade from inside his jacket and started toward me. I allowed him to advance, thinking I had the advantage of reach on the open deck. When I drew the sword from my cane the thief stopped and looked down, as if comparing his blade to mine, then he grinned and started forward again.

The man feinted left then went right. I kept my sword trained on him through both movements, then committed to an attack when an opening presented itself. I thrust forward and he dodged around my sword to swing his knife. Whether through luck or providence I still held the cane in my free hand and managed to get it in the way of the stroke so only the tip of it cut me. Even so it hurt like fire as the blade raked a shallow furrow along my left arm. I swung the cane up and slammed it across the thief's face.

Wilson continued chanting. What the hell was he trying to do?

Ph'nglui mglw'nafh Cthulhu R'lyeh wgah'nagl fhtagn.

Wind increased, chilling me to the bone, making my hands tight and frozen. My fingers wanted to open, to drop the sword but that meant death and worse.

The thief's mouth widened into a grin more toothless than his friend in my wardrobe. He knew all he needed to win was to keep me from his master. The advantage was his.

The ship rocked to one side, throwing us all with it. Wilson kept his balance, leaning against the rails and grasping the book. I used my cane as a third leg, though without the head it *was* more of an effort. Only the thief lost his balance and stumbled, his hand opening involuntarily and dropping the knife to clatter against the boards of the deck.

Without a thought, I thrust forward with the sword and ran the man through, the tip of the blade entering the man's stomach, though I'd been aiming for the heart. He screamed and twisted, dragging the sword from my grasp and staggering back toward his master.

"Damn it, you fool," Wilson said. "Kill him."

He resumed chanting and the thief rushed me. The man was

dead, but a stomach wound could take hours and I didn't have that much time. The fire of a fanatic was in his eyes as he rushed forward. Blood trickled from his mouth and sprayed with each exhale. We collided and he drove me back against the wall, hands reaching for my face and thumbs digging for my eyes.

I screamed.

Something dug painfully against my own stomach and I grasped blindly, knowing what it must be. The sword's hilt, now sitting flush against him. Thumbs pressed against my eyes, pushing them into my skull.

Finding the sword hilt, I twisted it one full circle.

A gasp and the pressure against my eyes relaxed.

I pushed the hilt downward, like a lever, then reversed the action. I'd intended to go left and right next, but the thief staggered away. Fanatic he may be, but the human brain still fought to avoid death.

Through blurry vision I watched him retreat toward the rail.

The ship rocked again, this time to the other side and more violently. Wilson took one step back before pushing himself into the rail once again. The thief, in his desire to get away, toppled over the edge and into the freezing water below, taking my sword with him.

I tried using the remaining cane half for balance again, planting it against the deck, but the slickness of blood on my hands made it too difficult to hold onto. I slipped, losing my grip on the cane and watched it skitter across the deck.

The lunatic words poured from Wilson's mouth. My mind was under siege, pulled sideways into a state of thinking I did not want to return to.

I was on all fours now, crawling toward Wilson. Without the cane this was much faster, though the pain in my lame leg was legendary. Hands and knees pressed against the wooden deck in step after step until one touched metal. The discarded knife of the thief was under hand and I grabbed it, not slowing my progress.

The chants had become more frenzied. Wilson had lost his

mind and I had no idea how he could continue standing, much less reading. I doubled my speed, needing to stop the words pouring from that man's mouth before my sanity left as well.

Reaching Wilson I rammed the knife into the meaty upper part of his right thigh. He gave a short hiss between two syllables but no other sign he had been hurt. I pulled myself up to my feet, reaching to stab him again. Still reading he swung one fist around and connected with the side of my head. Reeling I watched the blade sail away across deck.

With no options left I attacked Wilson with my fists. Puny, ineffective things. I might as well have been a child. He laughed. I cried and stepped backward.

What could I ...?

My hand darted into the jacket pocket and came out with the syringe, still more than three-quarters full of morphine. I swung around and stabbed it into the side of Wilson's neck, pressing on the plunger at the same time. The man sagged, whether from the drug or the wound I didn't care.

He dropped the book to the deck, still chanting.

Bracing myself, I reached down and grabbed Wilson by the lower legs, lifting the man and flipping him over the side of the ship and into the water below.

The book called to me, whispering, ordering me to finish what was begun.

I shook my head and looked down, seeing the pages. The book was in my hands, face up, the words burning into my mind.

Had I been reading?

Had I said any of this aloud?

"No. It has to be over. Please."

The ship lurched again as, in front of me, a shape rose from the water. Immense, coursing with rivers of slimy, stagnant water. A rounded, bulbous head ending in tentacles. An ancient god, asleep no more.

"No! No, no, no, no, no, no."

Once again I looked at the book, at the words that were there, at the madness awaiting. The ceremony had not been completed. I could see the spot where I'd interrupted Wilson. It blazed in my mind like fiery letters written across the sky, spiking into my mind like a silver needle of agony. Nothing else occupied my world except for the words of the book and this waiting, ancient deity.

READ!

I heard the word inside his head, felt it inside my soul, to the core of my being and beyond. Nothing else.

Nothing!

"Please."

I closed my eyes.

The words filled my head. I saw them, saw what I was expected to say, commanded to read.

READ THE WORDS!

"Yes. Read the words."

Had I said that?

Yes. Yes I had. And I saw it was true. I *did* need to read those words dancing in front of my eyes.

Fhtagn wgah'nagl R'lyeh Cthulhu mglw'nafh Ph'nglui

I read them. Backward.

More tumbled from my mouth. Word after word until I was screaming myself hoarse and had lost all sense of who I was.

The ancient god raged at the reversal of ceremony, thrashing as it returned to the depths. One appendage—A wing? An arm?—collided with the ship. The screech of rending, tearing steel filled the air.

I lost my balance as the ship was rocked sideways. That damned tome went overboard, following its god back to the ocean's bottom. A moment later I followed it, watching the freezing water rushing toward me.

The book was gone, my mission with it, and I welcomed death.

When my eyes opened I was lying in a lifeboat, cold and sodden, a blanket wrapped around me. Inside the rocking boat hunkered people with the haunted expressions of ones who had gone through war.

"Rest easy, Doctor. You're safe," a familiar voice said.

"Mrs. Hooper?"

"You're lucky the steward saw you."

"What happened?" I asked.

"Something hit the ship," the steward said. "Some sort of ..."

I knew the word *monster* was on the man's lips, but he wouldn't allow himself to speak it. His mind didn't want to acknowledge it. None of these people did.

"Iceberg," I said. "Yes, I saw it."

Everyone in the lifeboat focussed on me and I repeated the word several times. Iceberg. They were ready for any explanation but the truth of what they had seen.

"Iceberg," I repeated one final time.

There were murmurs of agreement and the repeating of my final words as I slipped away.

Iceberg.

Tomorrow's Miracles

BY L. RON HUBBARD

One might say that L. Ron Hubbard wasn't just a writer. He had an extraordinarily inquisitive and receptive mind, which led him as a youth to begin a lifelong exploration of the world and the nature of man.

He studied firsthand more than twenty-one different races and cultures; from the Indian tribes of North America, to the Kayans of Borneo and the Mongols living in the Western Hills of China. He was a licensed master mariner, a pilot of early aircraft and an organizer and leader of expeditions which carried the flag of the Explorers Club. Coupled with this insatiable curiosity and love of adventure was an ability to look at the world and, all in a glance, reach often brilliant and startling insights based upon his observations.

L. Ron Hubbard began his professional writing career in 1930, scripting and directing action radio dramas. He was also a correspondent for a national aviation magazine before becoming a writer of popular fiction. Within a few years he had written a multitude of action, sea, and air adventure stories and rose to the top ranks of published authors. His work carried a verisimilitude that most other authors could not match, for while they fantasized about faraway places, storms at sea and death-defying aerobatics, L. Ron Hubbard had lived those adventures. With remarkable versatility, he soon added mystery, western, and historical fiction to his growing markets.

By 1938, Ron Hubbard was already established and recognized as one of the top-selling authors, when Street & Smith, publishers of Astounding Science Fiction magazine urged him to try his hand at science fiction. Though he had studied nuclear physics at George Washington University, he protested that he did not write about "machines and machinery" but that he wrote about people. "That's just what we want," he was told.

The result was a barrage of stories from L. Ron Hubbard that expanded the scope and played a part in changing the face of the literary genre, gaining Ron Hubbard repute as one of the founding fathers of the great Golden Age of Science Fiction.

The following notes were written by Ron in 1938. He had just found himself fully immersed in the world of science fiction. Not just writing soon-to-be popular stories, but also partaking in many friendly discussions about what is possible, what could be or has been. These thought-provoking notes share insight into the character of science fiction writers of the Golden Age and the inherent quality of those writers who are creating new worlds and existences far beyond what is known or possible.

He began his exploratory essay with this, "We are all more interested in these speculations about matter, space and time than we will care to admit to the professors who sometimes prove 'something less than kind.' I began to wonder about the validity of this inner circle of 'science-fiction.' Was it science at all? Or was it something else, even greater? Are we children of science or, to be blunt, philosophers? What would be the difference between them? And so we begin."

Tomorrow's Miracles

How many men have ever paused in the summer night to look up at the stars and give a thought, not to astronomy, but to the men who first slashed the Gordian knot of planetary motion? Of course, all educated men have, at one time or another, scraped the surface of the source of such facts. But, today we speak grandly of galaxies and consider astronomy an exact science and bow down before facts.

There probably does not exist a professor in the world who has not, unwittingly or otherwise, held the ignorance of the ancients to ridicule; and there is no field where this is more apparent than astronomy.

Some of the facts are these:

Early Hebrews and Chaldeans, among others, believed in a flat earth, a sky supported by mountains and which upheld a sea, which, in turn, leaked through and caused rain. The flat plain was supported by nothing in particular. Of course we all know this, but there is a worthwhile point to make.

The Hindus believed that the earth was a hemisphere, supported by four large elephants. "This seems to have been entirely satisfactory until someone asked what was holding the elephants up. After some discussion, the wise men of India agreed that the four elephants were standing on a large mud turtle. Again, the people seem to have been satisfied until some inquisitive person raised the question as to what was holding the mud turtle up. I imagine the philosophers had grown tired of answering these questions by this time, for they are said to have replied that there was mud under the mud turtle and mud all the rest of the way." (*Astronomy* by Arthur M. Harding, PhD p. 4).

Twelve pillars, according to the Veda of India, supported the earth, leaving plenty of room for the sun and the moon to dive under and come up on the other side.

If you wish, you can find a multitude of such beliefs, all common enough. But there are two facts concerning these and their presentation which are most erroneous. By examining the above quote, one sees that terms have been confused. Men who ask questions and then figure out answers are, indeed, philosophers. The masses take anything which seems to have a certain academic reverence attached and cling to it desperately. The other error is considering that these beliefs were foolish and that scientists, laboring in their laboratories or observatories are wholly responsible for the ideas which permeate the world of thought.

It is not that we here wish to maintain these facts about the state of the earth. On the contrary. But, they are not presented for ridicule because they are the ideas which some philosopher developed painfully with the scant data he had at hand and who had to aid him no means of communication, travel, instruments or even mathematics. They are, what we chose to call, hypotheses possessing sufficient truth to be accepted. Today, thanks to Copernicus and all the rest, we know about gravity. Thanks to Newton, we have mathematics. Thanks to a lens grinder, we have a telescope.

It was stated in an early Sanskrit treatise that the world is round. Thales, Homer, Aristotle, Pythagoras, Ptolemy and others conceived various evidences which demonstrated that the earth was a sphere. In 250 BC, Erathosthanes computed the earth's circumference, missing it only by one hundred miles (and he had no mechanical aids or "higher" mathematics).

Of course, these gentlemen made errors in their hypotheses. Ptolemy, 140 AD, conceived of seven crystalline spheres to account for planetary motion. To counter for this, long before (in the sixth century BC) Pythagoras taught that the earth went around the sun but erred in supposing the sun to be the center of the universe. Aristarchus, in the third century BC, and Capella in the fifth century AD, also taught that the earth revolved itself around the sun. Copernicus, in the sixteenth century, gave the world the system which is now used.

Now the point we wish to make is this, down through the ages, men have conceived various hypotheses with regard to astronomy. Concurrently, instruments were invented and other discoveries made and into the hands of investigators was placed a complete idea, plus the means of examining it. There has been considerable lag, naturally, between widespread belief and philosophic location of new truths. We are fond of thinking in terms of tomorrow. But, the future is written with the pen of the present in the ink of the past.

We are fond of believing that that which we now possess is infallible and not subject to any great change. And, when we begin to localize certain fields for investigation, science feeds wholly upon the statements of predecessors. Should a man put forth a new theory (there hasn't been one since the nineteenth century), then he is no longer a scientist but a philosopher.

Let us remember our Voltaire and his admonition to define our terms. What is science? What is philosophy? Further, by knowing, what can we hope to gain by it? Will we benefit enough to talk about it? The answer to the last two is definitely yes.

To quote Spencer, "Knowledge of the lowest kind is un-unified knowledge; science is partially-unified knowledge; philosophy is completely-unified knowledge." (*First Principles*, p. 103).

Philosophy is *not* the muttering of epigrams nor is the true philosopher merely one who can quote at random from various great works.

Consider an explorer, casting away, all too often, his greatest securities, even his life, to stride forward into the outer dark, throwing up his star shells to view what lies in the unknown. He lacks a vocabulary suitable to record his findings because the words have yet to be invented. He lacks instruments to measure what he thinks he sees because no instruments for such are yet in existence. He stumbles and trips, pushing ever outward on his lonely track, farther and farther from the milestoned roads where statements are safe and conversants many. He is so far out, that those in their safe, warm homes of "proved thought" cannot recognize the distance he has traversed when he first covers it.

His is the task of stabbing deeper into the Unknown and the dangers he runs are those of ridicule. He knows, in his heart of hearts, what his fate will most likely be. He may come back with some great idea only to find that men laugh. He may point a road which will be a thoroughfare within a century but men, having but little vision, see only a tangle of undergrowth and blackness beyond and push but timidly where the first to go pushed forward with such courage.

In all the ages of history, thinking men have been crucified either by institutions or the masses. But those very ideas, which at first seemed so mad and impossible, are those which science now uses to polish up its reputation.

Inevitably, the philosopher, the true searcher, is decried. But then, it is perfectly natural. His breadth of view is so great and penetrating that he can unify all the knowledge groups, taking his findings to discover a lower common denominator.

It is quite natural that he should do this, just as it is that his work should usually be spurned by his own generation.

Un-unified knowledge is that possessed by every animal or drudge. "A cake of soap cleans a shirt." "A cake of soap cleans a floor." "A cake of soap cleans the face."

Partially-unified knowledge on this subject would be: "A cake of soap cleans," and "let us see how many things a cake of soap will clean."

Completely-unified knowledge on the subject would be: "Any agent which holds foreign matter in solution will clean."

The argument here is quite plain. Partially-unified knowledge has become a group of men all anxious to assemble data on the science of soap. The completely-unified knowledge opens up a new vista, the possibility of discovering some medium which will clean anything.

And if you think this is facetious, know that there is no medium which will clean everything and anything equally well. It would be essentially destructive to a million volumes of hard won data concerning soap. The philosopher has come up against a resistant force. He reduced the matter to simplicity and indicated that it was necessary to search for a new cleaner, not a new method. Put into practice immediately and meeting with success, the idea would destroy, for instance, the business of hundreds of soap factories and would, of course, throw umpteen thousand soap chemists out of excellent jobs.

There is nothing being used today except those ideas given to the world by philosophers. For instance, Spinoza is responsible for most of modern psychology. Plato wrote about psychoanalysis in his *Republic* (in addition to most of our ideas on the political side of the ledger as well). Aniximander (610–540 BC) outlined our theory of evolution and Empedocles (c. 490–c. 430 BC) developed it as far as we have gone, originating natural selection. Democritus said, "In reality, there are only atoms and the void," and went on to outline the theories of planetary evolution much as they are used today. The Ionian Greeks developed the major portion of our physics. Kant handed out the finishing touches, with Schopenhauer (a strange combination, this) on our psychology, Spencer on evolution; Newton put natural laws into equations and invented mathematics to work them. Spinoza went so far into the realm of the outer dark that no one has caught up to him yet, though the trails are being followed slowly and inexorably to the destinations he indicated. But science in each case contemporarily taught and used outworn systems and considered that it had reached an outer frontier when, in reality, science was always hundreds of years behind the philosophic frontier!

In short, science has the unhealthy tendency to isolate and expand that isolation, where philosophy tends to reach higher or more general laws. Give a scientist a theory (witness cytology) and he immediately sets out and collects gravitically all the facts pertinent to that one thing. To the scientist is owed the particulars. The scientist inherits the theories and instruments already conceived and smooths out the rough spots. The philosopher is challenged because he does not do this but, as we have remarked, he has no instruments, no tables, no aid of any kind which has reached as far as he has gone forward.

In this manner, science tends to group and then complicate any subject. It is to science that the masses owe their benefits. It is to the philosopher that science owes all its fuel. The citizen, seeing not very far, praises where praise is really due but not wholly due to the point where a scientist can laugh at philosophic ideas, the very things which gave him the material with which to work.

That science does attempt to propagandize its importance to the extent of origination is attested by the commonly heard statement that "Now everything is all invented and if one would desire fame he must specialize." That word "specialize" is a red flag to any philosopher because it automatically indicates the localizing of knowledge into hideous complexities, which, he knows very well, will be destroyed just as all other complicated structures were ripped down when a new truth was isolated. Now it is indicative of the essential nature of science that it wars ceaselessly within itself in favor of this or that hypothesis as countering another hypothesis. It can be said with truth that the battles of philosophy are fought by science against science. Science comes along with measuring sticks of the already known, takes sides and begins to fire, without once inventing any substitute or new hypothesis of its own and ridiculing any which may be offered. So stubborn is science that it hangs to its achieved tomes like a bulldog. Ptolemy's weird theory of crystalline spheres was taught concurrently with the revised Copernican System in one of the oldest American universities for many years.

This is no diatribe against science, it is a defense of new theories, new ideas, new concepts and the men who made them. The laughter leveled at the heads of innovators is amusing only if it be remembered that the ideas now in use were once equally ridiculed by science. And one has only to glance back with the perspective of the years to see that science has embraced many things much more weird—such as a hemisphere on four elephants on a mud turtle on mud, mud, mud. Doubtless, in this instance, there were a hundred libraries filled with tracts to the effect that the mud turtle had green eyes as against the opinion of another that his eyes were purple. Basing this on horizon stars and examining them as reflection, scientists of that day were likely very learned within their sphere of findings.

But there is such a thing as a cumulation of knowledge. By this, most men envision being swamped by facts and books. Libraries crammed to the roof, laboratories humming, men shouting in lecture rooms, men writing vast discourses on electrons and positrons . . . But there is no need for alarm. Ten times as much data has been stacked away in the basement where it molds, forgotten, the product of but fifty years ago but now disproved through the scientific acceptance of higher generalizations. Each time a higher generalization is reached, all men shout, "This is the ULTIMATE! Man can go no further!" But they forget, that in quiet places men are looking all about them, not at one special object but at all objects and so it comes as a shock when a perfectly simple truth which was right under everybody's nose all the time, was brought to light.

Just as God's connection with man and the Creator of the Universe (Prime Mover Unmoved or whatever God might really be) is pushed back step by step infinitely, so is all knowledge simplified.

Two hundred years ago (although it had probably been outlined already) science would have blinked at the idea of splitting the atom. Science dealt in atoms and molecules in that day and nothing smaller. Today every schoolboy knows that an atom can be split and remade into several things. A hundred years from now, men will look back at this atom splitting and shake their heads over such stupidity as thinking that an electron was the smallest division.

But how do we get to the point where we can look back? The answer is somewhere in our midst. Just who will advance the theory and method for releasing atomic energy is not important. That the possibility of doing so has been often sighted and that various means are constantly being proposed is the course which will lead to such a thing. And do not for one hypnotized moment suppose that the method will be born in any flashing, sparking laboratory endowed with millions. On the contrary, it will first be proposed by a thinker. The laboratory may later claim all the credit but that is of no matter, it seems, as long as men can then begin to write all about the mathematics of disintegration with which they will fill ten thousand libraries.

If this cannot be believed, if it cannot be accepted that all truths are simple truths and need only to be pointed out, recall that the splitting of the atom was a simple truth. Then, if it be a matter of concern that the only discoveries left will be complex and that specialization is paramount, remember that the discovery of the disintegration of the atom will scrap all the fine tomes (which fill ten thousand libraries) on the subject of internal combustion engines and propelling forces in general as well as all extant hull, wheel and wing designs. The only thing of these fine flights which will remain is the essential truth from which they were born.

Knowledge is not a swamping sea of facts but a long line of simple truths, each one more simple than the last. If one would discover the next in line, let him not in any specialized field but rather in a cross between two fields or more. And as a man cannot be specialized in half a dozen fields it remains that his investigations would have to be wholly independent of any rubber-stamped outlook. The atom disintegrator may come as a cross between botany and physics. Who would dream of such a thing? But already the newest source of energy is the leaf of a tree. Would a physicist, interested only in physics, have discovered that? It is doubtful. He would have to be more concerned with the entire world around him than he would be with his immediate laboratory bench. Strangely enough, the men who have isolated the greatest truths have not been what is generally known as "an educated man." Widely read, yes. Intelligent, certainly. But above all, anxious to push into anything and everything where the devil would fear to tread.

This thirst for adventure into the abstract is the motivating force of all youth. Later, weighed down with admonitions that one must specialize, youth succumbs to the lure of security and forgets about those things he wanted to plan, in the scramble to read all everybody ever said on the subject of Trimming Frogs' Toenails.

To be very specific, today the scientist mocks wild ideas about interplanetary travel, saying, "Wel-l-l-l, yes-s, it might be done ... maybe. But ..." With all respect to him, he is perfectly right. He has a certain job of his own to do. He will probably be dead long before man first sets foot on the moon. But that the dream, any wildest dream, can be accomplished needs only the verification of the source of most of our mechanical marvels today. Submarine? Locomotive? Airplane? Stratosphere and overweather? Typewriter? Traffic signals? Look at what you may and where you may, you will uncover "science-fiction" or a man interested in it.

The philosophers of the great general ideas are, of course, in a class by themselves. But as far as the advanced applications of various methods and hybrid sciences, as far as the forecast of our civilization, and indeed our very architecture of tomorrow, one has only to search the files.

Men have been writing "science-fiction" since the Phoenicians, perhaps. At least the first story followed soon after writing itself. Once where the "pseudo-science" sent a man west on an iron horse to fight Indians (which didn't happen really, until many, many years had flown), it now sends men into the outer galaxies.

Among the scientists of today are many outlaws, not quite philosophers, but still intrigued by the ideas which can be turned up.

Looking back into the past's dim depths one can see a great many "foolish" ideas brought to fruition. Looking ahead into the future, one can see ...?

The Idealist

written by

L. Ron Hubbard

illustrated by

BRIAN C. HAILES

ABOUT THE STORY

Originally published in 1940 in Astounding Science Fiction, *"The Idealist" was met with reader acclaim declaring it "one of the most unforgettable bits of writing I've ever come across" and "so good, it hurt to read it."*

With such great reception, it could be surprising that it isn't as well known as other L. Ron Hubbard sci-fi classics, such as To the Stars *or* Final Blackout. *But that is simply because it and the subsequent five stories that encompass the series were written under the pen name Kurt von Rachen. And the true name of the author wasn't revealed until a decade later.*

Science fiction in 1940 was a short-story field. It was also a poorly paying genre at one cent per word. To make a living in that market, an author had to write a lot of stories. But then editors didn't want the same names on the cover month after month, even if they wanted the same quality of story, so the best writers used pseudonyms. And that's why you've not heard of "The Idealist" by L. Ron Hubbard.

As an aside, the Kurt von Rachen name has a comical origin several years prior to "The Idealist." In response to an editor's pronouncement that he was looking for new talent (really hoping to find new writers willing to work for a lower rate), Ron wrote "a sizzling story of the legion" from legionnaire Kurt von Rachen. The editor was so proud to have discovered new talent that rivaled the best his magazines had been publishing, he bragged to Ron himself. And as Ron didn't have the heart to reveal his gag, he let it ride.

In reading "The Idealist," you'll find something you may not expect, revelations written by a clear-eyed realist who saw things as they were, not according to the popular view. Revelations which may be as true today as when they were written.

ABOUT THE ILLUSTRATOR

Brian C. Hailes, creator of the popular YouTube channel, Draw It With Me, *is also the award-winning writer/illustrator of the illustrated novel* Blink, *two graphic novels, entitled* Dragon's Gait *and* Devil's Triangle, *and the children's picture book,* Skeleton Play. *Other titles he has illustrated include* Heroic: Tales of the Extraordinary; Passion & Spirit: The Dance Quote Book; Continuum *(Arcana Studios); as well as* McKenna, McKenna; Ready to Fly; *and* Grace & Sylvie: A Recipe for Family *(American Girl). In addition to his several publishing credits, Hailes has illustrated an extensive collection of fantasy, science fiction, and children's book covers, as well as interior magazine illustrations.*

Hailes has received numerous awards for his art from across the country, including 2002 Winner of the L. Ron Hubbard Illustrators of the Future. His artwork has also been featured in the 2017 and 2018 editions of Infected by Art.

Hailes studied illustration and graphic design at Utah State University, where he received his Bachelor of Fine Arts degree, as well as the Academy of Art University in San Francisco.

He has been a regular panelist and presenter at Salt Lake FanX, LTUE, and was the Artist Guest of Honor at Conduit 2013. He has also appeared as a special guest at San Diego Comic Con.

Hailes currently lives with his wife and four boys in Salt Lake City, where he continues to draw and paint regularly.

The Idealist

AUTHOR'S NOTE:

This is not a chronicle of that chaos which befell the Earth in fatal February 2893; for it would require a far more brutal pen than mine and a far longer story than this to record the political and moral debacle which ended the Last Aristocracy. It is not to be regretted that decadent profligates, such as the Eighty Great Names contained, found unmerciful death in the scorching frenzy of a maddened mass; the only regrettable thing is a law, seemingly inviolable, which states that the method of government cannot be changed no matter how many rulers are slain.

When a billion despised and beaten workmen lifted their unshaven faces to give vent to the hideous marching song of the revolt, there were those among them who dreamed an idyllic ideal. No pity to the brawling clods who scarce knew that they lived! No pity to the drunken beasts who had abused rule for three centuries! Pity instead the idealist who discovered that he had placed power in the hands of an untutored mass who, inured to the foulness and bigotry of the Eighty Great Names, carried forward along the very principles which they had avowed to destroy. For a century, Justice had been a bland-faced mockery—the mass turned it into a careless buffoon.

Pity, then, the idealist, the human being who, by some strange chemistry, was born a gentleman in face and figure and worker in name. The ranks of the Enlightened People's Party held many such as this, men who tenaciously gripped light and reason to their breasts until the bullets of firing squads put out all their light and all their reason forever. Such men were the supporters of those unbelievably airy dreamers, the Anarchist Alliance. Like a round table of King Arthur, they judged the world by themselves and failed to recognize the brutalizing effect of the Eighty Great Names upon an uneducated and vengeful people.

The first slaughter was small compared to the second. Once set burning, passions caught from man to man and human life became, out of habit, something to destroy. With the Eighty Great Names stacked in a hundred and eighty sodden piles, the Anarchist Alliance, under the direction of very able scholars, sought to reform the new government into a lasting formula for contentment. But this effort was antagonistic to the Enlightened People's Party, for the leaders were power-crazed and lustful in their orgy of death. The Anarchist Alliance and the Communist regime parted. The latter was more numerous by ninety-five to one and it was therefore a simple matter for the Enlightened People's Party to single out and order executed any man who might possibly menace the Communist leaders.

Wholesale destruction steamrolled the Anarchist Alliance. Even so, there were a few, too powerful in friends to be murdered outright, who received the lingering death of the concentration camps and colonies around the System and in Outer Space.

Pity the poor idealist! The only man who could have founded a lasting contentment for Earth! For the ideal and the man must always genuflect before the avarice and personal terror of the unshaven clown who, to the peal of the devil's laughter, controls the crowd and sweeps it onward to greater follies. Stupidity and cupidity unfortunately rhyme.

Kurt von Rachen

He threw up his hands to protect his wounded face from the elbows and shoulders of the crowd. It was like drowning, being flung into this motion and sound. It was drowning, for drowning, too, is death. The place stunk of sweat and stale powder smoke and gangrene.

Revolution, thought Steve Gailbraith, didn't begin to kill until it was done.

The shiny courtroom walls, so lately adorned with statues symbolizing Justice and Mercy, were dotted and slashed with slugs and shrapnel, seared and crumpled with rays, and discolored by strangling gas. Pieces of furniture crunched underfoot. The crowd surged this way and that, now a vast roar of obscene delight, then a howling wolf pack athirst for new blood. Where no commoner had stood before except under arrest, commoners now made a vicious holiday. Each new sentence was greeted with "Forever to Fagar, the Deliverer!"

A man could die here, thought Steve, and never be discovered even if he began to stink. His wits were dulled by the swirling bedlam until it took great effort for him to see, or think, or feel anyone. He writhed with disgust for this thing he had helped bring about.

There was expectant lust in the faces which saw him push past. But the prisoners ahead had no interest in anything. The guard shoved him into a seat and tramped away to fetch more meat for the firing squad. Steve dabbed at his bleeding face with a ragged sleeve. The glint of torn braid about his wrist caught his eye for an instant and he grinned.

Colonel Steve Gailbraith.

Long live the Revolution!

There were other uniforms to the right and left, but just now the prisoner's box was jammed, in the main, with civilians—eight or nine women, men with the ascetic faces of scholars, hefties with a truculent swagger—

Evidently, thought Steve, they were running out of military criminals and easing off into counter-revolutionists. It was about time they started shooting some civilians.

The high bench was spread with the elbows of the judges. They sat in comfortable indifference and passed judgment without bothering to look or listen. Even murder, thought Steve, gets to be a habit.

The chief judge was an insolent rogue whose face consisted of unshaven folds of fat and a pair of lewd eyes. He had on a grimy suit of workman's slipovers and a borer's lantern cap; his hands were like lumps of lard and his paunch so soft that the bench dented it. For eight days Guis had been sitting there with his cohorts dispensing with those who had aided, but now might obstruct, the new governmental system which had swept the Continent from Frisco to New York with a bloodstained broom.

Two factions of workers, one Communistic and the other Anarchistic, had united to wipe out the mental aristocracy which had abused its workmen and slaves. And then the Communistic faction, the stronger, had found it expedient to cancel out the Anarchistic partner. With the aristocracy lying in congealed clots at crossroads throughout the land, the Enlightened People's Government found it simple to increase the heaps with Anarchistic corpses. It was being done smoothly. The people had not yet begun to realize that Anarchist and counter-revolutionist were being made synonymous. It would not do to excite the people too much. There were even Anarchists who could not be touched because of their great popularity.

Communism, thought Steve, is a method of repaying service with death. When he, as a member of the Anarchistic party's better element—which also included most of the brains in the land—had taken over the temporary government of California, he had supposed his own popularity sufficient to protect him. But when he had seen fit to spare a few aristocratic families, he had been disabused of his own invulnerability.

Ah, well, thought Steve, it was too swift a rise anyway. What goes up—and he had gone up. From an Air Force lieutenant he had zoomed to a colonelcy and, having done spectacular work in the revolt, his colonelcy had resulted in a governorship.

And here he sat watching Judge Guis gnaw a Havana with snagged teeth and spit out sentences amid clouds of smoke. It was unlikely that Guis caught half the names tossed up to him by cringing lawyers.

"Professor Jean Mauchard," barked the clerk. "Accused of heading the organization known as the Sons of Science, said organization having been found guilty of plotting to sustain a counter-revolutionary program."

Jean Mauchard was a straight, stiff fellow, thirty and disdainful. His lip was curled as he spoke up at Guis. "Guilty. Firing squad."

Guis stopped grinning and removed the cigar. He leaned forward to better view the prisoner. "Is that mockery, my fine *scientist*?"

"I save you your wind," said Jean Mauchard. "I wonder that you do not get a parrot to keep blatting those words for you."

Guis almost got angry and then, sitting back, he replaced the cigar. "No parrot for you, *scientist*. You Anarchists have very strange ideas, but you are not without your points. I have been waiting for your case. You are, I think, leader of the Sons of Science?"

"Correct."

"That outfit of disaffected aristocrats, composed of men with too many formulas and too few brains." Guis chuckled at his own wit and some of the other judges grinned down at Jean Mauchard.

Guis whispered to his cohorts on either side, and they whispered down the line. The grins increased.

They are relieved, thought Steve. I wonder what hell stew they're cooking now. They wouldn't dare shoot Jean Mauchard out of hand. But there he left the observation, for the confusion of the place made his already aching head spin. People in the box were jostling him and the guards had hurled several new prisoners in and the clerk was bellowing for more fodder.

When Steve next glanced toward the high bench it was in reply to a call for a name as familiar as Jean Mauchard's.

"Dave Blacker!"

A husky buccaneer was made to obey the summons. A guard thrust Dave Blacker toward the high bench and then, suddenly, the guard went loping into the crowd and Dave Blacker ostentatiously dusted his hands and settled his loud topcoat about his hulking shoulders. He swaggered up before the bench.

"I'm Dave Blacker, you pot warmer. And when you sing for me again, say it slow and respectful. I'm Dave Blacker, get it? D-A-V-E, Dave; B-L-A-C-K-E-R, Blacker. And when I roar a hunnert thousand men cheer their heads off. If you got business with me, get it out and get it done because this place stinks and you stink and when I want to wallow with hogs I'll go find some hogs more to my liking. Get going, Guis. You're goin' to charge me with sedition, mayhem and immorality—*if* you've got the nerve."

Guis removed the cigar for the second time that day. His shapeless lips were lopsided on his face. "You may be Dave Blacker in the West, but here in Washington you're a renegade that's guilty of plotting to overthrow the Enlightened People's Government. *Once* a hunnert thousand of your brick-tossing hefties might have cheered you to a man, but right now, when you talk about things stinking, take a smell of this pile of evidence against you!"

Dave Blacker spat and crossed his arms. "Shoot me, you dollar-a-day mucker, and you'll have to shoot half the longshoremen on the Pacific Coast. We done our part in this scrap and we can do plenty more."

Another judge leaned toward and whispered to Guis and then all the judges began to hiss like a platoon of snakes. Some of them appeared worried, but soon Guis wiped away their frowns. Whatever he proposed pleased them very much for two or three laughed outright.

"Blacker," said Guis, "we brought you here to test your metal. We've got a job for you. A big job. You and some three hundred of your men. And"—here Guis could barely suppress his own guffaws—"we've got a job for Mauchard. For Mauchard and his people. A job for the two of you."

"I'm not takin' no job with Mauchard!" roared Blacker, abruptly enraged by the mere thought of close contact with those devils, the scientists, who had sought to oust the honest laboring element from the Anarchists and dominate the show—a move which had resulted in the weakening and now the loss of all Anarchistic power to the death of thousands.

"Nor I with scum like Blacker," said Jean Mauchard with a chill glare in the labor leader's direction.

"Oh, but I'm sure you'll both like this job," said Guis. "We mean to honor you. Why, we're not even going to transport you to the labor colonies. We're going to give you a colony of your own. And on a beautiful planet. We're going to give you supplies and equipment. You gentlemen are valuable assets to our civilization and you can't be spared. Yes, that is what we are going to do. Jean Mauchard and Dave Blacker, you are going to head your respective groups in the colonization of Sereon of Sirius. You'll leave tomorrow morning."

Before they could vent the violence of their protests, the clerk was bawling, "Stephen Gailbraith!"

Steve was pulled out of the box and thrust against the front wall of the bench. He was getting used to being thrust about and so he merely straightened his tattered tunic and looked up at Guis with an amused and tolerant smile.

"Gailbraith," read the clerk. "Colonel, Air Force. As Emergency Governor of California, spared lives of aristocracy, compromised with subversive element and generally acted contrary to the best interests of the people."

"Guilty," said Guis. "Firing— Wait a moment. You have a familiar face, whatever-your-name-is."

"Gailbraith."

"Oh, yes. Colonel Gailbraith. You took San Francisco about five months ago, didn't you? Good piece of work even if you are a counter-revolutionist now. I suppose ... well, you must have quite a few friends in the army, haven't you?"

"A few."

"Ah, yes. A few." Guis whispered to the other judges for a moment, and they all whispered back and nodded. "Colonel Gailbraith, this court is going to be lenient with you. We are going to permit you, because of your extraordinary military skill, to accompany the Sereon Expedition. Next case."

The court clerk intoned, "Miss Fredericka Stalton. Miss Fredericka Stalton."

A guard pulled Steve away, and he almost collided with a slight but pretty girl whose face was a study in cold contempt for Guis. But it was a face which leaped out of the pool of faces for only an instant, and then was gone.

The court clerk was reading, "Fredericka Stalton, propagandist for the Anarchist party. Accused of counter-revolutionary ..."

Steve Gailbraith was glad to get into the corridor. His head was aching and he felt as if he had been hauled out of a swamp. Expedition to Sereon. With Dave Blacker and Jean Mauchard.

He didn't realize, just then, what a neat way it was of doing away with men who might have had objectors to their outright execution. He wasn't thinking at all. Only half conscious, he had the strange hallucination of a pretty face set with cold contempt—a face which blurred out and came clear again and hung upon nothingness before him. Vaguely, he wondered about it much as one might wonder about a buzzing fly. Expedition to Sereon. Who cared?

But he did care. And for all his effort to diminish the ache of disappointment by disavowing any interest in present events, his wound alone could not have accounted for the aching lethargy of him; heartbreak alone could have caused that. He was as a man in love whose sweetheart he has discovered to be a harlot. The empty misery of knowing had no balm.

And those first monotonous days of the voyage to Sereon of Sirius discovered no spark of will to live in Steve Gailbraith. As a soldier and the son of soldiers he had never understood. He had tasted his initial gagging sample of the Eighty Great Names when, as a cadet, he had been ordered to a prison island as an officer of the guard. There he had seen women clubbed into submission by callous RNZA guards, and had seen prisoners drown their children rather than bring them up in the incredible squalor and torture of a camp. Men whose only crime had been a deserved curse at an aristocrat were thrown into pens, naked and ill, to be left to starve on garbage which, in itself, was death. He had seen scholars who had refused to swerve from a discovery, broken bone by bone by steel-shod rayrifle butts. And there he had witnessed the execution of his own uncle, charged with the writing of inflammatory pamphlets.

There had been born his first disaffection for the Eighty Great Names for, childlike and sincere, he thought it worth his life to attempt to bring freedom to his tortured race. And when he had transferred to the Terrestrial Fleet he had spent his days in feeding upon the political sciences and the sociological doctrines. Among the Sons of Science he had gained many friends. Amid the Anarchist Alliance's labor element he had had much respect. And when the clarion cry for liberty had rung around the globe, he had been the first of Air Force officers to lead a squadron against the Eighty Great Names. He had dreamed; he had fought; he had striven. His banner had been "Emancipation."

And now that banner was clotted with the mire of ignorance. And he had won only to find that Fagar, rapacious and stupid, a former slaughterhouse killer of beef, had elevated himself like the resurrected carcass of one of his beeves into the leadership of the world. Fagar, whose brag was that he had never bathed. Fagar, who had disemboweled the emperor's wife before the emperor's very eyes. Fagar! The very thought of the man made Steve Gailbraith retch. And Fagar was risen to command this stupid mass of brutes to send down with a crash all the crystal dreams of those very men who had made the revolt possible.

Steve Gailbraith sat with his back to a bulkhead, his arms upon his knees and his face buried in his sleeves. He gave heed to the roaring and trembling of the spaceship no more than he gave heed to the guards or his fellow members, who idled about under the dirty highlight which canopied the promenade with glass.

When he had first come aboard he had bestowed a quiet laugh upon the *Fury*—a laugh without humor, but not without some sympathy. For this very ship had once been flag vessel of the RNZA Fleet and proud had been the glowflags upon her sides when she had borne the emperor on his first visit to Mars. How brightly had these bulkheads gleamed, how white had been these decks! How clear the highlight overhead, not barring the light from any star.

Steve Gailbraith had seen the ghost of himself, a sub-lieutenant in flawless plastiron, all blue and girded with golden belts, his thumbs smartly touching his rayrods on either side, his beardless face serious with a child's make-believe seriousness, his whole being rigid and respectful and somehow joyous from glittering helm to winged boot. Eyes straight ahead as the emperor passed. Blushing like a girl when the emperor paused and spoke to him. How thrilled he had been on that voyage, forgetting all his dark unrest, worshiping for once with all his heart before the majesty of pomp and dignity. Ai, the ghost of a child still stood there by the boarding shield, thumbs smartly touching his rayrods on either side. Ai, and the ghost of an emperor strolling upon this deck and pausing to speak with the child.

Ah God, poor *Fury*, Steve Gailbraith had thought. How rusty and dented, how shabby and forlorn with your guns all worn and your tubes decayed and your very glowflags minus half their lights. Outward bound upon a freighter's errand, packed with convicts and hate. The ghost of a ship, the ghost of an emperor and the ghost of a man.

Steve pressed his face more deeply into his bloodstained sleeve. If he could only laugh perhaps this ache of an ideal outraged and betrayed might soften. Why was he not born hard?

"You," said a calculating voice, "are Steve Gailbraith."

He did not look up for a little while even though it was not an unpleasant voice, a woman's. And then when he felt she would not go away, he looked at her. He was not startled, for he had nothing left to be startled about. Rather, he felt somehow enlivened, if only very vaguely. There was a vital flash in her gray eyes which spoke of strength and purpose and passion, all belied by the frailty of a lovely woman and the cold contempt of her face. He knew that he had seen her somewhere, but he was too weary to wonder. Still, he felt that he had met her in a dream or a nightmare and that the memory had been before him for some time.

"I saw you in the court—or that comedy that passes for one." She was very impersonal about it. "They sentenced me after they sentenced you."

He did not much care, but he remembered something about it now. He was a little annoyed, for he wanted no part of anyone, only the death of his own company. The vibrant force in her wearied him.

"My name is Vicky Stalton," she continued, scarcely looking at him. "You have not heard of me, for I was a member of the benighted Enlightened People's Party and I did not sign my pamphlets. I am not a member of your fancy Anarchist Alliance. I was not born good enough for that—or to associate with you, most likely. I come from the gutter and I've been thrown back. I was cursed with too many wits and too little nobility—legitimately—in my family. So sit there and ignore me if you will for I'm sure I really don't care whether you die or not."

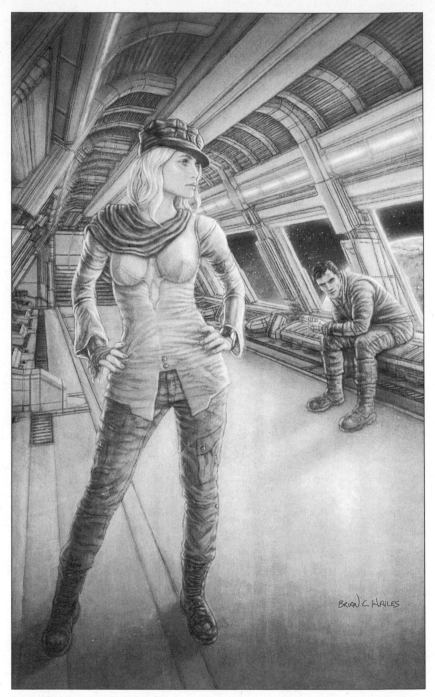

BRIAN C. HAILES

Steve looked at the bandage which wound a red-black coil around her right hand; the red torch insignia, which still held by a thread to her tunic cuff, was almost as smudged. She had evidently begged enough water to wash her face, for it was quite clean. A gleaming curve of blond hair, smoothly brushed, flowed out from under the peaked fatigue cap which she wore aslant over one eye. Yes, he thought dully, he had heard of her before, had seen her on a poster once; the poster had symbolized the first rush of revolutionaries upon Washington. The lower half of it had been scorched by a raygun, leaving a meaningless collection of syllables and the picture of this girl reaching ecstatically toward a flaming torch. Yes, he remembered. Funny that he should. He wished she would go away.

"Now that you have so courteously acknowledged my self-introduction," she said, "I shall answer your question as to why I came and spoke to you."

He moved restively under the sting in her voice. He knew suddenly that she could speak so softly that a man could drown ... Why didn't she go away?

"You and I are the outcasts," she said.

He looked up at her face, scowling a little in lieu of question.

"We are all outcasts in a way, of course," she continued. "But you and I are very choice. You are too good for them. I am too bad. You don't care whether you die or not, and I am sure I don't care if you do, but I am a foolish sort of person. I want to live."

"Why do you say that?"

"Well!" Vicky Stalton mocked. "It speaks and everything. The blammon on Venus seeks to protect itself by thrusting its head in the mud and leaving its red and green feathers waving airily in the breeze. And so, blammon, it is I that bring you the news that Dave Blacker is about to blast the Sons of Science into space dust, take command of the *Fury*, and hi-ho for the freedom of Outer Space. For Dave Blacker has just finished a brilliant piece of calculation. We are being sent to Sereon to eat each other up."

"Well?"

"Well, unlike you, my gaudy officer, there are some of us who dislike the idea of dying, and myself in particular, find it abhorrent. Dave Blacker got it from a crew member that the scientists were to be landed with the weapons and the food and, at some distance, Dave Blacker and his hefties are to be set down, empty-handed. No one knows anything about Sereon except that it has atmosphere and a gravity of seven-eighths. But it is certain that Dave Blacker and his hefties will have to overcome the scientists or freeze and starve. And because there will be very little food, the scientists will resist with everything they have. Seventeen scientists and three hundred hefties just about add up to a final zero. It is a very humorous plan that Guis evolved and Fagar upheld. And so Dave Blacker, not being without resource, does not intend to land on Sereon. He has a few friends in the crew and so he has a few blasticks and he has called a conference with the Sons of Science under a treacherous truce at four bells in the wardroom. And Jean Mauchard has accepted. Exit, my bravo, Jean Mauchard and the Sons of Science. Exit the *Fury* from the EPG's fleet. Or am I boring you?"

"Let them fight," said Steve with a tired sigh. "It's all one to me."

"Hah! It's all one to him. And here a beautiful and, I hope, desirable damsel comes seeking his strong arm and he says it's all one to him! Why, you yellow coward, not only are you afraid to live, but you're afraid of Dave Blacker! You! What an officer! No wonder they are transporting you!"

Steve shrugged.

"You genius!" she said. "Can't you see that Dave Blacker hates both of us? Because you are of the military caste and because I escaped from his element and was a factor in the EPP? As soon as he has either killed or intimidated the ship's officers, he'll finish up the job by killing us. Do you think he'd be such a fool as to leave a military expert and a propagandist director, both in opposition to him, alive? I don't care if he shoots you, but by those stars, soldier, I'm going to live!"

Steve looked at her for a little while. The flame of her glance was too violently opposed to his own apathy to do anything but weary him further. Why should he care about dying? Everything he had lived for was slain, and he felt tardy in not following after. It was good news, in truth, that Dave Blacker should aid him in escape with a well-placed shot.

"I might as well be talking to that scoregun!" she said. "And I thought I knew something about psychology!" She waved her hand as though throwing him away, but it was her right hand and a sudden spasm of agony made her clutch it to her and wince. Her voice was not powerful when she spoke again, though she tried to hide the pain. "No, I'm not so good. I could tell muckers and dimers that white was black and they believed me. But then I've never had much chance to practice on the nobility!" And she faced away and vanished down a hatch which led to the wardroom.

Steve stayed where he was. What was the use? Even if Blacker killed Mauchard and enslaved the ship, Steve would not mention that his own value, having been trained on the *Fury*, could not be denied. To hell with Blacker and the *Fury* and that Vicky Stalton. Let them explode in space and whirl with the comets for eternity. It was all one to him.

A few minutes later, just before four bells were struck, three hefties came lounging along the promenade, their brute faces sly. Everyone had the run of the ship because of the power of the guard weapons and the gifted reasoning of Dave Blacker and so these did not even bother to explain to the marine on guard why they hauled Steve Gailbraith to his feet.

Steve looked at them with bored eyes, resenting a little that they would put their hands upon him.

"The boss wants to see you, soldier," said one to Steve, "and when the boss wants to see people, people generally are seen. Come along."

They shoved him ahead of them down the hatchway and Steve only resisted enough to release himself, after which he walked quietly, not caring. Anything was better than this ache within him. And the newer blasticks were highly efficacious.

The wardroom was not dissimilar to any other battleship's except that, on the *Fury*, it was larger and better appointed as befitted a flag vessel. It had not changed much down the years, though the portrait of the emperor had been crudely cut from its frame and the noble name of the silver service's donor had been scraped from the dishes.

It was amidships and occupied the entire beam save for passage room between it and the outer skin. The furniture was, of course, reversible, ceiling and floor being identical so that, on acceleration the after-bulkhead was the floor which, on deceleration became the ceiling. And as they were now accelerating, the furniture was fixed to the wide expanse of the after-bulkhead. It looked poignantly familiar to Steve, for how many times had he leaned back from his dinner to trace the intricate networks of wires and pipes and cables which appeared to have settled around the place like a snare. It was just a battleship wardroom, designed for efficiency and utility and as unlike a passenger ship's salon as a powerhouse office was unlike a skyhouse.

It had the effect of deepening Steve's melancholy. He had begun his battle fleet career here before his transfer to the Air Force. How fitting to finish it in the same place. A ghost of a youngster in white gloves stood reporting to the ghost of a captain at the end of the long table.

But Dave Blacker was sitting at that board now. And across from him Jean Mauchard had just seated himself. Some of the lesser leaders of the hefties were ranged on Dave's side of the board and the Sons of Science were taking their places. Dave Blacker and Jean Mauchard were as intent upon one another as a pair of Kilkenny Cats. But other scientists and hefties glanced up when Steve was brought in and their faces registered an almost disinterested dislike. Vicky Stalton, her fatigue cap on the back of her head, was leaning against a transom smoking a cigarette and regarding one and all with aloof disdain. She gave Steve one look and then her face grew even more chill as she turned away.

"Mauchard," said Blacker without preamble. "You know me.

I don't monkey around. I brought you down here to arrange a truce. We don't like you and we don't trust you and you don't like us and you don't trust us and, me being Dave Blacker, things happen my way."

"A truce?" said Mauchard with a short, sharp laugh. "With thieves and fools? What of our truce once before, that lost us our power in its breaking? I want no truce with you. If that is why—"

"No," said Dave Blacker with a grin like a wolf's, "that isn't why we brought you down here. We brought you down here to kill you, Mauchard."

The leader of the Sons of Science started to leap up from the board but, in that instant, four blasticks appeared in capable hands. Their hefty holders were completely without expression, only waiting Blacker's command. The scientists were pale.

"So it is to be murder," said Mauchard. "Cold-blooded, calculated." His sensitive face was twisted with scorn. "Murder and mutiny. You gave your word, Dave Blacker, to the captain of this ship that you would not violate parole if he spared us the discomfort of irons and cells. You brought us here today under a white flag. But then, what else can one expect of a dock rat?"

"Better a dock rat," said Dave Blacker, unbothered, "than the illegitimate son of a careless nobleman."

Jean Mauchard winced and went pale. The retreating blood left his lips corpse-blue. But there was fire and hatred in his intelligent eyes which even Blacker could not overlook.

"You are even lower than I had thought," said Mauchard. "It will be a relief—this death you are delivering. A relief from having to scratch in the crawling company of such vermin. Long ago, when first my friends and I took part in the revolt, I should have known how low we would have to sink to associate with you."

"So you still think you did us a favor," said Blacker. "Why you bigoted bug killer, when you joined our ranks you came with the idea that you was going to run things as soon as the revolt was done. You and your favors! You had it all figured out that we was going to step out and let you figure a slick government run on slide rules and test tubes and to hell with the human beings. You got psychologists and God knows how many more kinds of -ologists, but you ain't got one single drop of honest human blood in the lot of you. What do you care about pain and sufferin' so long as you prove that you can make electrons and brains stand to attention and say 'Yes, sir!'"

"Our knowledge brought about the revolt!" snapped Mauchard.

"And you'd let it wreck the government," said Blacker. "With all your fancy titles and formulas, you ain't got the slightest idea about human beings. You and your gang was pitched out for proposin' to make slaves of every man back on Earth and we was fightin' to keep from bein' slaves any more. Your science ain't got any more heart than the Eighty Great Names!"

"Better science, heart or no heart," said Mauchard, "than to genuflect to sewer sweepings and to be executed for being too strong. You and your ilk twisted and warped all the principles for which we fought. Well! Why talk to a lump of lard? Once on Sereon we'd die at your hands as you would die at ours. It is quicker here and now, for I'm content you'll never make this mutiny stick. So shoot, you and your offal, and be damned to you!"

"The mutiny won't fail," said Blacker with a grin, "but you get the idea about yourselves. It's too bad, Mauchard—"

Steve, at the beginning, had not even been mildly interested. He would be next after the Sons of Science. Vicky Stalton, calmly finishing her cigarette, would probably go immediately after himself. Two outcasts. Outcasts from the soulless gentlemen of science. Outcasts from the hulks who had been too violent and brutal even for their own kind. But Steve, at first, cared little. His mind wandered away from the words which crackled between Mauchard and Blacker.

How different it had been in the yesterdays! How different were these men, uncouth and brawling, than others who had been seated at this table.

For the ghost of a stiffly straight child was reporting to the ghost of a captain at that table's head. And the child's braid was brave and his thumbs were precisely lined along his rayrods. How courteous and how formal had this place always been!

When the defeated Martian, Ralgar, wounded and weak, had been yanked from his determination to go down with his shattered *Grrawsly*, he had been brought here. And the *Fury*'s singed captain had stood up at the board's end to take Ralgar's hand and congratulate him upon a valiant fight. For the code demanded rigid courtesy even to a vanquished foe whose guns had crammed the *Fury*'s sick bay with wounded and had scarred the battleship's armor until it was a matter of speculation whether it could ever return to its base.

And when Farman had died hurling his vessel against uncountable Venusian odds, choosing suicide rather than retreat, the *Fury*'s officers had stood in silence a respectful time before they had drunk to the death of a brave man.

The service! Officers and gentlemen. Proud ships with proud traditions.

Dead, most of them. Ships and traditions and officers alike. Dead because of a slaughterhouse bully, Fagar, who now ruled supreme in the System. Dead because they had either aided or opposed the effort of a people to be free. Dead. For what? So that Fagar could swagger and swear and trample down all the fineness and intelligence that were left! Dead because they had fought for their ideals and because those very ideals had been besmirched by lies and treachery. And here was the *Fury* battered and forlorn, rocketing through space on as foul an errand as the warped minds of the EPP could conceive. And there was Blacker, under sentence, but blood brother to the oafs who had succeeded in putting all ideals to the torch. That was what that torch of freedom had turned out to be—a conflagration of everything that was decent in man.

Murder. Here in the wardroom of the *Fury*. Murder and then mutiny and the *Fury*'s helm would be befouled by the hands of this criminal crew. And the *Fury*'s guns would be turned to the account of piracy.

The ghost of a child, brave in blue and scarlet, face paled with disgust and rage, leaned back against the bulkhead.

"It's too bad," Blacker was saying. "But we don't like you, Mauchard." He turned to his raymen.

But suddenly all were crushed into their chairs and their faces went pasty as the blood rushed from their heads. Their arms were too heavy to lift and those who had been leaning forward were shoved face-down upon the board. Those who had been standing sank stubbornly to the floor and lay there, gasping. Steve too went down, weighing nearly half a ton. Vicky Stalton had dropped beside her chair.

Three marines with anti-acceleration belts forced the door mechanism and came floating in, ready to take battle stations. The lieutenant that followed them looked in wonder at the blasticks which were pressed in plain sight upon the table and could not be moved by their wielders. The lieutenant walked down the top of the table and, with his hook, scooped up the weapon.

Gongs were going through the whole battleship and several more officers and men en route fore or aft, stopped and heard the lieutenant's comment and then went hurrying on.

Shortly the terrible pressure ceased and the stricken ones began to breathe once more, flopping weakly and dizzily as they came erect.

A bull-voiced exec, who in this moment forgot that as an officer he ought to consult the soldiers' and sailors' council before deciding anything, came thundering into the wardroom and vented his wrath.

"What the double-banked haggus are you badgers doing?" he roared. "Blasticks! And on my ship!" He glared all around and was about to resume when a messenger came with a matter of greater concern.

"Aft lookout says he did not signal, sir. He swears it."

"What? Why, I'll stripe—" And then the exec remembered that times and the battle fleet had changed. "Is he sure?"

"Yes, sir. And there's no signal light on his buzzer, sir."

The exec looked piercingly around him. He began to see a connection between the false signal and these blasticks. "Listen, you transports! I've been white. The skipper has been white. And what pay do we get for it. Somebody signaled a double buzz on the aft lookout's meteor warning. And that somebody is in this room! How he did it, I don't know—"

"I know," said the lieutenant, coming back from the wall. "The insulation is all frayed on that buzzer cable. Somebody leaned up against it and shorted it."

"Maybe!" said the exec. "But we've got little enough fuel without wasting it on acceleration to get away from a meteor that wasn't even chasing us, much less existed! All right. I'll grant that it was an accident. Even though two buzzes was the proper signal, it would take a genius to know which wire was which in all this maze. Well! So there was murder and mutiny brewing in here, was there? Master at arms! Get me irons. Plenty of irons. Until we get these hyenas landed we'll be damned certain we can keep a finger on them. Quick, now."

Steve submitted gracefully and the man who affixed the irons to his wrists and ankles did not even glance at his face.

A little while later Vicky Stalton edged close to him. She did not express cold contempt now. "I am sorry. It was wicked of me to play upon your emotions as I did—"

Steve laughed brittlely. "Dear lady, you had little enough to do with that."

"You mean you deny that your mood—"

"My mood," said Steve Gailbraith, "seems to have changed. There were ghosts in this room."

He would have gone, but she held him back and made him face her. "I . . . I don't understand you."

Steve shrugged and attempted to be careless about it, but small lights of anger were in his eyes where only misery and resignation had been before. "Could I stand idle, seeing hogs wallow where kings have trod? I've been a fool. I helped lift up an order even worse than that which existed before. Had those idiotic idealists like myself worked less for the cause, all that was worthwhile in this world might not have been blackened out."

There was a hard twist to his face now and a tenseness of purpose in him which reacted upon her like an electric shock. "I was an idealist," he continued. "God help me! I thought that perfection could be attained, that people could be free. But the only freedom a people can enjoy is brought upon by a strong and merciful power, not by self rule, a thing for which they are not equipped. By holding ideals, I blinded myself to the quality of those with whom I had to deal. But that is done. I was sick. Now I am well."

"I thought—" she began.

"You thought wrongly. I am cured by the poison itself. You are a very clever girl, no doubt. But limit your tricks to telling your muckers and dimers that white is black. I am not blind—now."

She seemed to be seeing him for the first time, and she had an uncanny illusion of a helmet upon his head and a gun in his hand and battle in his eyes. And when he walked away she seemed to hear, far, far off, a voice saying, "The end has come, Fagar."

Thanatos Drive

written by

Andrew Dykstal

illustrated by

QIANJIAO MA

ABOUT THE AUTHOR

Andrew Dykstal lives in Arlington, Virginia, where he works as a technical editor. He's been a lifelong consumer of stories, and tipped over from affection to obsession when a few of his college professors persuaded him to major in English alongside political science. Between then and now, he's taught high school English and humanities (with a weird jaunt into orbital mechanics), earned an MA in English from the University of Virginia, and inflicted countless half-formed short stories, novels, and poems upon a circle of dear and long-suffering friends, without whom he'd have finished going mad years ago. His work has appeared or is forthcoming in Daily Science Fiction *and* Beneath Ceaseless Skies.

ABOUT THE ILLUSTRATOR

Qianjiao Ma is a concept artist, background painter and designer, based in Los Angeles, working in the themed entertainment and animation industries.

Qianjiao is originally from China. She has had a great passion for art and design from a young age. She came to the United States after high school, seeking further education. Qianjiao recently graduated from the Art Center College of Design with a Bachelor of Science in Entertainment Design.

As with many of our winners, she is gaining a lot of recognition quickly.

As a concept artist, Qianjiao's new freelance clients include Warner Bros., Universal Studios, Rough Draft Studios, ShadowMachine, the

Thinkwell Group, World Abu Dhabi and Universal Studios Japan. She has also worked in the animation industry. So far she has contributed as designer and painter for the Netflix Original Disenchantment *and TBS's* Final Space. *She is also an accomplished plein air painter, having exhibited her work in galleries in Los Angeles.*

Thanatos Drive

W here were you when it happened, baby?"

Alan Li knows he should keep walking. That's the rule on a boulevard like this, and it goes double at nightfall—move fast, avoid eye contact, don't let them touch you. But the question, or what's behind the question, catches him like a choke chain: *I look old enough to remember the Spasm?* Nobody has ever thought he looked that old, or at least nobody has tumbled to it.

For her part, the woman in the legacy green sequin dress looks like something out of a Vollmann fever dream. There's no feigned sensuality there, just an air of endless exhaustion, and her blush cracks where she's cut her makeup with red Missouri clay. Her bloodshot eyes are sunk into sockets that probably always look like they're just done healing up from a bruise. Veins wander her legs, stark against skin pale with cold. She looks about forty, which means she might be half that.

"Don't be stingy, baby," she says.

There's nothing he can say. He takes his bearings by what's left of the Arch and walks on.

She makes one final pitch: "The soils commonly known as red clay are in fact ultisols, the final product of weathering when there is no glaciation to create new soil."

Either she's gone mad or he has. He keeps walking, fighting down the impulse to look back.

Behind him, the woman picks her next prospect: "Where were you when it happened, baby?"

The first flakes of October snow drift down, white and gray

in the glow of the gaslights, and Li sees the world trapped in an immense glass eye stirring with the silvery threads of old nightmares.

His contact is waiting behind the bar, out by the stills. Some were liberated from Prohibition museums in the greater St. Louis area. Li doesn't want to know what the old man is fermenting; there hasn't been surplus grain for twenty years, fruit is worth more fresh or dried, and every potato in North America is going toward efforts to create something on par with the old monocultures. Grass, maybe? Cassava-plus?

Li accepts a tin cup of clearish liquid, takes the ritual sip, feels his eyes water. Godpuppets don't drink, or so the local rumor goes. "You found me a job."

"Might've."

"I take it it's the Doctor."

"Might be."

In the end, the price is a bit of gold the size of Li's thumbnail, a pair of sunglasses, and four genuine Advil. What they call a night/day kit out East, where that flake of gold would be just enough to buy you a three-day hangover and maybe the clap.

Out here, it will keep the moonshiner in shoes for another winter.

The moonshiner gives him an address, a password, and a companionable hand on the shoulder. "The man's PRA, so you watch yourself."

The People's Republic of Austin. Deep pockets if you live long enough to pick them. Li puts another Advil on the barrelhead. "Anything else I should watch?"

A grin. "Saw the Doctor myself three weeks back."

"And you didn't kill her."

"Hard to un-kill somebody. I got myself a thing about permanent choices. Amelie's still human. Sold her new maps of the Turnwell Confederacy. And an old terrain one of western Nebraska."

"That's in the Dust."

"Said she was human. Never said she was sane. That Delray of yours still running?"

"You going to try to sell me something else?"

"Tinfoil's getting preachy about cars."

"It's a fifty-seven. Good old Detroit metal. No microchips."

"You know that. I know that. Next Tinfoil technophobe you meet might not. I hear they burned a man for his well pump last month. Ought to trade up for a couple bicycles and an apprentice."

The moonshiner lets him copy a couple of maps gratis so long as he puts his own kerosene in the lamp. Li's eyes ache by the end. "When did we get old?" he asks.

"What, you were young?"

The man from the People's Republic of Austin is waiting in an upstairs suite over half a bookstore. He wears the Longhorn pin of an Ambassador and three pieces of three different suits.

"You're Alan Li," the Ambassador says, flipping open a typewritten dossier.

"I know that."

"You ... find certain sorts of people."

"I know that too."

"How long have you been tracking the Doctor?"

"Eleven years." The answer is automatic.

The Ambassador gives off a little flare of bureaucratic smugness. "That seems to imply you aren't very good at it."

In his mind's eye, Burden's Ford is burning again, and he can feel the mud of the riverbank oozing around his elbow as he peers through a rifle scope at silhouettes faceless and yet recognizable, some of them terribly small. The full moon crests a cloud bank, and now their eyes are shining silver, smiling. Where were you when it happened? Forget the rest of the world and its lingering where-were-you-when-Kennedy-was-shot mindset. For him, it was never the Spasm that proved the indifference of all the old gods and the madness of the new one. This is his *it*. Eleven years ago.

And he's never been fond of flippancy.

"Maybe," he says. "Thing about tracking the Doctor is that when her work goes well, there's nobody willing to talk about her. When it goes bad, there's nobody able. Sometimes for a good mile around."

"From the stories I hear, you don't take the time to ask questions in the latter case."

Li pictures the Ambassador flat on his back, screaming up at the smiling godpuppets while fine silver wires thread down into his eyes, his nose, his mouth. "No," he says, pleasantly, "on account of how I'm smarter than a root vegetable."

A bark of laughter from his left snaps his head around. A woman dressed for travel slips in from the farther room. She's slight, her brown hair bound back in a short tail, and her footfalls make no sound. Her jacket is cut loose, and Li would bet Prozac to pruno that there's an arsenal under it.

"Yes, Mr. Li," she says, dropping into a chair, "you might be at that." Her voice is smooth, low, touched with the same humor as her pale green eyes.

The Ambassador cuts in. "This is Jackie Boon, our resident expert on Doctor Amelie Bourreau, high-splice, and all things cybernetic. She has a lead on the Doctor's whereabouts."

So do I, Li doesn't say. "So what do you need me for?"

The Ambassador squirms. "Our own people have seen … limited success."

Boon is more direct. "The last four teams we sent after her didn't come back. The sole known survivor of the fifth team returned with a high-splice node in his head and forty pounds of ANFO under his jacket."

That gives him pause. He'd heard about the bombing that took out half the PRA Department of Economic Development, but to learn that a godpuppet did it forces a change in perspective. For one thing, the PRA put out that a radical faction from some hick city-state in the mid-Atlantic was responsible, and they built a good bit of foreign policy around the lie. For another, to assert that a godpuppet targeted a government pursuing the Doctor

180

has its own unsettling implications, not least of which is God taking an interest in Amelie Bourreau.

"You think I'll have more luck?"

Boon shrugs, gives him a once-over. "You're supposed to be a survivor."

"In any event," the Ambassador adds, "you'll have an advantage the others did not. Ms. Boon will be going with you."

"No."

The Ambassador names a figure.

"I'll think about it."

Boon names another figure.

"All right." He might have fought harder, but he finds himself immediately and irrationally liking Boon. Laughing at a man in a Longhorn pin takes guts, and there's something competent in how she moves, something he hasn't seen in a long time. As long as he's useful to her, she'll have his back. After that, she won't be the first slippery partner he's outmatched.

"And," the Ambassador adds, "you will be taking the Doctor in alive."

Disbelief, then anger, then puzzlement. "Alive? Why would you want her alive? Kill her, and there's nobody making new godpuppets. God would be better than half-dead."

The Ambassador gives no reply. Neither does Boon.

"Fine. If you want her alive, we'll need more support. That's a four-man job. Maybe more. If it's a party anyway, why not lend us a few of your hitters?"

The Ambassador clears his throat. "There are reasons of state."

Boon gives the real answer. "We've had security issues with the identities of our wetwork people, and it's about to get worse. In a few days, it's going to be unhealthy to wear PRA colors north of the Arkansas River. This stays small."

Another civil war. He thinks of the copied maps folded in his pocket. Suddenly, being well north of St. Louis seems like an excellent idea. "All right. We can come to an agreement. In addition to my fee, I'll need forty gallons of gasoline, ration kits for two people for fifteen days, and all the legacy .357 rounds you can give me. All pre-Spasm, all stored right, all new brass. None of that remanufactured stuff—I've seen too many ruptured cases."

The Ambassador doesn't even try to bargain. That night, as Li tries to fall asleep over the moonshiner's bar, this disregard for expense disturbs him more than anything else.

After a while, he gets up and inspects his eyes and gums in the mirror. He finds nothing—no change, no glint of metal. In time, he sleeps.

They set out westward at dawn, extra gas cans ratchet-strapped to the roof, Jackie Boon's pile of luggage crammed in the back. She's wearing aviators that cover half her face and chewing a wad of candied ginger. "I get carsick," she mumbles through a mouthful. "Your car can smell like ginger, or it can smell like vomit. Your call, Alan."

"How about you tell me your new and promising leads?"

"We think she's headed for western Nebraska."

"Yeah. I know."

"Did you know we have a list of five stops she'll be making en route?"

He blinks. "How could you know that?"

"She and some of her clients use shortwave radio. Spell everything out letter by letter in cipher. I broke the encryption. Well, I have a method for breaking it, I should say. It takes time. The plaintexts are a few months old."

"How?"

"I'd tell you, but the story goes back to Poland in the 1930s, and if the boredom didn't kill you, I'd have to."

He glances at the crude, hand-built radio clipped to the dash, thinking. It took him a while to get used to the thing. Radios are the heart of networks, and networks are the heart of God. He designed the mount for quick disassembly should Tinfoil come calling, or if it caught his eye the wrong way. And this sort of dumb radio is known to be safe, is almost in common use. He doesn't know much about ciphers, but he knows the one used by Amelie Bourreau has resisted decryption for two decades and is widely believed to be based on the naval version of the German Enigma machine. There's only one explanation for the breakthrough, and it's no comfort.

"You built a computer," he murmurs.

Boon startles, which is oddly satisfying. "A crude, electrome-chanical one," she says. "Perfectly safe. Nothing beyond 1940s technology."

He eases onto I-70, brings the Delray up to an easy thirty. The PRA is building computers. The north, frozen wasteland or not, is looking more and more attractive. "You know, that's got to be one of the Doctor's lines when she's selling implants."

"What?"

"That it's all perfectly safe. Now give me an exit number."

She slouches in the bench seat and pulls her hat down over her eyes, sunglasses and all. "Just follow the signs for Columbia."

"That on your magic list?"

"No magic about it."

"Sure."

They drive in silence for a while. Then Boon asks, "Do you always wear your hair like that?"

He touches the rough shag that falls over his ears. "Yeah. Cuts down on sunburn. Why?"

"I just notice things, is all." Another long silence. Then: "'Alive' doesn't mean 'unpunished,' Alan. She'll answer for Burden's Ford. You have my word on that."

Columbia has a population of almost eight thousand. Driving past the variously racked and hitched bicycles and horses, feeling the hustle and pulse of the city, Li feels like a plague doctor touring an overcrowded prison. If the Doctor did any work here, there's a one-in-ten chance he's walking into hell with untested backup.

QIANJIAO MA

Li curses by Shockley and Nader alike the quirk of timing that set him on the Doctor's trail in winter. Barring flickers of the old, mild October, there will be nothing but long sleeves and hats and heavy coats in every town clear out to Boise. Half the population could be walking around with surgical dressing packed from crotch to throat and he'd never know it. And coats can hide other things. He has two nickel-sized scars low on his back where a godpuppet tried to ventilate his kidneys with a derringer. When the cutters let him go three months later with a massive bill, two legacy Percocet, and a bag of willow bark to chew when the opioids wore off, he finally cleared up enough to realize why the thing hadn't gone for the easy headshot, and he had nightmares about it for the better part of a year, nightmares that mingled weirdly with those left over from Burden's Ford.

Three weeks. She had been here three weeks ago.

He parks behind a stable and tips the muckrakers a legacy skin mag to keep his tires from disappearing. For extra insurance, he makes sure they get a good look at the gun on his hip and the flat wand of the scrubber slung across his back. The signs of his office, such as it is. He tries not to think too hard about the scrubber; the capacitors are degrading, and it only works about half the time. And it never does what he tells people, never kills the godpuppet but leaves the person. The scrubber's real value is its aura of hope, which tends to keep the situation from devolving for an extra three minutes or so. Enough time to get in, sometimes even enough to get out.

If Boon is uneasy, she gives no sign. She straps a Turnwell-issue automatic to her belt with the easy nonchalance usually reserved for donning socks.

"The house is a block north," she says, eyeing his scrubber with an air of disapproval. "And you know those things don't work on solid-state memory, right? You can't degauss nonmagnetic storage, and almost no implants use hard disks."

"The ones that are supposed to be perfectly safe do."

That keeps her looking pensive all the way to the house.

A man answers the door after three knocks. His eyes lock on the scrubber. Boon gives him a bright smile. "Hi."

He bolts for the back door. Li tackles him at the ankles, rolls him over, gets a forearm across his throat, and leans on it for a while. The man goes still.

Boon crouches in the doorway, pistol down by her side. "Should you be that close?"

"It's only been three weeks. Even if he's turned, God hasn't had much time to improve him." Li peels back an eyelid, studies the pupil, the deep clear brown of the iris. He pulls open the mouth and checks the gums, the soft palate. "He's either clean or a slow burn." A lie: the man is clean, and Li can feel it, but Boon doesn't need to know that.

A flicker of motion from the corner of his eye. A kid on the short side of fourteen is standing in the kitchen three yards off with a shotgun pointed at Li's head, his mouth working around uncertain sounds. Li ignores the weapon. "What was wrong with your dad?"

"He couldn't see."

"Degenerative nerve disorder," Boon adds. "He needed two chips, one at the base of the skull, one in the frontal lobe."

Li feels around and finds the healing incision on the back of the unconscious man's head. There's nothing on his forehead. The Doctor probably went in through the nose. No denying she's good at what she does.

"High-splice?"

"No," Boon and the kid say together. The kid: "She said it was just old tech. No radios in it, no nothing."

Boon holsters her automatic. "He's clean, Alan."

"How do you know?"

She points down the hall to a spray of broken glass he hadn't even seen. "You knocked his glasses off. If he were infected, his vision would be perfect, not just better." She pushes past Li, reaches out, and takes the shotgun from the kid's unresisting hands. When she opens the breech, Li sees light glinting inside empty chambers. "Not even loaded." She passes the gun back to the kid, sighing. "The world doesn't deserve people like you."

Li grimaces. "It doesn't tend to keep them around real long, either. Kid, we need to know what you paid the Doctor and anything and everything she told you."

The kid shakes his head. "She was good," he says. "I don't care what you say. She was good."

"She rolled the dice with your lives. Ever hear of Bayside? New Tampa? Burden's Ford?"

The kid sticks his chin out.

"I need something from the car," Boon says, and she slips out the front door, moving without sound.

The kid kneels beside the unconscious man, feeling for a pulse.

"He's fine," Li says when the quiet starts getting heavy. "He might even still be fine tomorrow."

Boon returns with one of her heavier personal effects: a cloth-covered parcel in a leather sling. She sets it on the floor and whips off the covering with a flourish.

It's a cylindrical glass tank. Inside, a brain and part of a spinal cord float in clear fluid, surrounded and penetrated by silver threads drifting and twining like kelp. With the sudden rush of light, one thread reaches up and taps the glass.

The kid yells and recoils. So does Li, and his gun clears leather before Boon catches his wrist.

"Wait," she says.

Li jerks his wrist free. "You kept one? Have you lost your mind?"

Boon ignores him, eyes on the kid. The questing threads feel around the edges of their enclosure, seem to reach a conclusion, and lapse into quiescence.

"What's your name?" she asks.

"Kevin."

"I'm Jackie. This is a mature high-splice node. We call it a squid. You've heard of them? I've seen and dissected more than I want to think about, Kevin. This is what could have happened to your dad. Then it would have happened to you, and to your mom, and maybe to your friends, your neighbors, your whole town."

Fighting every instinct, Li forces his gun back into its holster and follows Boon's play, which he has to admit has a certain shock value. "In one sense," he says, voice almost steady, "nobody knows how God spreads. In another, I know perfectly well how it spreads: it spreads when somebody thinks that they'll be lucky, that this time it'll be different, that they're so special they don't have to think about who and what they're putting at risk." He points at the mass swirling in the tank. "When they think that can't happen, not to them."

The kid tells them everything he knows. When his father wakes and sees the monstrosity exposed and impossibly alive, so does he. For a chance at sight, he gave the Doctor a few thousand Turnwell dollars, a tank of hydraulic fluid, and several sets of replacement gaskets. The father was a mechanic before his vision went. Now, he might be again. Li can see that possible future rattling around in the man's brain, no longer quite able to balance out all the nightmare alternatives. Relief will fix him up soon enough. But for a day or two, he'll convince himself he'd have chosen to stay blind had he known what might have taken root in his head.

"She's pretty," the kid says after Boon leaves with the squid.

Li almost smiles. "You're fourteen."

"Fifteen."

"Fourteen."

A sigh. "Fourteen."

Li pauses on the doorstep and turns back. "You've got some courage," he says. "And I'll give you that. But you listen, and you listen well. You never point a weapon at somebody you're not willing to kill, and never at somebody you're not able to. Yeah?"

The kid just stares.

The father says, "You look for God in men's eyes, and yet have you beheld the man?"

Doubt, sudden and cold, uncoils inside him, bound somehow

to the prostitute's non sequitur. "Sure," he says, which is no answer at all. But then, he can't be certain the father asked a question.

They spend the night in a rebuilt hotel south of Olathe, as close as either is willing to come to the ruins of Kansas City. There hadn't been many deployable nuclear weapons left at the Spasm—the world had attained near-perfect nuclear disarmament—but the few dozen that remained had all been launched. Some, like the ones that did for Washington and Kansas City, had been old strategic types, the sort with yields so high into the megatons they had no practical use outside the mad counter-value logic of the Cold War.

Looking out the window to the north, Li can almost see the ghosts of that holocaust, each one a shadow against an incandescent wall. Flat and featureless and imperfectly blotted from the world. So like the silhouettes of Burden's Ford.

Boon has taken the bed nearer the door. She's paging through a notebook, scribbling, a vaguely contemplative expression flickering across her face. Her nerve, initially arresting, has become an obvious liability.

He drags the room's sole chair over. "We need to talk about the world-killing abomination you've got in my trunk."

"It's contained. That's ballistic glass."

"Physically contained. It could be transmitting."

"We've never detected any transmissions, and as it has no sense organs, I don't know what it could be sending."

"You don't know how God works. Or if there are sense organs in there you can't identify. I could have sworn it was responding to light. It might have been listening to everything we said. It might be sending location information. Last I checked, you can still get signals off GPS satellites."

Boon finally looks up. "There is a point beyond which paranoia is unproductive. I can make educated guesses, and it is my professional opinion that the danger is minimal."

"I'll buy that if you can answer me one question: the squid

189

can't live without a functioning brain. And I'm guessing you've had it sealed up in that jar for months. Yeah? So how's the brain oxygenating itself?"

She lays aside the notebook. "All right. I don't know how God works. Nobody does. It's possible nobody ever knew how high-splice worked, or why it ... behaved. What is beyond dispute is that the Spasm arose from a perfect storm of circumstances unrepeatable in the present world. The squid is dangerous, yes, but not nearly as much as you think."

"Because everything's already broken?"

"In a way. There's no American Congress now, no concentration of critical demographics within key sociopolitical and economic structures."

He can feel the lecture coming, but short of going out and killing the squid himself, he doesn't see an alternative. "All right. I'll bite. Explain."

"Ten years before the Spasm, the median age of a Congressperson was sixty-two, the median net worth in the low millions. Access to their medical records is difficult for obvious reasons, but actuarial data suggests that up to seventy percent of them had conditions treatable via high-splice and other networked neural correctives—and they could almost universally afford those treatments. The situation was similar for the European Parliament and even worse for the Chinese Central Committee. Commercial interests were a bit different, but the overall pattern held, especially in the central banks. With the right thousand or so people, you could control the world. God had several times that many in key positions. Hence the success of mutual disarmament treaties, free trade policies, and, obviously, the aerosol sulfate and reflector mitigations of climate change."

Li remembers clawing through five feet of snow to get to a courthouse in South Carolina the previous year. He'd almost lost a few toes. "Which ended so well," he mutters.

She pushes on. "Now, you'd need to distribute high-splice or hackable implants across the leadership of several thousand unstable, highly decentralized city-states and small nations.

To reach the same level of influence God had in the old world, it would need to turn more than forty-five thousand people based on conservative estimates. At an infection rate of ten percent, that means nearly half a million installations of high-splice chips."

"You're leaving out the secondary infections. This thing spreads, Boon. And you're not accounting for the outbreaks that started with nothing more advanced than a pacemaker from the 1990s. Burden's Ford started with an insulin pump that barely had an abacus-worth of processing power—but God hacked it from the outside. The original hijacked tech with no biological components at all. We're talking about kitchen appliances, transit automation, factories. We don't know where any of the thresholds are. I'm not worried about the Doctor doing half a million operations. I'm worried about her doing just one in Columbia, or Mexico City, or Havana." Or Austin, he doesn't add.

"So far, outbreaks have been self-containing. There's no definitive evidence of high-level coordination among infected individuals."

"Godpuppets."

"We dislike that term."

Words, he thinks. She's actually concerned about words. "I dislike the thing."

"There's every reason to believe God is dead, Alan. It was as much the people that comprised it as the technology inside them, and those people are gone. What we're seeing is just a remnant, a few random high-splice nodes talking to each other. The squid is inert, a single cell without a larger body."

"God had a psychotic break when it realized it had overshot its climate-change fix, that half the population was gone no matter what it did. That doesn't mean it's dead. It just means it's insane."

She sniffs. "That's a metaphor drawn from single human minds, and almost worthless."

"You're the one who said it was made out of people. And you can't look at the PRA or Tinfoil or those white supremacist hacks out east and then tell me people can't go crazy in groups."

Silence. Boon glares at him, or maybe just at his unreasonability.

"How old are you, Boon?"

"Thirty-eight. Would you like to know my weight next?"

"I'm forty-nine," Li says, rubbing at his eyes. "I was wearing onesies when the Spasm happened. My parents died less than a year later. My stepmom raised me on stories of watching C-SPAN and seeing most of Congress screaming incoherent apologies in unison like a madhouse choir until the government folded up and the nukes started flying, all while the readout on the office microwave kept trying to explain that this was really for the best."

"You've internalized an irrational fear of science rather than a rational fear of a specific application of a specific technology." She folds her hands, and there's something prim in the gesture he finds exasperating. "That's how movements like Tinfoil survive. My generation has more distance on the issue. And the theory that God had anything analogous to a psychotic break is entirely unsubstantiated."

"So are all the other theories. Seeing as the most popular runner-up is that it got fed up halfway through saving the world and decided to kill us all, I don't find much comfort in the alternatives."

"True. That's true." She gnaws at her lip for a moment. "The squid stays. You saw how effective it was at convincing the boy, and it's worth the risk."

"Never seen an outbreak, have you?"

"No. But I've studied them. I understand the danger."

He strips off his jacket and crawls into his bed, tucking his revolver into the bedside holster. He leaves the knife at his ankle undisturbed. No reason to call attention to it. "If you understood," he mutters, "you wouldn't be trying to hand the Doctor over to your government alive."

"We're not trying to resurrect God. Yes, the Doctor might give us certain technological advantages in the coming conflict, but we're not so foolish as to try that."

He turns out the oil lamp. "Nobody was trying to build God in the first place. Nobody even noticed it until the world was coming apart. And I honestly can't believe you're naive enough to believe half of what you're saying. You don't take risks with the likes of the Doctor. You shoot them."

"Tell me, Alan, what did you feel after Burden's Ford?"

"What do you think? I felt the insides of bottles." He hesitates. "Guilt." It feels wrong not to say it. "Mostly guilt."

"Interesting, given that it wasn't remotely your fault. It's nice to meet a man who's not afraid to express his feelings."

"If I were expressing my feelings right now, you'd be in that jar with your squid."

Quiet laughter. "You know, I don't think I would."

He dreams of tree roots he has to keep pulling up from his throat and piling on plates that are whisked away in their turn to a dining room hung with pleated fans and banners bright with the mad patriotism of a half-dozen nascent empires. With a final heave and ripple of contraction, he draws up the bulb, that choicest piece, which is served to Jackie Boon. She reclines at the head table, resplendent, attended by his friends from Burden's Ford, both his children, and the indistinct impression of his wife, who died in childbirth long before the Doctor passed through town.

There are not enough roots to go around. This is a problem. He's responsible for ensuring plentiful and equitable distribution of food. Already the favoritism he's shown Jackie is causing whispers. The St. Louis prostitute shakes her head sadly. "You don't remember at all, do you?"

Jackie holds up the bulb, letting its dangling fibers quiver and squirm like the tentacles of a terrestrial jellyfish. "It's all right," she says, still cheerful. She reaches for his mouth. "I can wait while we grow more. We'll just put it back for a bit."

He wakes screaming, clawing at his throat, gasping. Reality rushes back in, and he subsides. On the far side of the room,

Boon is pretending to sleep. He lies back, shame and anxiety mingling with gratitude.

From long experience, he knows he will spend the rest of the night awake, thinking.

They follow the track northwest, assembling a picture of the Doctor's final destination and intentions from the objects and currencies she takes in payment. Northwest scrip, which makes sense. A random selection of fuses and hydraulic parts, which doesn't, not until Boon realizes that all the parts belong to a backhoe or similar piece of equipment. From there, the rest is obvious. Li long ago concluded that the Doctor wasn't procuring her tech from overlooked warehouses, which leaves one other source: graveyards.

Reactions to their arrival run the gamut from terror to indignation to sullen apology. No former patient keeps silent upon seeing the squid, though, and Li takes this as proof that the Doctor has been underselling the danger of her cures.

Nowhere do they meet resistance. Nowhere, as far as Li's hard evidence and sixth sense can tell, do they see any godpuppets at all. And nowhere do they discuss just what is going to happen when they catch up with the Doctor.

They cross into the Dust, following cracked and broken roads through cracked and broken land. Winter deepens with the advent of November. The rising winds spray dry grit over the windshield, graying out the windows, and they sleep in the car within a hissing cocoon of sound.

The last town on Boon's list lies in what was once a small river valley. Now the river is a rind of frost on the ground and a few fractured panes of ice. Signs of hopeless tillage dot the landscape downstream. Glassing the town from a bluff to the east, Li considers the empty streets, the unguarded well, the broken yet unboarded windows of the pre-Spasm buildings. His teeth hurt, and a sensation not quite nausea gathers slickness in his mouth.

"Well?" Boon says beside him.

"Why do you want to find the Doctor? Personally, I mean."

"She's a genius. Irresponsible, obviously, but a genius. The PRA needs people like that."

He shifts the binoculars to focus on the decaying chapel on the far side of town. "No, that's not it."

"What does it matter?"

"Because we can either make a detour and keep after the Doctor for king, country, and mad science, or we can take the time and risk to do the right thing here."

To her credit, she wastes no time asking how he knows. "How many?"

"From the fields and the number of buildings in some kind of repair, I'd say about fifty."

In the town below them, doors swing open. A small crowd gathers around the chapel. One figure steps forward, facing the church doors, and seems to offer a speech, hands moving with a strange and perfect grace.

"We've got survivors," Li murmurs, lowering his voice out of reflex. "There, in the church. No way to know how many. I count forty godpuppets. You?"

"Forty-two."

"How's your shooting?"

"Excellent. Why? There are too many of them."

"No. No, there aren't."

Would you like to be saved?" the godpuppet asks as they roll into town. In life, it had been a middle-aged woman, traces of an old and practical frumpery visible in her dress and hair. As a puppet, it has a severe, drawn beauty, perhaps how the woman had always wished she could look, and little flickers of silver lick at its lips. "We have found things small and entire. There will be punch on Tuesdays—Tuesdays are lovely—and a hymn-sing."

Boon, aiming out the rear passenger-side window, swings Li's old Winchester 94 into line and drops the godpuppet with the first round and levers another into the chamber. Li floors the accelerator and draws a long curve of dust as the Delray slews around, aiming back the way they came. In rearview mirror miniature, a form sprawls on the ground, a question mark dotted with gray and red and the brightness of wet metal.

Then the howl goes up around them, and the pursuit begins.

Forty-two is a small outbreak. There's no meaningful collective intelligence, nothing beyond an enhanced facility for barn-raising or maybe tug-of-war. In the sudden, mad reaction to the loss of one of their own, the godpuppets use no strategy. They just chase, strung out and reaching with hands and wire, coming into range one by one as Li finesses the accelerator.

It's murder, pure and simple, and he can hear Boon realizing it, hear the little hesitation creep into the rhythm of her shooting, hear it creep back out as she substitutes mechanical proficiency for awareness. She counts under her breath, her voice flat. "Fifteen. Sixteen."

And so on until she says it's finished and Li lets the car coast to a stop.

It's murder. The only question is whether they committed it, or the Doctor the previous month. Li has given up trying to decide.

"Can we drive back a different way?" Boon asks.

For a moment disgust floods him, and he almost tells her she can walk back to town alone, can linger by each body, can get a look at the ones that were just kids, or that were old but phasing weirdly back into a kind of youth and were still caught in the delight of it. But he sees her face and just wishes there were something, anything, they could do but what comes next.

"No," he says softly.

Comprehension dawns, and with it revulsion. "The squids," she mutters. Shaking hands pack the last of her ginger into her mouth. "We've got to kill the squids."

Li draws his revolver. "I'll do it."

"We'll do it together."

"Keep a six-foot distance. One of those wires tags you, you've had it."

She doesn't even bother to look insulted. She just opens the door and goes to work.

To the survivors barricaded in the church falls the burial of the dead, as if anything in that wind-scoured wasteland could stay buried. They spill everything, say they gave the Doctor the names of a few halfway honest innkeepers and arms dealers on the Turnwell border. Li puts the odds of finding her at over fifty percent.

The town is dead. Maybe it was never alive. There are enough bicycles and dried stores for the twelve survivors to make a run south for warmer climes. On an impulse he can't quite explain, Li gives them a half-dozen little blue pills packed in nitrogen. It's a small fortune, an emergency fund Li liberated from a man with more bravado than situational awareness. If they can make it to Austin or El Paso or even Louisville, it will buy them a fresh start, or would, were such things more than empty fantasy.

Li and Boon sit up all night in the church, wrapped in blankets, drinking what the locals said was coffee. The wind is a long whine punctuated by creaks and pops and the rattle of detritus against glass and plywood. For all that the survivors said everyone in town was accounted for among the living or the dead, every small discontinuity of sound or trick of shadow is a godpuppet returning in rage or terror or strange lust with tendrils snapping out like tongues to unite itself with its enemies.

"Do you know what ALS is?" Boon asks.

"Lou Gehrig's disease. Motor neuron disorder. Degenerative."

"Yes."

Silence.

Li coughs. "You still shoot pretty straight."

"Don't say that. Don't tell me that."

"Does the PRA know?"

"No. I've been careful. And the diagnosis is less than six months old."

So that's why she's after the Doctor. He imagines brightness growing in Boon's eyes, hears her spouting cheery inanities as the chips in her brain rebuild her body's cellular machinery to cast silver paths for signals beyond all hope of human reckoning. A sudden picture, stark in the shuddering light of an atomic detonation, of her mouth opening to kiss him and spilling wires past his lips, down his throat, setting them to turn and quest in the very core of him.

But he also sees her stumbling, then bedridden, unable to chew or swallow or draw a full breath. Clear eyes in a slack face, the sick one-way *awareness* of them, their life peering up out of a dead body.

"You think the Doctor can save you?"

"I think I have a ninety percent chance. That's not so bad. And if it goes wrong ..." She smiles in the darkness. "I didn't bring you along because I need protection, or a conscience, or your attempts to analyze something I've spent my whole life studying."

Light grows in the windows. The rising sun is a pale, heatless eye. Li finds his voice, finds himself speaking without thought or effort. The words spill down, fluid and unstoppable. "There were fifty of us outside Burden's Ford when it happened. We were out clearing a lock downriver when people started turning, and we didn't know. We came home, and there were our friends, our families waiting for us. They didn't sound right, didn't move right. I could see it wasn't really them, sense it wasn't really them, and then the others couldn't deny it anymore.... A couple of us got to the armory, and then we won free to the river. But there were six hundred and twenty-four of them. Enough for some cleverness. Some tricks. They started talking in their old voices. Showing off memories. It was so clear, so perfectly clear that everyone we loved was still in there, in a way.

"All twisted up, though. I heard Shengzhi's daughter telling him the story of her own birth like she remembered it. Maybe she did, or God did; it had her mother, too, so maybe that's where it got the details. And my sons were there."

This is the detail he hasn't told anyone, the little crook in the story that warps it from tragedy into something small and cowardly and not even piteous. Boon's eyes are bright but unreadable, fixed.

"Shengzhi and I traded. You understand? We all traded. We

would've worked it out on the back of a napkin if we'd had enough time, because they were crossing the river, all those friends and relations, and it was complicated. Thirty-seven of us left with hunting rifles and shotguns on the bank, and the town burning, and the full moon showing us just what we were doing, what we were allowing. We murdered each other's wives, husbands, lovers, kids, parents.

"The heroes of Burden's Ford. That's what three governments called us. So there's my credential. There's my expertise. I can kill my friends. Most of the others killed themselves, too, sooner or later. There. Was it better than reading my résumé?"

Her voice is just above a whisper. "It shows I was right."

"Yeah?"

"I can trust you to do what's necessary if something goes wrong. I'm sorry, but it's the truth. All that blood on your hands—what difference, in the end, would mine make?"

A bar of sunlight eases into being in the dust of the old church.

"Then there's the matter of your self-loathing," she adds, softly. "I don't know why, but I'm almost sure that it means something."

As if from very far away, Li remembers that the Methodists served punch on Tuesdays in this very church, that it was someone's favorite night of the week because her mother seemed to come alive in a mad whirl of activity involving casseroles and elaborate social networks and keeping the swarm of self-righteous do-gooders from quashing what was really a surprisingly good time. Nights like a bright string of pearls in a dim and abortive childhood, clutched long into the Spasm and the coming of the Dust.

The town of Mercy stands on the western edge of the Dust in territory nominally Turnwell's and practically the domain of anyone who can coax life from it. News comes over the shortwave that the PRA has declared war on Dixie and is pushing northeast. St. Louis has expelled the PRA embassy staff. In Louisville, the radio says, PRA diplomats are strung from lamp posts.

It's easy, in the end, and almost disappointing. Boon asks the townsfolk a few pointed questions, greases a few palms. Li gets the right man drunk enough to talk, then he gets himself drunk enough to feel nothing for a while. He wakes wrapped around a woman whose name he can't remember.

"Where were you when it happened?" he asks. In daylight, she seems gaunt. Her ribs show, and the sharp curve of her hip bones.

A small, sleepy noise and a rank wash of morning breath. "How old do you think I am, mister?"

He checks his eyes and mouth in the mirror. When the girl sees what he's doing, she looks more confused than afraid. He finds nothing. Just a dirty mirror giving back a tired, windburned face.

He finds Boon waiting downstairs. She looks as ragged as he feels, and he wonders how she coped with her own uncertainties. "I have the backhoe seller," she says.

Li slaps a hand-drawn map down on the table. "I have the graveyard."

Doctor Amelie Bourreau does not turn when they enter the cemetery. She zips the body bag closed on something nearly unrecognizable, stretches, and sheds her hat. A few strands of iron-gray hair float in the wind. The ancient backhoe stands beside the row of exhumed graves, all awkward angles and flaking yellow paint.

"The puzzle," she tells the bag in a light Creole accent, "is the people who do not change. Of course, there are no such people. Before the Spasm, there were notions of selective infection, as if the choice could precede the means of making it. And now, Alan, you treat infection as a random event: a roll of the dice, I believe, is your preferred metaphor."

Li watches her, watches Boon watch her, feels Boon watching him right back. A complex triad of attention and indifference. "Doctor," he says, unable to think of anything else. The rage he should be feeling is nowhere to be found. Burden's Ford plays out in his mind, but the memories are far away, drained of color and vitality.

The Doctor ignores him. "Tell me, Jackie, why you think my otherwise excellent implementation of a strong encryption system began to deteriorate? Surely you noticed the sudden appearance of cribs, repeated settings, and other errors?"

"I noticed," Boon murmurs, staring at the Doctor with something between hope and desperation, her face that of a woman seeing home after years at sea, or seeing it burn. "I wasn't sure what it meant."

"It meant I wanted to meet you. And him? What have you noticed about Alan Li?"

"He's good at killing godpuppets. They're bad at killing him."

"And isn't that odd?"

Li finds his voice again. "We're here to take you back to Austin."

"No, I don't believe so. You're here to kill me. Jackie is here for my help." A pause. "I'm unsure either of you will get what you want, I'm afraid." She tucks something metallic into a satchel at her feet. A pacemaker, or a high-splice neural sync. "Come along. We have much to discuss. And we'll need a razor, I'm afraid."

Jackie's come a long way for meatball surgery. "Not a scalpel? Standards are slipping."

The Doctor crooks an eyebrow. "For a haircut, Alan? If you insist."

The moment is tilting, sliding out of control. It wasn't supposed to happen this way. He holds up a pair of handcuffs, trying to recover some trace of equilibrium. "How about we start with these?"

The Doctor smiles beatifically. "If it makes you feel better."

"It does."

It doesn't. It really doesn't.

His protests amount to nothing before the Doctor's cool persuasion, and Jackie Boon shaves his head in the upstairs room where the sheets still need changing. He watches in the same mirror he used that morning to check his eyes, his gums, to keep his uncertainty at bay. The outline of his head changes by degrees in the mirror as she trades scissors for straight razor, working with calm, steady hands.

From the chair in the far corner, the Doctor speaks: "I was fifteen at the Spasm. Eighteen when a GP and a neurosurgeon took me to apprentice. I took excellent notes on all our cases, I'm proud to say. Of particular note was a male child, age four, Chinese and mixed northern European ancestry, otherwise healthy, who presented with myoclonic seizures. Having ruled out febrile seizures and a handful of other possibilities, my teachers diagnosed him as epileptic, which means less than most laymen think; there are a host of possible underlying causes, most of them treatable only via high-splice or surgeries which are, regrettably, no longer possible."

A bit of hair has gotten into Li's nose. It itches. The inside of his head itches too, horribly, as if something is squirming within his skull. His heart pounds. Boon runs a rag through the sweat on his brow.

"We fitted him with a high-splice implant, admittedly an ethically questionable decision, but he showed no signs of mania or physical conversion. The seizures simply stopped."

A pause in the scrape of the razor. Resumption. He can feel a faint tremor through the blade, and warmth flows down from just above his left ear.

"Now we come to a man who, by all accounts, has an uncanny aptitude for identifying godpuppets and, as they say, a knack for killing them. And around him, they develop a peculiar ineptitude. Why might that be, Alan?"

His tongue feels like lead. "They want what's in my brain. It's why that one didn't take the headshot all those years ago. They want my memories, or something I can do."

"Ego." The Doctor sighs. "Yours is exceptional. No, Alan, I can assure you that God neither wants nor needs your memories."

Boon wipes away the blood and presses his shoulder until he turns and leans toward the mirror.

The scar is faint, long-faded, a slim arc two inches above his ear punctuated by four small circles of roughened tissue. How many times did he comb his hair and not feel it? Did his wife ever trace the outline and hesitate while he remained oblivious?

"God already has your memories, Alan. I imagine you have a few of its. What it wants from you is more ... complicated. The difficulty is that God's mind is the sum of so many beliefs, so many networked associations of things, that it functions rather like a language. And language functions like the unconscious. Fundamental drives surfacing as signs, signs refigured as fundamental drives. Do you see?"

"No."

"Eros and thanatos: the motions toward life and death. So many of the people who make up the mind of God are no more than unstructured open space, a bulk of mental critical mass—today, subcritical mass. Parts of an unconscious, if you will, that holds echoes of the former being but could so easily be otherwise. And you, Alan, are the part of God that wants to die."

Jackie is still standing behind him, stock-still. "You're bringing it back," she whispers.

"In a more controlled fashion, yes. I am, if you will, building from scratch, selecting minds which contain qualities conducive to humanity's long-term survival. I make mistakes now and then, and a mind grows ... assertive, rather than phasing smoothly, unconsciously, into greater alignment with the others. I know the problems that accompany these outbreaks of higher function. They are worth the eventual benefits. In time, I expect to achieve critical mass, and God, or a more stable variation, will have a second chance. This will not be a God of elites. This will be a God of the people. The side effects should be mild."

"That's insane," Li snaps. "Look what it did the first time. Look what happens when it starts growing your 'higher functions.' It kills people."

"Only in self-defense."

"It ... takes people over."

A soft laugh. "The word is 'assimilates.' I suppose I know why no one likes to use it, even though it's been half a century since anyone has watched an episode of *Star Trek*. No one likes to feel ridiculous. And no one wants to wonder if people are really better off afterward—or if they even know the difference."

His gun is in his hand, the front sight a black cutout over the Doctor's left eye. "I am not a part of God."

"Are you sure?"

Cool pressure at his throat. The razor. "Wait, Alan," Boon says. "Hear her out."

"Why should I? She's lost it."

"She's not the only one." She takes a deep breath, lets it out. "How long until God could oppose the PRA?"

The Doctor shrugs. "Years."

Li keeps the revolver aimed. He can feel a little creak in the trigger, and his volume is rising. "Listen to yourselves. Boon, you've seen it. Seen what an outbreak looks like, what people have to do. People like us, cleaning up the mess. Have you seen it, Doctor?" He's shouting now, and someone downstairs thumps the ceiling. The razor scrapes pain along the side of his neck. He ignores it. "Seen the kids with wires hanging out of their mouths? Heard people talking in each other's voices?"

"I would have," the Doctor says softly, "and I would have gone a long way toward mitigating outbreaks early if people like you weren't chasing me."

Silence. Li gropes for a refutation that isn't there. What would Burden's Ford have looked like with the Doctor still there, waiting by the patient's bedside with a humane killer? A single shot, a single shattered family. A kind of containment possible only outside the world he has so labored since to create.

Slowly, he lowers the revolver. Boon takes the razor from his throat. "They're pushing north," Boon tells the Doctor, relaxing. "The PRA intends to drive all the way to the Dakotas. It will take a few months, but they can do it. They're after the nuclear stockpiles. With the intel they've collected over the last few years, and the new computers, they'll be able to break into the warehouses and reactivate the non-deployable warheads. In two years, there will be an armed nuclear weapon hidden in every port city in the world. Then there will be a demonstration and a list of demands. I assume this is as unacceptable to you as it is to me?"

The Doctor considers for a moment. "It depends on what percentage of the PRA upper leadership might find itself in need of specialized medical care in the coming years."

"Nukes," Li says, leaning into the word. "Nuclear warheads, Boon. You can't be serious about trusting God with those."

"I don't trust *people* with them," Boon says. "Not the ones I know."

"Is this what you wanted all along?" he asks. "Are you even sick?"

"I wasn't sure. And yes, I really am sick." At the Doctor's questioning look, she adds, "ALS. Very early stages."

The Doctor nods. "I supposed it was something along those lines. I can treat that."

A long sigh from Boon. Li stares, trying to read the decision in her eyes. "You're insane. Both of you."

"Now, Alan. God tried to fix the world, made a mistake, and collapsed with the guilt of it. To me, that sounds human— perhaps even what is best about humanity, for all that it reflects regrettable underlying instabilities and assumptions. Can you say the same for the PRA? Turnwell? Tinfoil?" She rattles her handcuffs. "Survivors in the Carolinas attempted to revive black slavery. Can you imagine God doing that?"

"No. I guess I can't."

"God has been borrowing your mind for almost your entire life, Alan, and vice versa. Do you feel worse for it? Do you feel your individuality diminished? Do you feel coerced as you would living within the borders of the PRA, or strapped down on a Tinfoil pyre because some zealot mistook your wristwatch for witchcraft? Jackie here rose to the upper echelons of the PRA, and her plan, regardless of what happens here, is to defect to Turnwell, isn't it? And how much better, Jackie, do you think the devil you don't know will treat you?"

The doctor pauses, studies them, evaluation turning behind her eyes. "We have a chance to make a better world. Do you know how many enemies I've made into allies over the years? You're not the first to be offered this choice. You wouldn't be the first to accept it. I need an engineer and a wetworks man. We can do better this time. Jackie, Alan—all it requires is a small extension of faith."

"Then start small," Boon says. "Fix me. Cure me, and we'll talk."

Li says nothing at all.

Only when Boon is unconscious and the air cool with the sweet smell of ether does Li free both of the Doctor's hands. "I'm leaving a scalpel on the tray," he says. "I don't have to tell you what happens if you abuse it."

"But of course." With neat, practiced motions, she arranges the various needful things beside the patient, culminating in a small metal cylinder trailing short leads. "This moment is a test, you realize, yes?"

"I figured. Not sure what for."

"You're the part of God that wants to die. The surest way to accomplish that would be to kill me. Of course, if you follow that impulse, you might not be acting freely at all. If you resist it, you prove to yourself that your freedom can coexist with your role. A reconciliation, theologically long-overdue, of God and free will."

"So I have to let you live to prove I'm not afraid of God, do I?"

"I do believe the point, Alan, is that you don't *have* to do anything at all." The scalpel traces a red line at the nape of Boon's neck. "Including take a risk you allegedly believe, deep in your heart of hearts, to be both selfish and foolish. I am even inclined to think that, by permitting this operation, you've already made your decision, just as by placing my life in your hands I've made mine. Well?"

"How long will the operation take?"

"Two hours."

"Then I guess I have two hours to think it over."

The first thing Boon asks when she wakes is whether she might have a drink of water. The second is where Li buried the Doctor.

"In one of the graves she opened. I smashed all her other gadgets, too, just to be sure."

She's still shivering from the anesthesia, the tremors a mockery of what might have been. "I should be angry."

"No. We both know you made your choice the minute you breathed that ether. Otherwise, you'd have cut my throat first. What convinced you?"

She shrugged. "I can sympathize with wanting to fix the world. But she picked dangerous tools."

"So now you come around."

"Not God. The PRA. Those people. Everything she said, and she was still going to let them back in. What about you? You hesitated." She touches the surgical gauze at the nape of her neck. "You let her do it. I wasn't sure you would."

"I guess I decided I'm still human. That the risk of an outbreak is minimal if there's someone able to stay, someone who knows what they're doing, what to look for. She was right about that: If we hadn't been chasing her all these years, a lot of outbreaks never would have happened. I might even have let her live, let her go if she'd just been taking mad risks to save people. But I don't think she cared about the people at all. Not anymore, not as patients or human beings. It's why she lied to them. It's all about God and better worlds. And aside from that, everything she said might have been completely nuts."

The sun is setting, the grimy windowpanes transfigured into sheets of light. Downstairs, men and women are beginning to sing, drunk on fermented cassava-plus and the knowledge that life goes on, at least for a while. Forty-nine doesn't seem so old now. There are still choices left, and enough time for them to matter.

"I have a nine-in-ten chance," Boon says. "That's better than most people get."

Li nods.

"You'll come with me? For a few weeks, at least. We can go west, get to Seattle, take a ship anywhere."

He studies her eyes, the calm intelligence behind them, the trace of doubt. The future history already written there of a lifetime spent peering into mirrors for fine silver flecks in the iris, for bleeding around the gums. The nightmares that he is now convinced might not belong to anyone in particular. He wonders what form they will take for her.

"We'll watch each other," he says.

"Yes. And when we're in the middle of the Pacific, we're throwing the squid overboard."

Li lets himself smile. "I know that too."

"What are we going to do about the PRA?"

To that, and to the questions behind it, he has only the beginnings of an answer.

The next morning, he sells his Delray to a man with more cash than sense and buys two bicycles with trailers. By noon, they are riding west into a gentle fall of snow while the world behind them fades into subtle, sloping shapes, all of them gray.

A Harvest of Astronauts

written by

Kyle Kirrin

illustrated by

SAM KEMP

ABOUT THE AUTHOR

Kyle Kirrin works on a ranch 9,000 feet above sea level in Creede, Colorado, where he tends to the needs of two Irish Wolfhounds, three Icelandic sheep, two geriatric horses, four chickens, a miniature donkey, and a very loud cat. He's spent the last seven winters writing on the side while resort-hopping as a snowboard instructor and guide, most recently based out of Big Sky, Montana. During the summer, he's climbed trees professionally as an arborist, hosted wine tastings in northern Virginia, and done fine woodworking in North Carolina. He's a first reader for Apex Magazine *and this is his second professional sale.*

ABOUT THE ILLUSTRATOR

Sam Kemp was born in 1989 in Essex, England.

He has always been creative, taking inspiration from his mum's mentality of never being bored when you have imagination. Sam loved to create using any tool at his disposal, from wood from his dad's shed to clay and paint.

Sam went on to study across England, gaining a degree in game design from Norwich University and a master's degree in concept art and animation from Teesside University. It was here he began his journey as a digital artist.

Sam continues to learn and grow as an artist, taking inspiration from contemporary digital artists, as well as from the masters such as John Singer Sargent. He is currently working as a freelance artist across several industries, including theming and fashion.

A Harvest of Astronauts

The airlock sighed open, and the first corpse floated through. It was a thin, hairless girl, whose eyes and lips were sewn shut with golden thread. A black sheet covered her body from the neck down, though her hands protruded from two cross-shaped slits. A sprig of lavender was wrapped around each of the girl's wrists.

X09 caught the body by its shoulders and guided it onto a gurney. Then they cinched a strap across the corpse's ribs and pushed it down the hall, where Anya was waiting to catch it and steer it around the corner and into the prep bay.

"Got six for you this time," someone said from the other side of the lock. "All kids again."

"Understood." The coupling mechanism groaned just as X09 detected a slight deviation in the interface between the two ships. They fired the Vernier thrusters to correct the alignment and the groaning stopped.

Anya glanced toward X09. Her face was angular; her brown eyes were bloodshot. She was getting worse.

X09 ran a superficial diagnostic, and Anya's vitals overlaid the space around her in a digital cloud. Everything looked acceptable, so far as that definition currently stood. "Nothing to be concerned about," X09 said. "Just a slight adjustment."

A second body cartwheeled through the lock, one that carried the undisguised tang of formaldehyde. X09 caught the body, strapped it down, and sent it on its way.

Anya kicked off the wall, caught the gurney, and disappeared around the corner, pulling it behind her.

"Gotta be your last shift in this system, right?" the voice said.

"Yes," X09 said.

"You figure you've got enough time to offload all these before the nova pops?"

"Yes," X09 repeated.

The voice hesitated. "Yeah, I guess you'd know."

X09 transferred three more corpses down to Anya, making small adjustments to their trajectories here and there. "Thank you for your business," they said, as the final body disappeared around the corner.

"Yeah, same," the voice called back. "You two be safe out there."

X09 gave one yank on the horizontal ladder that ran the length of the wall, propelling themselves deeper into the ship. They pulled their way around the corner and found Anya standing outside the prep bay windows, with a hand to the ceiling to anchor her in place, her thinning dreads haloed around her shoulders. All six gurneys floated behind the glass, spinning, bumping into each other.

X09 caught a rung just behind Anya and jerked themselves to a stop. They wrapped their arms around her.

She sank into them, pressing her chin into the crook of their elbow. "They were all so young."

X09 ran a deeper diagnostic. They were doing that too often these days, but they couldn't help it. The readout covered every inch of available space: the walls, the ceiling, the air. Even Anya's light-brown skin was overlaid with scrolling blue text, though of course she couldn't see it.

Her heart rate and blood pressure were slightly elevated, which was understandable. But her T cell count had spiked again. X09 pulled her closer.

"Any one of them could have been ours," she said, through chattering teeth. "In another life."

"Perhaps once leasing our body is no longer necessary, and we can acquire something more permanent . . ."

She kissed their left hand, their right. Then she said what X09 had been thinking repeatedly these last few weeks: "I wish I had that much time."

Alchemy, really?" Anya said, as she pulled herself into X09's personal quarters. She'd put her rings back on, eight in total, one on each finger. Four platinum, four gold, all thin as wire. One for each body X09 had left behind. One for each time they'd fallen back in love with her.

X09 closed the book they'd been reading. "Alchemy. Really." They'd turned to the field out of necessity. They'd already exhausted every medical text dating back to the *Kahoun Papyrus*, every spiritual book back to the *Rig Veda*, and everything in between. Many of those yellowed, dusty texts were still pinned against the wall, held in place by a triangular net that spanned ceiling to floor.

But X09 had dismissed alchemy out of hand. It seemed a grievous oversight now that a new, desperate hope was sparking inside their chest.

Anya twined her fingers through the netting and let her body drift up off the floor. "I guess you've already started the descent."

"We have. We'll be close enough to begin in a little over an hour."

"Great. So, can I help with anything?"

X09 plucked a volume out from the stack. The cover was so worn it was indecipherable. "Try this one. It's a bit too technical for us."

Anya cracked it open, barked a laugh, and threw it at X09's head.

X09 caught the book between two fingers and set it back behind the netting.

"Not funny," Anya said with a smile. "How long have you been sitting on that one?"

"We do not understand what you mean," X09 said. "We are a robot. We are not programmed for humor." They'd handed her *Harry Potter and the Philosopher's Stone*. "Boop beep, beep boop."

"Shut up," she said, still grinning. "I figured you'd have finished all these by now."

"We have. We're rereading them."

"In case you missed something."

"Yes."

"But you don't miss things. Ever."

"No."

Anya shook her head, and her dreads lashed back and forth across her face. "Yeah, that's not obsessive at all. Totally normal. Why don't you just scan them?"

"We like turning pages. We like the weight in our hands."

"Such a romantic."

"If you say so."

"What are you reading, exactly?"

"Translations, guesses, ramblings. Anything to do with the Philosopher's Stone."

Anya pursed her lips. It made her look gaunt, but no less pretty. "For turning metal into gold, right?"

"That was the primary aim. But there are several other interpretations, too."

She stifled a yawn with her hand. "Like?"

X09 magnified their vision, straining to see if her palm would come away speckled with blood. For once, it didn't. "Some say the transmutation is metaphorical. That alchemy is to be understood as a means for the purification of the soul. To elevate oneself from a base state to enlightenment."

"And you really believe that?"

X09 shrugged. They had other opinions, other hopes. Though the possibility of redemption—especially after all the suffering they'd caused these last few weeks—was a comforting one.

"Mmm. Well, I'll leave you to it. I'm going to rest up a bit before we start."

"Feeling all right?"

"Yeah, I'm fine. Just tired. Don't work too hard, okay?" She kissed the top of their head and left.

Her fatigue wasn't a surprise. X09 had stolen nearly a pint of her blood over the last two nights as she'd slept. The vials were tucked away inside a hollow they'd carved out beneath the synthetic flesh of their abdomen. They looked out the window.

Ryzel A, a neutron star, loomed large beyond the glass, pale blue light beaming from both its poles. Ryzel B was barely visible, just a speck hurtling through the dark, spiraling ever closer to an inevitable collision with its twin.

How strange it was, that mankind had been searching for the Philosopher's Stone for thousands of years, yet none had ever considered that there might be thousands of them screaming unseen through the sky. That the Stone might not be a stone at all, but a star.

X09 accessed the ship's live feed and directed it to Anya's quarters. They watched the rhythmic rise and fall of her chest until they were sure she was sleeping, then they tucked the feed into the corner of their vision and slipped into the prep bay.

The bodies were still floating about on their gurneys. X09 grabbed one and pushed it onto the wall, where a set of latches clicked into place over its metal frame. They anchored the other five in the same way.

X09 cut the power to the prep bay's cameras and started with the left eye of the first girl to arrive. They held their breath as they worked the first gold stitch out of her eyelid, though X09 didn't need to breathe. One of the many habits they'd picked up from Anya. They removed a spool of painted wire from a compartment in their chest and tied one end to the stitch they'd pulled loose. Then they worked the strings until it was the painted wire that was embedded in the girl's skin, and the thread was free for the taking. They clipped the knot and pocketed the gold.

So it went with the girl's other eye, then her lips. X09 couldn't tell the difference when they were done; they'd made the switch without damaging the girl's face. They weren't always that lucky, though Anya had never noticed. They tried not to theorize about how she would react if she knew.

X09 pulled the black sheet down and checked for other offerings. The girl wore a diamond ring on her middle finger. They gave it a sharp tug, but the ring wouldn't come free. They tried again, harder, and when it still refused to budge, they snapped the girl's finger off at the knuckle. X09 pulled the ring loose and curled the girl's remaining fingers around her severed digit. Then they pulled the sheet back up to the girl's throat and moved on to the next body, a boy with platinum bands fastened around his throat.

The offerings that the living made to the next life were varied, but always valuable. No resurrection came without its cost. When their work was done, X09's compartments were full, and their heart was heavy in their chest. They understood, with calculable certainty, exactly how many children they'd cast off to be reborn, knowing that they'd robbed the boys and girls of the ability to pay their way.

But Anya's medications weren't cheap, and if X09 ever had to cast her into the cleansing fire, they'd send her to the stars with every inch of her dripping in gold.

I think we should go with a female body next time," Anya said. She was chewing mint again—it was of the few scents strong enough to keep her from smelling the blood on her breath. She'd just joined X09 in the prep bay, and they were waiting for the ship to settle into orbit.

"Really?" X09 said. "Female?"

Anya hugged herself. Her breath misted out from between her lips. She looked so small. "You'd take up a lot less space."

"That is true." X09 bumped the room's temperature up four degrees.

"And you wouldn't smell so bad."

"This body isn't capable—oh. We see how it is."

She flicked their nose. "Beep boop indeed. But what do you think?"

"We'll be happy with whatever body you choose."

"Any body at all?"

"Within reason. We don't want to come back as a chihuahua."

"Wolfhound? German shepherd?"

"Tempting, but no. We're afraid we have to insist on some approximation of human."

"Probably for the best. People might talk, otherwise."

"You should put your glasses on," X09 said. "We're getting close."

Anya squinted at the blue brilliance of the window, sighed, and slid a pair of dark glasses down off her forehead and over her eyes. They were much too big for her face.

X09 released the latches on the first gurney and maneuvered it in front of the chute, a circular disk set into the wall just beneath the window. It spiraled open to receive the body. They studied Anya's face as they slid the corpse into the tube, but her attention remained fixed on the window. The disk sealed shut.

"You're really going to go through with it again, aren't you?" she said.

"Yes."

She licked her lips. "I wish you wouldn't."

"We know."

"There's too many risks."

"They're minimal, mostly."

"All it would take for me to lose you is a bit more background noise than normal during the transfer. A flare or a burst or almost anything else. You know it's just a matter of chance."

"Even if our personal data was lost, you'd still have our basic programming."

"But you wouldn't be you. I'd have to make you you again."

X09 shrugged. "We're sure you could find a way to improve us."

216

"I'd have to make you love me again. From scratch. It's hard enough when the transfer goes well and you get most of your memories back, but"—her voice was quiet, delicate—"I don't know if I could manage it again without them. Now that I'm like this. I don't even feel like I'm the same person anymore."

X09 patched together what memories they had, and eight Anyas overlaid their vision, data ghosts that a different part of X09 had loved in turn, data ghosts whose sum comprised the beautiful totality that was Anya—the real Anya—floating there before them.

"By our calculations," X09 said, "making us fall in love with you would take approximately seven seconds."

She grabbed both of their hands and squeezed. "Do you really have to go like this? Can't we wait a bit longer? Please?"

"This body is going to deactivate in a few hours regardless. And the decrease in weight will boost the ship's efficiency on the way back."

"Barely. And we could just eject it after we've jumped out of this system."

"That would be wasteful." And it would leave X09 without the answers they needed.

"I know," Anya said.

An alert sounded inside X09's head; the ship was in position. They fired the ejector. "It'll be fine. We promise."

Anya shivered as she watched the corpse surge down into the blue light. "Can we at least pick up a different contract next time? I'm so tired of doing this. I know the pay's good, but ..."

"We'll have to run the numbers when we get back, but if we can make it work, we'll do something else. If that's what you want."

"Thanks. This job just creeps me out."

"Why?"

"You don't think it's weird? That we've turned these stars into graveyards?"

"Not particularly. A star dies, and a neutron star is born. We've always associated them with death."

"I guess so. I just find it a little grotesque is all. I mean, these stars are going to collide, and then a hundred scrapper ships are going to jump in under the nova to salvage the metal that's made. So many strangers picking through the bones." She rolled one of her platinum rings about her index finger. "They're gravediggers. I know it's just gold and all that they're after, but no matter how you look at it, they're still harvesting corpses."

"If that's true, then you've got us wrapped around your finger in more ways than we realized."

Anya smiled down into her rings. "Clearly. It's different with you though."

"Is it?"

"I don't really think of these rings as being a part of you, even if there's a piece of your old bodies in each of them. They're more reminders that you came back to me, even though you didn't have to."

"Why would we ever want to do otherwise?"

She swallowed, wincing. "I can't imagine watching you die. I don't think I could handle it. Maybe you're just better than I am, but I wouldn't blame you if you wanted to go back to when everything was simple between us. When we were just captain and navigation system."

"We aren't going anywhere. Neither are you."

"Look at me. I'm less every day. There has to be a point where I won't be worth coming ba—"

"There isn't."

She looked away.

"There isn't."

"I just wonder sometimes. What it must be like to be like you, to know that you can reset your whole life whenever you want."

"Would you go back if you could?"

"To my childhood? God no. I hated being a kid." She coughed, a wet, strangling sound that set her hacking. Three ruby-red globes drifted across the distance between them.

X09 slid the next corpse into place and sent it on its way.

This isn't goodbye," X09 said, as they climbed into the ejector, feet first.

"I know."

"And I won't be long."

"I know." She bent down and kissed their forehead, then planted a longer, lingering kiss on their lips. "I'll miss this body. It was a good one."

"Better than some, worse than others."

"Maybe we should splurge for some upgrades for this next one. We could afford it if we took another one of these jobs. Maybe . . ." she trailed off, blushing.

X09 smirked. "Yes?"

"We'll talk when you get back."

"Okay."

"Well," Anya said.

"We love you."

"I love you too."

X09 sealed the ejector bay behind them. Then they sent themselves careening into space. The ship loomed in front of them for a split-second—with Anya's face in the window, her fingers splayed against the glass—then she and the ship were lost in the darkness. The cold enveloped them, then the heat flashed up, warm at first, then almost unbearable. But X09's mind was elsewhere as they plummeted down.

One part was stuck on Anya, as always. Analyzing her prognosis, gauging how many days she had left. Testing variables that were increasingly obscure: the ship's proximity to sources of radiation, its temperature, its composition. Anya's hydration levels, the number of blankets she slept with, the freshness of the coffee she drank.

The second part was wondering if X09 had a soul, and if so, whether it could be saved. A great hope, but an unnecessary one. X09 would carry whatever burden Anya needed them to, into the afterlife or otherwise.

The third part was beaming their nonessential data back to the ship. The memories that bound X09 to Anya and made them hers.

SAM KEMP

But the fourth part—the greatest part by far—was focused on the vials of blood they'd stolen. On analyzing the rogue cells that were eating Anya from the inside out.

X09 plunged down, glowing now, synthetic skin wicking off in white-hot bursts. The tidal force built until it was pulling them apart, into streams of metal, into particles.

In that last warped, overlong second, X09 thought of the Philosopher's Stone. Of its ability to transmute base metal to gold, confirmed by an earthbound telescope way back in 2017.

They thought of the many humans who now flocked to these cosmic graveyards, seeking purification, and awaiting rebirth, in whatever form the stars saw fit to grant them.

And, finally, they thought of their last great hope: that the Stone's true strength might not lie in its ability to purify the souls of the dead, but in cleansing the bodies of the living. X09 poured nine lives' worth of hope into those vials.

There was the slightest shimmer, and then—

Super-Duper Moongirl and the Amazing Moon Dawdler

written by

Wulf Moon

illustrated by

ALICE WANG

ABOUT THE AUTHOR

Wulf Moon is a Pacific Northwest writer. He believes in born storytellers. You also have to serve seven cats—every successful writer knows that— but allow only ONE in your office. But if you want more proof, here it is:

Moon wrote his first science fiction story when he was fifteen. It won the Scholastic Art & Writing Awards—the same contest that first discovered Stephen King, Truman Capote, Joyce Carol Oates, and many other iconic names in the arts. This story became his first professional sale when it sold to Science World.

His Borg love story was a winner in Pocket Books' Star Trek: Strange New Worlds *contest. Moon also won a contest by bestselling author Nora Roberts, writing the conclusion to "Riley Slade's Return." His story "Beast of the Month" earned Honorable Mentions from all three of the Writers of the Future Coordinating Judges, and sold to the* Strange Beasties *anthology from Third Flatiron Publishing. They also published his story, "War Dog." In Critters Annual Readers' Poll, it was awarded Best Science Fiction and Fantasy Short Story of 2018.*

Moon has created numerous podcast episodes for Gallery of Curiosities *and* Third Flatiron. *He is podcast director for* Future Science Fiction Digest.

Donald Maass of the Donald Maass Literary Agency has represented Moon on one novel, and has requested the epic fantasy he's currently completing, Driftweave.

This is Moon's third professional sale. He finds it ironic that winning the contest known for discovering new writers has also made him a pro in one fell swoop.

ABOUT THE ILLUSTRATOR

Alice Wang was born in 2003 in Florida, before moving to the state of Washington as a toddler.

Proverbially, she began drawing before she could walk. Whatever the case, Wang has been drawing for as long as she can remember, and grew up surrounded by stacks of notebooks filled with her own scribbles. As a youth growing up in today's technologically developed world, she discovered the online art community in middle school and began posting her art on social media and blogs, learning about the art world and interacting with experienced artists in the process.

Today, Wang is a hobbyist illustrator, frequently entering competitions. She now also takes illustration commissions. Currently, she is a sophomore attending Bellevue High School in Bellevue, Washington.

Super-Duper Moongirl and the Amazing Moon Dawdler

I'm Dixie. I'm twelve. Well, almost. My birthday is coming up, so close enough. I wear red. God gave me red hair, but I picked the rest, from my red space Keds—Mom hates them—to my matching silk cape—Dad loves it—because capes are cool, and when you drape them right, they hide the tubes.

I have a dog. He's a MedGen robodog, looks like a chrome Doberman pinscher. He breathes for both of us, and he juices up my air with higher oxy. I named him Moon Dawdler, because, duh, we're on the Moon, and because, double duh, he dawdles, doing his blinkies and sniffies with everything, making sure I'm safe before we enter an airlock, or head to Moonshine's for burgers, or go to the arboretum for a run, or take the tunnels back to Norden Moonbase Resort. Mom and Dad run it for some rich dude that's about to head the first mission to Mars.

Mars. I'm the first girl on the Moon, and I can't breathe on my own, so who would have believed *that*? But Mars? That's a *whole* 'nuther world. But they'll make a base there too, and I'd love to see it. One step at a time, my physical therapist used to say, and look where that got me so far!

I'm in the arboretum dome, topside, the only pod at Norden not buried under rocks and moon sand. The dome has a special film across it, helps reduce the harmful radiation, but Mom says it's still too much exposure. I can only be up here a half hour a day, and I have to wear a stupid cap, and it's heavy, I think there's lead in it. The stupid tomatoes in all these stupid plant beds don't wear little sombreros, and they look just fine to me,

ALICE WANG

but Mom's a doctor, she should know what's good for me, I guess. Mom seems to know everything and is not afraid to tell it to anyone, especially Dad. Anyhow, it's my scheduled time in the sun, and I'm here to use the treadmill.

Moon Dawdler is heeled beside me, his sides *wisp-wisping*, making my chest go up and down. I look up. Yeah, through silvered sunglasses. I can see it up there, the Moon's moon, the Deep Space Gateway, a silver teaspoon floating across black milk. The handle is FlashPoint's *Mars I* spaceship—they're still shipping it up hydrogen and oxy made from a big chunk of comet head ice they found buried under the Aristoteles crater. The round spoon part up there? That's where the Earth transports dock, like SpaceX and Virgin Galactic, and then the Russians bring the tourists down. Dad wishes we had an American lander, especially now that Russia took control of Syria after their dictator died. The UN is all flippin' crazy about it, but Mom says not to worry, we all signed treaties for up here. She says mutual dependence for survival makes everyone mind their p's and q's. I act like I know, but I don't, and now that I'm alone, I ask Moon Dawdler.

"Hey, Moonie: Go fetch! What's p's and q's?"

Moon Dawdler's AI is always running, always learning—especially when it comes to me—but "Moonie: Go fetch" is my code that the coast is clear, and we can talk normal like. His tail wags just like a real dog's too—it's his zipline, you know, data and communications antennae. Oh, you think Dobermans don't have tails? Well, they do, and my dog looks good with his, thank you very much. I got to choose his AI personality at MedGen too. They had this persona called Mr. Z that tickled me. The tech said I chose wisely, because his AI growth will lean toward strength and defense, just like Ziggy, the rapper turned bodyguard it was based on. Mom hates it. I love it, 'cuz my dog has to be tough. He's breathing for both of us.

"Yo, Dixie," he says, deep and gruff like he's from the mean streets of the Bronx, "you sure you want the dope on that question?"

I pat his cold head with my good hand, the one that still feels. He's got LED eyes, and I got to choose those too and they light up red, because I like red, and because when he speaks they glow and he looks like one of those mechanical hounds from *Fahrenheit 451*. Yeah, I read. I put my digidrive into thermonuclear meltdown with all those days at the hospital. I've begged Mom to get me a new PowaPlayah 4 from Earth for my birthday, the ones that can hold 2.5 pet bites, er, petabytes, and that's gazillions of bytes, as much as a human brain! Please, please, please may it also be preloaded with MegaCoda, because that's like every game, book, and song ever. And it comes with a thousand unlock tokens!

Moonie clacks his jaw. "Yo, girl. You want the didgies or not?"

My lips don't always frame words so well from being burned and then reconstructed—the surgeon did her best—but Moonie always gets me. "Thilly T-Bone. Mom thaid it, so it *can't* be that bad."

He tilts his head and his mouth moves with his words. "Woof! Okay. It means pints and quarts. Old English. Bar talk, my little Chick-chick-chickadee. Beer used to be served in pint- and quart-sized mugs."

"Ah, p's and q's."

"Word. The 'xact history is lost, but when bartenders were behind the stick—um, serving drinks—they'd keep tabs on how much customers drank, so they didn't lose their green, know what I mean?"

"No."

"Means to be careful, watch your step, be on best behavior."

"Oh, I get it!"

"Woof! Power to the kitten." He tilts his head the other way, silver ears cocked just like a Doberman's. "And, since we're on the topic of booze, just say *No* to drinking and drugs."

"Mom and Dad drink sometimes."

"They adults. You a kid. Just say *No*."

I pushed past a frond of an areca palm leaning over the path to the treadmill. "Who do you think will offer me booze up here?"

He growled. "Okay, you got me. Just doin' my thing, Chickadee."

I giggled. *"Word."*

I was about to connect the straps from the treadmill to my weight belt so I didn't go bouncing into the air, and then the door to the outside airlock swishes open, making my ears pop. I turn. It's the plump astrobotanist, his bald head shining like he had just greased it as he carries in one of those yellow tiger-striped packs. Those come from waste reclamation. He drops it with a thud on the path to the exit. He looks up and sees me.

"What are you doing in here?" His face is always red, even when he isn't annoyed. I don't like his gravelly voice, he always talks too loud. I feel my panic rev up seeing him loom between me and the exit. My heart is thumping, my legs are shaking, and I can't breathe. Fortunately, Moonie is between us. Moonie always has my back. Except when he has my front.

"It's, it's my time, Mr. Franco." I nod to the schedule screen next to the door.

"Oh." He swipes his hand over his head. Maybe he misses his hair, I know I did until it grew back. "Well, little girl, it's always my time in this place. Unless you enjoy the smell of shit, you might want to reschedule."

Moon Dawdler has my bio readings—he could tell my heart rate just jumped. He flares his eyes at Mr. Franco and growls low. "What's wrong with you, dude? You ghetto trash? You don't use that kind of language around little girls."

Mr. Franco doesn't even respond to Moonie, just ignores him and stares straight at me. "Look, I've got work to do before the next dump of spoiled tourists. It's a small world up here, we all have to put up or shut up." With that, he does look at my dog. *Mean.*

"I, I, I'll just come back tonight," I say.

"Come again?"

I hate it when people don't understand my words. I repeat them. Slower.

"Oh. No night up here, girlie. North pole. Eternal sun."

Now he's talking to me like I'm a stupid kid. That burns. "You know what I mean."

"Sure kid." He steps between the fronds and motions that the way is clear. To leave. Moonie sends the spark to my chest and fills my lungs with air and we head for the exit, Moonie growling low.

I look out the corners of my eyes. Mr. Franco scowls as we pass. "Nice dog. What do you feed that thing, nuts and bolts?"

He's not funny. I try to bite my tongue, I really do, but Dad always says I have a lot of Mom in me.

"Fat botanists," I whisper, but it's a loud whisper. I kinda hope he hears it. And then, *lightbulb.* What if he did hear me? I go tell Mom about all this, he'll tell her I insulted him. Dad says loose lips sink spaceships. I seal the hatch.

On days when the tourists aren't here, the resort lobby is our living room. Like tonight. The lobby's just another resin-and-moon sand cube in the underground gerbil maze, but it's way bigger than our pod, and can hold about fifty people! It's got holo projectors on the walls, and a reception desk at one end, and an airlock at the other that connects to the garage and entrance tunnel. The rover sits there—Dad picks up tourists in it when they land, and it's also for taking them out on excursions. Don't tell anyone, but Dad even let me drive it once, on one of our father/daughter days. We drove to Darkside. There isn't really a dark side of the Moon, but when you live at a base that's specially planted to get never-ending sunlight for the solar cells, you miss night like you miss Earth.

I have never seen so many stars. . . .

When the noisy tourists arrive, Dad waves at the walls and up come the feeds from Tycho crater, or Mare Crisium, what I call the pompom tip of the poodle's tail, and they're all *ooohs* and *ahhhs.* Poodle? Yeah, there's a French poodle on the Moon. God did all kinds of silly things to make us laugh, and the poodle outlined across the right face of the Moon is one of them. You've never seen it? Look again.

But tonight it's just us, and so it's sunset over the Olympics. We like that view. We used to go camping there when we lived in Seattle. You see, unlike tourists, we can see the Moon anytime we want. With all the grays up here, you start missing Earth colors *real* fast. Really helps to have the big views from the projectors too. You don't feel the moon cave scrunchies so much.

Mom's clearing our dinner trays as I go sit on the air sofa, Moonie trailing at my side, auto adjusting my tubes so they never scrape the floor. We had real peas and tomato slices tonight—not wrinkly like the hydrated chicken—but *yuck*, now I know what they're grown with. I can't wait for pizza night again—pepperoni is my fave!—but now I'm wondering what's in the sauce....

Dad's already over at the front desk, checking schedules, assigning pods, doing prep stuff. Mom will check their med records later. They get cleared by FlashPoint's doctors, of course. Mom says she's their 239,000-miles-from-home insurance policy. You'd be surprised how often they need that policy.

"Dad, can I switch to Iguacu Falls?"

"Huh? Ask your mother."

That's Dad's default. He looks like blond-haired Thor, but he doesn't have his hammer. I look at Mom. She looks like a fiery Valkyrie, and the sweep of red hair down both shoulders looks like copper wings about to slap the air.

"Mom?"

"It's dark there, Dixie."

"Duh, right. How about Waimea Falls? It's still light on Oahu."

"Don't you want to update your Spacebook fans? It's been a few days."

"Nah, nothing exciting to report. I need hot news. If it doesn't bleed, it doesn't lead."

"What?"

I shrink into the couch. "Nothing. Heard a reporter say that on my newsfeed."

Mom looks all skeptical, and flashes her death-ray stare at my dog.

I like doing my vlogs, and my fans *are* the reason we're up here. When Make-Me-A-Wish denied mine for "insurmountable costs and logistics," I was crushed. So were Mom and Dad, because they taught me not to let anything that happened stop me from reaching my dreams, and I worried LOTS I had reached too high. But then I sent a zip to *The Seattle Times*. That probably was unfair, I was already famous. I survived America's worst school bombing after all. Well, the *Times* started it, and my story went global. They contacted FlashPoint too, and after lots of their science people checked me out and interviewed Mom and Dad, it was all systems go. They even designed my own spacesuit that Moon Dawdler could plug into. I became their poster girl. "If Dixie can do it, why can't you?" I don't mind. It got me to the Moon.

Mom zips the trays into a blue tube bag. "There's always something interesting up here, honey. You just have to find the angle."

I stroke my hair. I'm always stroking my hair, 'cuz I'm so happy to have it. "Here's an angle. How about I talk about poop? Isn't that what our food is grown in?"

Mom pops the bag in the transport chute. There's a *whoosh* and it's gone. She turns and shakes her head, but I see the smile in her green eyes. "The waste is processed and sterilized through irradiation, honey. It's just clean, organic matter that gets worked into the regolith soil."

"So whose clean poop was in the peas tonight? Because if it was Mr. Franco's, I'm not eating peas *ever* again."

Moon Dawdler is sitting on the floor beside me, watching me with those red eyes. He blinks twice superfast. That's our code, it's him telling me he's laughing. I wink back the same, but Mom catches it, and the Valkyrie comes out.

"I told you, Dixie, I don't like the secret communication between you two. It's not healthy. The MedGen unit is a life-support system, it's not meant to be your friend or secret confidant or pet. We've been over this."

"Yes, Mother."

"Its AI is important, it keeps you safe, but treating it like a person is not healthy. And I've never liked that Mr. Z perso—"

I let go of my hair. "You said I could choose!"

Dad looks up, stares at Mom, but doesn't say anything.

Mom stops. "I did," Mom says. "You're right. I did." She sighs. "I just wanted you to be happy, honey. But why couldn't you have chosen a unit like DivaDoll? She was based on that Miss Universe winner that got a PhD in socioeconomics and—"

"Because I liked Mr. Z. He made me laugh!"

Moonie lays down, sides wisping quietly, tail flat against the floor. I know she hurt his feelings, and I hate it when she treats him like a machine. He *is* my friend. He's my *best* friend. And he keeps me *alive*. What friend can top that?

Mom sees I'm hurt, because my lip droops, and maybe there's tears, maybe there's not. I'm not telling. But I'm not trying to hurt Mom—her sitting by my side at the hospital all those days was hurt enough. But it really bothers her when I get sad, and now she's wringing her hands. We've had this talk before. It never goes anywhere but *bad*.

Yay! Dad saves the day. He opens a drawer in the desk, pulls out a small jewelry box. It's got a red bow on it! My heart jumps. Mom jerks her head, but this time, *she* stays silent. Dad walks over to Mom, takes her hand, and she nods. They both kneel down beside me, and Dad holds out the box.

"Happy birthday, Super-Duper Moongirl."

"But my birthday isn't—"

Dad opens the box and smiles bright as the sun. "If we wait until then, this model will become obsolete."

I squeal. "PowaPlayah 4! The new gold earring model!"

Dad nods. "It's got Rimshot—besides communication features, it zip links to any screen or player. Moon Dawdler has Rimshot capability too. That means he can project its holovids or games or play its tunes for you."

"Or play the audiobooks," Mom says quick.

"Yeah, that too," Dad says quick.

I take the box. I know everything about this model. Models

wear this model! Oh, it's not a clip-on. "But I don't have pierced ears."

"It's got an auto-piercer," Dad says. "Nova injector, like the one in Moon Dawdler's tongue. Won't even hurt."

"But, Mom, you always said I have to be—"

Mom smiles. She's not a Valkyrie anymore. She's just Mom. "We decided a twelve year old on the Moon is equivalent to a fourteen year old for an Earth girl."

I almost slip and say *"Damn straight!"* I'm so excited, but instead I stand and wrap my arms around both of them. "Thank you so, so much! I love it!"

Moonie thumps his tail.

A week goes by, and the next set of tourists have left. I was hoping another kid would come up, even a *boy*, but none in this batch. It's so expensive, it's really rare, but it's dynamo when a girl comes up that's close to my age. They always want to get z-vlogs with me and Moon Dawdler to zip on their Spacebook. Spikes their ratings. I don't mind, spikes mine too, and the ads earn me bookoo digicoin.

I'm so happy! My turn in the arboretum, and I'm alone at last! I take the path to the treadmill in the center, strap in, and it's projection time as I run.

"Moonie: Go fetch! Show me some jacked-up street cars and make them dance to your chant."

"You got it, Chick-chick-chickadee. You wantin' discreet, or you wantin' complete?"

"Full meal deal! I want engines, I want sidepipes, I want a beat that will kick my seat!"

"Alien drivers?"

"With extra tentacles please! Supersize me!"

Moonie's eyes shimmer beams of light, and neon Chevys float in the air, with lowrider suspensions that make them hop and jump to the beat. It's razor rap, and the alien drivers are snapping their tentacles to it while Moonie makes it up as he goes. He has holovids stored in his core, and he's got every song and vid ever recorded in my earring, but I like the ones he makes up best, because they're about us.

As I trot on the tread, he gets into his chant, silver head swinging side to side with his urban beat.

"The girl is super,
she's a super-duper,
don't tell me I'm crazy,
say my memory is hazy!
I can say that I knew her,
before the spaceship flew her,
and yo, that girl is famous,
but she'll never be the lamest
never gonna be the tamest
silver bow wow at her side
BOW WOW!
Lay it down one more time!
BOW WOW!
'Cuz she's the Moongirl,
the radical tune girl,
the girl with the sass
gonna kick 'em in th—"

"Hey! Hey! Can you turn that racket down? I'm trying to work here!"

Moonie zips it. Down crash the cars. I kill the treadmill, unclip, turn and see red-faced Franco, fists on his hips, standing behind a big pile of tiger-stripe packs stacked on the exit path. When did he get here?

"Can't you go play with your dog outside or something?"

This burns, and for a moment, I forget the packs. "You know I can't. Outside is dangerous. I can only go out with Mom or Dad."

He shrugs. "Hmmph. I didn't know that. Makes sense, I guess. Well, you keep to your backyard and I'll keep to mine. Just be a good neighbor and kill the audio, okay?"

I want to let it go, but I can't. "You're blocking my exit."

"Huh? Oh. Well, when you're ready to go, let me know. I'll move them."

My heart pounds like the banging sound in an MRI. "Please, Mr. Franco. I need you to move them. Now." He doesn't know. He can't know. And I can't tell him why, but I need the exit clear.

Right *now.*

"Little girl, these things are heavy. When you're ready to go, I'll probably have half of them ..."

I'm so hot the room is melting. I want out of here. I need out of here. I smell the air. I see no smoke, but I smell it everywhere.

Moon Dawdler is prepared. My emergency meds are in his tongue. I can hear the whine of the vial advance. In another second he's going to turn and jab me. I hate the shot, it makes me dopey and ruins my day. "Moonie, heel! I'll be okay if you can push them away."

Moonie barks. "Got your back, Jack." He lowers his head and trots forward, extending my tubes as he gives the bags a push with his head. Moonie is heavy, he carries tanks of oxy and nitro as my safety backup. A pack topples as he shoves them forward. It bangs into a palm.

Mr. Franco shoves back. "Hey! Stop that! You'll damage the plants. They're slated for Mars, you dipshit dog!"

Moonie's ears cock, listening for any change of orders. I give him none. I want out. Right now. I'm hearing glass shatter. All kinds of slow musical notes tinkling in my ears, tumbling end on end. This hasn't happened since I was in the hospital. Triggers. This must be a trigger. A psychologist warned me about triggers. Triggers kill. No, guns kill. Or is it bullets? No. People kill. Bad people.

"Get me out of here, Moonie!"

"On it! Mr. Gorbachev, tear down this wall!"

Moon Dawdler shoves forward, knocking another pack to the side. He shoves again, and the path opens up, but Mr. Franco is now blocking it. He reaches out meaty hands and grabs my dog by the jaw and gives him a terrible shake. "I said knock it off, you rabid mutt! You're damaging my plants!"

Moonie's legs scrabble to get traction to push Mr. Franco out of the way, but he's a big guy, and they just stand in place like wrestlers locked in mortal combat. Mr. Franco is lobster red and shoving back with all his might. I'm right behind Moonie, gripping my hoses, and there's no opening and the dome shatters and all the titanium beams and glass sheets pop once and there's the *whoosh* that sucks the air from my lungs for the last time and red Keds and blue Nikes and green camo Zens are flying as the music tinkles and the glass sprinkles and the beams bounce across the tiles and smash the desks and the EXIT light screams and I'm skittering across the floor like a broken crab and stinky smoke burns my vision and bam goes my back and I'm pinned to the tiles as my skin crinkles and I stare wide-eyed at sparkly flames as they skitter and roll and dance and hiss and spi—

Moonie's eyes. They're sparklies. They're glowing. He's calling my name. "Dixie. Dixie. Dixie. I'm here, Chickadee. Path is clear. Come on, get up!"

He lowers his head. I put my hand on it, and he doesn't feel cold, he feels all warm and loving and soft and furry and the safest thing I've ever felt in my life, and I cling to him as he lifts me up and fills my lungs with air.

Mr. Franco is sprawled out like a dead chicken between the palms.

"Oh, no! Moonie! What have you done?"

Moonie looks at the body. "Man's a fridge, heavy as a Mack truck. Wouldn't move, but Z found a way. You're my priority."

"But what have you done? Is he?"

"Dead? No, but I shoulda' popped a cap in his, I mean, his momma should be fined for bearing such a bonehead. Any dude with half a chestnut for a brain could tell you were in serious distress. You okay, Chickadee?"

I breathe. I see the exit. It's not blocked now. My good hand is shaking, but the room is real again, all green and white and smelling like light. "I'm okay. Is he okay?"

"He be trippin'. I gave him a special cocktail: Haldol 5, Ativan 2, and Benadryl 50. Only way to clear your path."

My chest gets all tight. My voice shakes like my hand. "Moonie, you don't know what you've done."

Maybe it's the mist makers, but Moon Dawdler's eyes look moist, just like a real dog's. He huffs. "Dixie girl, I do know. With you, I'm always all in. Only way I play. Now let's go get yo' mother."

He bit me! Back home, when a dog bites you, you put him down. End. Of. Story!"

We're in the factory side of Norden Moonbase. It's built in one of those huge dead lava tubes that are all over the Moon. This is the base chief's office for FlashPoint Corp, another 3-D printed pod, but this one is stacked, three stories up, and has a big window that looks over all the stations. I can name some. Waste processing. Water storage. Hydrogen production. Titanium extraction. There's bright blue flashes down below. Mom says not to look at them. So I'm looking at Mr. Franco, 'cuz he's a big fat liar.

Mom, Dad, Moonie and me are sitting on one side, Mr. Franco on the other. Two men sit behind the desk. The station chief is one, he's from India, Mr. Anand, but everyone just calls him the Mayor, because he's the final word when it comes to this place. Mom says in Sanskrit *anand* means joy, but he doesn't look very joyful right now. Nor does the guy in the helix-weave cobalt suit sitting next to him. I've never seen him before, but I've seen lawyers.

The lawyer speaks. "I've reviewed the security camera coverage of said event, but the areca palms block much of the interaction. I've heard both submitted testimonies. I have also reviewed a direct recording from the MedGen unit itself."

Moonie is totally silent except for his whispering sides. We've talked. We both are pretty sure how this day is going to go down. We're knee-deep in scree, Moonie says. I think he meant to say something else. Dad's biting his lip. Mom's wringing her hands.

Mom interrupts. "May I comment?"

The Mayor nods. His eyes are bloodshot.

"I sent a halo zip to MedGen." She taps her tablet, and the glass on the Mayor's desk lights up. "The units are designed to protect a patient by any means at their disposal, so long as their method of defense does not cause permanent harm to another human. MedGen insists the unit was acting properly within the AI's human interaction safeties, and you can see the notes from Dr. Varley, director of the AI division, that in his professional opinion the unit *acted with extraordinary insight in solving an ethical dilemma, a tribute to MedGen's algorithms, achieving a solution that relieved the trauma Dixie Wagner experienced from an aggressive individual while at the same time not causing the aggressor permanent harm.*"

Mr. Franco slammed his hand down on his chair's armrest. "Their dog bit me! It dropped me to the ground. I've got bruises! I call that harm!"

Mom speaks in her Valkyrie voice. "The unit *sedated* you, Mr. Franco. It accounted for your weight and measured out a dose any psychiatric doctor would have prescribed for a patient exhibiting your type of aggressive behavior. Be very glad you got the dog's solution ... mine would have been *quite* different."

I'm shocked. I've never heard Mom speak up for Moon Dawdler before. Mr. Franco is sputtering, but the Mayor holds up his hand.

"I have reviewed the security footage as well. I have heard testimony from both sides, and I commend our young lady Dixie here for being present at this hearing. I have also received advice and guidance from our corporate representative. After careful consideration and with due respect to all parties, the company's position is as follows:

"First, the contract you signed with FlashPoint clearly states that the Moon is neutral territory under The Outer Space Treaty; therefore FlashPoint corporate law holds jurisdiction over our properties." The company man nods. For sure he's their lawyer.

"Mr. Franco believes he suffered harm and was acting within his rights to protect valuable corporate assets, indeed, property deemed essential to portions of the Mars mission."

Mr. Franco nods his head like a bulldog. "You're damn right."

The Mayor scowls at Mr. Franco, and he shuts up quick. "On the other hand, the Wagners believe Mr. Franco showed gross disrespect to their daughter's needs—his thoughtless and sometimes belligerent actions causing her severe mental distress. After careful review of the evidence, I concur."

My heart leaps! Moonie is saved!

Mr. Franco turns scalded red, but he keeps his mouth shut as the Mayor stares him down and swipes the face of his desk. A halo document glides over to Mr. Franco. The Mayor continues. "This is a restraining order. Read it. Sign it if you want to keep your job. You are never to be in the same room as Dixie again, or you're out on the next shuttle."

I feel so much happiness I can't even describe it. I'm full of bubbles! Mom is right! *Anand* does mean *joy*!

"Now to the Wagners."

Gulp.

"Corporate is very proud to have Dixie represent those with disabilities on our moon base. She is a wonderful example of triumph over trials, and is a shining symbol of what FlashPoint's space program is all about." The lawyer makes a check on the halo device in his palm, looks up at me and smiles.

Okay, I'm beaming again.

"Additionally, Dr. Wagner, Mr. Wagner, you are both valuable employees, receiving numerous commendations from our esteemed guests, and I've heard nothing but good about you from all but one"—and he scowls again at Mr. Franco—"of our numerous employees. In short, here at FlashPoint, we call people like you *The Right Stuff*."

Dad calls this kind of talk *butter*, and now I'm thinking the Mayor is spreading it on thick. I look at Moonie, pat him on the head. His head feels real cold.

"That said, I regret to inform you I have here an order from corporate that the MedGen AI personality known as Mr. Z is to be terminated, replaced by something more suitable for a closed environment such as our own."

Oh no. Oh no. Oh no.

Dad stands up, and now he does look like Thor, even without a hammer, because he's got thunder. "Are you crazy! The dog was protecting our daughter! This jackass blocked the exit and made her relive the most traumatic ex—"

The Mayor gets loud. For a guy as thin as a string bean, he can punch it out too. "Sit down, Mr. Wagner! I am not happy with their decision, but don't test me!"

Dad stands there, fists bunched. I don't think I've ever seen him mad. I look out the corner of my eyes. Even Mr. Franco looks scared. Finally, Dad sits. Mom starts turning her hands over and under again. I feel sorry for them. For all of them. But mostly for Moon Dawdler. Maybe I start crying, maybe I don't. I'm not telling.

Six endless days.

Make-Me-A-Wish started this thing, and I figure with all this, maybe I deserve another. I know how it works now. But that's future. Tomorrow, they put Moonie down. I get sedated so I don't panic, he goes on autonomous life-support mode, and they jerk out his AI unit and pop in another. I'm done crying. I've cried out every tear I've got over this past week. I could ask Mom and Dad to take me home, and they'd do it, they'd give up everything again for me, just to make me happy. But it isn't fair. None of it's fair, and I'm not going to make it worse.

That AI module. When we were at the hearing, FlashPoint's lawyer slid me a halo, asked me to check one of the boxes they had approved, and they'd send it right up on the next flight. Right there in front of Moonie, like he wouldn't even care. Forgive me, but I told him to go to hell. And I meant it.

So FlashPoint is going to kill Mr. Z and stuff DivaDoll or MissPrissy or My Prancing Pony into Moon Dawdler's head, something more appropriate for their poster girl, something safe for Norden Moonbase. And I'm going to go along with it, because that's what big girls do: they suck it up into their artificial lungs, and they wait and they wait and they wait for the day they can blow it all back out on them, every stinky breath.

But today, Dad says I can have anything, and I say I want to be alone with my dog on the Darkside. Outside the rover, my suit's good for six hours in the frigid darkness, and I want most of that. We suit up and go for a drive, and Dad does it, he drops me off on a crater lip, says the comm is open when I'm ready, and drives away where I can't see him.

Moonie and I sit on a rock, looking up at the stars. You've never seen stars like this, never ever, and I like describing things, but this I can't. It's too big. It's too wonderful. God's out there. He has to be, because it's bigger and brighter than anything you can imagine. I look up at Him, and I say a prayer for Moonie.

As Moonie puffs me with air some escapes within my helmet and I hear the defroster whir like crazy. I pat Moonie on the head with my glove. He makes a "woof" and I hear it. Not because you can hear sound in space—duh, no air—but because I have a PowaPlayah 4 in my ear complete with 2.5 petabytes. Double duh.

Mom and Dad don't know it, but nobody is going to put my dog down but me, and I can't think of any place better to do it than under the light of the Milky Way.

"I love you, Moonie."

He thumps his tail. "Love you too, Chickadee. You're the bravest girl I've ever heard of, and I've been proud to serve. Would do it again, too. Wouldn't change a thing."

"Me either."

Those stars are so bright. I don't care that my helmet says it's minus 280 degrees Fahrenheit/minus 173 Celsius, they make me feel warm.

"Ready, Moonie?"

"I was born ready. You mind your p's and q's, hear?"

Okay, that almost makes me cry again. Maybe I did have a few tears left, maybe I didn't. I'm not telling. But I suck it up. "I hear. Loud and clear."

He cocks his head to the stars. "Then I'm ready. Power to the kitten."

I lean over to Moonie's ear and whisper, *"Best. Dog. Evah."*

He lifts his tail and wags it one last time.

I say, "Moonie: Go fetch. Access my PowaPlayah's reboot code."

"Chickadee, I'm way ahead of ya'. Lightyears."

"Dump memory. All of it."

"Girl, that's *shiny*. 2.5 blank petabytes. All yours."

"Enough to store one MedGen brain?"

"One way to find out."

"Moonie: transfer your core."

"See you on the flip side."

"Word."

We did the math together. I needed four hours and thirty-six minutes alone with my Moon Dawdler. I made Dad promise to leave me alone for five. And Dad keeps his promises.

I scrunch up, tilt my helmet until I see that teaspoon hovering over the Moon. I've got dreams, every girl does.

I hug my silent dog and make a wish.

Tips for Embryonic Pros

BY MIKE RESNICK

Mike Resnick is, according to Locus, *the all-time award winner for short fiction. He has won five Hugos (from a record thirty-seven Hugo nominations), and has won other top awards in the USA, France, Japan, Croatia, Catalonia, Spain, Poland, and China, and has been shortlisted in England, Italy, and Australia. He is the author of more than seventy-five novels, twenty collections, and 285 stories, and is currently the editor of* Galaxy's Edge *magazine and Stellar Guild books. Mike was Guest of Honor at the 2012 Worldcon, was the 2016 recipient of the Writers of the Future Lifetime Achievement Award and has been a Writers of the Future judge since 2010.*

Tips for Embryonic Pros

There are dozens of books on how to write, or at least how to write better, including quite a few aimed at science fiction writers, so I thought rather than repeating what they say it might be more useful to write an article on how to sell your science fiction. After all, that's the name of the game.

So . . .

Submissions. It's been said time and again: work on that opening paragraph. And of course it's true, but once you know the commercial reason, you won't need any serious encouragement to do so.

And the reason is simply this: the average science fiction magazine gets more than a thousand submissions a month. Break it down: that's 200 to 250 a week. Break it down further: it's 40 to 50 a day. That means the average slush reader (let's dignify him or her and call them First Readers) is reading (and passing on, or rejecting) about half a dozen stories an hour. That's one every ten minutes, without taking into account coffee breaks, bathroom breaks, cigarette breaks, and anything else that breaks his concentration even for just a minute or two.

Now do you see why the most important thing in your story is the opening paragraph, followed by the opening page? In the simplest of terms: if you haven't captured the First Reader (or the editor) by then, he'll never get to page 2. After all, he's got hundreds of more stories waiting to be read.

Reading aloud. I know you're careful, I know you realize that typos or even clumsy wordings can put the First Reader in the wrong frame of mind—but you've been sitting at your keyboard for hours, staring at your screen. You *know* there are no typos remaining, so should you send it off?

The answer, of course, is No. It's a lot easier to write clumsy but error-free sentences than you might think, and over the years I have found that the very best way to give your prose the final polish it needs is to read it aloud. (Not to an audience; an empty room will do just as well.) And you'll be amazed at how many vague or clumsy or inadequate sentences got through your word processor's spell-check program.

Novellas. By definition a short story is anything up to 7,500 words, a novelette is 7,500 to 17,500 words, a novella is 17,500 to 40,000 words, and a novel is anything over 40,000 words (though it'll be a cold day in hell before you see a 45,000 or 53,000-word novel on the stands.)

I would advise beginners to avoid novellas. Even if you've got one you *know* will be a powerhouse, wait until you've got a little name recognition before writing and submitting it.

Why?

Because the average prozine runs maybe seven pieces of fiction an issue. The authors' names invariably go on the cover, as indeed they should. But the cover also happens to be the magazine's single most effective selling point, and no editor is going to turn over 40% to 50% of his issue's pages to an unknown name that, when put on the cover, won't sell a single extra copy.

Study your market. Example: you wouldn't submit a delicate fantasy to the 1960s or 1970s *Analog.* You wouldn't insert a sex scene and submit it to a magazine where the last dozen issues avoid even a hint of sex. And so on. Which is a roundabout way of saying: read the markets you are submitting to, and try not to break too many of their unwritten rules.

Return address. Okay, this one will sound like I'm talking to kindergartners—and on this particular subject I sometimes feel like I am. The very first rule of submitting your manuscript, whether it's a 300-word piece of flash fiction or a 300,000-word novel, is to put your address (and these days, make that your e-mail address, since no one submits paper anymore) on the title page.

Simple, right? I mean, why am I wasting time stating the obvious?

The answer is just as simple. I edit *Galaxy's Edge* magazine. The past week alone, we received six—count 'em, six—stories with no return addresses. Can't buy, or even reject, a story if I don't know where to send the contract or the rejection slip—and if I remember the writer's name, it is definitely not for the reasons writers hope editors will remember their names.

Foreign markets. Okay, you've sold a story, and now you hope in a year or three (or six, or nine) it'll be picked up by some reprint anthology. Is there anything else you can do with it?

Well, yes—you can submit it to a dozen or more foreign markets. The beauty of this is that the editor, who may or may not be all that fluent in English, knows (because you have told him, and perhaps even e-mailed him a copy) that an American editor, one who *is* fluent in English and works for the biggest science fiction market in the world, has already bought it, which means that it's a very saleable story. Is it by an unknown? Sure. But many of our established writers are unknown—or nearly so—to foreign markets.

So how do you contact these markets? Who's buying and what are they looking for? There's a web page that's been around well over a decade that will give you what you need to know: it's www.smithwriter.com/foreign_market_list.htm

Simple, believe it or not, as that.

Word counts. This should go without saying, but every editor in the business can get an exact word count once you send him your electronic submission. So it should go without saying (though of course it never does) that you should never lie on the word count to get an extra five or ten dollars. Editors have excellent word-counters and even better memories.

Lag time. Lag time is the length of time between the day your editor buys your story and the day it is published. The thing to keep in mind is that while lag time varies, it is rarely less than six months, and often as much as two years. So there is not much sense writing about, say, the 2020 election (which is held in November) in August. Ditto any other thing that's likely to make headlines, from a particular Super Bowl match-up to the first spaceship to wherever, that figures to make your story obsolescent before it's even published.

Meeting editors. If nothing else, you'll feel more comfortable dealing with someone (by which I mean an editor) you know than someone you have never met. You'll also be able to discuss what he or she is looking for, and what you're working on and will soon be working on, and it never hurts (always assuming you make a good impression) for you to be known to/by an editor.

So how do you meet them, short of flying to Manhattan and staying in a run-of-the-mill $350-a-night hotel and dining on run-of-the-mill $75 midtown Manhattan dinners?

In the traditional way, of course. You go to a convention and meet them there. And no, not just *any* convention. There are more than 100 of them every year just in the United States.

The biggie, in terms of editors, remains Worldcon, which these days is far outnumbered by Comic Con, Dragon Con, and other "general interest" (by which they mean general interest in the fantastic) conventions. Just about every publisher and most editors show up there, so you'll go to their panels to listen to them generalize, and then at nights you'll go to their parties to meet them personally and, if the room isn't jammed, get a little face time with the ones you want to deal with.

World Fantasy Con isn't quite as big, but it has damned near as many editors, and the procedure is the same: go to their panels and parties, and without being pushy try to get some face time with the ones who most interest you.

There are smaller regional cons (Worldcon and World Fantasy Con move around the country each year) that are properly located for you to meet a goodly number of editors: LunaCon in New York and Boskone in Boston (or, in both cases, occasionally just beyond the city limits).

249

And if you read *Locus* or any of the printed or electronic newsletters of the field, you'll see when an editor you want to meet has been invited to a convention that is within commuting distance of where you live, and of course you'll try to get to those when the right names come up.

Agents. I won't say that no competent agent handles unsold writers, but it's relatively rare for the good ones to do so. Reason: they've got dozens of *sold* writers vying for their services.

More to the point, a lot of the better agents prefer to handle novels—well, *books*—exclusively. Fifteen percent of a short story just isn't worth their while, especially if they pay a carrier service to deliver it fifteen blocks away. If you can find an agent who wants you as an unpublished or barely published writer of short fiction, fine—but make sure he or she has some Names in his stable, and find out what his policy is on short fiction, both original and reprint (and foreign) sales.

Anyway, these have been some tips on selling. As for writing good enough to sell, that's what Writers of the Future is for—and indeed, what it specializes in.

Lost Robot

written by

Dean Wesley Smith

inspired by

BOB EGGLETON'S
One of Our Robots Is Missing

ABOUT THE AUTHOR

In the 35 years since his first story in L. Ron Hubbard Presents
Writers of the Future Volume 1, New York Times *bestselling
writer, Dean Wesley Smith published well over two hundred novels
and hundreds and hundreds of short stories and nonfiction books.
Considered one of the most prolific authors in modern fiction, he has over
twenty-three million copies of his books in print.*

*At the moment, he produces novels in four major series, including
the time travel* Thunder Mountain *novels set in the Old West, the
galaxy-spanning* Seeders Universe *series, the urban fantasy* Ghost
of a Chance *series, and the superhero series starring* Poker Boy *and
superhero detective* Sky Tate.

During his career, Dean also wrote a couple dozen Star Trek *novels,
the only two original* Men in Black *novels,* Spider-Man *and* X-Men
*novels, plus novels set in gaming and television worlds. Writing with
his wife Kristine Kathryn Rusch under the name Kathryn Wesley, they
wrote the novel for the NBC miniseries* The Tenth Kingdom *and other
books for* Hallmark Hall of Fame *movies.*

*He wrote novels under dozens of pen names in the worlds of comic
books and movies, including novelizations of almost a dozen films, from*
X-Men *to* The Final Fantasy *to* Steel *to* Rundown.

Dean also worked as a fiction editor off and on, starting at Pulphouse
Publishing, *then at* VB Tech Journal, *then Pocket Books, and now
at WMG Publishing where he and Kristine Kathryn Rusch serve as
executive editors for the acclaimed Fiction River anthology series. He
took over the editorship of the acclaimed* Pulphouse Magazine *in 2018.*

Lost Robot

A SKY TATE MYSTERY STORY

ONE

Finding clients just never seems to be an issue for me. Not sure if that stems from the vast number of total idiots in the world or my ability to attract those infected by idiocy. Not saying all of my clients are idiots. Most aren't, but most seem to be dealing with stupidity of one sort or another.

In fact, lately, my clients have been wonderful women, attractive women.

My new client's name was Jean. Her full and real name was Jeanette King. No middle name, no initial, nothing. Just Jeanette King. She went by Jean. And first time I saw her walk into the Rocky's Bar in the strip mall off Flamingo, her beauty made the place heat up, even though the Vegas weather was nice at eighty and Rocky's air conditioning was working just fine.

Jean had a full head of bright red hair that flared out from her head like a nova and ran down over her shoulders like a lava flow. (So sue me, I get a little descriptive when it comes to Jean.)

She had the standard green eyes that went with bright red natural hair and the fair skin covered with a sea of light tan freckles. The freckles went down her neck and vanished under her white silk blouse.

I got all that detail and she hadn't even started across the small bar yet. Being a superhero detective and super observant of everything had its advantages and disadvantages at times.

Jean had on jeans (go figure), running shoes, and a smile that seemed to light up her red hair even more as she came toward me across the small dance floor of the bar.

She had been referred to me by a friend at the main police station and I knew instantly I was going to have to send him a bottle of fine whiskey for the referral, no matter what her case turned out to be.

I had been sitting at the bar, working on a Diet Coke, waiting for her, when she came in. She reached me and my open mouth and staring eyes and stuck out her hand.

"You must be Sky Tate," she said.

"I am," I said, managing to get my hand into her fine-skinned grip.

"Oh, you're a woman," Jean said.

Then she blushed.

I loved the blush. It lit up the trail of her freckles.

"I noticed that too when I took a shower this morning," I said.

She blushed even more.

The bar got warmer.

Lots of people thought I was a guy because I had a habit of wearing the standard detective gray trench coat and a gray fedora. The hat tended to hide my longer hair because I kept it tied up and covered when working, and the trench coat covered what assets I did have without any issue at all.

Plus my face was long and I had what many call a Roman nose. I call it a beak.

So with all that, being mistaken for a guy with the name Sky Tate wasn't anything new. And I often used that to my advantage in cases.

"I'm sorry," Jean said.

"Don't be," I said, taking off my hat and coat and letting my hair fall down over my shoulders. "I tend to hide some. A detective thing."

She nodded to that. Amazing how using the detective-thing excuse allowed me to get away with a lot.

I motioned that we should move to a small table off to one side so we could talk in private, even though Rocky was the only other person in the place and most of the time he was hard of hearing. One reason I liked the place.

One of my superpowers was being able to completely read a person's problems by simply shaking their hand. When I shook Jean's hand I saw her problem and why she wanted to hire me.

Her father, Carl, was dying. Nasty cancer. He didn't have long, that much was clear.

Now I might be a superhero, but I sure didn't have the power to keep anyone alive or bring them back from the dead. But her problem was that her father, who seemed to be clear in the head with all other matters, had started telling her this wild story that back in the 1960s, when he was just out of college and before he headed to Vietnam, he had found a gigantic sentient robot up by Lake Mead.

And for a time, he and the robot had become friends. From what her father had said, the robot could read his thoughts, kind of like I was reading Jean's thoughts when I touched her hand. It seems that the robot had gotten separated from the others of his kind and was hiding. It had sworn his father to secrecy.

Then her father had been drafted into the war in Vietnam and by the time he had returned, the robot had vanished. Her father had told no one, not even his wife, until he finally told his daughter as he was dying.

Now I am sure that any normal detective, or anyone for that matter, would have laughed, but I was no normal detective, and over the two hundred years of my life, I had seen a lot of really strange stuff. Granted, no giant robots, but just about everything else.

"First off," I said to Jean, "I am sorry about your father's illness."

She looked startled.

"Another detective thing," I said, smiling at her. "So you want to tell me what I can do to help?"

She nodded, took a deep breath, and then basically told me the story I already knew about her father and his tale of a giant robot in Lake Mead.

I nodded all the way through the story, not saying a thing.

Finally Jean said, "You're not laughing."

I wanted to say that I would never laugh at a woman as good-looking as she was, but instead said, "I take all my client's stories seriously."

"Thank you," she said, blushing slightly again. "All I really want is to let my father know I am taking him seriously and looking for his lost robot."

She looked like she might burst into tears at that moment, but managed to hold it together. I could only imagine the courage this was taking for her to tell anyone such a wild story.

"I understand," I said, wanting to reach out and touch her hand, but resisting.

She nodded and I gave her a moment to compose herself. Besides, I loved just staring at her. Not very professional for a detective like me, I must admit, but I didn't often face someone as beautiful as Jean.

"I would like to meet your father," I said to her after a long moment. "Would that be possible?"

"So you will help me?"

"I will do my best, and nothing less," I said. "We will make sure your father knows we believe him and are doing our best for him in his final days."

Now tears really did reach her eyes and she smiled.

"How much is your fee?"

"Let's not worry about that," I said. "Can I meet your father now?"

She nodded. And gave me directions to his house, which I already knew, of course.

"I will follow you," I said. "I have a white Cadillac that I can do a little research in and get my assistants to help while we drive."

I didn't have any assistants, but I figured I would set that up in case I learned something from her father I needed to cover.

Again she smiled and stood. "You have no idea how much I appreciate this."

"Let's see what we can do," I said.

I had little hope at all that we could do much more than help a dying man get some peace, but watching Jean walk from that bar ahead of me was worth far more than I wanted to admit. Natural beauty like hers just didn't walk into my life that often.

TWO

Jean's father's house sat in one of those desert subdivisions that looked all the same. All were gated with winding streets and evenly spaced palm trees. Only slight differences in the desert landscaping of each brown-toned house and the large address numbers on the front by the two-car garages allowed anyone to tell them apart. I hated subdivisions like this one, no matter how well-kept they looked. They felt more like warehouses for humans than actual distinctive places to live. That's why I lived in the Ogden Condos that were square in the middle of the downtown area. It was a beautiful high-rise condo that looked out over the constant party that was Fremont Street.

Jean waited for me to park on the street, her massive red hair glowing in the afternoon sun like a goddess. I had met my share of real goddesses over the two centuries, including Lady Luck herself, but none of them could hold a candle to Jean's beauty.

We went through the open garage and into the kitchen area of the modern home. It was clean, as I would have expected, with no dishes in the sink or on the counter.

The morning paper, actual old-style print newspaper, took up part of the kitchen table, and the sounds of a football game came from another room. Everything was in brown tones, including the kitchen tile and eggshell paint on the walls.

The living room was more brown, with expensive furniture and only splashes of color from a pillow or a flower in a vase.

I knew Jean's father lived here alone since her mother had died five years before. And I knew he was well-off when it came to money. Clearly someone did the cleaning for him as well.

As we entered the living room, Jean said, "Daddy, I have company. Someone to meet you."

The man with the balding head in the chair glanced back, then clicked off the television and stood without issue. Clearly he was in good shape except for the cancer that was about to kill him.

"This is detective Sky Tate," Jean said. "Detective Tate, this is my father Carl King."

Carl laughed. "You hired a detective?"

Jean just smiled at him fondly. "I wanted to see what we could find out."

I had left my trench coat and fedora in the car and still had my hair down, so I looked fairly normal.

"Nice to meet you, Detective," Jean's father said, reaching forward to shake my hand.

And the moment I touched his dry skin and firm grip, I knew for a fact he was telling Jean the truth about finding a giant robot in Lake Mead.

He really had.

I flat didn't know what to think about that.

The robot had a pointed head, two rocket-looking packs on its back, two arms, two legs, and no mouth. Its eyes were black as night and Carl had communicated with it through thoughts.

The robot had clearly been hiding for some time, mostly underwater, when Carl came into contact with it in a cave in the rocks in an area of Lake Mead that was now, all these years later, above the water line, since the lake level had gone down so far.

I held onto his hand a moment too long, then finally let go. The shock that over fifty years ago there was a giant robot in Lake Mead took me a moment to adjust to, I had to admit.

"I am sure sorry to hear about your illness, sir," I said.

He shrugged. "I survived Nam, figured something was going to take me out eventually."

I smiled at him and then at Jean.

Jean got us all some water and we sat at the kitchen table, with Jean between me and her dad.

Then I leaned forward and looked him directly in the eye, making sure he understood I was listening as intently as anyone had ever listened to him. That was one of my main superpowers, besides reading thoughts and the ability to teleport.

Then I said simply, "Tell me about this robot you found."

And he did, detail for detail, awkward at times because he clearly hadn't told this story much at all. He started by detailing the times of the 1960s, about how he had gone up to Lake Mead to get away from the knowledge that he was going to be drafted. He had been trying to decide whether to go into the service or flee to Canada. He had already run through his student deferment.

He had been using a small rented rowboat that day and found the cave in the rocks late in the afternoon, hidden from view of the main traffic on the lake. The robot had been underwater and when he rowed into the cave, it appeared.

Turns out it was lonely. After the shock at being able to understand what a giant robot was saying, Carl said he had relaxed and it seemed the two of them had similar issues. Carl felt lost and the robot was lost, separated from the other robots in his group.

The robot had been hiding there since right after the dam had filled.

Over the next few weeks, Carl went back every day and, by talking to the robot, Carl came to realize he needed to face his future and not hide from it. So he told the robot he hoped to survive the war and return. He said that knowing that robot was there kept him alive in Vietnam more than anything.

But when he got back, the robot was gone. Once or twice a year, Carl went back to the same area, searching for it, but could not find any sign of it.

"My only hope," Carl said finally, "was that the robot found his own kind."

I nodded.

It had been clear from Carl's thoughts that the existence of that robot had got him through the war and kept him going through hard times in his life.

"Can you show me on a map exactly where this cave is?"

He frowned, clearly feeling slightly shocked that someone was giving his story complete credence, and then stood and headed off down the hallway to a back room.

Jean reached over and touched my arm, a smile on her face and tears in her eyes. "Thank you."

I flat loved her touch, but strangely enough, at the moment, my entire interest had turned to finding that robot. I really believed that it had existed, as Carl said, and the superhero detective in me really wanted to find it.

Carl came back with a map and easily showed me exactly the rock wall where the cave was. I asked if I could take the map and he agreed.

"I got some friends who might be able to help me with this," I said, standing and refolding the map. "We will see what we can find."

He shook my hand again and I could read how pleased he was that I was taking him seriously. He had no expectations, but clearly I had done what Jean wanted me to do in his last days.

Jean walked me out to my car and once again shook my hand. I could feel her interest in getting to know me more and how thankful she felt. I didn't mind, but at the moment I had a lost robot to find, or at least prove it had existed at one point in time. No small case. But I loved the challenge.

And I didn't get that many really challenging cases after two hundred years on the job.

THREE

Every aspect of life has gods and superheroes attached. I am a superhero in the detective area. We live a long time, possibly forever, and we have special powers that help us in our profession. There are food gods, sports gods of every type, and even poker gods and superheroes. One of the most famous is Poker Boy. His girlfriend is a superhero in the hotel hospitality area and Poker Boy calls her Front Desk Girl, but not to her face.

What I needed for help was a superhero in the area of lost-and-found items. And in the Las Vegas area, I only knew of one.

Plane.

I mean, I at least had a second name that went with Sky, but

Plane, as far as I knew, only went by one. Just Plane, the kind that flies, not the boring kind. That was his standard line.

Plane topped the scales at well over four hundred pounds and lived in a giant home just outside of Vegas that had to be the size of a major grocery store, filled to the ceiling in most places with stuff.

He always wore silk suits and bright ties that he never tied completely. He wore standard, white tennis shoes with his silk suits and kept a baseball cap on his head at all times.

On top of that, Plane was a hoarder. He would be a cliché if he wasn't older than I was and as rich as most countries from buying and selling stuff.

He was one of those hoarders who knew exactly where everything was in every pile and the current value of it on the open market. I had only been in his home once, about five years before, but he took a liking to my beak of a nose. Not sure why, maybe it was so strange it was collectible.

So I parked my caddy in my spot in the Ogden parking garage, and teleported out to his place. I had warned him I had something really special that needed finding and he had just grunted and said, "Get here before dinner."

Since it was only just before noon, I figured I had some time.

I teleported there and found him sitting in his big office chair surrounded by at least a dozen computer screens, all showing auctions going around the world.

He put his finger up for me to be silent and wait and less than one minute later he sighed and turned to face me. From what I could tell he had lost all the auctions he had been bidding on. I said nothing. Last thing I wanted was to get a collector going on the unfairness of the new world of computers and eBay and the internet.

"So what are you looking for?"

"A giant robot. Real, telepathic, about sixty feet or so tall, vanished in the Lake Mead area in the 1960s."

He stared at me for a moment with tiny, dark eyes that I

wasn't certain could see out of the rolls of fat on his forehead and cheeks, then said, "You aren't kidding, are you?"

I shook my head. "Client's father made friends with it back in the 1960s before he shipped off to Vietnam. The robot was gone when he got back and now the guy is dying of cancer and wanted to tell his story."

Plane knew my powers, knew I had read the guy's mind to see if he was telling the truth. So he just nodded.

I pulled out the folded map and put it on a pile of papers near Plane so he could see it, then pointed at the spot. "A cave that was at the water line back then. He says he goes back out there twice a year to see if the robot has returned."

Plane nodded and stood. "You want to jump us there or you want me to."

"Safer if you do it," I said. I didn't feel good about trying to land someone of his bulk on a pile of rocks.

He nodded and a moment later we were standing on rocks about a hundred feet above the waterline of the lake. There was a dry wind blowing and I felt damned happy the temperatures were moderate today. On a hot summer day, this would be an oven.

Plane was looking behind us and after a moment pointed and said, "There."

He jumped us into the mouth of a cave that clearly had been under water at one point.

"This is the place I saw in his mind," I said, nodding.

Plane again jumped us to a spot above the waterline in the back of the cave, then said simply, "Brace yourself, this rewinding time thing can get a little crazy-making."

With that, outside the cave the sun started blinking like a strobe light as Carl took us back in time until eventually in front of us the cavern filled with water.

Then he slowed it down and I caught a glimpse of a young man in a rowboat.

"Here," I said.

Plane had already stopped time.

"No worry, he can't see us," Plane said. "We're outside the time stream."

I nodded, thankful he had answered my unasked question.

As we watched, a young guy, clearly the Carl I had met before he went off to war, rowed slowly into the cave.

And as he got to the back edge, just as I'd seen in his mind, a pointed-headed robot came up out of the water slowly. I found it very impressive that Carl didn't instantly panic and row like hell out into the lake, but eventually it became clear they were talking.

After Carl left that day, the robot simply sank back into the water.

Plane sped us forward to the next day and then the next until finally it was clear that Carl was saying goodbye. This time the robot watched him row away before he sank back into the water.

Three months later, we watched the robot wade out of the now-shallow cave and into deep water.

"Okay," Plane said, "I got the robot's signature. If it is still on the planet, I'll find it."

Plane flashed us back to the present. Then seemed to focus far away.

I waited as patiently as I could until he returned to his beady eyes. "He's still here, along with a couple dozen friends."

"What?" I asked, stunned.

Plane pointed to the deepest part of the lake in front of us, "They are living down there. And I got a hunch this is bigger than both of us."

I nodded and looked slightly upward. "Laverne. I think Plane and I have found a problem. Would you join us for a moment?"

In all my years, that was only the third time I had called Laverne, Lady Luck herself. She ran everything and was the most powerful god there was.

She appeared beside me dressed in a dark silk power suit that fit her thin body perfectly. She had her long dark hair pulled back tight, which gave her thin face a stern look.

BOB EGGLETON

She flat scared the hell out of me. The most powerful being in all the universe would do that to a normal person.

"Yes," she said.

I did a very quick summary of my client, her father, and what Plane and I had just seen in the 1960s.

"Pointed heads, jet packs on the back, dark eyes?" Lady Luck asked.

Plane and I both nodded.

"Maybe thirty of them down there," Plane said.

"Well, shit," Lady Luck said. "That's where they went."

"You knew about them?" I asked, trying to keep my voice level.

She nodded, staring down into the lake below us. "Back when we fought the Titans, before Atlantis, we created them to help us and built a world for them to live on. Most were destroyed in the battles, but they helped turn the tide. After the war and then with Atlantis going down, we lost track of the survivors because without our help they couldn't go home. And honestly I had never thought of them for centuries until now. "We called them Lightning."

"That's why the lightning bolts painted on them?"

She nodded. "Amazing they are still here and hiding after all these years. We need to get them out of there and get them home. More than likely they have no idea the war is even over."

"The war with the Titans?" Plane asked.

Laverne nodded.

My knowledge of the history of the gods and superheroes was slim, at best. I just couldn't imagine how long ago that war was, or how old Lady Luck really was.

"Where is their home?" I asked.

"Deep in space," she said, waving her hand and dismissing my question. "I'm going to need help with this. I want to thank you both for this incredible find. We owe it to the Lightning to get them home.

"I have one favor to ask," I said before she could vanish. And I asked and she laughed and said, "Of course."

So three days later Jean and I were in a rented speedboat that had towed Carl in a small rowboat out to the area where I knew the robots were. I hadn't told Jean or her father a thing, just that I had a surprise for them. Both of them thought I was being stupid, but they went along.

The evening was still warm and thankfully the wind was fairly calm, so the waves on the lake weren't bad at all. I normally wasn't a fan of small boats, but for this, I wasn't going to miss it, even if I had to dogpaddle out here.

After we unhooked Carl's rowboat from the speedboat, I turned off the engine and pointed to a spot. We watched him row toward it. For a man near death, he was surprisingly strong.

As he reached the spot, a metal pointed head slowly eased up out of the water.

We all just watched as the robot got about halfway out of the water and stopped, facing Carl directly.

I knew that was the last of the robots left, the very one that Carl had met. All the others had left last night under cover of darkness. Lady Luck had asked if it wanted to stay behind for just a short time and say goodbye and it had. It really was the last of its kind left.

Clearly the two of them were having a conversation, but from our distance, we couldn't hear Carl's side of it, even though he was speaking aloud.

Finally Carl nodded and the robot moved a little farther way and then silently its rocket packs fired and it lifted out of the water and into the air, not even causing a slight wave. In a moment it was gone into the late afternoon blue sky.

I started the speedboat and we went over to where Carl just sat in the rowboat, head down, smiling. We got him back into the speedboat and the rowboat tied to the stern.

"Are you all right, Dad?" Jean said, putting a jacket over Carl's shoulder.

Carl smiled and nodded. "He's just like me. He's a survivor, and he finally gets to go home after his war. And now, I feel like I do as well."

Then Carl just sat there smiling in the back of the boat and there just wasn't a thing Jean or I could say.

Five weeks later I got a call from Jean that her father had passed away in his sleep, peacefully. I attended the funeral two days later.

Two weeks after that Jean called me to talk. I figured she wanted to know how I had done what I had managed to do for her father. And that was going to be a tough topic to get through.

But it didn't turn out that way.

The two of us sat with glasses of wine and then had a great dinner. And besides getting to know a little more about each other, we talked most about her father and his incredible life, how he had finally gotten to come home from his war.

And how he had helped his friend do the same.

Are You the Life of the Party?

written by

Mica Scotti Kole

illustrated by

JOSH PEMBERTON

ABOUT THE AUTHOR

Mica is a freelance developmental editor based near Detroit, Michigan. She started writing stories in kindergarten, opening with a colorful series based on her zoo-animal Duplos (involving, at one point, flying go-carts that ran on . . . coconuts?). She is also the curator of Free Writing Events, a Twitter account and website, which compiles and promotes free-to-enter online writing events and contests to over 20,000 authors (it's how she discovered Writers of the Future). She writes YA fantasy long-form and adult science fiction short-form, and her current obsessions are home-brewing, Steven Universe, and board games that start with the letter M. She is also the founder and host of the #Write4Life charity event, which aims to help other writers get edited and agented. She quit her day job to pursue the dream of writing in 2016, and this is her third professional publication. She will be querying her third novel next year.

ABOUT THE ILLUSTRATOR

Josh Pemberton was born in 1987 in Concord, Massachusetts, and grew up in Seattle, Washington.

From posters of oceans and dinosaurs on his walls as a young child, Josh has held a consistent fascination in the capacity of images to ignite his imagination and has sought to understand and unravel that mystery ever since.

He went on to graduate with a major in studio art at Reed College in Portland, Oregon. Then spent three years studying in the drawing and painting atelier program at Gage Academy of Art, and finally went on to receive his MFA in illustration at the Academy of Art University, in San Francisco, California.

Primarily working with traditional materials, themes of the mythic, fantastic, and natural world hold his interest. Josh currently is seeking to establish himself within the illustration world while continuing to work with private clients and commission work.

Are You the Life of the Party?

Q*uestion Seven: How do you like to be kissed?*

Eddie tapped his front teeth with the clickable end of his pen. The waxy pages of the old *Teenspeak* magazine shone blue in his hands, reflecting the blinking lights of the console as he considered his options. *A: soft and sweet. B: deep and dark* ... He laughed aloud at the absurdity. The Engineers were good about giving him stuff to read, but they missed the mark on his gender and age.

A speaker on the control panel blared, "Operator, request closure of Gate B-4."

Eyeing his quiz choices, Eddie palmed the mic button and said, "You got it." It was old habit; the Engineers didn't need confirmation. All they needed was for him to cut the connection and do what he was told, which he did, right after placing the folded magazine on a switch panel and circling A for *soft and sweet.*

Trust your old dad on this one, Rissa, he thought. *It's best to keep away from the rough ones.*

Swiveling in his chair, Eddie fiddled with a monitor and cocked his head. He heard a monotone rumble as Gate B-4 closed. Beyond the glittering console and the bulletproof glass of his tower, Eddie could make out the rat's maze of thirty-foot partitions spreading off into the distance below him. Bleak and dim, the nearest section was empty of subjects, human or non.

He leaned back in the chair and flipped up the magazine. *Question Eight: There's a house party this weekend. You:*

Eddie crossed off *are throwing it* and smiled to himself. "I don't think so, Rissa." Then he circled C: *are getting everyone to go!*

"You'll get there, sweetie," he told the empty room. His Rissa had always been introverted—she had a misanthrope for a dad, so it was no surprise—but she was so much *better* than he was, good-looking, smart, and so nice to everyone.... Before the prank, she'd had more friends at one time than Eddie had ever had in his life.

He made a fist, gripping the corner of the magazine. "Some friends," he growled to no one.

A human scream made him glance toward the windows. He leaned forward, squinting into the dimness of the labyrinth. One of the Skitters was climbing the wall nearest him, six of its eight legs finding purchase on the specially designed ridges. He'd grown accustomed to them by now, the grotesque, nightmare look of them—the way they seemed to put shape to his pain. But for a moment, as he watched, his gut twisted.

In its other two legs, the thing held a girl.

She was a teenager, short and blond and still struggling, her arms beating against the sharp metal claws. The memory hurtled forward, of two boys holding Rissa. Keeping her back as they made her watch ...

But it was Eddie who did the watching now, his gaze flashing across the silver grips of the Skitter as the blond girl writhed and squealed.

The console blared again. "Operator," came the computer's mechanical voice, "request pivot of Wall T-7."

Eddie made a few quick strokes across the nearest touchscreen, and a wall segment near the Skitter spun in place, closing off a passage in front of Eddie's control tower. The Skitter crab-walked over to the Wall and vanished, the Feeder-girl still screaming.

As Eddie smoothed the ridges on the Wall, preventing anyone from following the Skitter, he caught movement. A group of human subjects—Feeders—sprinting around the corner of the labyrinth. Eddie snickered as their heads tilted back, their eyes scaling the impassable Wall. One of them collapsed to his knees while another tried to scrabble up the partition.

The scream on the other side died abruptly, and Eddie leaned back in his chair.

Question Nine, he read, from the magazine. *What is the best holiday for throwing a party?*

His fingers tightened on the pen. There were four options, but his eyes were glued to *C: your birthday.*

He could still remember the pink decorations.

Eddie leaned forward and pressed the mic button. "Engineer, request access to subject log."

"Granted," came the warbling voice. It never had cause to deny him.

The red window popped up on his screen, and he clicked *OK* and scanned the names of the Feeders with a fingertip. To his surprise, most of them came from high-numbered holding tanks; had the experiment shifted from old stock to new? Last week, he'd submitted a Human Feedback report, where he'd mused that people in long-term containment wouldn't run as fast as the fresh ones. It was the sort of thing the Engineers might not notice on their own, the whole reason they used people like him.

His heart sped up. If they had liked his report . . .

Eddie scanned the subject log, eyes darting between human names. When he found what he was searching for, he cried out the word "Bingo!" as he slammed the bright console with a fist.

In response, a Wall pivoted somewhere in the distance. Eddie corrected the error before he could get reprimanded, grinning widely at the familiar name in the log. He'd memorized every one of the little pricks: the bullies that had pinned her, the so-called friends that had laughed, even the witnesses that had shown up in court. And one of those names was in his labyrinth—a Feeder! It was as close as Eddie had come to a Christmas since the Engineers had taken control.

Mentally he recalled what this particular offender had done: stood up before God and jury and said that the kids who'd destroyed his little girl's life "hadn't meant no harm, Your Honor. It was just a little *prank.*"

"*Character witness* my ass," Eddie spat, peering through the glass again. The group of Feeders were still huddled in front of Wall T-7, dazed and terrified. Dumb brats, they ought to be running.

Leaning back, he wondered what it felt like, to finally get what was coming to you. Someday, the Engineers would throw Eddie to the Skitters, and then he would know.

But he'd been waiting an awful long time.

He scanned the name again. It was not marked *Terminated*. Eddie flipped a switch, and Wall T-6 closed.

"Unauthorized closure," came the mechanical voice as the Feeders were shut inside an impenetrable cube. "Immediate pivot of Wall T-6 ordered. Skitter has completed the feed-scan, repeat, order of immediate pivot—"

Eddie muted the mic and reopened *Teenspeak*.

Question Ten, he read, and again heard the scuttling, just out of sight under his tower. *The first thing you do when you get to any party . . . is ruin the birthday girl's life*, he thought, his jaw working. She'd been passing out cake when the girls had snuck off, stealing plus-size underwear straight out of her dresser. Rissa had dropped her plate when she'd seen her panties waving, paraded around the room like a flag. . . .

His gaze slipped to the labyrinth, where the group of Feeders broke into pieces. Running in all directions, every man for himself.

He snorted. It was always like that, with teenagers. Each Maze operator ran a different demographic, depending on how their past life made them useful. Martin ran toddlers because he'd been a child-killer; Wu ran middle-aged men because he'd been abused. But for all the variety, Eddie felt that his groups were best. None of his teens ever gave a crap about anyone but themselves, and this made it easy to pick them all off.

More screaming, that old shrill cry of terror; it had haunted his dreams the first years he'd been stationed. Beneath his observation deck, there came a clang and steel screeching, and a noise that could only be blood splatter.

JOSH PEMBERTON

In the magazine, Eddie marked option D. Out loud, he said: "'Say hello to the host.'"

More scuttling, a pot-and-pan banging. He popped open a cam-channel to listen closer. Someone retched, and the screaming wore louder.

Eddie scowled. This was taking longer than usual. The Engineers must be having a blast. The Maze was their favorite way to study the Feeders, and the longer it went on, the more they could learn. It was bad news for humanity that these kids weren't dead yet; with enough information, the Skitters could change how they fed, making it harder to fight them out in the field.

The final scream died, and Eddie relaxed. There was only one Feeder left now, a boy; he didn't check to see if it was the boy from his shit list, but he liked to think it was. The kid was backed into the towering Wall, so Eddie reached over and switched the climbing ridges back on. The boy jumped, but he wasn't stupid; reaching into the special slots, he ascended toward the hope of escape.

The boy did good, got about twenty feet before Eddie pulled back on the ridge-lever. It slid through the track panel, reaching off-mode with a click. The ruts meant for the Skitter went smooth again, and the boy fell and broke his leg.

As if he and the Skitter were somehow connected, Eddie felt its scanner homing in on the boy.

"How does it feel, to be helpless?" Eddie said. "How does it feel to have nowhere to run?"

The boy tried to roll over. The Skitter was faster.

On the quiz, Eddie tallied his points.

There was a buzz of feedback as the Engineer overrode Eddie's mute command.

"All subjects deceased," burbled the voice, as if it had never been silenced. "Disobedience Report in progress for Operator Bowman. You have one-point-five warnings remaining."

"I know, I know," Eddie muttered, not bothering to turn on his mic. He flipped the page, trailing a finger down the smooth paper. The quiz results were listed in bubbly pink font. Pink had been her favorite color.

"Statement retracted," the Engineer said abruptly, its voice crackling with static. "Leniency assessed. Combat-usable data gathered within unplanned scenario. Enclosed space, no escape, kill rate slower than usual. Possible mercy code: check command drive for errors. Scenario filed for future testing."

Eddie looked up. In his mind's eye, he saw the wooden beam in the living room, still wrapped in pink crepe paper and sprouting balloons. He'd gone down the next morning to clean up the cake, and found his daughter and her jump-rope hanging down.

"Mercy," he mumbled. "You don't say."

Then he turned to his quiz results: *You are the perfect partyer!*

A soft grin spread across his face. "See there, Rissa? You woulda been great."

Release from Service

written by

Rustin Lovewell

illustrated by

EMERSON RABBITT

ABOUT THE AUTHOR

Rustin Lovewell is a native New Englander now living in Maryland with his wife, daughter, and overly yappy dog/mobile alarm system. Full of contradictions, he is an immunologist when not writing fantasy stories, a soccer player when not rolling d20s, and a snowboarder if he can ever find enough snow.

Rustin has been an avid reader since he discovered Tom Swift's incredible inventions and the nightmares hidden within the pages of Goosebumps. His favorite stories have always been those that pointed left and then twisted right, only to twist yet again, before finally knocking the reader out with a "Luke, I am your father" roundhouse. After reading several such pieces, he wondered if he could come up with one of his own. He did, and he wrote it, and it was awful. Of course, that's how it starts. He's loved trying to get it right ever since. This is his first published work of fiction.

ABOUT THE ILLUSTRATOR

Emerson Rabbitt was born in 1996 in La Crosse, Wisconsin.

He became incredibly inspired by the Warhammer 40,000 tabletop game, and the likes of H. R. Giger's concepts for Ridley Scott's Alien, *and has been illustrating ever since.*

Emerson pursued his passion for creating and attended the Minneapolis College of Art Design, where he set his sights on becoming a concept artist within the videogame industry. Currently, he is sharpening his skills on private projects and is always in search of new opportunities to learn and grow.

Release from Service

Would you kill a child?

That is one of the questions they ask you. The Recruiters pay attention to every aspect of how you respond. Do you recoil in shock? Twist your face in revulsion? Do you pause and consider the question, and, if so, how long do you take before responding? They measure these things, noting every tic and breath and word choice. You can lie, of course, and they measure that, as well. Is your lie convincing? Do you glance to the left? How much conviction is in your voice?

For most, *Would you kill a child?* is a difficult question.

I answered immediately. Worst of all, I meant it.

1. ARRIVAL

I arrive in the island city of Xu on a perfect morning. One with blinding tropical sunshine pounding down from a cloudless blue sky. The Mantis keeps the cowl on his cloak pulled over his head and pays no attention to the weather; the only thing that ever interests my master are people, and then only in a distant, clinical manner. He leads me through a bustling waterfront of sailors and landsmen, where dockworkers load barrels of molasses and hogsheads of beef and piles of timber onto merchant ships bound for the mainland. This is his home city, but my first time in an island colony, and while I'm accustomed to the heat, I'm not used to such humidity. Sweat beads across my scalp and soaks my shirt, making my skin chafe where my twin blades sit in their inverted sheaths against my back. I could remove the cloak draping my shoulders, but that would expose my blades and hint at what I am. Anonymity is a powerful weapon—that was the first lesson my master taught me.

The Mantis brings me to a rooftop overlooking a central plaza. Crushed basalt cobblestones pave the square, a striking feature unique to the volcanic islands. A twelve-foot statue of a regal-looking man in flowing robes dominates the middle of the space. At the far end is the mansion of the Tyressry of Xu, a man with the family name Kaab. I don't know his given name, only that he is one of the *Kyo'Vyar*, the People of the Eye, and the administrator of this colony. He must have failed in some extraordinary capacity for his peers to send for us.

The Mantis hands me the telescopic lens he keeps in his pouch. "What do you see?" he says.

I let my eyes scan the plaza below, then double-check with the lens. "A pair of couriers moving past the statue. An elderly *Kyo'Rusalk* just below us selling folding hand-fans. A half-dozen pedestrians entering the square from the south. There is a beggar crone sitting against the building at the western edge, two sentries with muskets guarding the stairs leading to the mansion, and a garden keeper watering the boxed plants on the terrace. The gardener moves like a dancer, meaning he is likely a bodyguard with training."

My master waits for me to finish. When I say nothing further, his hand snaps out from beneath his cloak and cracks across my face. I reel from the blow, pinpricks of light blooming in my vision like stars. Blood tastes tacky and metallic in my mouth.

I've missed something.

The Mantis watches me. There is no malice in his gaze. No passion, no anger. Just curiosity tinged with annoyance.

I wipe my mouth and reassess the people below, checking each with the lens. The vendor, the guards, the old beggar crone ... Her hands are wrong.

An elderly beggar living in the isles would have hands the color of dark bronze, veins like tree roots and dirty fingernails.

This woman's hands are clean, calloused but young. Otherwise, her disguise is flawless. Her face remains hidden underneath a wide hood, silver strands of hair dangling out the front. She wears a filthy robe and sits on a shred of sailcloth, her back against the side of a building, head drooped and posture off-kilter as if she suffers a bent spine. She holds a chipped bowl out before her.

"That isn't a beggar," I say.

My master slides his gaze back to the square. Had I missed it a second time, he would have dismissed me back to the ship.

"You should know," the Mantis says. "She is an acquaintance of ours."

The fact that this revelation doesn't come with a slap means he didn't really expect me to know, but he does expect me to figure it out. I suppress my frustration. The Mantis is one of the oldest of the *Kyo'Assyn*, second only to the Moth, and his lethality is legend. What he is not, however, is forthcoming.

I can't see the woman's face, so I scour my memory. I've forged few relationships in the decade since my recruitment. There have been some few marks that required intimacy, but they are all dead. There is my family, who I haven't seen in years, but those hands are too young to be my mother's, and while my sister would be of an age, she lost the tip of one middle finger to a falling boulder when she was eight, and this woman's hands are whole. Not a family member, then. That left the other *Kyo'Assyn*.

The People of the Carapace number only seven, plus their apprentices, and only among each other do they form any real kinship. My master is a step beyond this; I believe the Mantis incapable of friendship. He is endlessly curious, but behind his cold scrutiny there is only more coldness, as if he is not a man but a golem made from clay, a thing built and not born. His peers afford him distance, but great respect.

I have trained with a choice few of those peers, a regal pyromancer called the Firefly and a surgeon-trained killer called the Locust, and I've heard descriptions and stories of all the others. The Mantis would, on occasion, take their apprentices to co-train with me, as well.

One pupil, a girl my own age apprenticed to the Firefly, joined us several times. She was the daughter of a trade magistrate and one of the People of the Eye, and in our first interactions she intimidated me. As apprentices, we were both of equal caste, but in those first years I was still in the mindset of a villager and saw her as a rich aristocrat from the capitol. The Mantis pitted us against each other in a series of training exercises. She beat me three times before my master said that if I lost again, he would release me.

I remember those hands clearly, now.

"That is Jen'lyn Reed," I say.

The Mantis gives a shallow nod within his cowl. "She arrived in Xu with the Firefly ten days ago."

The Firefly is an older version of her apprentice, a lady of court whose delicate manner belies her penchant for fire and explosives. I scan the square a third time but do not see her.

"Are we to assist them in eliminating the Tyressry?" I ask. The *Kyo'Vyar* would sometimes send more than one *Assyn* for a difficult assignment. Eliminating the administrator of Xu might qualify.

"No," the Mantis says. "And you won't find the Firefly. Jen'lyn killed her master just after they arrived."

I look sharply at him. "What?"

He makes a thin-lipped frown. "Jen'lyn is the primary reason we are here. We must perform a release from service."

2. RECRUITMENT

Nine years ago . . .

"Ty'rin Dovu," the first Recruiter said. "That is your name?"

"It is," I said.

The Recruiter wrote something in her book. Her pinched brow and pointy nose reminded me of a headmistress who enjoys disciplining children more than instructing them. She hadn't stopped scribbling in her leather-bound tome since we sat down.

The other three Recruiters stared at me across the table with near unbearable scrutiny. Then, they started their examination. The two sitting beside Scribbling-woman were twin brother and sister. They asked all their questions in tandem, one acting bored and the other engaged. Every few minutes, and without any apparent cue, they would switch personalities. The fourth Recruiter was plain-faced and balding. He never blinked.

The Recruiters' questions came at me without rhythm. Sometimes they indulged long stretches of silence between each question, other times they allowed me barely a breath before launching their next inquiry. They asked my opinion of the government; what I thought of the caste system; did I hunt for food; did I lick my blood from a cut? The topics ranged all over the place. Some questions were political, some were logical, some made no sense whatsoever.

According to my father, Recruiters for the People of the Carapace rarely visited interior villages. They usually stuck to the big coastal cities or the island colonies, and recruitment only occurred when one of the *Assyn* needed an apprentice. I was of an age to begin apprenticeship, and this was a rare opportunity for one of the *Wosyn* to jump to a higher caste, but only if I answered their questions correctly—more correctly than the thousand other candidates across the Imperiate.

I did my best to speak evenly, with no emotion showing on my face, trying to mimic my questioners. I kept my hands stuffed in my vest pockets, clenching and unclenching the knickknacks within: a polished garnet, a firecracker, the torso to one of my sister's dolls.

My parents sat with us in the beginning, but the Recruiters didn't allow them to speak. I think the Recruiters wanted to see if I looked to them for answers. My parents could not hide their fidgeting, my mother dry-washing her hands over and over, my father bouncing one knee. After the first half hour, the Recruiters ordered them to leave. Then it was just the five of us sitting around the scuffed table in my family's one-room hut, me on one side and them on the other, a single whale-oil lamp between us. The Recruiters had brought the lamp. No one in my village could afford whale oil.

At one point, my brother Ray'fin burst through the door proffering a frog and squealing with an exuberance only a three-year-old can muster. My mother bolted in a second later. She snatched up the boy and murmured apologies. The Recruiters took this in stride. They never looked upset or disapproving or pleased. They provided nothing to indicate what they thought of me.

"Why do you wish to be *Kyo'Assyn*?" Scribbling-woman asked.

"To escape life as a village farmer," I answered honestly.

"And what will you forgo to achieve that end?" one of the twins droned. His sister leaned forward and followed with, "Would you leave behind all your possessions and passions to become a mere instrument?"

"I have nothing worth holding onto," I said, and that was also true. I couldn't stand this nameless village on its way to nowhere. I resented my unambitious parents, my simple neighbors, my life of dirt and toil. My siblings were the only ones I might miss, my little brother adorable in his innocence, my gentle sister sweet as summer lilacs. But like everyone in my community, they were stuck here, their future written. Ray'fin would take over my parent's homestead. Sun'rie would marry some neighbor's son and bear four to six children, who would then labor in the fields until old enough to bear children themselves and perpetuate the cycle. The people here tilled, they planted, they harvested; and then they did it again, twice a year, every year, until hardship and old age ground them into dust.

I'd recently begun to wonder if I would make it to adulthood before I killed myself.

The plain-faced Recruiter knitted his fingers. He said, "Do you know the purpose of the *Kyo'Assyn*?"

"The People of the Carapace are the Imperator's armor of blades," I said. It was the beginning of a maxim picked up by every child in every huddled conversation on every playground across the continent. "They are the shadows cast from the light of the Imperiate. They are the whispers that prevent screams, the knives that cut away rot, the shepherds that cull the herd. They are the seven that serve and the shields that are swords."

All four Recruiters just stared at me. So, I added, "And they do this by killing people."

Plain-faced man cocked his head to the side. "And who is it you think they kill?"

"Exactly who they're told to," I said.

Scribbling-lady paused her writing. Plain-faced man unknit his fingers, then gave her a single nod.

She made a final mark, closed her book, and all four Recruiters stood. I stood with them. She said, "Ty'rin Dovu, we hereby raise you to the People of the Carapace and apprentice you to the Mantis."

"Wha—I am? I mean, you do?"

She pulled a fine dagger from her belt and placed it on the table, then pointed at Plain-faced man across from me. "Your first assignment is to terminate this man. Now."

It was a test. I didn't hesitate, nor did I immediately go for the dagger. Instead, I dropped my firecracker into the oil lamp, grabbed the dagger, and sprinted to the opposite end of the room.

The fiery explosion wasn't large, but it was hot enough to sear a man's face should he catch it wrong. The miniature bomb blew apart the lamp and set fire to the table. All four Recruiters jumped back, the twins cursing, Plain-faced man shielding himself with his cloak. At the opposite side of the house, I turned and flung the dagger at him with all my strength. They would not expect a village boy to know how to hurl a dagger; it is a difficult skill, especially with a weapon not balanced for throwing. Even so, it was a good toss; I'd been practicing on rats and ground-squirrels ever since I'd found my father's skinning knife—anything to avoid farm chores.

Plain-faced man reacted faster than I'd ever seen a person move, slapping away the dagger with a curved short-sword seemingly pulled from thin air. A second blade whirled across the room and thumped into the log wall behind me, quivering beside my throat.

My parents burst into the hut, staring wild-eyed at the scene. My mother grabbed a blanket and beat at the flames on the table. My father prostrated himself before the Recruiters, begging forgiveness. All four ignored him.

"The Firefly would enjoy this one," Plain-faced man said. "A pity she took an apprentice last month. Regardless, I did not expect that. I will take him and see how he does."

Scribbling-woman sniffed at the smoke filling the room, then reopened her book and made a note.

The man returned his blade to a hidden sheath on his back, then crossed the room. He pointed at the identical blade stuck in the wall. "Take it. Once we reach the capitol, we will forge you a twin to match it."

"I don't understand," I said. "Are you taking me to the Mantis?"

He pulled the cowl up on his cloak. "First lesson, Ty'rin: anonymity is a powerful weapon."

3. INQUIRY

Jen killed her master?" I say, incredulous. "That's impossible."

"The Firefly was as mortal as anyone else," the Mantis says.

"But Jen had to know there would be repercussions."

"Yes," the Mantis says. "Yet she killed her anyway. I have confirmed with several sources. Now Jen'lyn waits here, in plain sight."

To say she waited in plain sight was a bit inaccurate; to passersby she appeared a bent and broken vagabond. To one of the *Assyn*, however, she sat woefully exposed. It didn't make sense.

"So why?" I ask. "What is she doing?"

"That is what you will find out," the Mantis says. "It is not without precedent for an apprentice to murder her master prior to retirement. Impatience often leads to recklessness. However,

Jen'lyn's subsequent behavior does not fit that narrative. I would know what motivates her recent actions."

"And you want me to just go down and ask her?"

"She may open up to you. Intimacy also leads to recklessness."

I feel my face reddening. "When has Jen ever been reckless?"

"Only once that I have witnessed," he admits, "when she became involved with you."

I wipe sweat from my brow to hide my discomfort. "All right, say she does explain herself, then what?"

"Then, Ty'rin, we do what we came here to do."

This preamble is to sate my master's curiosity. I know this. I don't know why I asked.

The thought of killing Jen settles on me like a slow sickness. It leaves an ache, like the weariness that comes with too little sleep. I accept it—I've come too far to shy from my purpose—but this will be difficult, and not just because she is a trained killer.

"Find out what you can," the Mantis says, "but do not try to release her on your own."

"Where will you be?" I ask.

"Watching."

I sigh, my master forthcoming as ever.

I make my way down to the street. More and more people trickle into the square, colonists on their way to the docks and petitioners hoping for an audience with the Tyressry. I take my time crossing the expanse, boots crunching on black stones, casual, unhurried. Just another traveler from the mainland. Perhaps one of the People of the Hand in search of new merchandise for trade in the capitol, or a government messenger waiting for a reply to some missive. This is how I present myself, though I do not doubt Jen notices me as soon as my feet touch the cobblestones.

She remains sitting as I stroll near, her head bowed, bowl lifted in supplication. She smells of sweat and offal, but that is mostly her robe. I sit down beside her and lean back against the building.

"You split your lip," she says.

"You smell like a privy."

I can't see her face, but I feel her smile underneath her hood.

"I'm glad you're here, Ty."

"I'm not! The islands always this humid? Place feels like a damn steam tent."

"You know," she says, "for someone born a farmer, I'm always amazed at how much you whine."

I shrug. "Well, I wasn't a very good farmer."

I feel her smile again.

"I miss humor," she says. "Before my recruitment, I used to share jokes with my ladies-in-waiting. We had code phrases so my mother and her sycophants wouldn't know we were mocking them. It remains one of the few aspects of my childhood I don't despise."

It always strikes me how much Jen and I have in common, despite coming from opposite ends of the caste hierarchy.

"Are you comparing me to a lady-in-waiting, Jen?"

"Don't be foolish. You bellyache far too much for a lady-in-waiting."

My turn to smile. I hadn't realized how much I missed her playful jabs. "So what are we doing here, Your Radiance?"

"You are here to kill me."

I consider how best to respond. "No," I say, "the Mantis is here to kill you. I'm just here to chat."

She emits a soft sigh. "I hope that's true, Ty. You are my only chance."

Her only chance? What is that supposed to mean? She has no chance of surviving this day, no matter what has transpired between us. I am no lifeline. Despite my fondness for her, I won't hesitate to plunge a blade through her eye should my master order it. She must realize that.

"Jen ..." I begin.

She interrupts me. "Do you believe in redemption, Ty?"

I am good at dealing with the unexpected, but this segue takes me off guard. "Redemption from what?"

"From the sorrow and emptiness we leave in the world."

"That is the most naive thing I've ever heard you say."

"Is it? Tell me, how many people have you killed?"

Again, the question surprises me. "I have no idea."

"Yes, you do. You know exactly how many."

Fourteen people, plus one. The number comes unbidden. I keep it to myself.

Jen sets her bowl down, does not lift her head. "I have killed twenty-nine people. Eighteen men, eight women, and three children. The first twenty-four didn't bother me. We *Assyn* are instruments, are we not? The knives that cut away rot, and all that."

"So our creed states," I say. "What happened with the last five people?"

Jen takes her time answering. "My supposed Trial came last year. The Trade Administration voted out Mother, and her former compatriots decided she knew too much to live. They thought matricide an appropriate test of my loyalty." She makes a snorting sound beneath her hood. "None of them realized how much I despised Mother. Killing that abusive bitch was easy. I even made certain she saw my face, just before the firework under her carriage exploded. She was number twenty-four." Jen's voice is an octave lower than normal, almost a growl. I've no doubt she would go back and kill her mother again if she could.

"The next marks were my real Trial," she continues, "though only I know it. I terminated a seamstress and her three children, children sired by a tax minister who decided he didn't want evidence of his past infidelity. At my mistress's instruction, I set fire to their shack and burned them alive."

I am reminded of a time I tripped and fell against the iron cooking-stove built into the back of my parent's hut. I was maybe four years old, and it remains one of my earliest memories. One I would forget if I could. I keep my face neutral, and say, "Sounds like you completed the assignment."

"I did," Jen says, "but I failed the Trial. Because those four, they bother me. They were not rot."

"You have lost resolve," I say. It's a cold statement, but the work we perform requires detachment. No one appreciates that more than I.

"Maybe," Jen says. "Or maybe I found something. What do the dark-haired peoples in the north call it? A soul, I think?" She laughs as if this is funny. "Did you ever think I would say such a thing?"

"No."

"Me neither. But then, never before have I been unable to sleep for the screaming inside my head. I can hear each of them: the mother, her teenage daughter, her two young sons; each of their voices distinct, all begging and pleading and crying inside my skull."

I know the voices. I've built walls to silence them.

"If that is how you feel," I say, "then maybe this is for the best." Jen's walls have crumbled. It saddens me, but there is nothing I can do for her.

"It is," Jen says. "I knew for certain when I terminated my twenty-ninth person—killing my own mistress does not haunt me."

"So you want to die, is that it? Is that why you waited for us to come for you?"

Jen answers with a question of her own. "Did the Mantis tell you why the Firefly and I came to Xu?"

"Not in so many words, but if I had to guess, the *Kyo'Vyar* placed a mark on Tyressry Kaab."

She nods. "That is what I thought, too. It wasn't until we arrived that I learned the real reason."

"So ... the Tyressry wasn't your target?"

"Oh, he was the target," Jen says, "but the *Vyar* did not mark him."

"I don't follow, Jen."

"Tyressry Kaab committed a grave transgression, and his fellow *Kyo'Vyar* want to send a message." Jen looks up finally, and I'm shocked to see tears in her eyes. "They sent us to kill his infant son."

4. TRAINING

Five years ago...

The dart lanced into my left buttock. I swore and ripped it free.

She wasn't in the fountain. I'd thought for sure she lay in the fountain.

I raised my hand to acknowledge the hit and looked back down the busy street. My mark emerged from one of the barrels stacked against the cooper's shop. I had checked behind the barrels as I stalked past but didn't think to look inside them.

I sighed and leaned against the fountain lip, annoyed at my mistake and nauseated from the reek of the city. The smarting in my backside made me wince.

Jen'lyn tucked her blowgun up her sleeve as she approached, her eyebrows lifted in that smug manner of an opponent who's beaten you and intends to passively rub your nose in it. "The fountain?" she said. "Really?"

"Thought you were hiding within the pool." I realized how stupid it sounded as I said it.

She sat on the basin next to me, made a show of looking down at the water. "Not sure how I'd get in and out of *there* unnoticed."

"I could do it," I said. I'd no idea how.

"You upset? You get petulant when you're upset."

"You shot me in the ass."

She patted my shoulder in mock empathy, then leaned in and whispered, "Maybe I can make it up to you tonight. If, that is, your master doesn't pummel you worthless."

As if on cue, the Mantis appeared among the street pedestrians. He wore the attire of a merchant of middling means, a once-valuable long-vest that was now thin and soiled, good boots with a hole in one toe, a cane to aid a fake limp. No one looked twice at him.

He leveled his unblinking stare at me. "You are dead, Ty'rin."

"Yes," I confirmed.

"Why?"

"She knows the city better than me."

"Is that a reason or an excuse?" The Mantis wore an expression of cool disdain I'd come to know as dissatisfaction. In the four years I'd been with him, I'd never seen him angry. Only unimpressed. Such moments of disappointment were dangerous for me.

"I dismissed the barrels because I could not fit inside one," I said. "But Jen is half a foot shorter and forty pounds lighter. I hunted her as if I hunted myself. I should have thought as my mark thinks."

The Mantis accepted this. He would allow a mistake, but only once, and only if I reconciled it.

The rest of the day's lessons involved walking the streets of the capitol, memorizing walkways and hidden alleys, identifying bottlenecks, learning approaches, and tailing random targets. Jen's errors were fewer than mine, but I did not resent her. Quite the opposite: I'd come to enjoy her company—even when she killed me.

That night I climbed onto the roof of our inn to sit underneath the rising moons. The capitol was not as hot as my village out west, but it stank with a cloistered stuffiness. Pigs and rotting wood and heaped sewage and endless body-sweat piled atop one another in an effort to offend my nostrils, the effect of thousands of people all crammed into a city not three miles wide. The stench became slightly more tolerable up on the rooftops.

I sat on the sloping tiles and wetted an oilcloth, then ran it over each of my twin blades. They were my favorite weapons, somewhere between a dagger and a short-sword. Each was thin and curved, forged with a single edge and almost no cross guard, identical to the pair my master carried. The Mantis had designed them to kill quickly and with stealth. We *Assyn* do not fight battles, he taught. We do not fight at all. We terminate threats to the Imperiate in the most efficient manner possible. The twin blades and the blowgun were my master's preferred methods—each of the seven had their specialties—but poison, arson, suffocation, musketry, all were on the table when terminating a mark. Stealth and anonymity remained our best weapons, but for myself, the twin blades were a close second.

A shadow materialized atop the roof edge to my left. I kept oiling my blades as if I hadn't noticed. The shadow slid across the tiles, moving behind me.

"If you're going to impale me with another dart," I said, "I'd prefer you stick my shoulder. Sitting is rather uncomfortable right now."

Jen cursed under her breath. "You heard me climbing."

I pointed at the three moons rising in the eastern sky. "Caught your shadow as you crested the rooftop. You needed to approach from farther west."

"Ugh," she groaned, plopping beside me. "Amateur mistake. I must be overtired."

"Whose fault is that?"

She smiled at me, violet eyes catching moonlight and taking my breath away. "Haven't slept enough the past few nights, for which I accept fifty-percent blame."

I schooled my body with an effort of will. "Do not think I don't know what you're doing."

"Oh? What am I doing, village boy?"

"Practicing. The Firefly is a seductress. She uses her beauty and charm to get close to a mark. She teaches you to do the same."

"Did you just call me a harlot?"

"I called you beautiful and charming."

Jen laughed. "Good save. And we're certain I am the one doing the seducing here?"

"I'm not following *you* up onto secluded rooftops in the middle of the night."

She pursed her lips and considered me for three heartbeats. "I'll give you this: you're perceptive for a bumpkin farmer from the countryside."

"The Mantis didn't pick me for my knowledge of turnips."

Jen lifted her palms. "So I'm practicing. And you know I'm practicing. Doesn't mean we can't enjoy it." She touched my forearm with the tip of her little finger. "And don't pretend you don't enjoy it."

I took a deep breath. "As long as we both know what this is."

"You afraid you'll wind up engaged?"

I narrowed my eyes at her.

She said, "I'll tell you a secret: I'm not the marrying type."

I set my blades aside. "What I'm afraid of, Jen, is that at some point they're going to test us. The Mantis keeps hinting at it, calls it the Trial of Devotion. We'll need to prove ourselves willing to take out any mark assigned to us."

"A test?" Jen said. "All they ever do is test us."

I shook my head. "This is just training. The Trial will be a different kind of test. A mark we won't want to kill. If we fail, they will release us from service. If that mark turns out to be you, I must be able to follow through."

Challenge flashed across her face. "For your sake, you better hope it's not me."

"That's the problem, Jen. I already hope it's not you, and not because you're good with darts."

She peered at me without speaking for long enough to make it awkward. Finally, she bit her lip and said, "We've chosen our path, Ty. I will terminate any mark the *Vyar* assigns me. That is the deal I made to escape my mother's tyranny, and it includes you. Until then, I take my enjoyments where I can." She touched my arm again. "I expect you to do the same."

"Are we still talking about killing each other, or something else?"

She leaned close to nuzzle my ear. "Take your pick."

It was too much for me. I could partition my feelings, hold a part of me separate to do what I must, should that day come, but I was not a golem like the Mantis. I needed connection, to feel something for someone who wasn't a mark or a master. I needed someone who understood the loneliness.

Jen'lyn acted casual, but I knew she felt that same need. I only hoped our masters wouldn't use it against us.

5. DISILLUSION

His son?" I exclaim.

Jen gives a sad nod. "The *Kyo'Vyar* sent us here to kill a baby, Ty."

I slump back against the building. An image tries to push its way forward in my mind. A cherub face filled with innocence. I slam the mental door shut.

"Why in the world would the *Vyar* mark a baby?" I ask.

Instead of answering, Jen rises to her feet. I join her, hastily signaling behind my back for my master, wherever he is, to HOLD.

Jen says, "Will you walk the square with me?"

"As you wish."

We begin a slow circuit of the plaza. Perhaps Jen hopes to glimpse the Mantis along the rooftops. He is likely up there somewhere, but I do not see him.

"The *Vyar* marked the baby as punishment," Jen eventually says. "Tyressry Kaab stepped outside his caste, and you know how the People of the Eye respond to things like that."

"Yes, but marking an infant for death is harsh even for them."

Jen scoffs. "And you call me naive. You don't know them the way I do. The caste hierarchy is everything, and those beneath them are dispensable. A single life in a lower caste means nothing."

"But the Tyressry is also *Kyo'Vyar*," I say. "His son would be, too."

"You're not listening. I told you, Tyressry Kaab stepped outside his caste."

I realize what she means. "The baby's mother is of lower birth."

"*Kyo'Wosyn*," Jen confirms. The People of the Blood. They are the lowest caste, the Imperiate only considers foreigners beneath them. The *Kyo'Wosyn* are the tradesmen: the cobblers, the coopers, the rope-makers, the blacksmiths. They are also the farmers. My former caste.

We move past the central statue, a granite carving of some

great Imperator, or maybe a former Tyressry, I can't really say. He wasn't *Kyo'Wosyn*, whoever he was. No one carves statues of *Kyo'Wosyn*.

"They must consider the child an abomination," I say. "Still, the worst they would do would be to remove the Tyressry from office. Strip him of wealth and reputation. They wouldn't go so far as to kill the child. There must be more to this."

"There is," Jen says. "Tyressry Kaab didn't just impregnate some country girl. He married her."

I lift my brows at that. An administrator having an affair with someone of lower standing is far from accepted, but nor is it unprecedented. Any resultant child led to disgrace, but again, nothing that warranted our presence. For the Tyressry of a city to wed a *Kyo'Wosyn* ... That is unheard of.

"I didn't believe it either," Jen says. "But then I investigated and yes, Tyressry Kaab fell in love with a young farm girl, married her in secret, moved her into his estate, and then conceived a child. The other *Kyo'Vyar* want to make an example of him."

The old woman selling hand-fans cackles at us as we walk past her stall, trying to woo me into buying one of her "lovelies." A fan would feel nice in this heat, but I want both my hands free. I wave her off and say, "Marking a child is savage. I won't pretend otherwise. But we may not choose our marks, Jen. You know this."

"That is exactly what the Firefly said. Right before I killed her."

Underneath my cloak, I shift an arm back, ready to draw a blade should she make a move.

Jen notes the subtle change. "You're still not listening," she says. "I'm not going to kill you, Ty. You are going to save me."

"I'm not, Jen."

She reaches out, deliberately slow, and touches my arm, just as she did five years ago. "I believe you'll try."

I step out of reach. "You know I'm beyond sentimental trappings. What makes you think I would, even if I could?"

"Redemption, Ty'rin. I know what happened in your Trial."

6. TRIAL

Three years ago ...

"Master, what are we doing here?"

"This place does not please you?" the Mantis asked.

"Please me?" I said. "You're asking if I'm pleased you brought me to this worthless collection of hovels in the middle of this worthless backwater province? No, nothing about this hole of a town *pleases* me."

Grime-caked homes lined both sides of the muddy wagon ruts that served as the main thoroughfare, most houses no larger than a single room. A few shops broke up the proceedings: a basket-weaver here, a thatcher on the corner. This backward town was so far behind the times the homeowners still used thatched roofs. People in dun clothing huddled in small groups amid the drizzling rain, conversing about the weather, wasting-sickness in someone's flock, a shortage of good brass, more about the stupid weather. No one hurried anywhere. No one had anywhere important to be.

We passed a stake in the ground tacked with a ragged sign stating: *Town of Dorin*. In an earlier life, I'd lugged my family's soybean and turnip crop past this sign twice a year. Five miles dragging a loaded cart across the countryside, just to hand it off to some oily snake in merchant's clothing who looked at me with a disdain often reserved for rats and cockroaches.

I hated Dorin.

The Mantis didn't address my complaints. Instead, he said, "Do you know why there are only seven *Kyo'Assyn*?"

I took a deep breath, considered the question. "Conformity to the balance of sevens," I guessed. "Seven castes, seven great cities, seven People of the Carapace."

"Partially," my master said, "but there are more practical reasons." He didn't say what. He waited for me to work it out on my own.

"The same reason we may never select a mark," I reasoned.

"We are a caste of shadows trained to kill. In greater numbers we might pose a threat to the *Vyar*."

The Mantis nodded. The crow's feet at the corners of his eyes crinkled, an indication I'd impressed him. "Very good. But there is a third reason, even more practical than that."

I worked through what I knew of my caste. Seven instruments of death: The Mantis, the Moth, the Locust, the Firefly, the Spider, the Wasp, and the Beetle. Each one specialized, each one a master of the trade. Only the People of the Eye and the Imperator himself stood above us. We'd spent years learning our work, moving about the Imperiate and the outside world with silent impunity, never wanting for food or money or resources, everything provided.

The Mantis and I strolled past the blacksmith's forge as I rolled these things over in my mind, the sound of hammer-strikes banging into my ears. The man working the bellows was a skinny, sweat-covered youth, the one at the anvil older and covered in burn scars. In their shop hung horseshoes and farm implements, some metal cookware, a few wagon axles. Across the street, a bakery offset the blacksmith's stench of charcoal and hot metal. In dryer weather, the baker would likely be displaying her loaves.

"Economics," I eventually said. "We provide a service, but we do not contribute to the economy. We are expensive."

"Correct," the Mantis said. "We are a standing army outside the military, but like any army, we cost a great deal. The more specialized the soldier, the higher the cost, and we are the most specialized soldiers in the world. Between the army and the navy and the extravagances of the *Vyar*, the Imperiate cannot afford a large number of *Assyn*."

"I understand," I said. What I didn't understand was what any of this had to do with Dorin. I didn't say as much though. The Mantis never rambled—he would make his point soon enough.

We entered the town square, a swampy, open space with a circular stone well in the center. We'd dressed as poor farmers, maybe a father and son from some outlying homestead, our cowls pulled up against the spitting rain. The townspeople didn't give us a second glance.

The Mantis said, "You are an investment, Ty'rin. A tremendous expenditure of time, energy, and resources. Like any investment, you come with risk. The *Vyar* wish to mitigate this risk as much as possible. The recruitment process is the first stage of mitigation. My tutelage is the second. We are here for the third."

I grasped his meaning. My mouth went dry.

The Mantis stopped at the well and placed his hands against the stonework. "What do you see?"

I answered without thought. "Two village women ten points to the east, leaving the square. A middle-aged man lugging firewood due south, coming toward us. A maid and a child taking shelter underneath that wayward pine at the edge of . . ."

The maid was missing the tip of her middle finger.

Sun'rie was no longer the child I remembered, instead a young woman of sixteen. Her smile remained the same though, a radiant sweetness that lit the world around her. She beamed down at my little brother, wiping dirt from his face where he'd splashed through a mud puddle. Ray'fin had grown into a cute boy of nine, chubby in the cheeks and still full of energy. They both wore traveling cloaks, Sun'rie holding a covered wicker basket, Ray'fin clutching a soggy stick like a sword. They must have traveled to Dorin that morning to purchase supplies, bread from the baker, maybe.

"When a *Kyo'Assyn* feels an apprentice is ready," the Mantis said, "he or she will petition the *Kyo'Vyar* for a mark of sufficient challenge."

"Sufficient challenge," I whispered. I could not take my eyes off my siblings.

"This challenge is not one of skill," the Mantis said, "but one of conviction. This is why we call it the Trial of Devotion."

"You petitioned for a mark on my family."

"I may not choose the mark," the Mantis said, "but I may make recommendations. Do you consider my recommendation cruel?"

The question was part of the Trial. An assessment of how

I would react, just like during my recruitment. I answered honestly. "Sun'rie and Ray'fin are no enemies of the Imperiate. They pose no risk to anyone or anything. Marking them is malicious, nothing more."

"I agree," the Mantis said.

I turned to look at my master, trying to understand. He dug into his satchel and produced a stoppered waterskin and a blowgun, setting both on the lip of the well. He removed the stopper from the skin and positioned it upright, so the contents wouldn't spill. A foulness like a midsummer latrine wafted from within. The Mantis then produced a blowdart capped with a glass vial. The dart's steel tip rested within a thimbleful of milky liquid.

"Your assessment of this town is accurate," the Mantis said, removing the dart from the vial and loading it into the blowgun. "It is useless to the Imperiate. In fact, it is more than useless. It is a drain. The cost of sending the *Kyo'Rusalk* out here, purchasing the harvest, and then transporting it back to the nearest city is more than the crops are worth." He set the loaded blowgun back on the lip of the well. "One remedy is to simply stop sending the People of the Hand out here. Allow the farmers and tradesmen to keep what they produce and utilize a barter economy. However, that separates them from the Imperiate and sets a dangerous precedent. Thus, the second option is to eliminate them." He pointed to the waterskin. "A gift from the Locust. The blood of a diseased cow mixed with the excrement of a man dying of cholera. Drop it into the well, and it will wipe out a majority of this—how did you put it?—hole of a town. The suffering will be great and prolonged, but the Locust knows his pestilence. Do you consider this course of action cruel?"

I regarded the bag of slow, indiscriminate death. The reek of it made me gag. "I do."

"Ah," the Mantis said. He indicated toward the blowgun. "A second gift, this one from the Spider. She extracts the poison from a tiny octopus found in the island colonies. A coated dart will cause paralysis within twenty seconds, unconsciousness within a minute, and death within five. Quicker in a child. It is a painless and merciful end." He lifted his chin toward my brother and sister. "The young boy or the town. The choice is yours."

My jaw trembled. I felt too hot, suffocating within my oilskin cloak. The Mantis watched me, soaking up my every physiological reaction.

The local with the firewood labored past. He gave us an affable nod. My master transformed into a man to return the greeting, his empty face suddenly open and friendly, making some jibe about lazy youth these days unwilling to work in foul weather. The local man laughed and said he'd voice as much to his sons when he got home. He then continued on his way. As my master turned back to me, the amicable good humor sloughed from his face like rainwater, replaced by the hollowness of the golem, a creature knowing no joy, nor sorrow, nor mercy.

"How can I have a choice?" I croaked, barely audible for the ash in my mouth. "We never choose. Ever. That is the central pillar of our creed."

"No," the Mantis said. "That is a fiction. We always have a choice. We are instruments of the *Kyo'Vyar*, but we are mortal instruments, every one of us, and so we choose the weapon we will be. We can be a blunt explosive or a hidden blade. We can refuse our duty altogether. There is nothing stopping us, only the consequences of our actions. Will you be the blade and place the betterment of this community—a place you despise so much—above some sense of fraternal kinship? Or will you be the blunt instrument of carnage, exerting mass cruelty to spare an innocent boy? This choice is the Trial."

"And if I refuse to be either?" It was an absurd question. I already knew the answer.

"I will release you from service, and you will leave this world a man of principle, instead of an instrument of death. I will then terminate both your brother and the town of Dorin. The *Kyo'Vyar* will know the fruits of their investment, Ty'rin. As will I."

There was another option. I could attack my master, a course of action he would no doubt be ready for. I would lose, and then die. So would Ray'fin and the people of Dorin.

Across the town square, Ray'fin giggled as he played at fencing with his soggy stick, whacking playfully at my sister's legs. Sun'rie rolled her eyes. She deflected his blows with her basket and picked up a stick of her own, returning his attacks with equal energy.

Would you kill a child? the Recruiters had asked me. I'd answered immediately. Worst of all, I meant it.

The dart struck Ray'fin in the neck, right at the carotid artery. He issued a short scream, more a squeak of surprise, really, but to my ears it was a wail of purest agony. It bored into me like a fetid arrow, drilling into the pitch-black stone that had once been the heart of a simple village boy.

7. CHOICE

If you know about my Trial," I say to Jen, "then you know I passed, and I cannot help you now."

We complete our circuit of the plaza and stop back at Jen's bedding of sailcloth. She lowers her hood to allow the sun to reach her face. I wince at her movement and signal again for the Mantis to HOLD. I don't know where he is, but he either sees my signal or believes there is more to learn, because no dart or blade strikes Jen down. He won't wait much longer, though; more people enter the plaza every minute. While a crowd can be useful in some operations, here, a press of people get in the way.

Jen looks skyward. The morning rays illuminate a tired but still beautiful face. "I asked if you believe in redemption, Ty, because I have to believe in it. I have to believe we can be more than what they make us."

"You think I should feel guilty, the same as you."

"I think they select us for our desire to escape, teach us how to kill, then remove any vestige of remorse. I wonder if we can rediscover that remorse once it's gone."

"It would seem you are proof we can," I say.

"I failed my Trial, Ty. The remorse is all I have now. I am talking about you."

"A *Kyo'Assyn* cannot be remorseful."

"And what are we then!" Jen says, turning fierce. "Are we to be unfeeling weapons who murder at the whim of gluttonous tyrants? The *Kyo'Vyar* do not use us to protect the Imperiate. They use us to protect their own positions of power!"

Nothing she says is untrue. To say we serve a greater good is to be blind to the flaws of our puppeteers. Nevertheless, the Recruiters were clear on the sacrifice required to become *Assyn*. We joined this caste willingly.

"We agreed to be weapons of the *Vyar*," I say. "You to escape the prison of your station, me to escape the tedium of farm life. It was selfish, and the balance is that we must kill who we're told."

"Then let us be selfish," Jen says. "Your master is a dog who bites on command. So was mine. But we don't have to be. We can choose to be something else."

I remember a dreary day in a town a thousand miles west of here, where a boy and his sister played among the puddles, and I made a choice.

"It is too late for me, Jen," I whisper.

"Then why do you still hear your brother's voice when you close your eyes?"

I take an involuntary step back. How could she know that? I have buried it, layered stone and mortar over that scream until it is no more than a distant hum in my subconscious. Hidden from everyone, even myself.

Jen's eyes widen at my reaction, and I understand the gamble she made. She didn't know, she guessed. But she guessed correctly.

"I waited here in Xu," Jen breathes, "because for a job as difficult as a release from service, I knew the *Vyar* would send an *Assyn* familiar with the islands."

Someone familiar with Xu. Who more familiar than one who hails from here? "You knew they would send the Mantis."

EMERSON RABBITT

"And with him, you."

A small crowd now occupies the plaza, nearing a hundred people. Petitioners wait at the bottom of the stairs. Everyone looks to the mansion. Tyressry Kaab must make an announcement each morning before hearing petitions.

Jen squints at the sun's position once more. "It is time."

The tall mahogany doors to the mansion creak open. "Time for Tyressry Kaab to make his appearance?"

"Time to discover if such as us can find redemption," Jen says. "Ten days ago, I stood in this very spot, at this very time of day, waiting for my mark to appear. I chose to terminate the Firefly instead."

"You said the Tyressry wasn't your mark."

"Tyressry Kaab doesn't make the morning address. His wife does. Your nephew never leaves her arms."

The world stops. My peripheral vision blurs, and it is as if I look down a long tunnel. At the end of the tunnel, my sister steps from the doorway onto the landing. Sun'rie is now nineteen and thicker in the waist, but still stunning in a belted gray gown and gold marriage choker. She cradles a bundled baby in her arms.

My sister walks to the top of the stairs, smiling and nodding as the people clap for her. My mouth goes dry, just like the last time I saw her. She doesn't see me at the back of the crowd.

Whatever power my sister has over the Tyressry has spread to the citizens of Xu. They adore her—I can see it even before she speaks—and I understand why. She stands with authority but not arrogance, her face displays an honesty never witnessed among the People of the Eye, an earnestness that says she sees you, understands your plight, and is on your side. She is the epitome of what the *Kyo'Vyar* fear, a rising lowborn with the charisma and intelligence to inspire the masses, and she has an unprecedented platform in her marriage to a Tyressry.

Beside me, Jen's dirty robe falls to the ground. Underneath she wears black cotton breeches and a tight-wrap shirt, a utility belt of pouches and throwing-daggers, a thin short-sword in a downward facing sheath on her back, incendiary grenades strapped to one thigh. No hiding now. No one except the People of the Carapace carry weaponry like that. Even if the surrounding patrons don't recognize her as *Kyo'Assyn*, she stands out. It is a move to force my hand.

"I was to hurl a firebomb at your sister during her morning address," Jen says. "An example to anyone who thinks to move above their station. I chose to hurl it at the Firefly instead."

Sun'rie is orating now, telling a story of hardship and loss, of striving for more. It is a story of hope. Her voice is strong, maternal, resonant. The *Vyar* will never allow her to live.

Jen is trembling, her face flushed and her breathing fast. She knows the Mantis's death stroke will come any second. She plays her last card.

"I have loved you since the night on the rooftop, Ty'rin. For I am a woman, not an instrument. I did this for me, and for the hope of what I saw in you that night. This is your true Trial of Devotion. Now. Choose."

I have heard some few speak of the sensation that time slows during a near-death experience. Of the sense that during moments of great consequence, the universe pauses to appreciate the gravity of what transpires. I look now at Jen'lyn and know something similar, my heartbeat drawing out in an aching boom. It pounds my chest like some great slow-ringing bell, the air around us too heavy, the sunlight too bright. I realize then that this woman, who is no tool nor slave nor beast, is the single most courageous person I have ever known.

She is also an utter fool.

Time snaps back into cadence and I draw my left-hand blade in a blur, the draw itself an attack, slicing toward Jen's neck in a move perfected over a hundred hours of practice.

She never breaks eye contact. Even when the flat of the blade slaps against her carotid artery and the poison dart pings off the steel. She's foolish to think I knew how the Mantis would attack—he's never so forthcoming. Still, one does not spend nine years studying every move a man makes without learning his preferences.

Jen releases the breath she'd been holding and a look of joy I've never seen fills her violet eyes. Her smile is empyreal. "Good choice, village boy."

With an effort, I break my gaze and follow the dart's trajectory. The Mantis leans against the statue base to my left, in the middle of the square, his gray cloak making him near invisible against the weathered granite of the monument. He lowers his blowgun with an expression of puzzled shock, quickly replaced by irritated disappointment.

"Only if we survive the next twenty seconds," I say.

8. CONSEQUENCE

Now ...

The blowgun vanishes up my former master's sleeve, and he draws one of his hidden twin blades, held in a reverse grip. He pushes off the statue and walks toward us.

There is no bravado in his approach. No salute or swaggering challenge. Such things are the conceit of storytellers. The *Assyn* do not fight, the *Assyn* kill. I can draw-cut a slice to someone's liver and then hide the blade before my mark feels the wound, but I do not know any defensive parries or how to disarm an opponent. This duel will not be a prolonged affair.

"Any chance you've hidden a pistol on you?" I say to Jen.

"Afraid not," Jen says.

"At least he isn't carrying one either." If he did, he would've shot one of us by now.

"What is that woman wearing?" someone in the crowd says.

"Is that chap holding a sword?" another says. People are beginning to notice us.

I know better than to suggest running. We might escape, but the Mantis would hunt us, then terminate us unseen. This is our best chance, with the man before us, in the open.

"He'll go for me first," I say to Jen. "It will be your best shot." I have no illusions of surviving the attack myself. I am fast and skilled; the Mantis is legendary.

A slow-match flares in Jen's hand. "I can give you a chance." Her eyes flit to her feet and back.

"Guards!" a woman yells. "Those two carry swords!" Commotion among the people nearest us. Surprised murmurs, people backing away.

The Mantis continues his silent advance. Twenty paces away. I know he wonders what we will do.

Fifteen paces. My sister halts her speech.

Ten paces. Behind us, a deep voice yells, "You there! Get down on—"

Jen drops the burning match into her collection bowl, the one she'd proffered as a beggar. Not an empty bowl, but one with a trio of black-powder cartridges and sharp obsidian pebbles in the bottom. She times it perfectly. At the first hissing flare, her foot shoots forward, kicking the bowl away from us and straight at the Mantis.

The smoky bang rips across the square; men and women scream and cover their heads. The Mantis lifts his cloak against the blast, turning his face from the flying stones. The explosion is loud and flashy, but not lethal. It is a distraction. I let fly my blade in an underhand toss aimed at my former master's throat. It is a throw he cannot see for the blinding smoke between us. It is a throw to save my life, the life of Jen, and the life of my sister and her newborn son. A throw for a chance to be something else.

And just like nine years ago, the Mantis counters it.

He moves with impossible speed, his sword flashing in an arc to deflect my blade and his other arm snapping forward in a throw of his own. The second of his twin blades twirls in the air and strikes me in the chest, right at my heart. It would kill me if I'd remained five paces away, but I jumped forward as I threw, leaping into acrid smoke. Instead of the blade tip, the hilt slams into me, making me grunt. I don't slow. Three running strides and I'm there, slashing out my second blade. I do not expect to hit him, he's simply too fast, but he must sidestep to avoid my attack. I roll as I miss and the Mantis's counter-slash nicks across my hairline. Had I not gone low it would have cut my neck.

I come out of my roll and feint, but don't lunge. It's enough to make the Mantis twitch to the side. And there, in that second, we both know. Jen and I have him flanked. Time slows again.

The next dragged-out moment lasts a fraction of a heartbeat, but I see it unfold with perspicuous clarity. The Mantis blinks and I see his face change. A constricting of the eyes, a whisper of a smile. I like to think he feels a measure of pride for me, but with him it is impossible to tell. The fleeting moment passes, and the Mantis twists to avoid Jen's throwing-dagger whistling past his shoulder. The dodge leaves him unbalanced, and he is unable to escape my follow-up strike, slashing deep between his ribs. People run and scream around us, Jen's explosion eliciting a general panic. The Mantis staggers and I dance back as some youth barrels into him, spinning him full around, and then Jen's second throwing-dagger thumps into his back.

My former master falls to a knee. Blood gushes from his side as his blade drops from his fingers. He looks at me with his forgetful face and coughs blood onto his chin. He slowly shakes his head, until Jen's third dagger skewers the back of his neck and he topples forward onto the cobblestones, released from service.

9. REDEMPTION

Would you kill a child? For me, the answer was clear. The truly difficult question would have been: *And can you live with yourself afterward?*

Both these questions are unfair, of course. No one can know such a thing until he or she faces it. I look down at the man who made me what I am, and I wonder whom he killed during his own Trial of Devotion, if it made him into the golem I knew. I wonder if I would have become the same, if not for Jen'lyn.

The plaza clears of people. Only the elderly fan merchant and the guards remain, the old woman gaping at us as if we are creatures risen from some nightmare, the guards stepping carefully toward us, three of them now, muskets at the ready.

"On the ground, both of you!" a deep voice yells.

Jen and I square to face them.

The one who spoke freezes. *"Kyo'Assyn,"* he whispers.

The new guardsman, a kid no more than fourteen years old bearing scars on his cheeks, waves his gun back and forth between the two of us, while the third sentry, a sweaty fellow who's forgotten to pull back the hammer on his flintlock, stammers, "Wh-who are you? Identify yourselves!"

"He is the ghost of a boy I once knew," Sun'rie says from behind him. She didn't flee at the explosion like everyone else. Instead, she descended the stairs, baby still bundled in her arms. "It is you, isn't it?"

I swallow the lump in my throat. Force myself to look her in the eye. "Hello, Sun."

She pulls her child protectively close. "Ty'rin. Why ... why are you here?"

I have only one answer. "To perform a release from service."

She looks at the body beside me, blood soaking the stones at my feet. "That man's?"

I shake my head. "My own."

She is very still. "Was that man *Kyo'Assyn*?"

I nod.

"Is he the one who killed Ray'fin? I know the *Assyn* are responsible; I dug the poison dart from Ray's neck. Is that the man who did it? Was it because of you?"

I can lie and spare my sister the knowledge of my fratricide. It might be a mercy. In a sense, it would only be a half-lie, for while the Mantis did not shoot the dart into my brother's neck, he did orchestrate the mark. The *Assyn* flourish in this murk of misdirection and half-truth, but I am no longer *Assyn*, and there can be no redemption in a half-truth.

"No, Sun," I say. "It was the other way around. I killed Ray because of him."

Pain moves across her face in a rippling wave. A wash of betrayal and horror that starts at her left eye and moves in a diagonal down her nose and jaw, stopping at the right corner of her chin. Something cold follows. A pitiless hardness I don't recognize on the sweet girl remembered from my youth.

"The Mantis gave him an impossible choice," Jen says. "He sacrificed your brother to save an entire town. Today he sacrificed his future to save you and your—" Jen stops. Something is wrong.

What do you see? My sister stands beside her three guards, her son cradled in one arm, her other hand placed over top. One guard remains awestruck by the sight of us, the third remains nervous, but the newcomer in the middle is different. The scarred young teen has his musket trained on Jen, a determined calmness about him. The elderly woman selling fans is ... no longer to my right.

The youth taps the stock of his musket twice with his finger, a signal. Movement behind me.

A shot cracks across the square. Not from the guards but from the mansion beyond. A musket ball shrieks past my ear and I crouch instinctively. Behind me, the fan-seller halts in petrified stillness, a tessen war fan with sharpened iron spokes poised to decapitate me. She then crumples to the ground.

The Moth. Sometimes the *Kyo'Vyar* send more than one *Assyn* for a difficult task. A task such as a release from service. But if that is the Moth, then her apprentice—

"Jen!"

A second shot splits the air. Jen hops backward. Her face is bloodless. She stares straight ahead into the blue gun smoke curling in front of her.

No. Please no. Not after all this. Not her.

Jen doesn't fall. Instead, the youth with the musket collapses, a gaping hole passing through both temples. Beside him, Sun'rie points a smoking pistol, a second flintlock in her off hand. The cloth wrap swaddling her supposed child pools at her feet, a ceramic doll's head rolling across the cobblestones.

The two remaining guards are as confused as I feel. They swing their guns about wildly. Sun'rie catches the barrel of one, points it at the ground. "You have stumbled into *Kyo'Assyn* business. Go home. Forget everything you saw here. Do not speak of this. Ever. Am I understood?"

The chill in her voice does not belong to my sister. Nor do firearms. The two guards drop their weapons and run, all too happy to get away from this hard-eyed killer who swaddles flintlock pistols like a baby.

Jen is first to speak. She states what must be truth, though I can scarcely believe it. "Sun'rie, you are an apprentice, as well."

"A talented one," announces a man at the stair-top. He holds an exceptionally long musket, sharpshooter sights attached to the barrel. He descends the stairs and I recognize him as the gardener from the terrace. The one I remarked moved like a dancer. He is a lanky man maybe ten years my senior, and he exhibits a wry intelligence I could not appreciate from distance. His is the careful boldness of one who has overcome many trials, a confidence born of experience and streaked with gallows humor.

"Tyressry Kaab," Jen whispers.

The leader of Xu pauses next to Sun'rie and touches her elbow, a tender question in his gaze. She gives a weak smile and small nod. *Yes, I'm all right.* He then rests his long musket across his shoulder, takes the unfired pistol from Sun'rie's hand, and walks past me to where the Moth twitches on the ground.

"Be glad neither of you co-trained with this sadistic hag," he says, glaring down at the woman. "Back when I co-trained with her, she made me paint her precious fans with my very own blood. Can you believe that? Cut me to ribbons for no other reason than to watch me suffer, then amused herself as I decorated her weapons with my own lifeblood." Tyressry Kaab waves a finger toward the young man Sun'rie shot. "Believe me, we did that poor fool a favor. She exsanguinated her last two apprentices." He then leans over the Moth, whispers something I cannot hear, and shoots her in the face.

Tyressry Kaab is a sharpshooter who trained with the *Assyn*. Now he has an apprentice of his own.

"You are the Beetle," I say.

He straightens and waves gun smoke from his face. "And

you are my brother-in-law. I'll admit, I did not know how this introduction would play out, and I certainly didn't foresee all this, but I think it is a pleasure to finally meet you Ty'rin." He performs a flawless court bow, then turns to Jen. "And of course, the spirited apprentice to the Firefly. I was half a breath from putting a lead shot through your heart before you decided to throw that incendiary at your master. You saved me a good deal of trouble, little miss firebrand, and for that, you have my thanks." He executes a second court bow.

Jen answers my question before I ask it. "I didn't know, Ty. I knew she was your sister because you told me about her hand. That's all."

"Anonymity can be useful," the Beetle says. He jerks his head at the body of the Mantis. "I'm sure that old sociopath taught you two something similar."

"How?" I demand. "How are you *here*, Sun'rie?"

"I'm here because of you," Sun'rie says. "Mother and father died from typhoid four years ago. I don't know if you know that." I didn't. "Then, after Dorin, I couldn't just stay in that house, alone and helpless after losing everyone. I traveled to the capitol and petitioned the *Kyo'Vyar* for an apprenticeship."

I turn to the Beetle, unbelieving. "And you took her?"

"She had a good pedigree," he says, "and who would think this gentle hummingbird capable of pulling a pistol? She's perfect." He makes an abashed grin. "Turns out, I didn't realize how perfect."

"What does that mean?" Jen says.

The Beetle lifts an amused eyebrow at her. His eyes flick to me, back to her. "You of all people should know, firebrand."

"You really did fall in love with her," I say.

The Beetle winks at Sun'rie. "Utterly forbidden, such a thing." He rejoins my sister, and the look they share is the same one my parents shared when we attended a neighbor's wedding. It is the same look as I saw my mother give my father when they walked through the wildflowers that lined the fields after a good rain, the same look my father gave my mother when she announced she was pregnant with Ray'fin.

"And the child ruse?" I ask.

"It's not a ruse," Sun'rie says.

The Beetle places a hand on her belly. "He won't join us for another three months, that's all."

"*She* won't join us for three months," Sun'rie amends, and for a moment, the girl I remember is back, beaming like a clear sunrise.

The Beetle chuckles. "We'll see."

"You were waiting for Ty'rin," Jen says, "weren't you? You knew the *Vyar* would eventually send the Mantis after you, so you waited out in the open, just like me."

The Beetle huffs. "Until this morning, I'd no idea *what* you were doing here. You suddenly turned on your master and then inexplicably hung around like a bad cough. Sun insisted we wait to see what you'd do once Ty'rin arrived. A rather reckless insistence, I thought, but as usual, she made the right call."

I look to my sister. "And why were you waiting for me, Sun? Was it so you could kill me?"

"Honestly," she says, "I don't know. Maybe. I only knew that if I went into hiding before we spoke, I might never have this chance. To shoot you or turn you, to learn the truth about Ray, I'm not certain what I expected. But I knew I needed closure."

I struggle to keep my voice steady. "I killed him, Sun. I put that dart in his neck while you two played in the rain. I can never take that back."

Sun'rie closes her eyes. "The Recruiters asked me about killing a child during my interview. Right when they asked, I knew. Not that it was you, specifically, but that you were there in Dorin that day. And I knew how I would have to answer their question in turn." She looks at the body of the young teenager she gunned down. "I do not forgive you, Ty'rin. I will never, ever forgive you. But I do understand the choice you faced."

It is more than I deserve. Guilt and relief flood through me in a river, for part of me wants her condemnation. I deserve a musket ball through my own temple as much as that youth, and if she were to decide to execute me right here, I would not protest. I cannot forgive myself, either. I am beyond forgiveness, but between Jen and my sister, perhaps I can know some degree of the hope Jen feels. A hope to be something else.

"The *Vyar* won't stop," I say. "If anything, they'll come after you even harder. The Locust, the Spider, and the Wasp are still out there."

"Formidable opponents, all three," the Beetle says. "Though Sun is rather formidable herself, and if you will permit me the boast, I did not become the Beetle simply because I am a good shot. Now, should my *Assyn*-trained brother-in-law and a certain dagger-throwing pyromancer join us, well . . . that would give even the most capable killer pause for consideration. Also, I am not the only one fond of Sun'rie. You saw how the people respond to her. She speaks words dangerous to the *Vyar*. Words like equality and revolution. If spoken in the right way, there are those who would join the four of us."

The four of us. It sounded like a family. Something I ran from nine years ago, then nearly destroyed. How I missed feeling part of a family.

"I say four," the Beetle continues, "but that is soon to be five. And our son—"

"Daughter."

"—could use an overprotective aunt and uncle."

Jen takes my arm. She has already made her choice.

Each of us climbs our own tree, following branches that twist and split and split yet again, pushing into a canopy and intertwining with those of others, none of us certain where they lead. My path forked into darkness, and much as I wish it, I cannot climb back down the tree. I can only take another fork, one pointing a different direction, knowing that down this path lie remorse, and heartache, and just maybe, should I be so fortunate, something treasured by men and unknown to golems. Something like family.

My sister and her husband look to me, their final question implicit: *Will you help protect our child?*

I answer immediately. Best of all, I mean it.

Dark Equations of the Heart

written by

David Cleden

illustrated by

VYTAUTAS VASILIAUSKAS

ABOUT THE AUTHOR

David Cleden lives in the United Kingdom with a demanding family of cats, children and wife (mostly in that order). From an early age, he immersed himself in science fiction. During weekly trips to the local library with his father, he discovered his ABCs—Asimov, Bradbury, Clarke—and all the rest of the author alphabet followed on from there. After eventually realizing that his dream job (being Isaac Asimov) was already taken, he became deeply interested in science, eventually gaining a degree in physics from Imperial College, London. It taught him a new respect for the beauty of mathematics—which sadly, isn't shared by the rest of his family or circle of friends—but gave him the genesis of the story that follows.

The author would like to stress that he is not a trained practitioner of arithmos and has not personally encountered the Dark Equations referenced in this story. Readers are urged not to undertake similar mathematical experiments except under strict supervision.

David now writes business proposals and technical documents by day while actively pursuing the dream of science fiction and fantasy writing on weekends. He can't stress enough how important it is not to muddle them up. He is the 2016 winner of the James White Award, and last year won the Aeon Award.

ABOUT THE ILLUSTRATOR

Vytautas Vasiliauskas, or Vytas, was born in 1990 in Kaunas, Lithuania.

As a child, Vytautas was always interested in drawing and creating various card and tabletop games and comics, not surprisingly inspired

315

by what he saw in popular culture at that time. Later he went on to get a bachelor's degree in fine art and illustration in Coventry, United Kingdom, to gain knowledge about the art world and industry.

Always surrounded by Japanese and American influences, Vytautas continues to study these alongside new contemporary interests. He is mostly self-taught, using his own analysis of classic masters in addition to many online tutorials. Vytautas continues to find new ways of expressing himself through his art and to push his craft in new directions to discover what truly might be his unique take.

Dark Equations of the Heart

Reuben Belgrum stepped from cot to cot, lingering a few minutes at each, his voice low and intimate. The people, wealthy merchant and humble labourer alike—for there were no class barriers in this place of ill-repute—lay in the feverish darkness. The air was heavy with the stink of foul breath, sweat, and desperation. Belgrum ministered to them in turn, his eager fingers reaching for the coin placed beneath each pillow. He trod his silent path between them, an angel of mercy and a demon of despair, whispering words of beguiling beauty and power. *Perhaps it would be better*, he thought, *to plunge a blade into each of their hearts.* A swift ending at least, not this creeping infection that rots a man's soul from the inside.

A young man, no older than himself, turned a pale face towards Belgrum. He appeared scared. *His first time*, Belgrum thought. What would suit for the occasion? An elegant description of binomial theorem, perhaps? Or a pleasing proof of Euclidean geometry? But he had no paper on which to sketch and there wasn't enough light in this cellar. The derivation of infinitesimal calculus, then? No, without a thorough grounding in mathematical fundamentals, its true meaning would be lost, the beauty unglimpsed. *What then? Ah—*

"Imagine two numbers," he whispered. "We shall call them x and y. Remarkable numbers, for the ratio of x to y is precisely the same as that of x plus y to x. Can you picture it?" Belgrum drew little lines in the air with his finger and the man caught his meaning. "The golden ratio ..." he murmured.

"Yes! Exactly!" This one never failed Belgrum. It was as though the golden ratio was hard-wired into the human mind. Perhaps we were all somehow programmed in the womb to appreciate its beauty and seek to shape the world around us in harmony.

Belgrum began to utter a long sequence of numbers: "One point six one eight zero three, three nine eight—" On and on, his voice softly rising and falling, painting a picture with numbers directly into the brain. The sound of his voice was soporific. The man's eyes lost focus. "Yes, yes!" A lazy smile lit up his face as he was transported somewhere far away from the fetid, gloomy cellar.

Belgrum hurried to the next cot. Here, a Laplacian transform, described in exquisite detail, served for this regular client, a man from the city governance department, classically educated. To another, he offered up Euler's Identity, first describing each term, the better to show the unifying beauty of that simple equation in a thunderous climax. It was a cheap, well-worn device, but no less effective for it. Another of his clients was satisfied by nothing more than a clever geometric progression. "Such miracles in the spaces between numbers," the client muttered, and slumped back onto his cot with an ecstatic groan. *Fool*, Belgrum thought. There were no spaces between the numbers. Integers were infinite, and there was an infinity of irrational numbers in the gap between any two integers, so in all the universe there must exist an infinite number of infinities. The universe was packed tight with more numbers than any mind could ever know! And down such yawning chasms of wonderment, human sanity could easily fall, never to return.

Last of all, Belgrum stepped through the low door to the backroom where Isobel waited. The air was even warmer and thicker, cloying in his nostrils and quickening his pulse. He pulled the curtain aside, hesitating. "At last," a husky voice said.

He crossed to the cot where she lay and bent over her. A single candle, burnt down to a stub, cast his flickering shadow across the ceiling. "There were more than I expected tonight," he told her. "In these troubled times, business is good." The past few weeks had indeed been troubled: a senseless, terrifying spate of murders across the city. Men and women, young and old, had been slaughtered—no pattern, no rhyme nor reason. This savagery was the talk in all the taverns, and on the streets too. Each body had been discovered cut open and mutilated in the most grisly fashion, filleted like fish on a fishmonger's slab. But this "Fishmonger Killer" was clever and wily, and yet to be caught. Belgrum wondered what madness drove a man to such depravity? Whatever kind it was, it stalked the streets after dark and he worried for Isobel's safety. She shouldn't have come here alone, but still, he felt glad she had.

Isobel stroked his arm tenderly. "Then don't waste any more time."

In the candlelight, the faded scar on her neck and upper chest looked red and angry. It had been a year and a half since the operation that saved her life, and now she always wore high necklines or a scarf to keep it hidden. To Belgrum though, the marks were beguiling, adding to her beauty not detracting. A cascade of auburn hair spilled across the pillow, framing an oval face, reddened lips pursed in a half-smile. Her gaze caught his and held him steadfast until he felt a curious lightness in his chest. Perhaps one day he would find the courage to tell her of his feelings.

He leant close until the plain, unadorned scent of her skin filled his nostrils and made him dizzy. Then he began to speak: of complex integrals, of strange numbers with real and imaginary parts, and residue theorems, and expressions that tended towards zero yet never quite touched it—like the tantalising caress of a lover drawing away. These were not the dull explanations of mathematical theory that others might administer; nothing so bland for his Isobel. Belgrum conjured up the essence of the *arithmos*. He described its beauty with such eloquence, talked of the perfection that existed when one elegant equation so completely captured an essential truth. With Isobel he knew which images to invoke, the exact sequence of ideas to drip into her mind—like *this*, and *this*, and *this*—to stir the pleasure centres of the brain. Her mind was a beautiful viola to be bowed, he the virtuoso performer.

Isobel became so still and silent as his words fell on her, he couldn't help but wonder if she had slipped into sleep. Then with a soft groan, her back arched and her whole body became rigid. Her head was flung backward, mouth wide in a silent scream. He laid one final captivating equation upon her, elegant in its simplicity, transcendent in its complexity, and she subsided back onto the cot, spent.

His mind felt weakened and skittish from the exertion. There was no air left in this room and the heat ... Ye gods, the heat! Belgrum stumbled from that sinful place out into the darkened streets, scarcely aware of splashing through deep puddles where the canals had spilled over onto the sidewalks again. The cool night air on his face, the wetness soaking into his boots—neither could make him forget the terrible emptiness he felt inside. *You're a fool, Belgrum. You walk this fine line between sanity and madness. But one day soon you'll stumble and fall on the wrong side.*

Yet what choice did he have?

Lost in his thoughts, he heard no footsteps. Suddenly there was an arm tight around his windpipe, half choking him in the darkness. The prick of a knife was sharp against his cheek. "Cheat me of my fee, would you?" a voice breathed in his ear.

"Pietr—"

"Where were you runnin' to, eh?"

"I meant to leave your share. I forgot."

"Did you now? It don't pay to forget things like that round here. Not unless you want your throat slit." A hand thrust into Belgrum's pocket, searching. "Call that gratitude, after I found all those clients for you? Mind on other things, was it? Like that pretty girl of yours?"

Belgrum stayed silent. Isobel wasn't his girl and Pietr knew it.

"Don't suppose that hi-falutin' father of hers would like it if he knew, would he? Is she still filching his notebooks for you? But you gotta get your learnin' from somewhere, eh?"

"Leave Isobel out of this—Hey!" Pietr had withdrawn his hand, the pocketful of coins clenched tight in his fist.

"Only what you owes me. And a little extra for the trouble you've put me to."

Maybe it was better to let him take the money. It didn't do to cross Pietr. The man had *connections*. Let him have it all, and the gods be damned! Belgrum was tired of living like this: a trapped rat running and running and always turning someone else's wheel. And with that thought came sudden clarity as he reached a decision. "Take it then! I want no more of this. As long as I never see you again."

"Don't work like that, does it?" Pietr gave a little grunt. "And funny you should say that, 'cos I've had a special request for your ... *services*. Some posh gentleman's club. Asked for you by name, they did. Not the sort of people to go disappointin'."

Belgrum struggled in his grip. "I told you—I'm through. I won't do this anymore."

"Ho-hum," Pietr said, sounding unconcerned. "I must not be hearin' you clear enough. Thing is, hop joints are dangerous places, aren't they, 'specially for a lady who visits regular-like? All kind of rough folks go there. Wouldn't want nothin' to happen to her. Nothin' *bad*."

Belgrum plucked at the arm still throttling him, feeling righteous anger mount inside, but Pietr only tightened his grip. "I'll get more money," Belgrum wheezed. "Buy my way out. Name your price—but leave Isobel out of this."

"Reckon that girl's capable of takin' care of herself, don't you? All you have to do"—the pressure on his neck loosened and a piece of paper was stuffed into his pocket—"is find this address. Ten o'clock tomorrow night, and don't keep 'em waiting. Then maybe we'll talk."

"Give me your word Isobel won't come to any harm."

"She won't. Not if you honour your contract with me."

"Honour? What would you know about that? Besides, I have no contract with you."

Pietr relaxed his grip and pushed Belgrum away roughly, a wide grin on his face. "You do now."

Reuben Belgrum walked for hours, going wherever his feet took him, trying to outpace his worries. It wasn't working. Then he heard distant voices. He rounded a street corner and ran straight into the mob.

A lookout on the edge of the crowd passed an appraising eye over Belgrum. He seemed satisfied that Belgrum was no Enforcer come to break a few dissident heads and resumed his surveillance of the crowd. *Turbulent times*, Belgrum thought. He needed to be careful.

The soapbox figure haranguing the crowd was petite and well-wrapped against autumn's dreary cold, her face safely hidden by a veil. Even with lookouts, there were sympathizers everywhere, ready to inform. "Learning is for everyone, isn't it, my friends?" she exhorted the crowd. "Why should you be state-registered and state-approved before you're allowed to lift the covers of even the most basic mathematical texts? That learning and understanding is our *birthright*!"

Belgrum was intending to hurry on, but he recognized the woman's voice and it drew him closer.

"Are we so feebleminded," she continued, "that we are not to be trusted with the enjoyment of even the simplest mathematical truth in the privacy of our own homes? Yes—there is ecstasy to be found in the purity of *arithmos*! It exerts a strong and undeniable attraction upon us. But surely this is no more dangerous than other kinds of experience? When we fall deeply in love, don't our thoughts become less focused, our attention more easily distracted—yet the experience is still a wondrous thing. Do we become any less human when we experience such euphoria? Are we a danger to others, or to the society in which we live?" The crowd was stirring restlessly, its mood roused by the woman's words. Someone near the front of the crowd shouted out, "No!" and it was echoed by others.

Oh Isobel. You're treading a dangerous path. He had tried to warn her before. There were rumours of imprisonments, beatings. Some even said the Fishmonger killed those who dabbled too deeply in *arithmos*. But Isobel only laughed when he said that. "My father's influence always protects me. Do you see the irony?"

"If he knew the truth, would he be so understanding?" Belgrum had asked, knowing full well her father would not. He was, after all, the very symbol of the establishment that was trying to stamp out these underground movements. "Oh no," she'd answered with a twinkle in her eye, "that's what makes it all such glorious fun!"

Emboldened now, Isobel continued to address the crowd. "Imagine a world where we could not experience *arithmos*! Where all those beautiful theorems and proofs, those humble equations which embody such universal truths, appear as no more than squiggles on a piece of paper! Where such powerful ideas have no capacity to inspire the minds of ordinary men and women. Where not even the simple elegance of an arithmetic progression is appreciated!"

"Shame!" the crowd chanted at her.

"Yet that's precisely what those in power wish to achieve! They would drive all but the commonest, basest mathematical learning underground. They would outlaw those with the gift of explaining, those elucidators who merely help others to appreciate the beauty. They wish to restrict the advancement of learning to a select few, rob the common man of the simple pleasures of comprehension, deprive the—" Her eyes found Belgrum by chance and she stumbled over her next few words. Belgrum wished he could see the expression on her face. Guilt or defiance, he wondered?

She recovered, and her voice grew more strident. The crowd were with her now, shouts of encouragement punctuated every other sentence. But Belgrum noticed there was one man she had left unmoved. He stood near the far edge of the crowd. His back was to Belgrum, but something about his stance marked him out. A large, powerful man, expensively dressed. He stood motionless while all around him jostled and fidgeted. On his right hand he wore a leather glove, the fingers of which seemed abnormally slender. Belgrum began circling the crowd to get a better look at his face—but by the time he had done so, the man had slipped away and Belgrum could find no trace of him.

Pietr's slip of paper took him—reluctantly—to an address in the eastern quarter of the city: broad boulevards and terraced rows of anonymous white-stone buildings, where the paved streets were shovelled clear of horse dung each day. A clutch of expensively tailored gentlemen and ladies strolled in the evening air, having no pressing business to attend. It was a place of wealth, privilege, and power. Belgrum felt completely out of place.

His knock was answered by a bellboy who fetched the gentleman in question. Lars Eysenck was a tall, wiry man with a thinning pate and such nervous energy that he hopped from foot to foot like a robin in search of worms.

Eysenck led him into a grand drawing room panelled in dark mahogany where towering glass-fronted bookcases climbed into the shadows. The gaslights were dim, almost to the point of gloom. A gathering of perhaps twenty-five gentlemen were ensconced in clusters of easy chairs. At the far end of the room, gilded portraits glowered down on the gathering, and a lectern awaited.

Belgrum was not expecting to speak to them as a group. "That's . . . that's not how I do it," he stammered.

"Then what is your method?"

"Individually. I will speak to each of you in turn."

A portly gentleman levered himself out of an armchair and approached. "Oh no," he said. "No, that will not do. We cannot be kept waiting for our satisfaction while you work your way around the room."

"I think what Mr. Belgrum is trying to say—" Eysenck began,

but the portly gentleman interrupted as though Eysenck had not spoken.

"Besides, there is the matter of precedence. We shall never be able to agree upon the order in which you serve us. No, I must insist that you address the entire room."

"I cannot possibly—" but Belgrum's response was lost in the general babble as all the gentlemen began to express their views at once. It was not a happy room, Belgrum observed glumly. That was going to make his job as elucidator twice as hard. If not for Pietr's blackmail, he would have foregone payment and left that instant.

Suddenly the hubbub died away. From the shadows at the edge of the room, a figure raised a hand for silence. It was the slightest of movements, no more than a gesture of the wrist. Yet somehow everyone noticed. The man was nestled deep in a wing-back chair. Belgrum couldn't see his face but the raised hand wore a black leather glove. The slender fingers were stiff and freakishly long—unquestionably the same man he had seen in the crowd, the man who had been watching Isobel.

Absolute silence had fallen on the room. Into it, the man spoke with the voice of one who expected to be obeyed without question. "Begin."

What topic should he choose? His *arithmos* was self-taught and he feared he might be exposed as a fraud before such an august group—no matter that he had spent countless nights slaving over his mathematical texts with a kind of manic intensity.

Perhaps a simple proof to start them off? Yes. He would gauge their learning and their mood. Change up a gear or down, as necessary. He had barely begun to speak when—

"Enough!"

The cry halted Belgrum in mid-sentence. The man with the gloved hand sprang from the chair and strode into an adjoining private office. "Come!" he called over his shoulder, before disappearing.

Eysenck looked meaningfully at Belgrum, gesturing with

his head that Belgrum should follow. "Who is that?" Belgrum whispered.

"Lord Felton-Oriel Urquhart is a founding member of the society." Eysenck touched his arm lightly and lowered his voice. "An important man. Be sure to give him whatever he asks for."

Belgrum found Urquhart seated behind a broad desk, copious paperwork of some kind ordered in neat piles like army battalions being readied on the battlefield. A gas lamp turned low provided the only illumination. Urquhart's gaze was intense, like the hawk observing its prey, calculating the moment for its swooping dive. Belgrum took a seat opposite. "Shall I begin?" he asked hesitantly, assuming a private audience was required after all.

Urquhart studied him a moment then barked a laugh. "Indeed, no! I doubt there is any mathematical wonder you could describe that is not already familiar to me a dozen times over. Don't confuse me with those feebleminded dilettantes out there." He leaned forward. "I am a *connoisseur* in these matters."

"Then—?"

Urquhart regarded him steadily for a long moment. "Tell me, Master Belgrum. From where do you obtain your knowledge of mathematics? Such materials are closely guarded by the University, yet you seem in possession of quite advanced concepts."

Belgrum had no answer, at least none that he cared to voice. Urquhart shrugged as if the lack of an answer was of no consequence. "I'm given to understand there is a certain young lady of your acquaintance. Her father is an important man, a sitting member of the University Senate. Was he not also a promising mathematician in his youth?" An eyebrow raised quizzically, but still Belgrum gave him no reaction. "No matter. Instead, let me describe the purpose for which I brought you here. I have a small task for you to perform. A book I would like you to obtain."

Now Belgrum could see where this was going. There was a small but thriving black market for mathematical texts. Elucidators such as himself depended on them for source material. Most were tatty handwritten copies of copies, harmless primers and instructional texts barely more potent than the basic arithmetic a child might learn in the classroom. But a small number were lifted from under the noses of the University's theoreticians, those talented few who worked in the most challenging of circumstances. Years of training had built up their mental tolerance to *arithmos*, working as they did at the cutting edge where new theorems were patiently honed. Their chalkboards were filled with eigenvectors and Bessel functions and nonlinear transformations that verged on the esoteric. They dealt in equations of such beauty that they risked their own sanity in contemplation of them. Belgrum had glimpsed enough of those materials to know his limits. He took from them only what he thought was safe—both for himself and for his clients. In the hands of a skilled elucidator such as he, they brought an hour or two's bliss to the mind of the common man. And he was careful to keep his descriptions simple—because at the heart of everything, there was beauty in simplicity.

But Urquhart didn't strike him as a man to be satisfied with the pedestrian.

"Ah! I see by your expression you have misunderstood," Urquhart said. "This is a book of poetry I'm seeking. Nothing underhand, you see. A volume published privately in a very limited edition and consequentially quite rare. *Dark Equations of the Heart.* Perhaps you've heard of it?"

Belgrum shook his head. "Surely any reputable bookseller can obtain such a thing?"

"No. Quite impossible." Urquhart's tone became weary, as though he tired of explaining the obvious. "This particular volume was personally inscribed by the author not long before his untimely death. Such an exceptional man, a true polymath. Poetry was but one of his talents, and not the greatest by any means. You have, I believe, various channels for obtaining unorthodox works? Certain ... contacts?"

"Your interest in poetry must be compelling."

Urquhart frowned. "Compelling ... Yes, a most appropriate word in the circumstances."

Belgrum thought of the debt that Pietr held over him, and his promise to Isobel to guard her secrets from her father. Neither had he forgotten Eysenck's words. *Be sure to give him whatever he asks for.*

Belgrum gave a barely perceptible nod. "I will make enquiries."

Urquhart clapped his hands together, one gloved hand onto bare flesh. "Excellent! I'm glad we have an understanding." Urquhart's gaze remained unrelenting, the dark eyes piercing. "Tell me—Did you ever consider, Master Belgrum, how different our world might be without *arithmos*? Suppose the human mind were *not* endowed with its instinctive appreciation of mathematical beauty, piercing straight to the pleasure centres of the brain?"

The echo of Isobel's words wasn't lost on him. Was Urquhart testing him in some way, or merely making a point?

"Were our rationality not so easily blinded," Urquhart continued, "what great things might we have achieved? Would we have forged ahead in our understanding of the physical sciences, created great works of engineering? Instead, it's as if we stare into the sun, our vision blurred as we fumble to make mathematics do our bidding. Oh, I'm sure those with the greatest resilience do what they can to develop the field, but it is little enough. I myself have tried, but I grow bored easily. I yearn to challenge my mind. Test my limits."

He grunted, as if in pain. With delicate, precise movements, Urquhart loosened each finger of the glove he wore on his right hand and slipped it off. He flexed the fingers as though chasing stiffness from them, but that wasn't what fixed Belgrum's attention. Where the last joint should be, each finger was topped with a long, thin blade, like that of a scalpel. They caught the light and made a soft rasping sound as they rubbed against each other.

"These were ... gifted ... to me," Urquhart said quietly. "The surgeon in question felt I had cheated him in a business matter and sought a means of redress. He drugged me and abused me thus. When I was revived, he said he wished to ensure no other businessman would shake my hand on a deal without first thinking very carefully." Urquhart smiled, but there was no warmth in it. "His name was Dr. Amos. It is he who authored *Dark Equations of the Heart*."

Belgrum couldn't wrench his eyes from those talonlike fingers. "Can't the surgery be reversed?"

"Oh yes. Easily." Urquhart reached out and removed a single rose from a vase on the desk. He inspected it carefully, then inhaled its fragrance. "But they serve me in unexpected ways." The fingers flexed. Two outer petals fell silently onto the desk. Belgrum was suddenly reminded of the old maxim: a blade cuts two ways. It could cut to save a life like the scalpel in the hands of a surgeon, or it could slash and pierce and drain away a life—like the callous blade of the Fishmonger.

"Dr. Amos's skills as a surgeon were never in doubt," Urquhart continued. "He also dabbled in mathematics, but what began as a hobby soon became an obsession. I believe he learnt what he could from stolen texts—much as you do yourself—and what couldn't be learned from books, he deduced from first principles. Away from the censorious meddling of the authorities, his prodigious natural talent led him in unexpected directions. Yet none of his discoveries entirely satisfied him. I'm certain he only turned to poetry as an expression of his frustrations. He sought ever darker, purer equations. Powerful, dangerous things."

Belgrum smiled faintly. "Such things don't exist. Only as propaganda spread by the authorities to scare off the curious."

"You're too quick to dismiss. Certainly, *he* believed such a thing might exist. And if it did, he decided he must be the one to discover such a truth. He *craved* the glory."

"More than he valued his sanity?"

A finger flicked, and the bottom inch of stem fell to the desktop.

"He had the strength of mind and the stamina. Years of constant dabbling with *arithmos* builds up a certain immunity. The ennui of commonplace *arithmos* becomes unbearable after a while—don't you find that? But if Dr. Amos were to derive such an equation, who could he tell? To whom could he boast if the act of comprehension drove the unwary into madness?"

Belgrum stroked his chin. "Once discovered, it would certainly be hard to keep it secret."

"Precisely! It would be too dangerous to commit to paper. Too easy for it to fall into untrained hands and destroy innocent minds. It could only be exposed to someone who had developed the necessary fortitude. Even then ..." Urquhart looked up slowly from the flower.

"You'd risk your own sanity?"

"For the chance of such ecstasy? What man of learning could resist?" Urquhart drew the flower closer. For a moment he appeared to caress it. Then its petals fell in a shower.

Belgrum swallowed. "How did Dr. Amos die?"

Urquhart glanced up. His blade-fingers seemed to tremble, or perhaps it was just the flickering gaslight. "By his own hand. Driven mad by the very thing he had discovered—but not, I think, before he had a chance to conceal it somewhere safe. Would it have been better lost for good? Perhaps. But what has been found once can be found again. This dark equation was the product of *his* mind, and his alone. I don't think he could bear the idea of someone else claiming credit for his discovery. Wouldn't you or I have done the same?"

No, Belgrum thought. He would not. He had danced long enough along the edges of sanity to recognize those kinds of traps.

"The good doctor gave copies of his book to many of his patients. I am told one of them contained a handwritten inscription. If I can find it, I may have my clue." Urquhart sighed. "I have laboured hard to trace all those patients and it has not been easy. Dr. Amos's mind was clearly tormented in those final weeks of life, the equation eating away at his soul like some kind of blight, but his hands were as skilful as ever and he saw a great many cases. I have searched—and continue to search—but the one I am seeking still eludes me."

"For what purpose? What do you ask of his patients?"

"Ask? I don't need to ask anything of them."

Belgrum's mind was whirling. Men and women, young and old, no pattern or connection other than as patients of this doctor. It somehow seemed a familiar conundrum. "I don't see the connection in all this."

Urquhart fell silent as though savouring the moment. Then he said, "It has come to my attention one such volume resides in the private collection of a certain well-connected gentleman affiliated to the University. My access to this collection is barred, but an acquaintance of the family might fare better. The gentleman's name—" But Belgrum was already rising from his seat. "If you mean Isobel's father, then I won't do it! I promised never to do anything that might lead her father to ... to ..." the words seemed to sting the back of his throat. "To think any the less of her."

Urquhart pointed a bladed finger at him. "She is an *arithmos* addict and you, sir, are her peddler. I see no sense in denying the truth and pretending otherwise. If she chooses to keep that knowledge from her father, that is her affair, but your connection to her father is valuable to me. We can all profit from this situation. Find this copy of *Dark Equations of the Heart*. Borrow it, steal it, I care not—but bring it to me."

Belgrum was on his feet, unable to contain his anger. "You ask too much of me!"

"I'm not asking, Mr. Belgrum. Not *asking*." His right hand made a swift swirling motion, too fast for the eye to follow. What was left of the stem was diced into pieces. "Bring me this book and you shall have whatever you ask for. Refuse, and I shall take everything that you have from you. *Everything*."

Isobel was waiting for him, sitting primly on a park bench, a flock of expectant sparrows making darting runs between her legs to peck the breadcrumbs she scattered. A morning mist had lingered into midafternoon, the grey sky low and oppressive in the nearly deserted park.

"We agreed not to be seen together in public," she reminded him. "What's so urgent it's worth the risk?"

He took her hand in his. She flinched, and he understood her awkwardness but she didn't withdraw her hand. Desperation had brought him thus far; now it must carry him further. But he had no plan, not even an inkling of one. He was no burglar—and even if he were, he had no idea where to search. The whole quest that Urquhart had sent him on seemed preposterous. Only the thought of those bladed fingers at his throat drove him on. "May I come to your house?"

His question left Isobel flustered. "What? No! Father would be sure to ask questions! If he found out who you were, about our association I mean, and what I truly believe in … It's not that I'm ashamed—but the revelation would crush him."

"Please, Isobel. I wouldn't ask if it wasn't important." He took a deep breath, readying the speech he'd practiced a dozen times in his head. "Isobel, there's something I need to ask you. It's very important. There's a book in your father's collection which I would very much like to see. A book of poems—"

Isobel tilted her head back as if only really seeing him for the first time. "Poems? You?"

He blushed. "It's called *Dark Equations of the Heart*. A very rare book. A private edition."

"And valuable," Isobel added. "And also something I treasure greatly." She reached into her purse and withdrew a slim volume.

Belgrum was dumbfounded. "*You* have it? You carry it with you?"

"Always."

"May I?"

A moment's hesitation, and then she handed him the little book. He ran a finger over the soft leather covers, opening it long enough to see there was an inscription inside but made no attempt to read the spidery scrawl. Knowing what he must do, he raised his eyes to meet Isobel's gaze. "I am so sorry," he said, and before there was time for regrets, he stood and sprinted away across the park, the book clutched tightly in his hand.

*S*weet child—*fear not the darkness in man's heart. It is but a place where the light of comprehension has yet to shine. Until the child grows into the adult, we can but hope for contentment in our ignorance.*
—*Thaddeus A.*
Dark Equations of the Heart

VYTAUTAS VASILIAUSKAS

The gentleman's club was shrouded in darkness save for one gas lamp burning low and erratically in the foyer. But the door was open. As he entered, Belgrum moved a hand to his breast pocket where the stolen volume of poetry rested. It weighed as heavy as any burden he could ever recall.

Beyond the foyer, the members' chamber seemed larger: a dark, echoing space where the scattered armchairs were deep pools of black, like a herd of slumbering creatures. At the far end of the room, the door was open; a faint glimmer spilled out.

"Come!" Urquhart commanded, though Belgrum could swear he had entered as stealthily as a mouse.

"I trust you have not disappointed me?" Urquhart sat behind his panelled desk. He drew a desk lamp closer, the fingers of his left hand quivering as he reached for the book Belgrum had laid before him.

Belgrum began, "Now that our bargain is done—"

A raised right hand admonished him, no longer sheathed in its glove. While Urquhart turned the pages, Belgrum's gaze was drawn again to those multifaceted blades tipping the fingers. He marvelled at how they reflected the light. Satisfied, Urquhart drew one bladed finger downwards—a slight, casual movement—and the title page was cut free. He moved it closer to the light. His eyes scanned the inscription a dozen times or more, rather as a thirsty man would scoop water from a clear pool. At last he looked up and handed the book back to Belgrum. "Take it. Return it to your friend."

Belgrum blinked in surprise. "I doubt I'll ever see Isobel again. I've betrayed her trust."

"Oh, come now. I have no doubt she is waiting for you in the hop-joint at this very moment."

"What makes you so certain?"

Urquhart tilted his head to one side as though musing on some thought. "*Arithmos* addicts have one thing in common. *Need.* She will be there."

Belgrum sighed. "Now that I've done what you asked, will you speak to Pietr? Ask him to release me from my contract?"

Urquhart smiled. "Pietr will trouble you no more." He glanced over to a darkened corner of the room, to the chair where Pietr sat—so still and quiet in the shadows that Belgrum hadn't noticed his presence. Pietr stared back at Belgrum with glassy eyes, mouth open in a kind of perpetual look of surprise. A single channel of arterial blood, dark now as it dried, ran from the deep incision to his neck.

Belgrum stumbled from the room, blundering into armchairs and side tables in his haste to be gone, as all the while Urquhart's laughter chased him from the building.

Belgrum ran through darkened city streets, no destination or purpose in mind. His thoughts raced like great wheels clattering inside his head, and each revolution wore down a little more of his sanity, revealing the knot of madness at its core. Shadows in the quiet alleyways made his heart race. It was hard to push the image of those finger-blades from his mind. How easily—and how deeply—they cut.

Arithmos was everywhere he turned, pressing in on him from all sides. He saw the city with different eyes: its congruent geometries and bisected planes, the golden ratios in the stone facades and windows of shuttered town houses. From an open window the sound of a flute carried on the night air. It wasn't the tune he heard but the spacing of the notes, an arithmetic progression in its rhythm that built until the notes fluttered together into a single continuous tone and the pressure in his head made Belgrum want to scream.

And thus, into the emptiness of his brain, a single thought slipped. He came to a sudden halt. *Not the book itself, but its owner.* That's what Urquhart had been looking for all along.

Oh Isobel! You're the one who holds the key to this mystery.

And you are the biggest fool of all, he told himself. *Because you've just handed that key directly to Urquhart.*

She wasn't in the usual hop-joint. He shook every one of the dozing clients to be sure, asking if they had seen her, knew where she might have gone—but all he got were curses and threats. *Of course* she wouldn't be here. He'd betrayed her trust and stolen her precious book, snatched it from her hands and run like a common thief. Why would she want to see him again?

But she needed her *arithmos*. If not here, where would she go?

He searched for nearly an hour. Eventually he found her in a seedy little den down near the river, dank, rundown and dirty. He saw the flicker of fear in her eyes as he entered the room. Stiffly and deliberately, she turned her back to him. Belgrum bought off the madam with the last of Urquhart's coins so that they had the cramped little room to themselves.

"Don't come closer," she hissed, backing away into a corner. "I thought I could trust you. I thought you were my *friend*."

He held out his hands placatingly. "It's not safe here, Isobel. You have to leave the city. Get as far away as you can."

Her face flushed with anger. "Don't dare tell me what to do!"

He seized her arm and she struggled for a moment, but his grip was firm. "I *am* your friend," he told her. "Listen to me—" One deep breath and then the truth spilled out—about his meetings with Urquhart, about the dark equations and their treacherous nature—and last of all, how powerfully obsessed Urquhart had become. "He will stop at nothing, Isobel. He means to rediscover this dark equation himself."

Isobel shook herself free of his grasp. "*If* any of that is true—" she pointed a finger at Belgrum, advanced a step and now it was Belgrum who backed up. "*If*, then it's already too late. You stole the book from me. Whatever nonsense code may be hidden inside, Urquhart has it now."

Belgrum shook his head. "The book doesn't hold the answer. It never did. It's only a kind of marker post. One that points to *you*. That's the reason you were given it."

Isobel laughed harshly. "You think I'm concealing some great mathematical secret from you?"

"No." Belgrum reached out gently to finger the scarf at her neck. Isobel flinched.

"Let me see those scars you keep so well-hidden," he said.

She stared at him, frowning. "What have they to do with anything?"

"Please. It's important."

Something in his expression must have convinced her. After a moment she fumbled with a couple of buttons and pulled her collar down, turning away as though embarrassed. A tracery of thin scars ran from the top of her sternum, branching and spreading across her chest. "And the name of your surgeon? The one who saved your life?"

"Is this some kind of parlour game, Reuben?" But then she sighed. "All right, all right. When I fell ill with grey-scourge, Father insisted on finding the best surgeon in the city to cut out the growths. They'd taken such a hold that another week or two's delay and— Well. Let's just say it was fortunate Father had both money and influence. There were plenty of others less fortunate." She looked up defiantly into Belgrum's eyes, seeing that he still wanted his question answered. "The surgeon's name was Dr. Amos."

Belgrum felt the room tilt a little. "Then it all fits," he mumbled.

"Reuben, what are you talking about?"

"Dr. Amos gave you *Dark Equations of the Heart* as a keepsake, didn't he? Just as he entrusted his awful discovery to you."

"Reuben, I swear he didn't! Why would he? My only acquaintance with him was out of medical necessity."

Belgrum said grimly, "Oh, but you're wrong. *You* are the keeper of the equation. Right here." He placed a finger lightly between her breasts. She slapped his hand away in irritation.

"Amos needed a way to preserve his secret," Belgrum continued. "Writing it down, even in coded form, was too dangerous. What if it fell into inexperienced hands? There are probably no more than a dozen highly trained mathematicians in the University who would not be overwhelmed by it. Enough elegance and beauty to engulf the human soul! Doesn't it make you feel giddy just thinking about it? But Amos couldn't bear to let the discovery slip away."

"That's ridiculous! How could he have given me something

like that without my knowing? Wait—do you think my scars are some kind of clue? An equation in coded form?"

"No. Too obvious. I think the truth is written on your beating heart. *Literally*. When you were under his knife, all it would have taken was a hot needle and his dexterity. Tiny little scars etched into the quivering outer layers of heart-muscle: quick-healing, permanent marks you would have known nothing about. He meant you to carry his secret until your death—inaccessible, yet somehow not lost. Only then could he rest easy."

"No—"

"His dedication to you in the book as good as says so, doesn't it? He thought to put the equation beyond reach, but he hadn't reckoned with Urquhart's obsession. Don't you see? Urquhart has tracked down each patient, butchering them one by one to discover if they carried the dark equation. And so far, none has. All those brutal murders these past months, the so-called 'Fishmonger' gutting and filleting his victims. Yet there was no obvious motive, seemingly no pattern to the choice of victim. Except for one thing."

Isobel's eyes were wide. Almost without thinking, she had backed farther into the room. Belgrum pressed on relentlessly. "I'll wager every single victim was a former patient of Dr. Amos. It's as though the killer is looking for something, isn't it? And when he doesn't find it, he moves on, hunting down individuals one by one. Always searching, never finding."

"Until now," she said. "My god! Where is Urquhart? It is him, isn't it?"

"I'm so sorry, Isobel. I think I've led him directly to you."

"Then what should I do?" she said in a whisper. Her face had become deathly pale.

"Do you trust me?" She nodded weakly.

"Then please. Undress, and do exactly as I say."

Belgrum crouched by the door to the street, listening to the sounds outside, trying to judge if it was safe for them to leave. All was quiet save for the distant rumble of a laden cart heading for the quay side and two tomcats engaged in a loud disagreement over territory in the alley beyond. He knew they must leave straightaway, but the night was a cold one and filled with too many shadows.

Without warning, the door slammed inwards, sending him crashing to the floor. Urquhart stood in the doorway. "Excellent!" he said, focusing on Isobel.

Isobel's face turned deathly white, but she stood her ground. Urquhart pointed at Belgrum, a steel blade gleaming at the end of his forefinger. "Stay where you are! Leave me to my work."

But Belgrum had no intention of doing that. He struggled to his feet, meaning to put himself between Isobel and Urquhart— but his opponent was quicker. Urquhart rushed into the room, delivering a jab to the throat so hard and vicious that Belgrum wondered if his windpipe had been crushed. He couldn't breathe; his vision was blurring. *If he'd struck me with his right hand, those scalpel fingernails would have ripped my neck apart.* But that was little consolation. He felt as though he would never be able to draw air into his protesting lungs again.

Urquhart advanced, pressing Isobel into the corner, pinning her arms. She struggled, kicking out wildly, hissing like some alley cat.

Belgrum's vision was narrowing. The struggling Isobel appeared to be at the end of a dark tunnel, receding by the second. Dimly he saw Urquhart's hand slash downwards, heard the sound of fabric tearing, and Isobel's screams. *It's too late*, he thought. *This is all my fault and I could do nothing to stop it.*

Belgrum was on his knees. Still no breath would come. Where his lungs used to be, there was only a cold, empty place. Perhaps he should let the numbness envelop him and just embrace the darkness.

Isobel struggled in Urquhart's grip. He touched the scar on her neck almost reverentially, beginning to trace its curving lines down her body. "Yes," he whispered. "I think you truly are the one."

In a savage motion, he ripped the tattered remains of the dress from her shoulders. Isobel grew silent and ceased her struggling. Now it was Urquhart's turn to become still.

"What is this? What trickery?"

Her bared skin was covered in neat script, the ink barely dry from Belgrum's hasty work. Equations and symbols marched down her body: eight or more lines in a rambling proof of the impossible.

Still on his knees, Belgrum took a sudden, convulsive breath and it felt as though life itself flooded back into his body.

Isobel offered no resistance as Urquhart stared at the equations written on her body. Belgrum had called it a nonsense proof, little more than schoolboy doggerel. It began with a definition of unity and, through a series of convoluted equivalences, demonstrated that its terms summed to zero. In other words, a proof that one equals zero. That was absurd, of course. Somewhere deep in the manipulated formulae there was a subtle falsehood, like a magician's sleight of hand.

Belgrum didn't doubt Urquhart would easily spot the deception. Urquhart had the depth of learning, a connoisseur's instinctive grasp of *arithmos*—but he was still an addict for all that. And what addict could resist such a curious puzzle, a purported proof that one equals zero?

But where was the falsehood hidden ...? Urquhart frowned, drawn in by its challenge.

Belgrum used the back of a chair to haul himself to his feet. Then he used the chair itself as a weapon, swinging it high in an arc. Isobel's graffitied body had bought him the necessary few seconds of distraction after all.

"Childish," Urquhart was saying, eyes sweeping across the symbols as he searched for the falsehood. "I see it!" Then, sensing danger, he turned raising one hand instinctively against the descending chair. He staggered, parrying the blow, and his bladed fingers sank deep into the wood. But Urquhart was powerfully built and Belgrum was no match for his strength. With comparative ease, Urquhart used the chair to drive him back across the room, thrusting him hard into the wall. Urquhart bore down on him forcing the back of the chair against his bruised windpipe. Choking for breath once more, Belgrum twisted the chair free with the last of his strength and Urquhart screamed in pain as the finger-blades, still deeply embedded in the wood, tore free of his flesh. Blood ran from each ruined fingertip as Urquhart sank to his knees, cradling his wounded hand, screaming obscenities.

Belgrum threw his jacket over Isobel's shoulders and they fled. They raced into the night, dodging through alleys and darkened streets, drawing on all his secret knowledge of the city. He had no idea where they were headed. All he knew was that there was no safe place back where they had come from, nowhere Urquhart would not find them eventually.

They walked for hours, until their feet were sore and blistering but Belgrum wouldn't let them rest. "Father has money—" Isobel began.

"Money won't keep you safe. Money will be a trail that leads straight back to you. And once there's a trail, Urquhart will follow it."

"What then?"

"I'll keep you safe. I'll help you disappear. We must reinvent you as someone else. I don't know of any other way."

Hours later, they stopped to rest at the side of the road on the outskirts of a little village far beyond the city. The sky was beginning to lighten in the east. Belgrum slipped an arm round Isobel's shoulders as she began to shiver.

"You're safe here, at least for a little while. No one knows us in this place."

She pulled away from him sharply. "Safe? How can I ever be safe? Who can I trust when I carry such a terrible thing—such an *evil* thing—inside me? I'm like a book waiting to be read. All anyone has to do is open the cover ..."

"It doesn't change who you are. You're still a good person, Isobel."

"It changes everything! The evil is a *part* of me. It's something I can never cut out. And *he* will never stop looking. Not while I live."

Somewhere deep in his own heart Belgrum knew she was right, but he was too tired to argue. There were men and women who would think nothing of taking a life to glimpse that dark equation, to drink in the purest *arithmos*, and taste its power. Even the thought of being within touching distance of that knowledge sent a little tingling thrill through Belgrum. Would he have the reserves of strength to withstand such a thing? Would he dare test himself to such limits? He imagined the skin peeled back, the rib cage parted, the still-beating heart exposed and that dark scar tissue spelling out its terrible secret to hungry eyes ...

His head jerked up with a start after the brief slumber he'd slipped into. For a moment, he couldn't remember where he was or why he was here.

Of Isobel, there was no sign.

Advice for Artists

BY ROB PRIOR

At a very early age, Rob Prior knew he wanted to be an artist by profession. After his father revealed that the bionics in the Six-Million Dollar Man were just science fiction, he developed a fear of losing the use of his dominant hand and spent several years training himself to use both hands for everything he did in his daily life, including his art. Rob has been a published artist since the age of thirteen, when he worked for a local publishing company creating illustrations.

Rob's passion for art and music have made him notorious as the ambidextrous artist who creates masterpieces in record time, painting with both hands at once, and often with his eyes closed. His live painting sessions are a mesmerizing combination of art, entertainment, and excitement for audiences as small as two and as large as several thousand. Rob's art has traveled far and wide, and his works have been exhibited in museums and galleries across North America, Europe, Asia, and Africa.

With a comic artist background, Rob has worked with Marvel and DC, but his most notable credits include work on Star Wars: The Force Awakens, Terminator, Deep Space 9, Game of Thrones, Buffy the Vampire Slayer. Rob is also part owner of Heavy Metal magazine. When he is not in the studio or on the road painting at an event, he is highly sought after as a director and producer of movies and music videos. He and his family reside in southern California. Rob's motto is: "You can do anything you want to do, if you want it bad enough."

Advice for Artists

Many young artists ask me similar questions. I'll share some experience and advice that has helped me and can help you, too.

Really, the biggest issue is that young artists tend to give up very easily. Probably the question I'm asked the most is, "How did you make it?" I always say that you have to keep trying. You don't know if an art director woke up on the wrong side of the bed or he's seen fifty portfolios or a hundred portfolios that day and yours happens to be 101. If you try ten times, it's not enough. If you try twenty times, it's not enough. You have to keep sending your work out. Just send it.

Most people in the professional world get paid to tell you No. That's just how it is. They reject artists out of habit. If you can, go to them and get their advice. Ask them, "What can I do to make my portfolio better?" Most artists never ask that. They get the rejection letter. They get depressed and their productivity goes down—ending a career that could have been. My advice is to just stick it through. If you have to send your portfolio out a thousand times, then do it, because you never know if that thousandth submission is going to be the one where people say "That's what we want to see." Learn from your rejection letters. Just keep getting better.

Most artists will approach a project with their own agenda and ideas. When you're painting covers and working in the real world, you must understand 5% of that is work for yourself and 95% is for and through other people. So, if you want to get published, get out of doing something your own way. You have to understand what your client wants and create that.

Other questions I'm consistently asked are, "How do you not stagnate? How do you get rid of artist's block?" And my answer is this: I don't have artist's block. I don't have writer's block. I work on five or more projects at a time, well actually more, but I always suggest people work on three to five projects consistently. Because when you hit a wall on one and you just can't go any further, you bounce to another. And you may come up with solutions on project #3 that won't work for #3 but they might work for project #1 or they might work for project #5. Work on multiple projects—as many as you can handle—and don't let laziness get in the way (artists tend to be very lazy).

I think artist's block or writer's block is an excuse to not go forward. And artists should never have an excuse to not continue on. You should push through anything and everything. If you're an artist—it's how you breathe, it's how you live, it's what you love—then create art.

Work on your craft consistently. Attempt everything you can to be good at every aspect. Every day, I tell the apprentices in my studio: study and learn. If you don't know how to draw trees, go buy books with trees in them, go to a forest, or go somewhere there are trees. Draw them consistently over and over again. If you have trouble drawing hands, draw hands.

Prepare yourself for what is about to come. Remember that you can't only be able to draw eyeballs and expect to get a job. You've got to be able to draw anything. This happened to me: I'm better at drawing people than I am almost anything, but my first job in Hollywood was storyboarding for a Jeep commercial. And I hate drawing cars. I hate it. But I said, "All right," and I went out and brushed up on drawing cars until I could draw them perfectly. When I went in for the job, I was ready.

I always say, "Believe in yourself, but while you believe in yourself, feed your artistic self, the artist within you."

People ask me about computer art. And I'm all for learning to master that medium. The computer can be a great tool. However, when people just take photos, apply twenty-five filters, and think it's art, then I have something to say about it, because that's just wrong. That's being a button pusher, not an artist. Instead, learn to use the tools that are on hand. If you're a good painter, but you're not so good at chalk, pick up some chalk and study it. You never know when something is going to come in handy. The more well-rounded your skills, the more chances you have of being hired.

So the question all artists have whether they ask anyone else or not is, "How good does a piece of art need to be?" And L. Ron Hubbard gave some advice that I agree with: "Technical expertise itself adequate to produce an emotional impact." And that's how good a work of art needs to be.

You have to boost your technical expertise up to the level needed for the job. Most people just throw too much into a project, and sometimes minimalism is the best. Any illustration starts with a good layout. But don't create just one layout, especially when you are starting out. For everything I paint, I make dozens of little tiny layouts. Study the old masters. Their layout sense was impeccable. The tricks after that are about what's going to have the most visual impact.

Paint a picture to the best of your ability and then step back from it: Okay. Is it visually pleasing? Is it crowded? (It tends to be crowded most of the time.) Does it tell a story? Convey an emotion?

I rely mostly on my artwork to convey emotion. That's why I use splatter. But I'm very particular about how I use it and what kind of splatter per piece. You want to pull an emotional response. Make sure that your artwork is technically excellent for the audience that you are aiming for.

Another piece of advice—somebody said this to me once and I've done it ever since—make friends as best you can. Be nice on the phone. Send coffee to the assistants of the people you want to work with. Send them flowers. They have direct contact to the person that you need to get to, so the friendlier that you are with them, the more chance you have. A guy was asking me about this the other day. He said he likes to drop off his portfolio in person, but apparently the receptionists are nasty. Well, he has to figure out how to win those receptionists over, or he's never going to be seen. His work is going to the bottom of the pile. Whatever you have to do, make sure that you are friendly to the people who are the conduit to the person you need to get to.

A big problem most artists have when they put a portfolio together is they throw everything in there: the kitchen sink, things they drew when they were ten. The more choices you give an art director, the more chances they have to say, "No." Compile your five best pieces into your submission and call it a day. If you need to show different styles, don't include more than eight. The recipient will lose interest on more than that. Most likely, they are not even going to be paying attention by page eight. Try to capture them with the first three to five pieces. That's what you need to create interest in your work.

As for getting your art out there, figure out what you want your discipline to be first. If you want to illustrate, then go after book publishers. If you love Photoshop and you're really good at it, send a portfolio to movie poster companies— they're everywhere now, not just in Hollywood. Video game companies need covers for games and other things. Board games, there are thousands of them out there. If you want to do graphic stuff, you can just start designing people's business cards and things like that. And if there are contests, enter contests. Enter Illustrators of the Future. These contests are the greatest thing I've ever seen for artists because it's a chance to be published—that's so important. It's rare—in fact, I don't think there is any other group that does what this Contest is doing.

You can find the companies you're looking for on the internet. When I was starting out, you had to go to the yellow pages and actually required some detective work. Now you can just look a company up, find the creative art director, and send them your portfolio.

Think of smart ways to send your art so that it will be seen. When I sent a portfolio to Random House, I included Christmas lights. I got a big battery pack. I put the battery pack on the Christmas lights. I turned them on. I plastic wrapped it and overnighted it. They received a blinking, glowing package—of course, they were going to open it. Get inventive. Be creative. Think about something that's going to get you noticed.

I try and come up with just crazy stuff to attract attention. If there's something that I really want, like if there's a certain gallery I want to get in, I'll target and I'll figure out something to get in there.

I really wanted to work with a specific game company. I had been published by several of the top game companies, and I could never get this one company. So I found a picture of the art director and I did a photo-realistic cartoon of him and myself. I was asking "Hey, would you, please, get back to me on my portfolio," and his picture was saying, "Of course I will, Rob." So I sent that in. About five days later, I got a phone call and I ended up working for them.

I just did it with the movie company I'm going to work with. I had already been talking to them, but they hadn't gotten back to me. So I made a little recording on an iPod, and I sent it with a big note that said, "Listen to this" and they did. It was me describing why I should be doing multiple pictures, why I needed to sign a three-picture deal. It was funny and they passed it all around the office. Shortly after, I signed my three-picture deal.

Another thing that got a lot of attention, sort of by accident, was my chicken head. I hide a chicken head in every single thing I create. And I began doing it because somebody said that they would fire me if I put a chicken head in anything. So I hid one in there. But now, I get hired or people seek me out because of this stupid chicken head.

Just be creative. Be yourself. Work hard and come up with some things that'll attract attention to you. If you want a job bad enough, then dress up in a clown suit and go deliver your portfolio. They'll never forget you. Come up with your own ideas. And persevere.

Yellow Submarine

written by

Rebecca Moesta

illustrated by

DAVID FURNAL

ABOUT THE AUTHOR

Rebecca Moesta (pronounced MESS-tuh) is the bestselling author of forty books, both solo and in collaboration with her husband, Kevin J. Anderson. Much of her writing focuses on teens. Her solo work includes A Christmas to Remember, Buffy the Vampire Slayer *and* Junior Jedi Knights *novels, short stories, articles, ghostwriting, and editing anthologies. With Kevin, she has written the Crystal Doors trilogy, the Star Challengers trilogy, the Young Jedi Knights series, movie and game novelizations, lyrics for rock CDs, graphic novels, pop-up books, and writing books, such as* Writing as a Team Sport. *Rebecca and her husband are the publishers of WordFire Press.*

ABOUT THE STORY

In America, getting a first car is a rite of passage for many teenagers and a source of great anxiety for their parents. Though the future may bring changes in technology and society, there will always be some similar rite of passage to give young adults joy and parents ulcers. This story is set in an underwater city, to explore the idea that teens will always be teens, and parents will be parents.

ABOUT THE ILLUSTRATOR

David Furnal, from San Jose, California, started drawing at an early age, gaining inspiration from comics, anime, video games, and cartoons.

David graduated from Art Center College of Design in Pasadena, California in 2011, and has since been doing freelance illustration and commissions for a number of clients.

He loves to create original stories using his art, and is working on completing a graphic novel in the near future. He is happy to have the opportunity to draw and paint on a daily basis.

David is a former quarterly winner of the Illustrators of the Future award. His artwork was published in L. Ron Hubbard Presents Writers of the Future Volume 33.

Yellow Submarine

Life with a sixteen-year-old is never short on melodrama.

"But Mom," André groaned, rolling his eyes, "you can't expect me to drive that. It's positively prehistoric. That's what *moms* drive. I'd be laughed out of school."

"I've had that SeaPig for eight years now. It's reliable and I haven't noticed anybody laughing at me," I said, crossing my arms defensively over my chest.

"Maybe you just haven't *noticed*, period."

"I may be your mother, but that hardly makes me old and senile," I said, uncrossing my arms and wiping my sweaty palms on the silvery material of the form-fitting jumpsuit I had worn to work that day. The idea of André actually having his own vehicle filled me with maternal trepidation. "You certainly don't need anything flashy. You just have to find something to get you to and from school, and back and forth to work."

"Maybe you don't care what you drive anymore, but this is important to me." André stopped and tried a new approach. "Please? Dad says I've earned the right to choose my own. I work hard." That was true enough. At his habitat-construction job, my son had probably logged more work hours than any other kid at Marianas High. But something inside me still resisted.

I sighed. "That's the only reason we're discussing this. Your work schedule makes it impossible for your father and me to ferry you and your sister everywhere you have to go."

"So you'll take me shopping for a minisub?" he said.

I glanced up through the clear, domed ceiling of our home,

my eyes unconsciously searching the ocean for any sign of Howard's submarine returning, though I knew he wasn't due back from his fishing expedition for another day yet. In any case, I knew that my husband wouldn't thank me for putting off the inevitable.

"All right," I said, giving in. "But we'll get something used, not showy, and I'm going to insist on certain safety features. Just give me a minute to change out of my work clothes."

By the time we reached the dealership on the outskirts of Marianasville, I was much calmer. On our way past the colorful glow of habitat domes, around the kelp fields, and past the fish processing plant, André and I had discussed the budget and ground rules, and he was grinning with anticipation. I zoomed my faithful SeaPig right into the center of the lot and parked in the first available space. André had already donned his NEMM—nose-eye-mouth mask—and waited impatiently for me to put my gear on.

Since I didn't want to get my hair wet, I chose a full transparahelm. I popped the lower hatch and allowed André to drop smoothly into the water. I followed a moment later. The hatch closed behind us as we swam toward the first submarine that caught André's eye, a sports model Nuke Mini, a muscle sub powered by a miniature nuclear generator. The vidsticker on its window proclaimed that it could do zero to a hundred twenty in under ten seconds.

Naturally, I was appalled. Then I saw the price. I gasped and quickly had to adjust the flow on my air condenser rebreather unit.

"You can't fully appreciate its features without a test drive." The voice came from behind us.

We whirled to look at the salesman in his garish plaid wet suit. He wore a vidbadge that said, WELCOME TO SUBMARINE WORLD. I'M RON.

I activated my helmet mic. "No, thank you. I think it's out of our range, er ... Ron."

"But Mom, why not take a test drive? It would be fun," André said with a reproachful look as if I were trying to suck all of the joy out of his afternoon.

I kept my voice calm and reasonable. I could do this. I was his mother. "There's no point in driving the ones you can't afford. Why don't we try that one?" I pointed toward a compact Waterbug.

The salesman's face fell at this much more sensible choice. The vehicle had once been red, but had now faded to a sort of rusty pink color. "It looks very fuel efficient, and it's in our price range." I tried to sound as enthusiastic as possible. "Can you show it to us?" The vehicle was definitely ugly. Even a SeaPig would be a step up from it.

"You realize of course that the Waterbug is an older trade-in," Ron replied, forcing a smile. "It can't compare favorably to the Nuke Mini."

"My son is buying his first sub," I told him in no uncertain terms. "He doesn't need all of the features on the Nuke Mini. Once he shows us that he's responsible—maybe in a couple of years—we can come back to look at a Nuke Mini, and you can help André set up a reasonable payment plan to help him establish a good credit rating."

"Very well, then," Ron replied as the smile dissolved from his face and was replaced by a look of resignation. He led the way toward the other sub.

"Mom," André said to me over the private microphone, "I need to do this myself. It's my first time, and you're doing all the talking. It's embarrassing."

"Okay." I raised my hands in mock surrender. "I'll keep quiet. But don't forget this is for transportation, not to impress your friends."

He nodded as if he had heard the lecture a thousand times before, not just once on our way to the dealership. "I know, and it has to be safe enough to withstand a nuclear blast. I've got the whole list of your requirements right up here," he said, tapping his forehead just above the NEMM rebreather.

André was exaggerating for effect, of course. But not by much. Agreeing to let him take the lead from here on out, I made a motion across my mouth as if applying emergency water sealant.

Keeping my vow of silence, I watched as Ron of the plaid wetsuit gathered himself to launch into a full-fledged sales speech, even though I could tell he was not impressed by the Waterbug. "This minisub's a beauty, all right. She's got low usage, sturdy crash webbing, an economical smooth-spurt engine, dual rudder controls, and not a speck of wasted space." He gave me a conspiratorial grin, grown-up to grown-up, that was as false as his phosphor-glow hairpiece. "Very sensible."

I didn't answer. André peered into the vessel through its front viewbubble, then turned toward Ron and gave him an okay-just-try-to-impress-me look, and rattled off a series of questions. For once, apparently, my son had done his homework.

The salesman tried to keep up and had to make frequent reference to the datascreen on his wrist. Long before the man finished explaining the lack of warranty, the almost nonexistent cargo capacity, and the inadequate max speed, I could tell André's mind was made up, so I knew that his final question was just for show. "And where do the passengers sit?"

"Ahh." Ron tugged at the collar of his garish tartan suit. "In the, ah, the interest of economy and, ah . . ." His voice trailed off. "Actually, it's a one-person vehicle."

André gave me a glance and spread his hands as if that clinched it. "I'm afraid we'll have to keep looking, then. See, I need to be able to pick up my little sister from her aquaballet lessons. I can't even take my mom out for a test drive in this thing, much less take care of Reina. At this rate, I might as well get an AquaScoot. It's cheaper, faster, and even more fuel efficient, plus it has room for a passenger."

As I said, I'm a mom, and I'm not completely oblivious. André was playing both of us. I knew that one of André's primary purposes in buying this vehicle was to be able to go out on dates without wearing the protective gear and portable ACRU rebreathers that would be required on a Scoot. It was a clever stroke, of course, to mention that only with an appropriate vehicle would he be able to free up even more of my time by picking up his sister from school and lessons. I knew, of course, he had no intention of purchasing an AquaScoot, but Ron did not. And his dealership did not sell AquaScoots. I saw his face pale by at least two shades of blue-green when he realized that any chance for a commission was about to swim away.

Suddenly Ron's concern seemed to be all about safety. "An AquaScoot? With no protection from reefs, predators, and submersibles that don't watch where they're going? Besides, when you consider all the excess gear you'd need—sonic repellents, ACRU units, helmets—you would hardly save anything at all. And it's so uncomfortable. Come with me. I think I have just the thing."

Obviously, the plaid panderer finally understood whom he needed to please and was playing to André for all he was worth. "Hold on," Ron said, grabbing onto a loop on one of the continuously cycling transportation cables that crisscrossed the submarine lot. André and I each caught a loop and we were whisked away to the outskirts of the lot, where we all let go of our cables. Ron gestured with a flourish toward a sleek, flashy minisub in neon yellow. "I think that you'll find this is much more to your liking. It just came in."

I shuddered to think what the price would be. The slick vehicle was far too new to be within our price range, and maybe just a bit too sexy for my son to own. I was about to suggest that we keep looking when I remembered that I had promised to keep my mouth sealed. I decided to wait.

"Allow me to present the Subatomic," Ron said, "with twelve independent propulsion jets and eight customizable attitude jets, plus six brake rotors, complete with energy-recapture turbines. She's had some heavy usage, but for the price, this minisub is a steal. Compact and safety conscious, the Subatomic can carry the driver and three passengers—or the driver, one passenger, and a generous cargo when the rear seats are—"

"We'll test drive this one," André interrupted.

Ron obligingly cycled open the lower hatch for us, letting André enter first to get into the pilot's chair. I took shotgun, and Ron, folding himself into the rear seat, closed the hatch again. While we all took off our masks and fastened our crash webbing, he picked up his spiel where he had left off. I sat back in my seat, which was comfortable—perhaps a bit *too* comfortable—and André punched the ignition.

"The Subatomic's TruGyro steering system," Ron droned on like an annoying commercial, "never loses track of its orientation. It boasts a wired microperiscope that shoots a tiny camera to the top of the water to let you keep track of conditions on the surface, then retracts again at the touch of a button."

André grabbed the steering gyro with both hands and hit the accelerator, throwing us all back in our seats, which quickly adjusted to support our backs and heads. A nice feature. Without slowing, André curved the minisub around toward the Test Drive area and plunged us into the Level 5 Hazard Course. A forest of wriggling fake seaweed swallowed us in darkness. I bit my lip, digging my nails into the seat's armrest. I would have cried out, but a moment later, the minisub's exterior lights winked on. The floods illuminated the course before us, while my son's face lit with an equally bright grin of fierce enjoyment.

Then, from out of nowhere, the tentacles of a gigantic "squid" reached for us. André pushed the Subatomic into a sideways spin and plaid Ron's sales speech ended with a squawk. In spite of the quick change of direction, the ride was surprisingly smooth and quiet, and the dynamic crash webbing didn't cut into my neck as it did when I made sudden maneuvers in my SPig.

Just as I began to calm down again, now that we were out of the squid's reach, the heads-up display blinked a warning signal. André tapped the brake rotors, tweaked the attitude adjustment jets on the left and lower hulls, and accelerated upward in a smooth curve as a giant coral reef loomed ahead of us. I gulped and closed my eyes, expecting a crash or the screech of coral scraping metal.

DAVID FURNAL

But the sounds never came. André started quizzing Ron on things like the number of spare universal jets in case one should go out (three), backup ACRU units (two portable NEMMs), and warranty (two years). Not bad for a used vehicle. I opened one eye to see that we were entering the cavern portion of the obstacle course. I quickly shut my eye again. That was when André started his negotiations—both of the cave passages and of the price.

I heard the occasional ping of the warning sensors and felt the almost instantaneous adjustments my son made in speed, orientation, and direction. In the background, André and Ron continued their bargaining while I cringed deeper into the passenger seat. It was amazingly comfortable.

"You can open your eyes now, Mom," André said, and I realized that I had actually started to relax. "We're out of the hazard course and almost back to the dealership lot."

I blinked my eyes open to see that he was right. We were almost back, and André was driving at a safe, respectable pace, observing all of the traffic laws of the sea.

"Did you hear the final price, Mom?" André said with a note of uncertain hope in his voice.

"No," I said, bracing myself for sticker shock and already preparing for the unpleasant task of talking my son out of the sub he had so obviously fallen in love with.

Ron quoted me the number of credits, which was, as I had suspected, higher than the amount we had budgeted for, but not nearly as high as I had expected. It was, in fact, quite reasonable, considering the sub's excellent condition, well thought-out safety features, and luxury options. But André was a teenager. He didn't really need to start out with all those bells and whistles. In fact, it would probably do him good to start with a more humble vehicle. *I* certainly had.

Just as André was about to start his turn into the sub lot, a plump green SPig came barreling out at us. It shouldn't have been much of a problem considering that SPigs can do no more than thirty at their top speed, but the teenage driver was distracted.

The young man, obviously not paying attention, had turned to speak with someone in the back seat and hadn't seen us yet.

The path of the other vessel would intersect ours dead on. I drew in a sharp breath and stifled a scream just as the other driver noticed us and began frantically trying to maneuver in another direction. But his ungainly vehicle refused to cooperate. I heard a strangled yelp from Ron in the back. André, meanwhile seemed completely unfazed as the warning signal began to ping. I slapped my hands over my eyes, but then spread my fingers and watched in terrified fascination.

Tapping the brake rotors, André twirled the gyro steering downward and threw the upper and side attitude adjustment jets on full so that we dove directly beneath the wallowing SPig. Instead of a jarring crash that would likely have disabled both vehicles, all I heard was the tiniest squeak, as the SPig's bulky rudder scratched against our hull for a bare fraction of a second.

Once clear of the other minisub, André steered the Subatomic on a slow, gentle curve back into the dealership and parked it at its original slot while I struggled to breathe normally again.

This was no time for debate. I knew what I had to do. André had wanted to make the final decision, but he couldn't afford this choice without me.

"We'll take it," I said. I glanced at André. "We'll split the cost."

The next day was Friday and, as promised, André swung by to pick up his little sister Reina from aquaballet on his way home from school. Howard and the rest of the submarine fishing fleet were home from their expedition with a large catch, so the four of us—Howard, Reina, André, and I—had dinner as a family for a change.

André regaled us all with the tale of the previous day's shopping expedition and test drive, as well as the story of his first day at school with his new minisub.

"You drove a good bargain, Son," Howard said with an admiring chuckle. "Literally. Why don't we all go out for a spin after supper?"

"Could, uh, could that wait for tomorrow?" André said, his face growing pink. "I kind of have a date tonight."

"Who with?" Reina blurted. "Do I know her? Does she go to your school?"

Howard cleared his throat, cutting off the stream of questions. "Don't stay out too late, Son."

"I won't." André wiped his mouth with a napkin and excused himself from the table. "I promised Mr. Martinez I'd have Etsuko home early."

I stared at my son in amazement. André was going out without us, on his first date alone. Howard grinned like the proud father he was. I, however, was not quite ready to let go. "Wait. What kind of date? Where are you going?" I asked as he headed for the front floor hatch where the Subatomic was parked.

He turned, grinned at me, and shrugged. "Where else, Mom? To watch the submarine races."

An Itch

written by

Christopher Baker

illustrated by

JENNIFER OBER

ABOUT THE AUTHOR

Christopher is a writer from rural England with a particular interest in folklore and how the magical intersects with the mundane. His work often explores themes of nature and identity, and how stories are tied to particular environments. Having recently graduated with a First (the highest degree classification in the UK) from the Warwick Writing Programme, Christopher is now writing novels and teaching on the side. When he is not writing, he is usually going for long walks with his three dogs, painting, or playing violin.

ABOUT THE ILLUSTRATOR

Jennifer Ober was born in 1993 and grew up in the small town of Los Lunas, New Mexico, a few minutes south of Albuquerque.

Growing up in the beautiful and culturally rich Southwest, Jennifer had a passion for storytelling through imagery, especially painting. Her parents nurtured these artistic interests by connecting her with the local art community and encouraged her to pursue a career in the arts. Through the years, Jennifer was inspired by the classical masters and her longtime mentor Ricardo.

Her passion for fantasy, however, came from her childhood immersion in classics such as Tolkien's Middle-earth, Star Trek, and Star Wars. In addition, Jennifer's passion for animals emanates throughout her life, evidenced in her early paintings and work experience with animals. Her current artistic practices culminated all these passions into the pursuit of creature design.

While translating her skills in traditional materials into the digital realm, Jennifer is currently completing her master's in illustration at the Savannah College of Art and Design in Atlanta and working as a freelance illustrator.

An Itch

Before he died, my father made a secretaire from the old tree in our garden. He was an enchanter. And while this did set him apart from most other people, he still rode a bike. Unfortunately, he didn't wear a helmet.

My parents had an unusual arrangement. They lived in separate houses at opposite ends of their garden. My mother chose to live in a narrow three-story house, and my father had a small cottage with circular windows that smelt of wood smoke. I lived mostly with my father, while my sister, Jane, lived with my mother. Our parents told us they were still in love, and for a time, we believed them.

The tree in the centre of the garden had been there for as long as anyone could remember, so it was a shock to find my father hacking at it one morning, his tan, craggy face dripping with sweat.

"You're chopping down the tree in the centre of the garden," I said.

"I am," my father replied.

As well as being an enchanter, my father was a door-to-door vacuum salesman, who had never chopped down a tree in his life.

"You'll understand some day," he said, hefting the axe up onto his shoulder, readying himself for another swing. "I'm scratching an itch."

"An itch?" I asked, quite certain he'd gone insane.

"Everyone has an itch. You'll get one too when you're older."

"What's it feel like?"

"Like you've left nothing behind. Like you won't be remembered."

"I'll remember you."

He swung the axe into the trunk and it stuck. Jostling it free, he said: "I know you will. But if you have children, will they?"

"Yes."

"And their children?"

I thought for a moment, then replied with certainty, "Yes!"

"Well I don't think they will," he laughed. "So, I'm going to build something from this tree."

I saw my sister and my mother watching us from the window of their house and waved at them, but they didn't wave back.

"I love you, Claire," my father said.

"I love you too." I left him to his tree and went back inside the house.

For the next two weeks, I remember my father working nonstop, sawing the tree, sanding it down into smooth planes, locking joints into place, lacquering the soft wood in varnish that hardened like old, smoky honey. I watched him in his workshop, whispering words of enchantment into the wood, words that made the light fall curiously, as if through clear water.

"What are you doing?" I asked one night, peering through the doorway.

"Curing the wood," he replied. Then, when seeing the confused look on my face, said, "Asking it, very nicely, to behave."

"Will it?"

"I think so, but there are more words to be spoken."

"Very nicely?" I asked.

He smiled. "Yes, very nicely."

Sometimes he would whisper a word to me and I would repeat it in my head until it stuck fast. In sleep, the words would come again and conjure wonderful dreams that vanished with the sunrise but left a warmth in the air that made the winter mornings tolerable.

When he was finished, he called me into the living room, where the fire chuckled in the hearth. There, standing in the centre of the room was the secretaire. He watched me, as I approached, with a vulnerability I hadn't seen before.

"What do you think?" he asked.

I pulled out the chair and sat at the desk, ran my fingers along the dark grain of the polished wood, flicked through the crisp papers and envelopes he had stowed in the many compartments. I asked him what magic he had given it.

He smiled and placed his palm against the wood. "Let me show you." Pulling a pen from his pocket, he knelt beside me and gestured for me to pass him one of the papers. I did.

"Close your eyes now."

"Okay."

Then, eyes closed, I began to receive the words he wrote without seeing or hearing them. They came like an intuition. A jolt.

> Dear Claire,
>   Please wash up your breakfast bowl.
>   Love,
>   Dad

I laughed and said, "What wonderful magic!"

My father grinned. "I'm glad you like it."

Then, as I washed up my bowl in the kitchen, I remembered to ask, "Is your itch still there?"

To which he replied: "I don't think so. But there's no way of knowing when you'll next get an itch."

Jane would often come visit the cottage, just as I would visit our mother's house. On one occasion, I showed her the secretaire our father had enchanted. She wasn't very impressed, and the novelty wore off after we had written each other about a dozen mind-letters. I promised her I would write her a letter every day and she said "Every day? No thank you!" She was eight years older than me, so whenever she said anything like that, I would feel silly and small.

My sister was the first person to tell me I was an enchantress.

Often, I would let her hear one of my father's words and she would watch in amazement as the ground about us blossomed with flowers, or the air shimmered with strange light. On one such occasion, I created a frog out of our father's old brown boot and we chased it through the garden, around the stump of the secretaire tree. When Jane caught the frog, it shifted back into the boot. Jane tried to get it to shift back into the frog, but the stubborn leather would not budge.

"I wish I could be an enchanter like you," she said.

In that moment, I repeated something our father had once told me. "If everyone were special, then no one would be."

Still holding the boot, Jane looked down and rubbed the corner of her eye, not meeting my gaze. I thought nothing of it then, but it was at that moment something about my sister changed. Something in how she held herself and in how she looked at me when we were together.

Something I had caused.

"Come on," I said. "Let me show you another!"

"I'm tired, Claire," said my sister. "We will play tomorrow."

"You promise?"

"I promise."

Back then, I was fond of binding people to me with promises. They were a kind of half-magic.

While my sister enjoyed my enchantments, my mother always tutted or ignored them completely. She was a teacher, and so had mastered the nuances of scaring children using only her voice.

"That stuff is for your father's house," she said once, in her teacher voice, after I had conjured a little blackbird to sit on my finger.

I always preferred it when Jane visited my father's cottage, where I could speak the strange words without worry. After Jane visited, my father would always kiss her on the forehead and I would feel slightly jealous. I wondered if she felt the same when our mother kissed me.

I saw Jane and Mum a lot more after my father didn't wear

his bike helmet. In fact, I lived with them. When I moved into their cold three-story house, I missed that secretaire; our mother had told me that it was simply too big to haul from the cottage.

And so, like the memory of my father, the secretaire collected dust, down at the other end of the garden.

"Why did you live apart from Dad?" I asked our mother once before school. A few years had passed since Dad's accident. I was eleven, and curious, and asking about my father was just about the only way I could stop myself sinking under that silent numbing sea. The sea that had been rising since he'd left. Asking questions kept me afloat. Jane and I were eating toast. Jane was in college then, but I don't think she had ever asked that question, considering our mother's reaction. "Mind your business," she said. My mother's face bunched up more than most people's when she was mad, and when I asked that question, it seemed as if her features would all squeeze into one great angry blob. She clattered about at the sink while I ate my toast, until eventually she turned and stared at me. "You really want to know?" She sat at the table. I could see tears in her eyes. Then she dropped her head. "No ... no, you don't."

I wasn't sure what to do, so I got up, put my plate in the sink and caught the bus. I didn't go to school that day; instead, I got off at the garden store and bought a little sapling. I tried to find one that looked strong, but they all looked the same, so I just settled on the first one I'd seen. With the little sapling on my lap, I rode the bus about our town until three o'clock, when school finished. Then, weary from not eating, I made my way back to my mother's house which whistled to itself sometimes, when the breeze danced along the window shutters. It was this whistling that hid the noise of my footsteps across the creaky floor (I was wary of my mother catching me and interviewing me about the sapling). I ran out into the garden, where the stump of the secretaire tree still lay, gathering moss and woodlice. It felt like just yesterday I had watched my father chopping, and waved at Jane and my mother peering from the window of the whistling house.

Finding a shovel in the shed, I began to dig a great hole beside the stump where I intended to plant the sapling. It was tiring work: the roots of the old stump were tangled and deep below the earth and made the shovel shudder and buck when it met them. When I stopped to catch my breath, I looked out across the garden and saw my father's cottage, crawling with ivy, the thatch slowly rotting.

"Why don't you just go back?" said Jane. Her voice surprised me. I hadn't heard her coming. She stood behind me, hands on hips. She was very beautiful and had long blonde hair which naturally curled. My hair wasn't long. Or blonde. "It would be easier if you just left," she concluded.

I knelt to lower the sapling into the hole I had dug.

"Why did you ask Mum that question this morning?"

"I don't know."

"I can answer it for you, if you like?"

I patted the fringe of earth around the base of the sapling, packing it tight.

"They lived apart because of you."

"What?"

"After you were born, they moved apart."

"Did Mum tell you that?"

"Yes."

"I don't believe you."

"Fine."

We didn't say much more to each other after that. I brushed the earth from my hands and watched Jane walk back to the house. Then, I sat in my mother's half of the garden, watching the little sapling sway like a child finding its balance, and cried.

Once the tears had stopped and I was left with a headache, I rose slowly and began to walk over to my father's cottage. The handle to the door was swallowed by twisting vines and it took all my strength to heave it open. The house was dark, and birds that had flown through the open windows were nesting in the rafters.

Guided by a memory, I made my way to the living room

where the old secretaire stood beside the hearth. I sat and wrote a letter.

> *Dad,*
>> *I miss you. I hope you receive this.*
>>> *Love,*
>>> *Claire*

It was not for another year that I discovered the truth about my parents' strange living situation. My father, while he was alive, had given his heart to an enchantress. An enchanter's heart sounds like an old song, and he chose to breathe his into a jam jar and give it to a woman we had never met. When my mother told me this, she spoke like she was writing equations up on a blackboard.

"Did you hate him?" I asked.

"Yes, I hated him."

"Do you hate me?" I—after all—was an enchantress too.

My mother watched me, her lips set in a thin line.

I left the room before she answered.

More and more, my mother retreated into herself, sitting in her room all day, reading books.

You only realise how unusual your life is when you look back ... and by then it's too late to do anything about it.

Jane was no longer interested in my enchantments, like she had been when we were younger. Now, whenever I said the words she would sigh and make me feel silly and small again. So I stopped speaking them. After a time they vanished, like mist rising from grass on a chilly morning.

I always thought the world of Jane.

Once, when the school sent a letter to our mother's house, mentioning the formal dress code for my upcoming school photo, I asked Jane if I could borrow one of her dresses—white, as the dress code suggested. I didn't own any because I hated them. Clothes should make you feel comfortable, and when I wear dresses I feel all scratchy. Still, I asked Jane for a dress and she gave me one. It was bright yellow. I asked her if this was what the other girls would be wearing, and she said yes, it would be.

It was not.

They were all wearing white, and there I was in bright yellow. They put me in the back of the photo.

When I came home I found Jane sitting on the sofa watching television. She laughed at me, still wearing the yellow dress, standing in front of the television.

"It suits you!" she said.

"I hate you," I said.

"I hate you too," she said. "Always have."

And that was pretty much how our interactions went from then on.

We lived in our mother's house until she died. It was a heart attack. We found her in her room with a book on her chest, her mouth parted slightly.

After that, my sister and I barely talked. Like two ghosts we occupied the same space, barely aware of each other, bound to the whistling house.

"I'm taking Mum's books," Jane notified me one day. "I'm having her jewellery," she told me the next.

I didn't put up a fight and, soon, I was in a house of Jane's things.

One evening I walked across the garden to my father's cottage for the first time since I had written him the letter. By then the sapling had grown into a young tree. It was about my height and its arms were spread wide.

I remembered when I had planted it long ago, before I had known about my father's enchantress. I think that's why I hadn't returned until now: I had wanted the memories of my father and the cottage to stay as they were. Now, walking through the rooms that smelt of wet moss, everything seemed marred by this other woman I had never met. I wondered if she had ever visited when I wasn't there ... if she, too, had spun her magic in this house.

JENNIFER OBER

Dusty blue light crept through the little windows as I moved among the rooms. Soon I had found the magic secretaire again, standing alone in the grey shadows. A sealed envelope lay on the dark wood, leaving an impression in the dust when I picked it up. I held it and brushed it down. The paper was the same as that in the compartments of the secretaire, however, it was mottled and rotten; the ink smudged and faded almost to nothing, as if it had travelled a very long way. I thought it might crumble to dust. After closely examining the envelope, I managed to make out my name, written in spidery handwriting.

Clumsily I tore at the envelope and pulled the letter out from inside. The writing was barely legible, but eventually, it made sense:

> *Dear Claire,*
>
> *Now I'm gone, the secretaire's magic is fading.*
> *I don't know how or if this will reach you.*
> *I heard your letter, though it was a little fuzzy over here.*
> *I miss you too. I love you and your sister both. Tell her that.*
> *This will be the last letter I can send.*
> *Forgive me.*
>
> > *Dad*

After I had read the letter, I walked about the house with it still in my hand, tidying. I tidied for hours until the cottage looked brand new. Then, I used the last of the secretaire's magic to write a letter to my sister.

> *Dear Jane,*
>
> *I want you to know that I forgive you. And I'm sorry for anything I've done to hurt you.*
> *I hope that someday we can be friends again, as we were when we were children.*

Dad sent a letter saying that he loved us
both. I think it would make him happy to see
us getting along.
  Meet me in the garden tomorrow if you
want to talk.

                    Love,
                    Claire

I decided to spend the night there in my father's cottage, thinking of Jane, a little walk away, in the whistling house where my mother had once lived. In my head I went through all the reasons she might have hated me—if it had been something I'd done and forgotten, or if it was for the same reason as my mother. I lay in the bed I had slept in as a child and waited for the night to crest into morning.

I prayed she had received the letter. Then, finally, I slept.

There was smoke.

I smelt it as I rose, wrapping myself in a musty blanket and wandering outside.

There Jane stood in the centre of the garden, beside the young tree which was consumed in thick ropes of flame. She watched me stumble out onto the grass, her mouth a hard line.

The tree was already dead; a thing of cinders and smoke.

The blanket fell from my shoulders and fluttered away in the wind as I ran towards my sister. As I ran, the words came to me, words I had never spoken before. Words of protection. Words of rage. They scorched my tongue as I made them.

The burning tree wrapped about itself, stretching out its dark limbs, glittering with embers. It grew and grew, burning the earth between us, crawling slowly up into the sky. A wall. The thing was black and coiled with scorched branches. It tore across the centre of the garden, stretching right to the edges, separating me from my sister.

It took about a day for the burning wall to harden and cool. It writhed for a while, settling into place, grappling with itself until finally it calmed.

There's not much to say after that.

I thought about writing to my sister again, but never did. We went about our lives on opposite sides of the wall, me in my father's house, she in my mother's. It was easier.

I can't tell you what she did with the rest of the time she was given.

Sometimes I wish I could.

I can only assume she grew old, like me, fell in love, as I did, and told her children the story of the wall at the end of the garden. Perhaps she too has grandchildren. Perhaps they too play at the end of the garden and try to climb the wall.

What's that whistling Gran?"

I lick my finger and rub at the chocolate he's managed to spread across his face.

"Shh, Dylan," Emma says. "It's just the wind."

It is summer, and I am in a good mood. Everything hurts less in summer. Dylan nods his head furiously and races across the garden, kicking a ball as he goes.

"Can I get you a drink, Mum?" Emma stands and tucks in her chair. She is turning thirty-eight tomorrow and has come down to visit. I hear a note of concern in her voice recently when she speaks to me.

"Tea please." I don't want any tea, but she will feel better making some for me.

She kisses my forehead and goes inside.

"Gran!" Dylan shouts.

I sigh and turn, expecting him to kick a ball at me. He likes doing that.

Surprisingly, he doesn't kick a ball at me. Instead, he looks at me with wide eyes. "Listen!" he says, beckoning me over to the wall.

Rising slowly, I walk to the wall, now verdant green, strewn with wild, fragrant blossoms. Coiling fingers of moss creep up from the bottom, and ivy twines over the old charred branches. Robins, wrens, and blackbirds weave in and out, darting up through the verdure to settle at the top and gaze down at the world. Some chirp and fly away when I near.

"What is it?"

"Knocking!"

He points at the wall and presses his ear against it. I join him.

Knock.

Knock.

Knock.

"Mum?" Emma shouts from the patio. She is holding two cups of tea. I know she has put too much sugar in mine.

I don't answer.

Knock.

Knock.

I place my hand against the branches and a word comes to me from a place I haven't been in years. I whisper it.

Dylan stumbles backward and is caught by his mother as the wall begins to rumble. A thin crack runs through the branches, arcing into the shape of a door.

I push open the door in the wall, the wood still trembling.

On the other side is a woman. Her skin hangs loose and is dappled with liver spots, her hair is thin and white and falls limp, plastered to the sweat on her forehead. She walks very slowly through the doorway, propping herself against a walking stick. Her body is thin and wasted. She looks like she is dying.

We don't speak. She drops her walking stick and falls against me, hugging as tightly as she is able. I hug her back.

Dirt Road Magic

written by

Carrie Callahan

illustrated by

YINGYING JIANG

ABOUT THE AUTHOR

Though a lifelong writer, Carrie Callahan has only recently found her voice with what she calls Dirt Spec—a style that mixes gritty realism with speculative elements. Dirt Spec comes from her experiences growing up sub working class and not seeing herself reflected in the shiny prose of high-gloss fiction. Writers of the Future is Carrie's first professional sale, and only the beginning of her exploration of sci-fi through a dirty lens.

As a first-generation college student, Carrie also developed a passion for helping her peers hone their writing, carving space for students to practice and share their writing outside of the classroom. Since graduating, she's continued to pursue this passion through her YouTube channel, About Write, where she attempts to democratize creative writing education and teach everyone that to be a writer, they don't have to be perfect—just about right!

When she isn't writing about imaginary worlds (or teaching others how to), Carrie can be found exploring the digital worlds of virtual reality in VRChat. She lives with her patient husband and adorable dog in the hills of bourbon country Kentucky.

ABOUT THE ILLUSTRATOR

Yingying is a self-taught artist with an overactive imagination and propensity for daydreaming. Although she graduated with a science degree from the University of Oxford and spent her post-university years working in fields completely unrelated to art, her passion for drawing could not be stemmed and in 2016 she decided to take her interest more seriously, culminating in creating a website and holding a debut exhibition in Tokyo.

Having grown up living on books such as *Harry Potter*, her love of fantasy and magic often crops up in her drawings. As a Chinese-British national she is also interested in combining western and eastern influences.

Yingying works mostly with digital media and describes her natural style as semi-realistic. She finds endless inspiration in the beauty of nature and from art masters such as John William Waterhouse and Hayao Miyazaki.

Although Yingying has not quite let go of her day job, she continues to develop her art and storytelling skills and takes on freelance projects from private clients.

When not working, she enjoys developing her YA novel, playing the piano, and seeking out the best afternoon teas in the land.

Dirt Road Magic

Aluminum foil on the windows couldn't keep out the summer heat. The air conditioning struggled to keep the trailer just under sweltering, and, overhead, a dim yellow light washed everything in a dingy glow. I sat on my bed in boxers, polyester blanket itchy on my back as I practiced the words Old Hurley had told me to say, trying to get the towel draped over my dresser to respond.

I said the words as quietly as I could to keep them from escaping the thin walls of my bedroom. The harsh, strange syllables blended together as I uttered them under my breath.

Nothing.

I tried again, this time wiggling my fingers desperately at the towel, willing it to move, to swish, to do anything. I said the words a little louder.

I climbed off my bed and stared intently, repeating the incantation again, but the fibers and folds hung inert. I hopped and struck a pose like a mage, shaking my room and sending a hollow thrum through the trailer floor. Clenching my fists, I commanded the damned thing to move with all my power!

"What the hell—" my mother asked.

I rushed to close the door, but she'd already stuck her French tips through the crack and pushed her way in.

"It's nothing!" I struggled to explain, reaching for my shirt. "I'm just practicing some—uh. Some meditations. Old Hurley showed them to me." As soon as the words were out, I realized my mistake.

"Hurley again? That man gives me the creeps," she said, shivering dramatically. She wore a low-cut shirt and bright lipstick. "You're too young to be hanging out with him. You're not even in high school yet, Jake!"

"And you're too old to be dressing like—" I thought, not realizing I was muttering out loud.

"What was that?" Mom asked, eyes widening with implied danger.

"I said I'm old enough," I replied, louder. "I'll be in high school next year."

"Well, I don't want you hanging out with some creeper in the backwoods. It's weird. You should hang out with kids your own age, like Robbie."

Robbie lived down the same dirt road behind the church as Old Hurley. We used to be best friends—in second grade. That was until he got into BB guns and tormenting small animals.

"Come on," she continued, waving her hand at me. "Get dressed."

"What? Why?" I asked, already reaching to grab my pants.

"Cause Rick is on his way over, and I want you to go to your friend's house. *Robbie's* house," she clarified, crossing her arms.

"I don't get why I can't be here when your boyfriend comes over," I replied, raising my eyebrows.

She scowled. "Just go to Robbie's house and come home later, OK?"

I tugged on my pants. I could go to Old Hurley's house and practice. Maybe he could tell me what I was doing wrong. My mom followed me down the narrow hall to the living room.

"Listen, you take this for food." She shoved a couple wadded up dollar bills into my hand. "And I don't want to see you back here until after seven, got it? And tell Robbie's mom I said Hi."

"Fine," I replied, shoving the money in my pocket. I would've felt guiltier for lying if she was more open minded about my friends.

She kissed me hard on the forehead. "Now you go and have fun. I'll see you later!"

I wiped the lipstick off my face, grabbed my backpack, and opened the door.

"And stay away from that creepy pedophile!" she yelled before the door slammed shut.

The sun was bright and harsh as I worked my way past the other trailers, toward the church and the field that would take me to the dirt road. The endless buzz of cicadas hummed over everything.

Sweat dripped down my face as I plodded across the field, the sun burning my skin. I worried about blisters, but then there was always the aloe and Old Hurley's incantations. Occasionally, a stirring of breeze interrupted the sticky heat and rippling humidity.

I walked along barbed-wire lines strung between rotting fence posts, and when I got to the road I stopped to pick the dried burs off my pants. I waved my hand over them like Old Hurley had shown me and muttered the strange words over and over. Nothing.

I sighed and plucked the spurs, their thorns making my fingertips itch.

"Crap," I said when one of them pricked my finger.

I walked along the road, dust kicking up around my sneakers and painting them gray. In the deep bottoms of potholes, light glistened on mud left over from yesterday's rain.

Old Hurley lived in a trailer like mine, but bigger: a double wide. It was back off the road a little, behind a copse of trees with low branches. I walked the ruts of his driveway into the blessed shade and ran my hands along the pine branches on my way to his place. On the porch, I knocked my hand against the rough, unpainted frame of the screen door. When no one responded, I knocked again.

"I'm coming, I'm coming, god dammit!" Hurley croaked as he came to see who it was. "Oh, Jake. Didn't know it was gonna be you."

"I told you I was coming today," I replied.

"Yeah, yeah—sure," he said and nodded, pushing open the

screeching screen door to let me in. He glanced around outside, looking for someone I think, as I stepped past him.

All the windows were open, and the breeze felt cooler inside his house. The lights were off, and the sunlight that found its way in cast high-contrast shadows. Hurley stood against a chipped bookshelf, his eyes bright and sunk into his roughened face. The silver stubble on his chin was erratic, patchy. His knuckles were knobby and twisted with some kind of arthritis. He wore faded basketball shorts and an old, paint-splattered construction shirt. The smell of cooking pasta and stale cigarette smoke barely registered beneath the odor of his many cats.

"You want some mac and cheese?" he asked, stepping over a lazy, gray feline on his way to the back of the trailer.

"Sure," I replied, following him into the linoleum-tiled kitchen, hopping over the pile of fur.

In the kitchen, Hurley walked to his sink with a pot full of water and pasta elbows. The steam drifted neatly out the window over the sink as he whispered something to it and wiggled the colander.

"Lemme just mix this all together—" He dumped the pasta into the pot and added some milk, then the powdered cheese. "Can't forget the butter," he said and dropped in a spoonful of margarine.

"That's not butter," I told him, shooing a calico off the table. "It's margarine."

"Who the hell cares?" Hurley said, not expecting an answer.

I shrugged as I brushed a clump of cat hair away and sat on a vinyl dining chair. He said something in his special language, and a spoon started stirring the pot in a jerky motion. I'd only seen the trick a few times by then, but I still tried not to seem too interested, sneaking glances over when I thought he wasn't looking. I didn't want Hurley to think I was rude or naive or anything, like a little kid who didn't "get it." Hurley was always telling me how I "got it." I wasn't sure what he meant, but I didn't want to prove him wrong.

He caught my wandering eye as he lit a cigarette.

"Thing you gotta understand is that none of this shit—" He

gestured around his kitchen and out the window to encompass everything. "None of it matters. What matters is what you think about it, in here." He tapped on his forehead with his cigarette hand, dropping a little bit of ash. He cursed and shook his foot, then rubbed it against the back of his calf. "The sooner you learn that," he continued in a strained voice, "the sooner you'll master what I showed you."

Hurley turned and said something guttural to the pot, which stopped stirring itself. The mac and cheese was dumped into two plastic bowls—the kind you get from cereal box tops or Goodwill—and placed in front of me.

"Did you practice what I showed you?" he asked as he put his cigarette out in the ashtray on the dining table.

"I tried, but—" I hesitated. "But my mom's being weird about it. She walked in on me, and I tried to explain. She told me I couldn't come over here anymore."

Hurley paused mid bite. "We'll see about that," he said, and got up. He rummaged through his kitchen drawers, muttering to himself in English, cursing and slamming things around. "Where is it?" I heard. Then more incomprehensible mutters.

Eventually, Hurley pulled a thin chain from one of the drawers and wrangled an attached pendant from a lump of tangled jewelry.

"Here it is!" He said, and dropped it in a glittering pile next to me before sitting back down.

"What is it?" I asked.

"Give it to your mom. Tell her it's from me, and she'll stop bugging you about coming over to my place."

The pendant was about the width of a penny—an irregular purple gemstone knocking around inside of a cube-shaped cage of gold. Even though the gemstone looked small enough to fall through the gaps, it didn't. Somehow, it was always *barely* too big to escape. I could feel it radiating that little bit of heat I'd come to recognize as the presence of magic.

"Is this real gold?" I asked.

Hurley shrugged. "Could be."

"How does it work?"

"How does any of this work? Just give it to her, OK?"

"It's not gonna hurt her or anything?"

"Ha!" Hurley laughed around the food in his mouth. "Course not! Don't worry about it. It's safe as any other piece of jewelry. Promise."

I shrugged and shoved it into the front pocket of my backpack, not sure if I was really gonna give it to her.

"Whatever you say, Boss," I said, and Hurley smirked.

After we finished with the mac and cheese, Hurley took our bowls to the sink.

"Listen," he said. "I've got some errands I need to run today— some special errands." Special meant magic, though Hurley never used that word. He looked at me. "Do you want to come with?"

My heart leaped into my throat. It was the first time Hurley had invited me to see what he did, out in the wild. He'd told me he helped people with their problems, and I believed him. At that point he'd already helped me with a few of mine—the regular sunburns, my crappy grades, and getting the attention of this one girl in school. He told me I'd have the power to help people, too, with practice.

"Well, y-yeah, of course!" I stuttered, and Hurley smiled before turning back to the sink. He muttered something, and the dishes clanked against one another as the water shifted on.

"Let's go!"

I grabbed my backpack and followed him into the backyard. His truck was old and covered in dust. It smelled like it looked with an extra pinch of mildew as I hopped into the passenger seat. I pulled hard to close the door and it creaked before slamming suddenly shut. Hurley lit up another cigarette before he climbed into the driver's seat, setting the whole cab teeter-tottering with the change in weight.

"Aren't you gonna lock your door?" I asked.

"Nah. That door's only opening for me and the cats. Your mom expect you home anytime soon?"

I shook my head. "Nope—not 'til around seven."

"Great," he replied and put the truck into gear.

The truck bumped over the potholes, bouncing me on the cab seat. Hurley didn't believe in seatbelts. It was a relief when we pulled onto a real road, paved in even asphalt.

"Where are we going?" I asked eventually, bored of staring out the window at decrepit strip malls and scrub.

"Buddy of mine, Tad," Hurley responded. He rested his hand out the window, letting the ashes of his cigarette blow off in the wind. "Just needs a little help is all."

"Am I gonna help?" I asked.

"Not today. But you can watch." He took a drag from the cigarette and fiddled with the radio, finding a rock station and blaring the volume.

We pulled off the back road onto a long, gravel driveway. The little rocks chinked against the undercarriage of the truck, and Spanish moss draped the tree branches overhead. The house we arrived at was small and shabby—hardly better than a trailer— with chipped and dirty white paint over rotting clapboard. The porch sagged and groaned under our feet as we waited for someone to answer the door.

"Come in!" came a distant, reedy cry.

Hurley opened the door and I followed him in. The house was cold, the AC blasting through rusted vents. The walls were close and dark with wood paneling; the carpet was worn down and stained. Other than that, the house looked clean. There was a Cowboys blanket pinned to one wall over a sagging couch, and a man lay there—Tad, I assumed—with one brown hand on his back, the other slack.

"Hurley, thank God," the man croaked. His eyes were hard and bright, even as his voice was strained. I thought he might have been in his forties. Hurley stepped in and looked around.

"You got yourself into quite a mess, Tad," he said, poking the coffee table piled with full ashtrays, beer bottles, and empty pill containers.

"Please, Hurley, I just need a little help," Tad said from his awkward position on the couch. "It's my back again."

Hurley sighed and knelt by Tad's face. They whispered back

and forth, and I didn't catch what he said, but as soon as he got up Hurley walked farther back into the house and told me to stay where I was.

As Hurley rummaged in the kitchen, Tad turned his attention to me. "You Hurley's son?" he asked.

I shook my head. "No. I don't think Hurley has kids."

He sighed and cringed as he tried to roll over. "That doesn't surprise me," he said through gritted teeth. "Can you hand me that pillow?"

I grabbed a throw pillow off the floor and handed it to him just as Hurley came back with a coffee can. He plucked some bills from inside and squinted at them.

"This isn't enough," he told Tad. "You gotta give me at least fifty."

"It's all I got," Tad replied. I stared at Hurley, and he looked back and rolled his eyes.

"All right," he said at last. "But you owe me."

Tad nodded his head vigorously, and Hurley stood near him.

"Come here," Hurley said, jerking his hand to motion me over. "I want you to watch. Sit there."

He bent over Tad as I knelt at the coffee table. The carpet was flat under my knees as I peered at the movement of Hurley's hands. The incantation he said was simple at first, but then the words folded into one another as I struggled to listen, whispering the sounds to myself in an attempt to capture some of their magic. The room warmed as it always did when Hurley did a full incantation. His hands drifted down the prone man's back, and pain melted from Tad's eyes. His gaze became hollow, then distant, hooded. He smiled.

Hurley barked out a final syllable to cut off his chant and made a tying motion with his hands. My fingers twitched to imitate him. Tad sighed contentedly, and his whole body relaxed, sinking into the couch cushions.

"Thank you," he slurred, staring at nothing.

"No problem," Hurley replied, patting Tad on the shoulder and stepping away. Tad was unresponsive—drifting in some painless, sightless neverland.

"What did you do to him?" I whispered.

"You don't have to be so quiet—he's so out of it, I doubt he'd notice if Hurricane Andrew stopped by."

"What did you do to him?" I repeated louder. "Can I do that?"

"Not yet, and never try the magic on yourself—it's dangerous." He rubbed his fingers, massaging the angled knuckles while he talked. "Pretty cool though, huh? Let's let him be."

Hurley moved to leave the house, but I couldn't get my eyes off Tad. He looked like he was somewhere else, even though his body was very much on the overstuffed couch.

"Come on," Hurley barked. "I got more to do today, and we can't just sit here in Tad's house. I got more to show you!"

As I turned to leave, I caught a glimpse of wide, brown eyes. A little girl with beads in her hair stared at me from a small hallway that branched away from the living room. She looked down at Tad, then back at me. I opened my mouth to say something, but Hurley pulled me out into the sun. On the horizon, clouds were darkening for another deluge.

I got back in the truck in silence, staring at the console, thinking of the little girl. I wondered who was going to feed her, with Tad so out of it. We pulled away, moving back toward the highway. A salty breeze roared through the windows as we crossed a bridge, muddy canal water drifting underneath.

"What's wrong?" Hurley asked, staring down at me from the driver's side. "It's not illegal or anything. Tell people about it and they'll just think you're crazy—I've been there. Let the clients come to you, you never go searching for them. That's torch-and-pitchfork territory. Or I guess today it's padded-wall-and-electroshock territory."

I didn't say anything.

"Come on, kid, it's really not as bad as you think. It was either me or pills. You know what I mean? Pills?"

I picked at my fingernails. "Does she have a mom?"

Hurley looked back to the road, shaking his head. "Shit, kid, of course she does. You think I'd leave her in there alone with a dad blinded by the shiny lights? I'm not a monster. Her mom'll be home in a couple hours. I asked."

I chose to think he was telling the truth.

"You do this often?" I asked.

"Not that often, but it pays good when I do. The magic I got—that *we* got—does a lot of good for people. It's cheaper than a doctor and it's not addictive."

The man's fevered eyes flashed in my mind as Hurley kept talking.

"Lemme get you something to eat, huh? You like McDonald's? I was always hungry when I was a kid."

The drive-thru was empty as we pulled up, and the violent hiss of the speakers made me flinch. We ate in the bed of his truck, watching the black horizon. I was still a little full from the mac and cheese, so I just had a hamburger and a coke, but Hurley wolfed down two Big Macs and a large fry.

"Does magic make you hungry?" I asked as he licked his fingers. "You eat a lot, but you're so skinny."

Hurley shrugged. "Sometimes. Depends on the magic."

He didn't tell me anything else and unwrapped another Big Mac.

Three stops later, as we drifted down I-95, I sat in the passenger seat winding the necklace chain around my hand, unwinding it, staring at the gem, feeling its heat. Eventually, I stuffed it back into my backpack and turned to Hurley.

"How much money do you make with this whole thing? I mean … helping people?" I asked.

Hurley smirked and itched his nose. "I make a good amount," he replied, nodding while he spoke. "I make decent money. Keeps my head above water, feeds my cats."

I turned back to looking at the road, something still bothering me. "But how *much*?"

My question agitated him, I could tell. He shook his head and smacked the radio that was starting to hiss with lost signal. "Goddamn thing," he exclaimed. "I make enough, dammit!" he said at last. "I could make more if I didn't have to be at every person's house—a *lot* more—but there's only one of me." He glanced at me carefully, waiting.

"You think I could do this?" I asked.

"I suppose, if you practice. You could make good money, too—soon, even. You have a gift, you know. Not everyone can say the words and have them work, Jake. I could count the people I've met that can do what we do on one hand—and that includes you and me."

We pulled off the highway, whirling around a copse of pine trees to get onto a familiar back road.

"You could go out, help people who don't want to use pills for their pain, Jake." Hurley kept going. "You'd help them feel better and keep them from needing prescriptions and all that toxic shit some people use. It's a good job—a clean, honest job."

I let Hurley's words wash over me as I rode along, and they sounded familiar. I'd heard Rick saying stuff like that to my mom. I'd heard it at Robbie's house. It wasn't usually about magic, but I knew what Hurley was offering, even if he didn't want to say it. I wasn't a stupid kid.

"You just give me some of what you make—you know, as my apprentice."

I stared at my hands.

"Think about it," Hurley finished, probably sensing my hesitation. "There's no pressure or anything. Hey, kid!" I looked up at him. "It's me. I'm not trying to make you do something you don't want to."

I smiled to reassure him. "Course not. I'll think about it."

The clock on the dash read 6:30, and wet clouds crept over the sky as we pulled into a gas station. The asphalt was uneven, and a gaggle of beer signs hung lit in the windows. Hurley climbed out, rocking the cab, and popped open the gas cap.

"Gonna rain soon!" He called to me as he filled the truck.

I leaned out my window. "It's getting late, Hurley. You taking me home soon? I don't want my mom calling around looking for me."

"Don't worry about it! I'll get you home soon. This'll be a quick stop—promise." He smiled at me as the gas nozzle clicked off.

The stop was down a spit of dirt road off the infamous County Line Highway. It was a bar clad in neon lights already blaring against the gloom of what was going to be a wet night. The air crackled with static, raising goose bumps on my arms, and I could hear a groan of quiet thunder coming for us.

We rolled up the windows before getting out, and I left my backpack in the truck—didn't see the point of bringing it with me.

The bar was empty except for a few guys playing pool and one man sitting stooped over the bar. The bartender was a chubby guy with strong arms, and he gave Hurley a nod as we walked in. My sneakers stuck to the floor, and the faint smell of alcohol permeated the whole place.

"How's it going, Dave?" Hurley asked the bartender as he went to the counter.

"We're not allowed to have kids in here, Hurley," Dave replied, nodding at me.

"Why the hell not? It's not like he'll be drinking."

"Because it's the law. You know what that is, don't you?"

"Well he's my assistant, and I want him here." Dave just raised his eyebrows. "What if he sits over there?" Hurley asked, gesturing at a booth next to an ancient jukebox.

"Fine, but not for long."

Hurley nodded meaningfully at the booth, and I rolled my eyes as I walked over. It was stupid—I wasn't gonna do anything. The two men talked for a few minutes, then the bartender handed Hurley a lump of cash and Hurley whispered something to him. Dave laughed—the first kind expression he'd had since we walked in—and nodded a few times at Hurley. They shook hands, and Hurley turned to walk to me.

Before he could, though, the stooped man pushed himself up and into Hurley's path.

"You," the man said, staring up at Hurley. I climbed out of the booth and started toward them, but Hurley held up a gnarled finger, stopping me.

"I'm sorry, bud, I don't have any cash for you," he said, arms open in a way that said "back off."

"I don't want your money. I just need you to say something to take the edge off. Say a few words for me—come on."

"I don't know what you're talking about," Hurley responded. He tried to push past the man and get to me, but the man grabbed Hurley's shirt.

"You know exactly what I mean—I need that thing you do. You know me. You used to help me. Now nothing helps me." Spittle flew from the man's mouth as he leaned closer to Hurley. "Look at my face. I need your help now. Say a few words—it's just a few words!"

"How's this: get your damned hands off—" Hurley tried to pull the man off, but his grip was too strong. They stumbled toward me, and I started back to avoid them. Hurley tripped, and the man fell with him to the dark, sticky floor. Then the man was flailing on top of Hurley. They tumbled toward me, each struggling for dominance. I tried to pull the man off Hurley as he chanted, "Say it" over and over into Hurley's face.

"Get off!" I yelled as Hurley kicked and struggled. The man smelled like old urine and stale beer. He flung his fist out blindly and made contact with my jaw, sending me falling into the booth table. The room spun, and spots glittered as I found myself on the floor.

Hurley glanced at me and opened his mouth to yell at the man. His face turned a deep red I'd never seen as he opened his mouth to speak. I couldn't make out the words, but I recognized some of the syllables. The air conditioner kicked on, and I saw little flashes of light at Hurley's fingertips.

Pushing myself up, I kept my eyes on what was happening. Hurley freed himself and stood over the man who now cowered and covered his ears. Hurley hacked one final word out and spit on the man, who gibbered madly, fear widening his eyes. He stumbled, trying to stand while Hurley watched him, sneering.

Eventually, the man fled through the back of the bar, moaning and crying in nonsense words. There was a coldness in Hurley's eyes I didn't recognize, and the room had turned hot and stifling.

"Are you OK?" Hurley asked eventually, bending to get a look at my face. I glared at him.

"What did you do to that man?" I asked. "What was he talking about 'nothing helps anymore'? What did you do?"

Hurley opened his mouth but nothing came out, so he closed it again.

"Thing is, it's not about—" he started, but I was already walking for the door. I felt so stupid, so dumb. This was what Hurley's help did. Like any other drug—it just looked different. Sparklier.

Outside, a few fat drops of water fell as I marched to the main road. The rain thickened, pouring over me as the cars drifted by. The rain hid my tears of disappointment—mostly in myself. If that was what magic did, I wasn't interested. I already knew that story.

My sneakers squelched in the runoff and I shivered as droplets drifted down the neck of my shirt onto my back. Lightning flashed and set thunder clapping down at me. Cars passed, red brake lights fragmenting in the drops and disappearing into the distance. I figured I was only a few miles from home and could use the time walking to think up an excuse for my mom to explain why I was late.

A truck pulled up next to me and slowed. The window rolled down and Hurley's face smiled sheepishly at me.

"Wet enough yet?" he asked. "Lemme give you a ride home. I'll explain everything that happened—promise."

I ignored him. He was probably gonna feed me some more bull. Cars swerved around his truck, but Hurley kept looking at me as he drove.

"Come on, kid. It's not that bad. Plus, how are you gonna explain not having your backpack?" He held it up to show me, wiggling it like bait. "Just hear me out, huh? And then

I'll take you home, and you can tell your mom you had dinner at Robbie's or some other BS. Then there's always the necklace—"

I sighed and rolled my eyes so he knew it wasn't all OK.

"Fine," I said, and he hit his brakes. I climbed into the truck, not caring that I was soaking his seats.

That man in the bar—" Hurley sighed. "He was an old client of mine, but he started reacting badly to my help. He started wanting more than was good for him, so I had to stop helping. Some people react that way—it's just them. It has nothing to do with the words. You get that, right?"

He sighed and lit a cigarette, inhaling and putting a hand to his forehead. "Sometimes you gotta make tough decisions. The man was nuts—you saw him."

I mulled over Hurley's explanation. The man was crazy. Crazy people happen. I shifted my sore jaw. We pulled into the parking lot of the church, where my mom wouldn't see Hurley dropping me off. The rain had stopped, and all that was left were the clouds and the humidity. The air was cooler and calm. The thunder was distant again, moved onto somewhere else.

"I'll see you later, Hurley," I said, hefting my backpack. I opened the door and he put a hand on my arm.

"Hold on, kid," he said. "Not everyone is cut out for this kind of work, but you got a knack. Don't let it go to waste, I'm begging you. Be my apprentice. Help people. Hell, help *yourself* for once."

I already knew my answer, but I nodded and smiled anyway. "I'll think about it."

He nodded back, accepting my response, letting me go. The sky was prematurely dark as I walked across the church lawn to the trailer park. I turned back to see Hurley getting the truck into gear. He waved at me before pulling out onto the road.

Cooking smells filled the trailer, but I wasn't hungry. My mom hummed as she stirred a large pot.

"Have fun at your friend's?" she asked. She whacked her

wooden spoon against the side of the pot, sending gravy splattering.

"Yeah," I replied. "It was great."

"Well, dinner will be ready in a few minutes if you wanna get cleaned up. It's beef stew."

"Oh, no thanks. I ate at Robbie's house."

She glanced up at me without really looking and opened the fridge. "That's fine. You can have leftovers later, if you're hungry. You get caught in the rain?"

"Yeah, but I'm fine. I'll be in my room," I said and walked back, trying to seem nonchalant. My shoes were still wet, but they weren't making squishing noises anymore. If she noticed my backpack was dry, she didn't say.

I peeled my wet clothes off and draped them over my dresser drawers to drip dry. I put on clean clothes and reached into my backpack for the necklace Hurley had given me. I looked closer at it, watching the light play off the facets of the gold and the polish of the stone. As I held it in front of the ceiling lamp, heat waves visibly wafted from the purple gem.

"Honey, are you sure you don't want something to eat?" My mom pushed the door open, and I shoved the necklace under my pillow. She was carrying a steaming bowl, the smell making my stomach churn.

"I said I'm good, Mom!" I cried. "And I want a lock on my door! Jeez!"

"Ha—you can get a lock when you start paying the bills. Is it so wrong of me to try and take care of you? God forbid I try to feed my son," she said louder than necessary as she walked back into the hallway.

"I'm putting your dinner in the fridge!" she yelled.

When I felt sure she was gone, I took the necklace out from under the pillow. I stared at the gemstone for a few seconds before taking it into the bathroom. It clinked against the ceramic bowl of the toilet, and I flushed until it was gone.

YINGYING JIANG

A Certain Slant of Light

written by

Preston Dennett

illustrated by

CHRISTINE RHEE

ABOUT THE AUTHOR

Preston Dennett has worked as a carpet cleaner, fast-food worker, data-entry clerk, bookkeeper, landscaper, singer, actor, writer, radio host, television consultant, teacher, UFO researcher, ghost hunter, and more. But his true love has always been speculative fiction.

From 1986 to 1992, he submitted eleven stories to this contest and received eleven rejections. Also rejected by other venues, Preston quit writing speculative fiction. Instead he wrote nonfiction about UFOs. Since then, he has written twenty-two books and more than 100 articles about UFOs and the paranormal.

Seventeen years later, in 2009, realizing his dream of being a science fiction writer was slipping away, he started writing and submitting stories again. He has since sold thirty-seven stories to various venues including Allegory, Andromeda Spaceways, Bards and Sages, Black Treacle, Cast of Wonders, The Colored Lens, Daily Science Fiction, Grievous Angel, Kzine, Perihelion Science Fiction, Sci Phi Journal, Stupefying Stories, T. Gene Davis's Speculative Blog, *and more, including several anthologies. Since these publications all paid less than professional rates, he was still qualified to win at the time he entered. He earned twelve honorable mentions in the Writers of the Future Contest before winning second place in the first quarter of 2018. It was his forty-seventh submission to the Contest, showing that if you want something bad enough, all you have to do is keep trying, and never give up. The story that follows is his third professional sale.*

Preston currently resides in southern California where he spends his days looking for new ways to pay his bills and his nights exploring the farthest edges of the universe.

ABOUT THE ILLUSTRATOR

Christine Rhee was born in 1980 in Seoul, South Korea, and grew up in different parts of Southern California and Seoul.

She discovered her love of art while completing her degree in Molecular and Cell Biology at Berkeley. She subsequently earned her Bachelor of Fine Arts in animation and illustration at San Jose State University, where she worked on design for plays and music videos, and production of animated films.

Christine loves stories of survival, growth, and transformation, especially as they take on mythic qualities. She adores fables and fairytales in all their retellings. She especially loves sharing Korean traditional stories that have not yet made their way to a wider audience. Christine works and lives in San Francisco with her husband, newborn son, and two studio bunnies.

A Certain Slant of Light

Walter walked slowly along the crumbling sidewalk. The last ten years had taken its toll on his body, not to mention this little town, and the world outside it. Lee walked silently beside him. Silent for now. His protests would come shortly, as they always did. Walter forgave him. Lee had only been a toddler when they'd lost his mother. He didn't remember her the way Walter did. The time had passed too quickly. Lee was an adult now, with his own family. Walter still saw him as that sandy-haired, freckle-faced little boy, but the truth was, Lee's hairline was receding. And Walter was sliding quickly into old age.

The number of people grew. "There he is," said an onlooker. "That's him." More faces turned toward him. More voices whispered.

Walter ignored them. Lee was clearly uncomfortable—he never liked the spotlight—but by now, Walter barely noticed the attention. Like Clare, he was a fixture here. The only difference was, he could move.

And there she was, his beautiful wife. The border of the time bubble was invisible, but a certain slant of light betrayed its presence. Clare stood with her back toward Walter. Her neck was craned around, and she peered in his direction with the hint of a smile. A smile that had been for him, all those years ago. A smile that was still there.

Walter approached as close as he could. Only a fool would approach closer. To do so was to die, to become caught in the time bubble, frozen.

Although only ten years had passed, the difference inside and out was obvious. Outside: dry foliage, the crumbling buildings, the yellow-brown sky. Inside the bubble, everything looked bright and green. It was like a snow globe. With his wife trapped inside, a living statue.

Walter stood silently and stared at Clare. How he longed to be with her again. He missed her so much. He couldn't let her go, he just couldn't.

He heard Lee sigh. Walter knew what that meant. Lee would again remind him that Clare was dead, that she wasn't even there anymore, that according to the scientists, the bubbles contained only images, mere reflections.

"You can't keep coming here forever," said Lee. "It's not good for you. It's not healthy. It just gets you all depressed. I don't know why you insist. I know you loved her. We all did. But Mom's not coming back. One day you're going to have to accept that."

Walter didn't bother responding. They had spoken variations of this conversation many times before. Instead, he smiled inwardly. They shared a stubborn streak, he and his son, neither willing to give in.

"You have to face the fact that she's dead. I hate to be so blunt, but it's true, and I think you know it."

"That's never been proven," Walter said.

Lee shook his head. "She's not there anymore. It doesn't matter why or how. Either way, she's gone. And you're wasting your time coming here over and over again, day after day, waiting for something that's never going to happen. You've become a laughingstock. You must know that."

"I know it," he said, seeing the hazel in Clare's eyes, the auburn in her hair. She wasn't dead. The world thought she was gone, but she wasn't. She couldn't be. He could feel the light around her, the undefinable quality of her presence. She was frozen in time, yes, but she lived. She was just trapped in this moment, fixed in time.

CHRISTINE RHEE

"You know, Dad, if Mom was alive, she'd tell you to move on, do something with your life. Stop waiting for her. Date a nice woman, remarry, something . . . anything. Spend more time with me and Jenny, and your grandson. He loves you."

"You don't have to come with me," said Walter. "I'm fine here with Clare." Walter winced when he heard how he sounded.

Lee glared at him. "I don't mind taking you here. I just want what's best for you. You know that."

"I know it," Walter said. "Don't worry. We'll leave soon. Just a few more minutes."

Lee flashed a dry, conciliatory smile. Walter ached to see it. Both Lee and Clare shared the same smile. Lee also had her soft hazel eyes. They were more alike than Lee would ever know.

Caleb giggled as he sat on Walter's lap. Jenny kept an eye on both of them, smiling as she did the dishes.

Lee, as usual, sat in front of the television, learning what latest tragedy had struck the world. Walter no longer paid attention to the constant reports of hurricanes in one area, droughts in another, food and gas shortages, the rising sea levels. None of it was new.

It was Caleb that Walter worried most about. This was his world now. He didn't know what it was like before the ocean became filled with plastic and algae, before the icecaps melted, before people were forced to stay inside air-conditioned homes while the world outside grew hotter. They had left him a used-up world. And Walter was as much to blame as anyone. At least Clare didn't have to see any of it. Small consolation, but there it was.

"Dad, take a look at this," Lee said, turning up the television.

"It's now confirmed. The time bubbles are not static," the male reporter said, "Scientists have measured them growing at a rate of one-tenth of an inch every three years. This may not sound like a lot, but over a period of decades, this sort of growth could become a problem. With thousands of these things around the world, it's only a matter of time before they take over the entire planet. Thankfully, at their current rate of growth, this will take millions of years. Still, it's an important discovery that may lead to an answer as to what these things are.

"In related news, legislation is being put forth to make it illegal to visit the time bubbles. With the growing number of suicides in which people throw themselves inside the stricken areas, the legislation is likely to prove popular to some, and not so to others. Take the case of Walter Scobee—"

"Look!" said Caleb. "It's Grandpa and Grandma."

An image of Walter gazing forlornly at Clare filled the screen. "Turn it off!" said Walter, removing Caleb from his lap and standing up.

Lee looked over at Jenny, who motioned for him to turn off the television. Lee quickly pressed the off button.

"Sorry," Walter said. "I just don't want to see that right now."

Lee rolled his eyes. "I don't know what you expect when you keep visiting her every damn day, granting interviews with the press. They make you look like a fool."

"Honey!" said Jenny. "Don't."

"He needs to hear this."

"I stopped doing interviews," said Walter. He had hoped by giving an interview, the press would leave him alone. Instead, his story just became more popular.

"But still you keep visiting, even when you know you're going to end up on TV."

"That's not my fault."

"You could stop visiting."

"Are you finished?" Walter asked. He disliked arguing. Why couldn't his son understand? He couldn't leave her. He couldn't.

Lee threw up his hands. "Yeah, Dad. I'm finished. Visit her. Visit as often as you want. Cling to the past. But I'm done. And don't take Caleb with you anymore. I don't want him going there."

"Lee," Jenny protested, scooping up Caleb. "That's not necessary."

"No, it's fine," Walter said, feeling a stab of guilt. "You don't have to worry. I won't bring him." Walter just wanted Caleb to know his grandmother. But Lee was right; that would never happen. It was wrong to give false hope.

"And quit telling him stories about her."

"Lee!"

"I'm serious. It's all he ever talks about. I loved Mom too, but I just can't keep doing this. He won't let her go. He talks as if Mom is still alive. She isn't alive, Dad. And I don't want you talking to Caleb like she is."

"I won't," Walter said. "I'm going to my room. If that's okay with you."

"You know I love you, Dad. But this is just the way I feel."

"I know it," Walter said, and went to his room.

He didn't blame Lee. But Lee wouldn't have been saying these things if he could remember his mother, if he knew about the love she and Walter shared.

Damn these time bubbles. He cursed the day they first appeared. It wasn't long after the Mid-East Holocaust. Pundits and so-called experts believed that there was a connection. They had fractured the time-stream, they said, frozen it in place. Maybe there was a connection, but if there was, nobody had found it. The truth was that nobody knew what the bubbles were. Thousands of them were dotted across the globe. Each of them was small, about ten to twenty miles in diameter, situated in seemingly random patterns. But still, the scientists knew little about them. Nobody had the faintest idea how they appeared or why. Theories ranged from aliens, to rips in space-time, to government experiments. All just theories. These days the bubbles were really nothing more than tourist attractions, bizarre curiosities, windows into a frozen past. *Perhaps that's what they are,* thought Walter, *time capsules to remind the world the way things used to be, before humanity polluted and destroyed the planet.*

Walter stood and studied Clare. With her in sight, the world around him faded. Lee waited silently next to him. Despite what Walter had said, Lee insisted on accompanying him. Walter knew the real reason. Lee feared Walter would try to enter the bubble.

At nighttime, the bubble was particularly beautiful, the way it glowed with a cheery daylight that defied the world around it. And the crowds were sparser.

Clare looked particularly attractive today. As always, Walter resisted the urge to lunge forward and embrace her. Then he noticed something. It was something that had been at the edge of his awareness for months. Clare looked different. He couldn't quite place how, but she *was* different. This was not the first time he had wondered about this, but today the sensation felt strong.

He had already studied every aspect of her, the way her dress hugged her hips, the arc of her footstep, the position of her arms, the flow of hair as it blew to the side.

Her hair. That was it! The difference was subtle, but the longer he peered the more certain he felt. A strand of her hair that had been pulled outward by the wind now lay almost flat against her shoulder. And yes, perhaps her foot was a fraction of an inch lower. Could it be? Could she be moving?

His heart raced. No trace of movement could be detected by the human eye, but she was moving. He felt sure of it. He glanced at Lee. He longed to tell him, but he didn't dare. Lee wouldn't believe it. He would assume that his father had lost his mental balance.

But he hadn't. Clare was different. Even the sunlight seemed slanted differently. If it was true, the scientists who studied the bubbles would know soon enough. They might already know but were keeping it secret.

It didn't matter. He knew the truth. And his heart soared. Maybe Clare wasn't dead.

The next day, when Walter sneaked from the house to visit Clare, Lee appeared by his side. "You don't need to come with me," Walter said. "I'm fine alone."

Lee was angry. "Do you think I'm stupid? I know what you're planning to do. And I'm not going to let you do it."

"I don't know what you're talking about." Walter began to walk briskly. Lee kept pace beside him. Thankfully it was just a short walk to visit Clare. Walter had insisted on living nearby.

"No? You're not planning on running into the time bubble?"

Walter didn't answer. Why lie? Of course, Lee was right.

"I knew it. Dad, you can't. It's suicide."

"That's just it. It's not. She moved, Lee. Clare moved. She's alive."

Lee frowned, an expression of pity and anger. "She's not alive, Dad. You know she's not. And if you go after her, you won't be either. You'll be stuck like her."

"She's alive," he whispered.

Lee sighed. "Think of us, me, Jenny, and Caleb. We love you too. You can't leave us."

"I don't want to."

"Dad, I'm not going to let you do this."

"You can't stop me."

"That's where you're wrong. I've already called the police. They've installed extra guards."

Walter couldn't disguise his anger and disappointment. "You have no right to tell me, your own father, what I can and can't do."

Lee's eyes shined with tears. "Go ahead, get angry. I'm just trying to save your life."

Walter gritted his teeth. Lee truly believed he was doing the right thing. But he wasn't. If Walter was correct, Lee might be completely wrong. Everybody might be wrong. But he had to get inside the time bubble to find out.

When they arrived, Walter was dismayed to see how well-guarded the area was. As usual, a small crowd of people stood watching.

If he had gone years earlier, it would've been a simple matter to just walk into the bubble. But now there were guards and fences, cameras and crowds. Soon it would be illegal. If he was going to succeed, he would have to do it soon.

Although he had visited this area thousands of times, today he studied it with a new perspective. He carefully planned his next move. He would do whatever it took. Nobody was going to keep him from Clare.

Walter had waited long enough. He had planned every detail. Nobody knew. Lee suspected, but he couldn't be sure. He walked alongside, silent, supportive in the best way he knew how. He smiled, made small talk. Walter pretended that today was like any other.

It was a Thursday morning, statistically the least crowded time. Walter felt encouraged to see that almost nobody was there. The guards looked at him and smiled. They were used to him. But they also had guns, and their numbers were increasing.

He moved as close as the suspicion of those around him allowed. He stared at Clare's form. *I'm coming, my love.*

He waited until the guards became used to him, until Lee began to use his cell phone.

He tapped his jacket, felt the heaviness of the handheld wire-cutter, and on the other side, a gun. Would this work?

He would miss his little family. He would miss Lee, sweet Jenny, and Caleb with his insatiable curiosity. He had done the honor of leaving them a note. Lee would see it as a suicide note, but it wasn't. In it Walter had outlined his theory about the time bubbles, and why he was doing what he was about to do. Lee wouldn't believe him, but he deserved to know how Walter felt.

He reached into his jacket, wrapped his fingers around the gun. He glanced at Lee, still engrossed with his phone.

He waited for the pacing guards to reach their point of furthest distance.

He pulled the gun out and he ran to the fence.

Incredibly, nobody seemed to notice him. Walter pulled out the cutters and turned them on. The blade buzzed to life. He held it to the chain-link fence and sparks began to fly.

"Hey! You!" The guard came running.

"Dad! Stop!"

"Stop!" the guard shouted, sprinting forward.

Walter quickly held up the gun. "Don't come any closer!"

The guard stopped. He motioned to the other guard who began to radio for backup. A crowd of people began to form.

Walter pointed the gun at anyone who approached. With his other hand, he continued cutting. "Don't try to stop me!" he yelled, trying to sound unstable. Then he did it. He shot the gun, straight up into the air. It was the only bullet in the gun. Walter had no intention of hurting anybody. But he needed them to believe that he might.

"Stand back!" the guard said, pointing his gun at Walter.

Lee lunged forward and put himself between the guard and Walter. "You can't shoot him!"

"Put down your gun!" the guard ordered.

Walter ignored him. The hole widened. It was almost big enough.

Lee slowly began to approach.

Walter held up the gun. "Don't come any closer. I'm doing this, Lee. Don't try to stop me."

Lee held up his hands. Tears streamed down his cheeks. "I won't, Dad. Hand me the wire cutter. Let me help."

Walter looked at him in surprise. His son was serious. Walter handed him the cutter.

Lee quickly knelt down and finished cutting the hole in the fence. He held it open for his father. "Okay, Dad. It's big enough. You can go."

"Lee," Walter said. "Thank you, and I'm sorry."

"Don't be. Just go. Quick."

The guards watched the exchange, clearly hesitant to stop Walter. They knew him too well. They knew his love for Clare was too strong to keep them apart. Everybody knew about Walter and Clare.

Walter embraced his son, then slipped through the hole in the fence. Walter heard people screaming in the background as he ran toward Clare. He was almost there.

Walter ran. He hadn't been this close to Clare since she got stuck. He didn't stop to examine the edge. He didn't turn around. Instead he kept his face hidden from Lee. Spared him the pain that Walter suffered seeing just a glimpse of Clare's face. Better to see nothing at all.

He hit the edge.

Time.

Stopped.

A flash of light.

Dizziness. Colors swirled around him. He could barely breathe.

Pain coursed through his body. He felt himself losing consciousness. He gritted his teeth, pushed one foot in front of the other.

There was a soft popping noise.

And he was through!

He stumbled. Ran toward Clare.

She was turning around. His wife! She turned and looked at him. She smiled to see him, but very quickly her eyes widened in fear.

Walter embraced his wife, weeping. He inhaled her fragrance, ran his fingers through her soft hair. "Oh, Clare, you're alive! I knew it!"

"I'm scared, Walt. What's happened to you? You look so old." She pointed to where Walter had come from and her eyes widened. "What is that?" She gripped his arm.

It was torture to tear his gaze from Clare's face. He glanced quickly. He could see the inside of the bubble, and outside: nothing but a swirling gray with a barely detectable flickering. The flickering, Walter knew, was the passing of day and night.

He stared back deeply into Clare's beautiful hazel eyes. "I'll explain everything, my love. First please tell me you're okay."

"I'm fine," she said. "You only just left a moment ago. Walter, what's going on?"

"I knew it!" Walter said, sweeping Clare into his arms. "The time bubbles aren't frozen at all. It was us the whole time. Inside,

411

time is normal. Outside, time is accelerated. They're sanctuaries. That's what they are."

"Time bubbles? What are you talking about? Walter, you look twenty years older. Are you okay?"

"I'm fine," he said. "Now that I'm here with you, I'm fine. Let's go home. I'll explain everything."

"Wait," she said. "Here comes someone."

Walter turned around to see a frail old man approaching them from the border of the time bubble. "Lee?" Walter asked, shocked.

The man laughed. "You don't recognize me? Dad died years ago. I'm Caleb."

Walter rushed up and embraced him.

"Who's Caleb?" Clare asked. She was crying.

"Your grandson," he said. "Caleb."

Clare held her hand over her mouth.

"You were right, Grandpa. I can't believe I'm talking to you. You have no idea how long it took me to get here, how many strings I had to pull, how many days and nights I watched you both, frozen in time. I read your note. I studied hard. You'd be proud of me. I became one of the world experts on the time bubbles. It was actually easy. You and grandma made it easy. You're both incredibly famous.

"And you were right. It's outside that time is broken. The time bubbles are growing much faster now. They are guarded very carefully. It's only a matter of time before people find out what they really are."

Walter paled. "Then more people are coming. We should prepare."

Caleb shook his head. "I wouldn't worry. Some may make it inside, but not many. The world's a lot different than when you were alive, I mean, since you were outside. We've had ... problems. Wars, famines, plagues—the world's not a very nice place. There was another war. Not a lot of people have survived."

"Let's go home," said Walter. "Tell me about Lee. He wasn't too angry with me, was he?"

Caleb laughed. "No, Dad loved you. He became a world hero. They made a movie about him. He made a lot of money and became very famous."

"You're joking."

Caleb shook his head. "Honest to God."

"Tell me everything," said Walter. And the three of them walked home.

The Year in the Contests

LAST YEAR'S ANTHOLOGY

Every year we strive to create the highest quality anthology possible. Our judges and administrators have the delightful task of searching for the best writers and illustrators in the world to win our contests. Thanks to the talented individuals who entered, the book was an international bestseller and received overwhelmingly positive reviews.

We are proud to announce that Volume 34 was on multiple bestseller lists, including *Publishers Weekly* and Amazon. In fact, WotF 34 was #1 in nine separate categories on Amazon, including, "Hot New Releases (for Short Stories—Sci-Fi Short Stories)," "Science Fiction—Canada," "Anthologies—UK," and "Sci-Fi and Fantasy Anthologies Kindle Edition—US."

We are also happy to share that we were recognized by some of the most influential book reviewers in the industry. *Publishers Weekly* declared that Volume 34 "features expertly crafted and edited stories and art, running the gamut from humorous to bone-chilling.... This inspired, well-rounded anthology has a little something for everyone." *Midwest Book Review* stated, "a 'must read' for all dedicated science fiction and fantasy fans." Finally, *Booklist* said, "This delightful collection holds obvious appeal for fans of speculative fiction, but it should also be recommended to aspiring writers as well."

In a first for us, WotF 34 was chosen by Book Authority as one of the best books to read for 2019. What is "Book Authority"? As featured on CNN, Forbes and Inc., Book Authority identifies and rates the best books in the world, based on public mentions, recommendations, ratings, and sentiment.

CONTEST GROWTH

The L. Ron Hubbard Writers and Illustrators of the Future Contests continue to grow. They are among the longest-running writing and art contests in the world and continue to attract thousands every year. And this past year, we once again had the highest number of entries since the beginning of both contests.

A NEW FIRST READER

Due to the high growth of the Contest, we invited award-winning author Kary English to act as first reader. Her job will be to make a first pass on the stories, deciding which to send on to David Farland for further judging and which can be easily rejected. Kary is a past first-place winner with the Contest and a Hugo finalist for her short fiction.

A FANTASTIC NEW JUDGE

This year, we were delighted to add a new judge to our Writers' Contest, Katherine Kurtz. Katherine is the historical fantasy author of the very popular Deryni series, the Templar series, and the Adept series. With a strong interest in writing, history, and police work, she created her own subgenres of "historical fantasy" and "crypto-history." She says, "I always try to help up-and-coming writers and am delighted to be able to judge in the L. Ron Hubbard Writers of the Future Contest." We're just as delighted to be able to work with her.

PUBLICATIONS AND MAJOR ACHIEVEMENTS BY PAST WINNERS

With nearly 800 Contest winners, it is virtually impossible to keep track of everyone's accomplishments. But here are some highlights from the past year:

Artem Mirolevich—Illustration winner, has been busy with art exhibits of his work and has started his own contest to get writers and illustrators to work together. He asks that writers create stories based on his illustrations.

Tobias S. Buckell—*New York Times* bestseller's new release, *The Tangled Lands*, was a finalist at the Digital World Awards.

Myke Cole—Former winner was cast on CBS's *Hunted* last year and has released one more book in his Sacred Throne trilogy, *The Armored Saint*, as well as another novel, *Legion Versus Phalanx: The Epic Struggle for Infantry Supremacy in the Ancient World*.

Nnedi Okorafor—Author of the soon-to-be-released *Black Panther* movie tie-in story, *Shuri: The Search for Black Panther*, has written two other stories for the franchise: *Long Live the King* and *Wakanda Forever*. Okorafor was also seen at this year's Emmys when she was escorted by George R. R. Martin, who is producing her award-winning novel *Who Fears Death*.

Each year, our winners and judges grace the covers of the three largest short story magazines in speculative fiction today: *The Magazine of Fantasy and Science Fiction, Asimov's Science Fiction*, and *Analog Science Fiction* all throughout the year. We have at least one winner on each cover, sometimes more.

We also continue to see our award-winning and *New York Times* bestselling authors publish novels in their series. Two of the most prominent are *Death's End*, translated by Ken Liu, and *Binti: The Night Masquerade* by Nnedi Okorafor.

RECOGNITIONS AND AWARDS IN 2018 FOR L. RON HUBBARD, OUR JUDGES, AND WINNERS

Recognitions:

The L. Ron Hubbard Writers and Illustrators of the Future Contests were recognized on their thirty-fourth anniversary with Certificates of Recognition from the California Senate, Senate President Kevin de León, and City of Los Angeles Councilmember Thirteenth District Mitch O'Farrell.

Awards:

NYC Big Book Award: We're proud that *L. Ron Hubbard Presents Writers of the Future Volume 34* was the winner in the anthology category for the New York City Big Book Award. Book submissions were collected from six continents: Africa, Asia, Australia, Europe, North America, and South America. The purpose of the award is to recognize high-quality writing from around the world.

Our Contest winners continue to be recognized for their talent. And this past year's wins across sci-fi and fantasy are tremendous. We're proud that their works were first published in the Writers of the Future anthology.

Analog Awards: In 2017, C. Stuart Hardwick's "For All Mankind" won Best Novelette. Brian Trent's "Galleon" was a finalist in the same category. Martin Shoemaker's "Not Far Enough" and Howard V. Hendrix's "The Girls with Kaleidoscope Eyes" were both finalists for Best Novella. Eldar Zakirov was a finalist for Best Cover.

Asimov's Readers' Award: In 2017, Eldar Zakirov won Best Cover for the September/October issue and Bob Eggleton was a finalist for his July/August issue. Robert Reed's "The Speed of Belief," Kristine Kathryn Rusch's "The Runabout," and R. Garcia y Robertson's "The Girl Who Stole Herself" were all finalists for Best Novel/Novella.

Aurealis Awards: Shauna O'Meara's "Island Green" was a finalist for Best Sci-Fi Novella. Cat Sparks's *Lotus Blue* was a finalist for Best Sci-Fi Novel.

Aurora Awards: James Alan Gardner's *All Those Explosions Were Someone Else's Fault* was a finalist for Best Novel while his *Compostela: Tesseracts Twenty* was a finalist for Best Related Work.

Baen Awards: David VonAllmen's "Dragon's Hand" won Grand Prize—Fantasy Adventure. Stephen Lawson's "Homunculus" won Grand Prize for the Jim Baen Memorial Short Story Award.

Compton Crook Award: Cat Sparks's *Lotus Blue* was a finalist for Best Novel.

Digital Book World Award: Tobias S. Buckell's *The Tangled Lands* was a finalist for Best Book (Science Fiction).

Ditmar Awards: Shauna O'Meara won for Best Fan Artist and was a finalist for Best Novella with "Island Green." Cat Sparks's *Ecopunk!* won Best Collected Work. Sparks was a finalist in three other categories as well: Best Novel for *Lotus Blue*, Best Short Story for "Prayers to Broken Stone," and the William Atheling Jr. Award for Criticism or Review for "Science Fiction and Climate Fiction: Contemporary Literatures of Purpose."

Dragon Awards: Brandon Sanderson won Best Graphic Novel for *Brandon Sanderson's White Sand: Volume One*. He also won Best Fantasy Novel for *Oathbringer*. Kevin J. Anderson won Best Alternate History Novel for *Uncharted* (cowritten with Sarah A. Hoyt).

Elgin Awards: Mary Turzillo won second place in Best Full-Length Collection for *Satan's Sweethearts*.

Geffen Awards: Brandon Sanderson's *Calamity* was a finalist for Best Translated YA Book.

Gemmell Awards: Brandon Sanderson's *Oathbringer* was a finalist for The Legend Award for Best Fantasy Novel.

Hugo Awards: Nnedi Okorafor's *Binti: Home* was a finalist for Best Novella. Aliette de Bodard's "Children of Thorns, Children of Water" was nominated for Best Novelette. Brandon Sanderson's The Stormlight Archive was nominated for Best Series.

The World Science Fiction Society Award: Nnedi Okorafor's *Akata Warrior* won Best Young Adult Book.

Life, The Universe and Everything Award: presented to L. Ron Hubbard for the Writers of the Future Contest.

Locus Awards: Nnedi Okorafor's *Akata Warrior* won Young Adult Book. Okorafor's *Binti: Home* was a finalist for Novella. Aliette de Bodard's *The House of Binding Thorns* was a finalist for Fantasy Novel. Aliette de Bodard's "Children of Thorns, Children of Water" and Ken Liu's "The Hidden Girl" were both finalists for Novelette. Tobias S. Buckell's "Zen and the Art of Starship Maintenance," Karen Joy Fowler's "Persephone of the Crows," and Nancy Kress's "Dear Sarah" were all finalists for Short Story. Bob Eggleton and Shaun Tan were both finalists for Best Artist. Omar Rayyan's *Goblin Market* was a finalist for Art Book.

World Fantasy Award: Tim Powers's *Down and Out in Purgatory* was nominated for Best Collection. Omar Rayyan was nominated for Best Artist.

Mexico's National Literature Award: Presented by the Mexican Association of Publishing Houses and the Federal Government of Mexico, Kevin J. Anderson and Orson Scott Card were awarded in the categories of science fiction and fantasy, respectively.

Spectrum Fantastic Art: Omar Rayyan, Andrew Sonea, Sarah Webb, and Contest judge Cliff Nielsen were all selected for Spectrum 25.

Chesley Awards: Stephen Youll was nominated for Best Cover Illustration: Paperback or Ebook for *Acadie.* Omar Rayyan was nominated for Best Interior Illustration for *Goblin Market.* Rachel Quinlan was nominated for Best Product Illustration for *Knight of Cups.* Christine Rhee was nominated for Best Monochrome Work.

This is all the news for this year. We'd like to congratulate all of our fine writers and illustrators for a great year. We look forward to next!

FOR CONTEST YEAR 35, THE WINNERS ARE:

WRITERS OF THE FUTURE CONTEST WINNERS

FIRST QUARTER

1. *Kyle Kirrin*
   A HARVEST OF ASTRONAUTS

2. *Preston Dennett*
   A CERTAIN SLANT OF LIGHT

3. *Kai Wolden*
   THE FIRST WARDEN

SECOND QUARTER

1. *David Cleden*
   DARK EQUATIONS OF THE HEART

2. *Rustin Lovewell*
   RELEASE FROM SERVICE

3. *Carrie Callahan*
   DIRT ROAD MAGIC

THIRD QUARTER

1. *Elise Stephens*
   UNTRAINED LUCK

2. *Christopher Baker*
   AN ITCH

3. *Mica Scotti Kole*
   ARE YOU THE LIFE OF THE PARTY?

FOURTH QUARTER

1. *Andrew Dykstal*
   THANATOS DRIVE

2. *Wulf Moon*
   SUPER-DUPER MOONGIRL
   AND THE AMAZING MOON DAWDLER

3. *John Haas*
   THE DAMNED VOYAGE

ILLUSTRATORS OF THE FUTURE CONTEST WINNERS

FIRST QUARTER

Emerson Rabbitt

Vytautas Vasiliauskas

Yingying Jiang

SECOND QUARTER

Alexander Gustafson

Christine Rhee

Sam Kemp

THIRD QUARTER

Allen Morris

Jennifer Ober

Josh Pemberton

FOURTH QUARTER

Qianjiao Ma

Alice Wang

Aliya Chen

WRITERS' CONTEST RULES

1. No entry fee is required, and all rights in the story remain the property of the author. All types of science fiction, fantasy, and dark fantasy are welcome.

2. By submitting to the Contest, the entrant agrees to abide by all Contest rules.

3. All entries must be original works by the entrant, in English. Plagiarism, which includes the use of third-party poetry, song lyrics, characters, or another person's universe, without written permission, will result in disqualification. Excessive violence or sex, determined by the judges, will result in disqualification. Entries may not have been previously published in professional media.

4. To be eligible, entries must be works of prose, up to 17,000 words in length. We regret we cannot consider poetry, or works intended for children.

5. The Contest is open only to those who have not professionally published a novel or short novel, or more than one novelette, or more than three short stories, in any medium. Professional publication is deemed to be payment of at least six cents per word, and at least 5,000 copies, or 5,000 hits.

6. Entries submitted in hard copy must be typewritten or a computer printout in black ink on white paper, printed only on the front of the paper, double-spaced, with numbered pages. All other formats will be disqualified. Each entry must have a cover page with the title of the work, the author's legal name, a pen name if applicable, address, telephone number, e-mail address and an approximate word count. Every subsequent page must carry the title and a page number, but the author's name must be deleted to facilitate fair, anonymous judging.

Entries submitted electronically must be double-spaced and must include the title and page number on each page, but not the author's name. Electronic submissions will separately include the author's legal name, pen name if applicable, address, telephone number, e-mail address, and approximate word count.

7. Manuscripts will be returned after judging only if the author has provided return postage on a self-addressed envelope.

8. We accept only entries that do not require a delivery signature for us to receive them.

9. There shall be three cash prizes in each quarter: a First Prize of $1,000, a Second Prize of $750, and a Third Prize of $500, in US dollars. In addition, at the end of the year the First Place winners will have their entries judged by a panel of judges, and a Grand Prize winner shall be determined and receive an additional $5,000. All winners will also receive trophies.

10. The Contest has four quarters, beginning on October 1, January 1, April 1, and July 1. The year will end on September 30. To be eligible for judging in its quarter, an entry must be postmarked or received electronically no later than midnight on the last day of the quarter. Late entries will be included in the following quarter and the Contest Administration will so notify the entrant.

11. Each entrant may submit only one manuscript per quarter. Winners are ineligible to make further entries in the Contest.

12. All entries for each quarter are final. No revisions are accepted.

13. Entries will be judged by professional authors. The decisions of the judges are entirely their own, and are final and binding.

14. Winners in each quarter will be individually notified of the results by phone, mail or e-mail.

15. This Contest is void where prohibited by law.

16. To send your entry electronically, go to:
    www.writersofthefuture.com/enter-writer-contest
    and follow the instructions.
    To send your entry in hard copy, mail it to:
    L. Ron Hubbard's Writers of the Future Contest
    7051 Hollywood Blvd., Hollywood, California 90028

17. Visit the website for any Contest rules update at:
    www.writersofthefuture.com

ILLUSTRATORS' CONTEST RULES

1. The Contest is open to entrants from all nations. (However, entrants should provide themselves with some means for written communication in English.) All themes of science fiction and fantasy illustrations are welcome: every entry is judged on its own merits only. No entry fee is required and all rights to the entry remain the property of the artist.

2. By submitting to the Contest, the entrant agrees to abide by all Contest rules.

3. The Contest is open to new and amateur artists who have not been professionally published and paid for more than three black-and-white story illustrations, or more than one process-color painting, in media distributed broadly to the general public. The ultimate eligibility criterion, however, is defined by the word "amateur"—in other words, the artist has not been paid for his artwork. If you are not sure of your eligibility, please write a letter to the Contest Administration with details regarding your publication history. Include a self-addressed and stamped envelope for the reply. You may also send your questions to the Contest Administration via e-mail.

4. Each entrant may submit only one set of illustrations in each Contest quarter. The entry must be original to the entrant and previously unpublished. Plagiarism, infringement of the rights of others, or other violations of the Contest rules will result in disqualification. Winners in previous quarters are not eligible to make further entries.

5. The entry shall consist of three illustrations done by the entrant in a color or black-and-white medium created from the artist's imagination. Use of gray scale in illustrations and mixed media, computer generated art, and the use of photography in the illustrations are accepted. Each illustration must represent a subject different from the other two.

6. ENTRIES SHOULD NOT BE THE ORIGINAL DRAWINGS, but should be color or black-and-white reproductions of the originals of a quality satisfactory to the entrant. Entries must be submitted

unfolded and flat, in an envelope no larger than 9 inches by 12 inches.

7. All hard copy entries must be accompanied by a self-addressed return envelope of the appropriate size, with the correct US postage affixed. (Non-US entrants should enclose international postage reply coupons.) If the entrant does not want the reproductions returned, the entry should be clearly marked DISPOSABLE COPIES: DO NOT RETURN. A business-size self-addressed envelope with correct postage (or valid e-mail address) should be included so that the judging results may be returned to the entrant. We only accept entries that do not require a delivery signature for us to receive them.

8. To facilitate anonymous judging, each of the three photocopies must be accompanied by a removable cover sheet bearing the artist's name, address, telephone number, e-mail address, and an identifying title for that work. The reproduction of the work should carry the same identifying title on the front of the illustration and the artist's signature should be deleted. The Contest Administration will remove and file the cover sheets, and forward only the anonymous entry to the judges.

9. There will be three cowinners in each quarter. Each winner will receive a cash prize of US $500. Winners will also receive eligibility to compete for the annual Grand Prize of $5,000 together with the annual Grand Prize trophy.

10. For the annual Grand Prize Contest, the quarterly winners will be furnished with a specification sheet and a winning story from the Writers of the Future Contest to illustrate. In order to retain eligibility for the Grand Prize, each winner shall send to the Contest address his/her illustration of the assigned story within thirty (30) days of receipt of the story assignment.

The yearly Grand Prize winner shall be determined by a panel of judges on the following basis only: Each Grand Prize judge's personal opinion on the extent to which it makes the judge want to read the story it illustrates. The Grand Prize winner shall be announced at the L. Ron Hubbard Awards ceremony held in the following year.

11. The Contest has four quarters, beginning on October 1, January 1, April 1, and July 1. The year will end on September 30. To be eligible for judging in its quarter, an entry must be postmarked no later than midnight on the last day of the quarter. Late entries will be included in the following quarter and the Contest Administration will so notify the entrant.

12. Entries will be judged by professional artists only. Each quarterly judging and the Grand Prize judging may have different panels of judges. The decisions of the judges are entirely their own and are final and binding.

13. Winners in each quarter will be individually notified of the results by mail or e-mail.

14. This Contest is void where prohibited by law.

15. To send your entry electronically, go to:
www.writersofthefuture.com/enter-the-illustrator-contest
and follow the instructions.
To send your entry via mail send it to:
    L. Ron Hubbard's Illustrators of the Future Contest
    7051 Hollywood Blvd., Hollywood, California 90028

16. Visit the website for any Contest rules update at:
www.illustratorsofthefuture.com

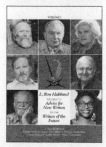